"EVERYONE HAS A WEAKNESS. WHAT'S YOURS?"

Brodie stopped and looked her over, his direct gaze lingering on her honey-colored hair before meeting her eyes. "Women with blond hair and green eyes."

Over his shoulder there was the sparkling silver ribbon of a waterfall, but Jessica didn't notice it or the fellow sightseers scattered along the trail. She was aware of nothing but the man in front of her and the sudden tightness that had gripped her throat.

"Is that right?" She tried to make it a breezy retort, but it came out breathless.

"Yes." Relentlessly he held her gaze. "I read somewhere that a gentleman shouldn't kiss a lady until the third date. Counting lunch, this is the third time we've been out together, Green Eyes. I don't remember if it said when a gentleman is entitled to claim his kiss, but . . ." His hand molded itself to the curve of her neck, his long fingers sliding into the silky length of the hair at the back of her neck. His other hand cupped the side of her face, lifting her chin with his thumb. "I'm not going to wait any longer."

BOOK YOUR PLACE ON OUR WEBSITE AND MAKE THE READING CONNECTION!

We've created a customized website just for our very special readers, where you can get the inside scoop on everything that's going on with Zebra, Pinnacle and Kensington books.

When you come online, you'll have the exciting opportunity to:

- View covers of upcoming books
- Read sample chapters
- Learn about our future publishing schedule (listed by publication month *and author*)
- Find out when your favorite authors will be visiting a city near you
- Search for and order backlist books from our online catalog
- Check out author bios and background information
- Send e-mail to your favorite authors
- Meet the Kensington staff online
- Join us in weekly chats with authors, readers and other guests
- Get writing guidelines
- AND MUCH MORE!

Visit our website at
http://www.kensingtonbooks.com

ALWAYS WITH LOVE

Janet Dailey

ZEBRA BOOKS
KENSINGTON PUBLISHING CORP.
http://www.kensingtonbooks.com

CONTENTS

SENTIMENTAL JOURNEY

Chapter One

Overhead, the sun was bright with the promise of spring. Its direct rays were warming, but the nipping north wind retained the cool breath of winter. A sudden gust whipped up dust and sent it whirling across the busy intersection, sweeping the street and bouncing off traffic.

Jessica Thorne strolled along the sidewalk, glancing into store windows, her hunter-green coat unbuttoned to the brisk air. She adjusted the shoulder strap of her handbag and slipped her hand back into her coat pocket. The teasing wind played with her silky blond hair, but Jessica made no attempt to smooth it into place. There would be time enough to freshen up when she returned to the office.

A twinge of restlessness swung her gaze to the Tennessee hills rising around Chattanooga. Evidence of spring was visible in the delicate shading of green on the hillside—new leaves, new grass, new life. Soon the dogwood and redbud would be blooming. The knowledge shadowed the already dark green of her eyes. But Jessica was unaware of it and would have been at a loss to explain why it should.

Her shoulder brushed against a passerby, returning her attention swiftly to her surroundings. "Excuse me," she murmured in apology, but the woman was already several steps beyond her and didn't hear.

The traffic light at the intersection was green. Jessica quickened her pace to catch the light. As she reached the crosswalk, it turned to amber, a Don't Walk sign flashing beneath it. Traffic surged forward and she had to wait with the other pedestrians on the curb.

A man stood beside her. His imposing height attracted her glance. Coatless despite the invigorating weather, he wore a dark business suit and tie. When Jessica would have looked away, the breeze ruffled his black hair and memory clicked in her mind, elusive yet strong.

She studied his craggy profile. There was a quality of toughness in his lean, hard features that was familiar. Jessica was certain that she knew him, but she couldn't place where or how. He wasn't the kind of man she would easily forget, which made it all the more confusing.

He had to be someone from her past. Time had etched lines around his eyes and mouth, hinting that he was somewhere in his middle thirties. That eliminated the possibility that she had gone to school with him, since she was only twenty-three.

Perhaps the clothing or environment was wrong. The dark suit was hand tailored, the material expensive. He wore it with an ease that indicated that he was accustomed to such clothing, yet Jessica had the distinct feeling he hadn't been so well-dressed whenever she had met him. What had he worn? A uniform? The answer eluded her.

Becoming aware of her scrutiny, the man glanced at her. His eyes were a shattering blue, narrowed to have the piercing effect of a hard blue diamond. The look was familiar, but Jessica experienced a sense of unease that bordered on fear. She felt her pulse fluttering in alarm as she felt an impulse to look away and avoid any further contact with the man.

Then recognition flickered uncertainly across his face. His raking gaze made a swift study of her, noting her honey-colored hair and the clouded green of her eyes. So thorough was the inspection that Jessica had the sensation that her coat was stripped away to allow him to examine the slender curves of her figure.

Dark eyebrows drew together in a frown. "Do I know you?" The voice fitted the man, low-pitched and demanding in its curiousness. It struck a familiar chord, but still Jessica could not remember his name. The shake of her head was more uncertain than negative.

"I'm not sure."

"That voice." He paused and seemed to search his memory while his gaze never left her face. "My God!" Recognition glittered in the hard blue eyes, tempered with a hint of skepticism. "Can it be? Jordanna?"

"Jordanna is my sister." Eight years older than Jessica, there was a similarity between the sisters despite the age difference. Besides, all the Thornes had honey-blond hair and either green or blue eyes.

"Of course." His mouth quirked at the corners with amusement. "I should have realized you're too young to be Jordanna. You're about the same age Jordanna was when I left. Guess I didn't make allowances for the amount of time that's passed."

Neither noticed the traffic light change, but as the other people at the curb brushed past them to enter the crosswalk, they became aware of the fact. He took Jessica's elbow to guide her across, and his strong, firm grip sent a tremor of unease through her. The physical contact increased the feeling that she should stay clear of him.

As he escorted her across the intersection, Jessica was still no nearer to remembering who he was. She had searched her memory, trying to recall the men her older sister had dated. None seemed to resemble the man striding beside her.

Stealing a glance at him, Jessica sensed his wary intelligence. For an instant, there was an animal look about him—a very powerful animal.

It occurred to her that, ultimately, he would always get what he wanted. It didn't seem to bode well.

Safely across the street, he stopped, his hand halting her.

"Small world, huh?" His lazy smile looked pleased. "Almost my very first day back, I meet a Thorne. It's an amazing coincidence."

"Yes," Jessica agreed, although she didn't know why it was. "Were you a friend of my sister's?"

"A friend?" he repeated in a faintly cynical tone. "No, I wasn't a friend. I had met your sister, but we never reached the stage of knowing each other well, through no fault of mine."

Jessica was intrigued by his answer. She didn't know what it meant—whether her sister hadn't wanted to get to know him better or whether her sister was too complicated to know well. She would have pursued the subject, but he changed it.

"Where is Jordanna now? Married, I suppose."

"Yes, she is. She has two children, a boy and a girl. She and her husband live in Florida."

He removed his hand from her arm and Jessica breathed a silent sigh of relief, as if she were once again in full possession of herself. He slipped both hands into his pants pockets, a seeming concession to the brisk air except that his suit jacket was pushed open. The thin material of his shirt hinted at the muscular wall of his chest and the trimness of his waist and flat stomach.

When Jessica had first noticed him standing at the crosswalk, she'd had an impression of a man on his way somewhere. Now he seemed prepared to stand on the street corner and chat away the day. It was a confusing reversal.

"What about your parents? They're well, I hope," he commented.

Did he know them, too? "Yes. Daddy retired two years ago. They moved to Florida so mother could be near the grandchildren." Jessica wondered if she should be telling him all this. She didn't even know him. Of course, there was a lot he seemed to know already.

"And your brother, did he get his degree from Harvard?" There was something almost sardonic in the question.

"Yes. He joined a law firm in Memphis. He's doing quite well." Jessica found herself defending her older brother. She thought she had detected a note of sarcasm when the man had referred to Harvard and it irritated her.

"A Thorne couldn't do any less than very well for himself."

The man smiled cruelly when he said it, and behind the joking response, Jessica suspected a taunt. "I never did ask—did Jordanna marry that rich Radford guy?"

"As a matter of fact, she did, but money had nothing to do with her choice." Jessica bristled. "She happens to love Tom."

"Did I imply otherwise?" He seemed genuinely taken aback by the suggestion. "I apologize for my choice of adjectives to describe Radford. I meant nothing by it."

Was he sincere or merely acting? Jessica couldn't tell. She had been anticipating that he would introduce himself, but obviously he wasn't going to.

"I'm afraid I can't place you." She forced him to make an introduction. "You do look familiar, but . . ."

"I doubt that we've met before," he said, not at all disconcerted. He withdrew his hand from his pants pocket and offered it to her. "The name is Hayes, Brodie Hayes."

His name brought her memory of him into clear focus and a chill shivered down her spine. "You're Jordanna's sister, but I don't know your name."

Shock at his identity made her pale. Through the tightness in her throat, she managed to answer, "Jessica." Automatically she reached to shake his hand. The instant contact was made, warm skin against warm skin, she pulled her hand free.

Brodie Hayes! Her disbelieving eyes swept over the expensive clothes he wore, the fine leather shoes visible beneath the precise crease of his trousers, and the large signet ring on his finger. Only after these changes were noted did she see the bemused and mocking look on his ruggedly masculine features.

"You do remember me, don't you?" he said.

"I've heard about you." Jessica recovered some of her poise. "I believe I saw you once or twice."

"I vaguely remember that Jordanna had a younger sister," Brodie Hayes admitted. "A cute little thing with braces on her teeth."

Jessica didn't smile, nor attempt in any way to reveal her now-perfect teeth. "You seem to have done very well for yourself, Mr. Hayes," she commented a trifle frigidly.

"Brodie," he corrected, and glanced down at his suit, giving the impression that its cost was of little importance. "I've come a long way, considering that I started out on the wrong side of the tracks."

A long way, Jessica agreed silently. He was a rough diamond that had been cut and polished into an expensive gem. But the outer look didn't change the fact that inside he was still that hard, rough diamond capable of cutting through anything.

Finally Jessica obeyed the impulse that she had felt so strongly from the first moment he had looked at her. "I know I must be keeping you from something important. It was nice seeing you again."

Before she could take a step away, he was speaking. "You're not keeping me from anything." Brodie Hayes briskly disposed of that excuse.

"Surely you must have some old friends you want to look up," she insisted.

"My old friends?" He seemed to consider the idea with bitter regret. "Unfortunately they wouldn't feel comfortable with me anymore. That's one of the prices you pay when you climb the ladder, Jessica. You leave people behind. It isn't often that you can help them come up with you."

"If they're your friends—" Jessica started to protest.

"If you meet someone you haven't seen in years and if he's a success while you're still struggling to make ends meet, you get the feeling you're a failure, whether you are or not. It's not a feeling many people want to experience," Brodie reasoned with unquestionable logic and the bitter taste of experience.

"I suppose you're right," she conceded, and glanced pointedly at her watch.

Brodie took the hint. "Am I keeping you from an appointment?"

"Well, lunch is over. I have to be back to work in a few minutes." Actually she had plenty of time to spare, but common sense demanded she spend no more time in his company.

"So you're not a lady of leisure. Interesting." He seemed mildly surprised by the discovery, as if he had expected her parents' wealth was a reason for her to be idle.

"Living a life of leisure can be boring. Perhaps you haven't reached the point where you've discovered that yet." This time her response was faintly acerbic.

Brodie Hayes seemed to find it amusing. His mouth remained in its half-curved line, but there was a sparkle of mocking laughter in his hard eyes. It didn't endear him to Jessica.

"Perhaps I haven't," he agreed.

"It was nice seeing you again." She repeated her earlier exit line with the same result as the last time.

"Have dinner with me this evening," Brodie invited her before she could move away. "Your husband is welcome to join us."

"I'm not married," Jessica answered, then realized she had fallen for an old gambit.

"Your boyfriend, then. You do have one?" His once-over seemed to say any woman as attractive as Jessica had to have a boyfriend or there was something wrong with her.

"Thank you, but I'm afraid I can't accept," she refused as graciously as her clenched jaw would permit, and purposefully adjusted the strap of her shoulder bag.

"Please reconsider." His slow smile was packed with compelling male charm. Jessica was aware of its potency and wavered under its spell. Only a woman made of stone could be immune to it, and she was definitely not made of stone. "Take pity on a lonely man who's tired of eating his meals by himself."

"If you eat alone, I'm sure it's by choice. There are probably any number of people who would be delighted to join you." She felt a drawing fascination and fought it vigorously as she discounted his appeal.

"My dinner companions generally want to discuss business or money, directly or indirectly." Brodie Hayes didn't deny her statement. "Yours is the first remotely familiar face I've seen since I returned. I'm a stranger returning home to find no one here to welcome me. I'd love to spend an evening with you and reminisce about old times." It was difficult to refuse in the face of his persuasiveness. He was making her feel guilty and heartless. Only the sensation that he was a little too smooth made Jessica persist in her rejection.

"I doubt if I could do much reminiscing, since your 'old times' weren't mine. And I don't know a thing about your contemporaries or where they are and what they're doing today," she argued, hiding her annoyance behind a smile.

"I'm sure you've heard your sister and brother speak about their friends." A gust of wind ruffled his midnight-black hair. With a careless gesture, his fingers combed it back into order. "You'd probably be surprised at how much information you've unconsciously gathered."

"Possibly." She had to concede that he might be right.

"Shall I pick you up at eight o'clock?" Brodie didn't repeat his invitation, but rephrased it to take her acceptance for granted.

Jessica hesitated, finding herself at a loss to battle him with words. With a sigh, she released the breath she had unconsciously been holding and flashed him a quick smile.

"Eight o'clock will be fine," she agreed, and glanced at her watch. "I have to run. See you tonight . . . Brodie." Her tongue tripped over his given name.

"Tonight," he agreed with an arrogantly pleased smile.

But Jessica was already moving away, not allowing him another chance to detain her. She hurried down the sidewalk, not looking behind her to see if Brodie Hayes was watching her leave.

There was no sense of triumph in having bested him. She had agreed to the dinner invitation for the simple reason that it was the easy way out. She knew she wouldn't be going with him when she had accepted. Not because she was going elsewhere that evening. The fact was that Brodie Hayes didn't know where she lived, and her phone number was unlisted, so there was no chance he could find her. A man like Brodie Hayes would not take kindly to being stood up, but with luck she would never bump into him again.

At the building where she worked, Jessica paused to glance behind her. She scanned the people on the sidewalk and felt silly for thinking that Brodie might have followed her. With an impatient shake of her head, she pushed open the glass door and walked in.

Riding the elevator, Jessica shrugged out of her coat and tried not to let her mind dwell on what she had just done. But her expression was downcast and slightly preoccupied as she entered the outer office area.

Ann Morrow, the receptionist, glanced up and frowned. "I wasn't expecting you for another twenty minutes, Ms. Thorne."

"I came back early," she answered abruptly, and immediately tempered her sharpness. "I wanted to look over the Atkins account."

"I took the file into Mr. Dane's office a few minutes ago." The girl looked at her apologetically.

"That's all right." Jessica hadn't really been interested in looking over the account, at least not overly so. Now that her uncle, Ralph Dane, was going over the file, there was no point in her looking at it. "I'll be in my office if anyone calls for me."

As Jessica turned away, she found herself thinking that Brodie Hayes wouldn't call. He didn't know where she worked, either.

A door opened and a tall, distinguished-looking man came striding out. His dark hair was grayed at the temples, a pair of horn-rimmed glasses were in his hand.

"Ann . . ." he began, glancing up from the file he held. At the familiar sound of her uncle's voice,

Jessica paused instinctively. His peripheral vision caught her presence and his attention immediately shifted to her. "Jessie, you're back already. You're just the person I wanted to see. Come into my office."

He didn't wait to see if she was coming as he retraced his path, leaving the door to his private office open for her. Jessica hesitated for only a second, then tossed her coat over the back of the chair beside the receptionist's desk and followed him. Closing the door, she walked to a leather-covered chair and set her bag on the seat.

"Back early from lunch, aren't you?" he said in his terse, clipped voice. "Not that I mind. This Atkins account is a shambles." He dropped the file on his desk and pushed back the cuff of his jacket to glance at his watch. "What are you—a glutton for work? Twenty minutes early."

"I had my lunch. There wasn't any shopping I wanted to do, so I came back to the office." Jessica shrugged.

"No shopping, huh?" Ralph Dane grunted. "I'd celebrate the day your Aunt Rebecca ever said that!" Hitching up his trousers, he sat down in the swivel chair behind his desk and opened the file holder. "I've just looked over the Atkins file. The ad campaign is . . . hokey, for want of a better word. Parts of it are worth saving, but this . . ."

A red pencil began slashing out lines of copy while Jessica moved closer to the desk, turning at an angle to see what he was eliminating. Her concentration held for two minutes until the words "success" and "hometown boy" made her attention stray. They came too soon after her encounter with Brodie Hayes for her not to apply them to him instead of this old and valued account.

"Are you listening to me, Jessie?" her uncle demanded impatiently.

She winced, both at her inattention and his use of her nickname. "Sorry, I was thinking," she admitted.

"Not about this, obviously." He flipped the pencil onto the desk top and leaned back in his chair, folding his hands in his lap. "Out with whatever it is that's on your mind so we can concentrate on this."

"It wasn't anything important."

"Important enough for you not to pay attention. Get it off your chest," he ordered.

Jessica knew her uncle well enough to know he would persist with his questions until she came up with a response. She had never been any good at making up stories, so she settled for the truth, or a portion thereof.

"On my way back to the office, I met a man who lived here several years ago, a hometown boy who's doing quite well now. The comparison with the Atkins campaign clicked in my mind."

"Who is he?"

"Brodie Hayes." Jessica was surprised by how naturally she spoke his name.

"Never heard of him," her uncle grumped. "Anything else?"

"No." Nothing that she was going to tell him. The trick she had pulled on Brodie Hayes was strictly private. It wasn't something she was proud of and she wasn't going to confide in her uncle. Despite their family connection he was still her boss, and she didn't want him to know she had used devious means to handle a situation. He was too open and aboveboard in his dealings to condone such behavior.

"Take this file, look over my notes, add some of your own, and take it back to the copywriters. Tell them they'd better come up with something better than this or they're fired.'' He closed the folder and handed it to her.

Hiding a smile at his false threat, she nodded. "Will do.'' In the outer office, she paused to pick up her coat. Ann Morrow was on the telephone. Jessica pointed to her office to indicate to the receptionist that that was where she would be, and the girl nodded.

Her office was small, containing no more than a desk, two chairs and a filing cabinet, but then she was a very junior member of the staff. Jessica's first year with her uncle's advertising firm had been spent in the back room, learning the fundamentals. When her apprenticeship had been served, she had been elevated to handling accounts.

In truth, most of the accounts were with old established customers, and Ralph Dane worked closely with her on these. Jessica knew she had the job because she was his niece. But she also knew that if she weren't capable, family ties would not guarantee that she would keep the job.

Sighing, Jessica settled into the lumpy seat of her chair and opened the file. She skimmed over the cuts and read the notes in the margin. Some of the changes she would have made; others she wouldn't have noticed. Her uncle had an instinctive knack for what pleased the public. Perhaps she would learn this talent in time.

In time. Time. How long had it been since she had last seen Brodie Hayes? Ten years? She had been eleven or twelve.

Chapter Two

Jessica decided she had been eleven years old. It was surprising what an indelible impression Brodie Hayes had made on her. She could even recall vividly the first time she had heard his name. It had been on a Saturday afternoon in July. She had been in the family room with her sister and brother, listening to new CDs.

Despite the vast age difference, they had never minded Jessica hanging around them. Her adoration of them had bordered on hero worship. They were so much older, had done so much more and were permitted to do so much more that Jessica got a vicarious thrill out of quietly listening to them talk.

Her father had walked in and raised his voice to be heard over the noisy music. "Jordanna, there's a rather scruffy-looking young man at the front door who wants to speak to you."

At first, her sister had only expressed mild surprise that someone was calling to see her, but as her father's words had sunk in, her expression changed to one of apprehension and dismay.

"It couldn't be," she protested. "Brodie Hayes wouldn't come here."

"Brodie Hayes?" Her brother, Justin, frowned in surprise.

"You never mentioned that you were seeing him."

"I'm not," Jordanna protested, while Jessica looked on with mounting interest. Her brother had sounded angry and faintly outraged. It made Jessica wonder who this Brodie Hayes was. "A bunch of us went swimming at the lake a couple of weeks ago," Jordanna explained in defense of her brother's accusation. "Brodie was there. I talked to him, just to be polite, and he's been bugging me to go out with him ever since."

"He's no good, Jordanna," Justin stated flatly. "Stay away from him."

"I intend to." Jordanna was emphatic. "There's something about him that scares me."

"If you feel that way, Jordanna," her father spoke up, "I'll tell him that you don't want to see him."

Jessica sat quietly on the large, boldly colored rug in front of the fireplace, glancing from one speaker to another, her head turning back and forth as if she were watching a tennis match. With every word that was spoken, her ears had figuratively grown bigger and bigger.

For Jordanna, so self-possessed and so popular, to be frightened of anyone seemed beyond Jessica's ken. And Justin's warning only added to her wide-eyed interest.

"No, dad." Jordanna hesitated before refusing the offer. "I'll talk to him."

But, by her expression, Jessica could tell that her

sister wasn't looking forward to it as she left the room. Justin then walked over to turn down the volume on the sound system. Jessica had the impression that he expected their sister to call for help and he wanted to be sure to hear her.

Her father remained in the room. Turning to Justin, he demanded, "Just who is Brodie Hayes?"

Justin appeared to hesitate, frowning. "He was in my class in high school—that is, when he bothered to come to class. He was smart, though. He wasn't in school half the time and still managed to pull above-average grades. But he dropped out when he was sixteen. He runs with a rough crowd. Reform school, rehab, jail, you name it."

"I don't like the idea of Jordanna getting mixed up with that sort." Her father's expression of concern deepened. He took a step toward the door. "I think I'd better send him on his way."

"No, dad, let Jordanna handle it," Justin insisted. "Believe me, it's better that Brodie doesn't develop a grudge against the Thorne family."

Her father looked grim, but didn't argue. Neither man had been paying any attention to the silent Jessica. Silently she slipped from the room and darted up the open staircase to her bedroom. The reason was simple and obvious: from the window of her room, she was able to overlook and overhear what was going on below.

Her first glimpse of Brodie Hayes fulfilled all the expectations her vivid imagination had conjured up. Coal black hair, black as the devil's, gleamed in the sunlight. Tall, with a powerful physique, he towered over her slightly built sister. His faded jeans showed signs of excessive wear, and his bare arms were corded with sinewy muscles. His aura of toughness was doubly intimidating to Jessica when she remembered what her brother had said about him.

Jordanna appeared composed on the surface, but Jessica, who knew her well, saw the nervous trembling of her smile and the distance her sister tried to maintain from Brodie. From her lofty perch Jessica eavesdropped on the conversation.

"Are you engaged?" Brodie Hayes demanded.

"No," Jordanna answered defensively.

"Are you going out with anyone?" He had taken a step closer and Jessica trembled in sympathy for her sister.

"Not right now, I'm not," Jordanna said casually.

"Then I don't see what's stopping you from accepting my invitation." It was more than a challenge.

"I'm sorry." Jordanna walked several feet away, escaping from his intimidating closeness. "I've already told you I'm busy. I'm sorry you've come all this way for nothing, but you should have called first."

"Yeah," he agreed cynically, "all the way from the wrong side of town."

The remark seemed to make Jordanna uneasy. "I said I was sorry, Brodie."

"And I'm supposed to say it's all right. Forget it." The mockery in his voice was harsh. He took a deep breath, the muscled wall of his chest expanding to strain the few buttons of his shirt that were fastened. "Okay, consider it said. But there's one other thing—I haven't given up." Peering from her window, Jessica shivered with fear because it had sounded like a warning. "I like you more, Jordanna, than all the other girls I know put together. I'll be seeing you again, you can bet on it."

On that ominous note, he turned and started down the long sidewalk to the driveway. Jessica heard the closing of the front door, indicating that her sister had come inside, but she wasn't able to take her eyes off the tall, dark-haired man striding away.

There was something about the way he moved, lithe and supple, that reminded her of a wild animal. She remembered the sensation she had felt when her parents had taken her to a zoo in California and she had seen a large wolf loping across an enclosure designed to resemble his native habitat. She had sensed she was looking at something ruthless, predatory and dangerous.

Staring after Brodie Hayes, Jessica had the same feeling. And as with the wild wolf, she experienced the same compelling fascination to watch Brodie Hayes from a safe distance. But she knew that if she ever met him face to face, she would be terrified.

Her knees were shaking when he drove away in a battered Jeep 4 x 4. Part of her wanted to curl up in the big, overstuffed chair in her room until the trembling stopped. But the stronger urge was to race downstairs to discover her sister's reaction to the meeting.

It was as easy to slip unseen into the family room as it had been to slip out. Her sister was standing at a window, staring at the expansive rear lawn, and Justin was watching her. There was no sign of their father.

"You should have told him you didn't want to see him again," Justin said with undisguised impatience.

"He wouldn't have listened." Jordanna moved away from the window and began nibbling on a fingernail. "Guess what he told me, Justin." She laughed, but nervously. "That he liked me more than all the girls he knew!"

"Hey, considering the kind of girls he knows . . . well, you know their reputation. If you go out with him, people will say the same stuff about you." Jessica checked herself just in time from asking what people would say. That wasn't the moment to interrupt the conversation with questions. She kept silent and played the little mouse in the corner.

"I know that. Believe me, I'm not going anywhere with him," Jordanna stated emphatically.

"Better not!" Jordanna shuddered and rubbed her arms. "There's something about him that frightens me. His eyes—they're so piercing. I get the feeling he's looking into my soul. And even when he smiles, his eyes don't."

"What color are his eyes?" Jessica had piped up, forgetting her vow to remain silent.

"Blue," Jordanna answered automatically, then exchanged a quick glance with Justin as they both realized she had been listening.

Since her presence had been noted, Jessica tried to include herself in the discussion. "I thought he looked dangerous," she added. "When have you ever seen him?" Jordanna frowned.

But Justin smiled. "I'll bet it was from your bedroom window, wasn't it, Jessica?"

"I wanted to see what he looked like," she answered in defense of her action.

"You shouldn't spy on people like that." The admonishment came from her sister.

"What's the matter?" Justin teased. "Afraid of what little sister might see when you and Tom kiss good-night?"

"Oooh!" Jordanna picked up a pillow from the sofa and threw it at her brother.

Much to Jessica's regret, the conversation never got back to Brodie Hayes. She knew it was because she was there.

The second time Jessica had seen Brodie Hayes, she and her sister had been in the house alone. Justin was off playing tennis with some of his buddies. Their father was working and their mother was at a committee meeting of the local planning board.

Skinny and shapeless in her bathing suit, Jessica was swimming in the pool in the backyard. Just as she entered the house through the rear sliding glass doors, the bell at the front door rang.

"I'll answer it!" she shouted, and raced barefoot to the entryway. She flung open the front door. Instantly the smile of greeting died as a shaft of cold fear rooted her to the ground. Her hand continued to clutch the doorknob. On the threshold stood Brodie Hayes with his black hair and cool blue eyes.

"Is Jordanna home?"

To Jessica, it seemed more like a demand than a question. Sudden fear kept her from uttering a sound. Brodie Hayes took her silence and the fact that the door was opened so wide as permission to enter.

Her heart was pounding so hard she thought it would explode as he stepped into the foyer. She watched his gaze sweep over the interior of the house. She wanted to run, but as if she were in a nightmare, her legs were paralyzed.

"Who was at the door, sis?" Jordanna's voice called from another room.

Jessica wanted to scream a warning, but not a sound came from her throat. She heard her sister walking toward the entryway and noted the way Brodie had turned to face the sound. Inside, she was crying for being so frightened. She could have told him Jordanna wasn't home if only she hadn't been so terrified.

It was too late when the footsteps stopped and Brodie said, "Hello, Jordanna." And Jessica noticed that his eyes didn't mirror the smile parting his mouth.

There were more footsteps. Jessica nearly jumped out of her skin when her sister's hand touched her shoulder, and she looked up into the nervous smile of her sister. Her cloudy green eyes were rounded in apology and Jordanna's hand tightened in reassurance.

"You'd better go up to your room and change out of that wet swimsuit." Her sister provided her with an excuse to escape.

The touch of Jordanna's hand broke the grip of paralysis. Jessica raced up the stairs two at a time, but she went no farther than the top. There she huddled against the wall to listen, shaking like a leaf.

"I happened to be in the neighborhood," Jessica heard Brodie say, "and thought I'd drop by to see if you'd like to go for a ride. It's a beautiful afternoon."

"I'm sorry you made another wasted trip. I can't go with you," Jordanna refused, then hurried an explanation. "There wouldn't be anyone here to stay with my little sister. I couldn't leave her alone."

Hiding at the top of the stairs, Jessica cringed. She didn't think her sister should tell him they were alone. What if he decided to rob them?

"How old is your sister?" Brodie Hayes asked. "Nine? Ten?"

"She's eleven."

"Old enough to stay by herself. Nobody hung around to look after me since I was eight."

"That doesn't matter," Jordanna insisted. "We don't do that. Besides, Jessica is a girl, so it's different."

"Then you won't change your mind and come for a ride with me?" He sounded as if he expected her to say no.

"I can't. I told you, I have to stay here."

"In that case, I'll keep you company."

At his statement, Jessica breathed in sharply. Alarm trembled through her, bones knocking together so loudly that she was sure they could hear her in the foyer below.

"I'm sorry, but I'll have to ask you to leave, Brodie. Our parents don't allow us to have friends over unless one of them is here as well," Jordanna explained, quite bravely, Jessica thought.

"Do you always do what your parents tell you?" He seemed to be mocking her.

"My parents don't make unreasonable requests." Jordanna didn't say any more in defense of her parents or her stand.

"If I come back later this afternoon, when your mother or father are home, would you go out with me then?" Jessica held her breath, knowing her sister was going to refuse, yet wondering what excuse she could make for not going with him.

Jordanna's answer, when it came, was straightforward, her voice slightly breathy. "No."

"Why?" Despite the quiet, even pitch of his voice, it contained the threatening ring of challenge. Upstairs, Jessica quivered as an eternity of seconds ticked away in silence. "Are you afraid of being seen with me?" His voice was so controlled, so lacking in emotion that it sent chills down Jessica's spine and she was able to imagine how her sister felt. "Or are you just afraid of me?"

"It's nothing like that, Brodie," Jordanna hastened to assure him.

"If it isn't where I live or what you think I am, would you mind telling me why you keep turning me down?" His tone was skeptical and taunting.

"Because—" Jordanna paused for a fraction of a second before completing her answer, "—I'm not interested in seeing you. There's someone else . . . that I like."

"Radford," Brodie Hayes concluded. "Your parents would approve of him. But they wouldn't welcome me here, would they?"

"I wouldn't know." Her sister's voice was faintly haughty. "The question never came up."

"Probably because everyone knows the answer."

"That isn't fair," Jordanna protested.

"Fair?" Brodie Hayes repeated in a laughing sound. "At least I know where I stand with you . . . and why," he added in a voice that indicated he'd drawn his own conclusion. "Would you like to know where you stand with me?"

That apprehensive note made Jessica peep around the wall. Her eyes rounded in fear when she saw her sister flattened against the wall, Brodie's arms on either side, caging her there. Afraid of what he might be planning to do to Jordanna, she rose to clutch the banister. He leaned intimidatingly close, all but blocking her sister from Jessica's view.

"Brodie, please—"

He made a harsh mockery out of her words. "Please, what? Please, get lost?" Jordanna made no response, holding her ground and meeting his look. "Okay, if that's what you want." He pushed away from the wall. "I guess I just stepped out of my class, didn't I?" Jordanna opened her mouth to say something. "Don't bother, I can show myself out. Unless I have to leave by the back door."

"No, I—"

But Brodie didn't give her sister a chance to complete the sentence, turning and walking to the front door with swift yet unhurried strides.

When the door closed, Jessica sped down the stairs, racing toward her sister. "Are you all right, Jordanna? I was so scared!"

"Jessica!" Her sister caught her by the shoulders and looked at her in surprise. "I thought you were in your room."

"I waited at the top of the stairs," she admitted. "I didn't think you'd be able to send him away. I thought he might hurt you."

"You have a vivid imagination," Jordanna sighed.

"I saw him," Jessica protested. "He'd backed you up to the wall. I just know he was going to do something."

"He was only trying to scare me a little because I hurt his pride by refusing to go out with him. But he didn't do anything, Jessica. You see, I'm all right." Jordanna smiled brightly. "Now go on upstairs and change out of your swimsuit. Mom would have fits if she caught you around the house in that wet thing."

Jessica obeyed, but she wasn't convinced that her fears for her older sister had been groundless. She had never forgotten the scene nor the sense of peril she had experienced licking through her veins.

Three weeks later she had seen Brodie Hayes for the third time, and the last time until today. As before, the doorbell had rung and Jessica had raced to answer it. Part of it was almost a replay of the previous time. She had stopped short at the sight of Brodie Hayes.

"Is your sister home?" he asked.

Robbed of speech by the memory of the other scene, Jessica shook her head. Jordanna had gone out with some friends for the afternoon.

"Do you know when she'll be back?"

Again her head moved swiftly from side to side. If she had known, she would never have told him. As it was, she didn't have to lie.

"Give her a message, okay?"

This time her head bobbed in agreement.

His mouth quirked at the action. "Can't you talk, kid?"

The taunt stung Jessica into speech. "I can talk."

"So that's your problem, a mouthful of metal." As soon as he spoke, Jessica pressed her lips tightly together to hide the braces he had seen. "Tell Jordanna that I stopped to tell her goodbye. I'm leaving town." Jessica nodded and Brodie Hayes started to turn away. Then he hesitated, his piercing blue eyes glancing back at her. "And tell her when I do come back, I won't be out of her class."

He walked away. Jessica couldn't remember his name ever being mentioned after that, not coupled with success or failure.

His statement on that long-ago yesterday echoed clearly in her mind. On the surface, he seemed to have succeeded. That proud chip on his shoulder hadn't been in evidence, unless it had been hidden by the superb cut of his suit. But why had he come back? After all this time, what had he hoped to find? Jessica shook her head, not finding any logical answer.

It was nothing to her. He was nothing to her, except part of an incident in her childhood, one that had probably been dramatized out of proportion by her imaginative age. It was only by sheer chance she had seen him again. The odds didn't favor a repeat, so she attempted to push all the memories, past and present, to the back of her mind.

As the rest of the afternoon progressed, it became easier. The Atkins account demanded her attention; conferring with the artists and copy-writers in the larger office to come up with a winning campaign.

It was after five before she finally left the office for her apartment. It was a spacious, two-bedroom place, much larger than she really needed. The spare bedroom had been used often by her family, since they all liked to drop in without warning for visits. Justin had stayed with her while on a business trip as recently as a month ago.

Entering the apartment, Jessica deposited her bag and the mail on the coffee table in the living room and opened the bamboo blinds concealing the sliding glass doors to a small balcony. In a pattern that had become routine, she continued to her bedroom. There she changed out of her office clothes into a silky T-shirt and faded jeans.

On her way back to the living room she stopped in the kitchen for a glass of chocolate milk, then plopped into the sofa to read the day's mail. It was her time of the day to relax and unwind from the pressures of the office.

In the mail, there was a letter from her mother filled with news of her grandchildren—Jessica's niece and nephew. Normally Jessica would have read the letter through at least twice, but this night she put it aside after one reading and picked up a women's magazine, choosing to immerse herself in an excerpt from a best-selling novel instead.

Chapter Three

As engrossing as the story had turned out to be, Jessica found it impossible to ignore the rumblings of her empty stomach. She turned down the corner of the page and set the magazine aside. Paying no attention to the chiming of the clock, she walked into the kitchen. A plate of cold chicken and a pasta salad were in the refrigerator. She set them on the breakfast bar and walked to the cutlery drawer of the kitchen cabinets.

The buzzer at the door to her apartment interrupted her, and she frowned, wondering who it might be. Her friends generally phoned before coming over. Well, guessing served no purpose. Jessica entered the living room and crossed to the door.

Opening it, she was carried back to that long-ago yesterday, and her hand froze on the doorknob. Shock struck the words from her throat. She could only stare at Brodie Hayes.

A half smile touched his hard mouth, but he seemed oblivious to her surprise. The clear blue of his eyes and the jet black of his hair was intensified by the sweater he wore, the pale color of smoke, and charcoal gray slacks. He was a compelling figure, all male, totally at ease.

Leaning a hand against the door jamb, he eyed her somewhat mockingly. "How did you know that I planned for us to have a very informal dinner this evening? Can you read minds, Jessica?"

The shock receded into astonishment. "How did you know where I lived?" she breathed incredulously.

"I called your office and explained to your uncle that we were having dinner together tonight, but that you'd forgotten to give me your new address. He actually knew who I was." His answer did not hold any underlying tone of mockery, as if he genuinely believed the omission of her address had been an oversight.

"But—" it was too much for Jessica to take in, "—how did you know where I worked?"

"Simple deduction." Brodie straightened and stepped over the threshold, forcing her backward into the living room. "I couldn't believe that a Thorne would be entirely on her own. There had to be some member of the family who would be in frequent contact with you. Luckily for me I remembered your uncle owned an advertising agency."

"Yes, it was lucky, wasn't it?" Jessica was breathing unevenly, not quite sure that he believed what he said. "If you hadn't remembered, we both would be dining alone tonight."

"Something neither of us would have enjoyed, isn't that right?" For all the smoothness of his response, there was a trace of a challenge in his voice.

It was the first indication that perhaps he believed she hadn't given him her address on purpose. But Jessica couldn't be sure. At this point, it would be rude to admit it and it was imperative that she somehow conceal the truth. Her uncle wouldn't have given out her address unless he thought it was safe to do so.

Some of her poise had returned, but her pulse had not yet regained its normal rate. Turning away from him, she nervously licked her lips and made up a story in her mind.

"Oh, right . . . my address." She laughed stiffly. "I didn't realize it until I was back in my office, and by then it was too late. And I didn't know where to reach you."

On the last word, she turned to face him, lifting her hands in a gesture that indicated there had been nothing she could do. The half smile remained in place, the blue eyes unblinking.

"You could have checked the hotels. There aren't that many of them in Chattanooga," Brodie pointed out. Then he shrugged. "But hey—a Thorne wouldn't call various hotels searching for a man."

Jessica almost breathed her sigh of relief aloud. "Um, no. But I wasn't even sure if you were staying in a hotel."

"And you didn't check," he said blandly.

"No, I didn't check," Jessica admitted quite freely. "Do you blame me?" she countered. "I barely know you."

"I don't blame you at all. If the roles were reversed, I might do the same."

He released her gaze and glanced at the mantel clock. "Have you eaten yet?"

Should she lie and claim she had? Jessica toyed

with the thought. But she was hungry and the growling of her stomach would tell him she was lying. His sharp gaze was back on her, waiting for an answer.

"As a matter of fact, I was just fixing myself something when the doorbell rang," she admitted. "So I haven't eaten."

"Good, then we'll be able to have dinner together." His eyes briefly noted her casual, body-hugging clothes. "No need to change. Where we're going, anything else would be out of place. If you're ready to leave, we can go now."

"Give me a couple of minutes to put away the food in the kitchen," she asked as he inclined his head in silent agreement.

Her hands were shaking as she set the chicken and pasta salad back in the refrigerator, and took a deep breath to calm her rattled senses. She would get through the evening somehow without letting him see how his company affected her, she vowed to herself.

"Ready?" A dark brow lifted when she reentered the living room.

"Yes." Jessica took her bag from the coffee table and slipped the long strap over her shoulder.

Brodie held the door open for her and waited in the hallway while she locked the deadbolt. Side by side, they walked outdoors. His hand came up to rest on her backbone above her waist. Its guiding pressure was light, but sufficient for Jessica to be aware of the contact and to be unnerved by it. He directed her to a dark blue Jaguar parked at the curb, unlocked the passenger door for her and helped her in.

When Brodie slid behind the wheel, Jessica ran her hand over the cream leather upholstery. "It's a beautiful car,'' she said to break a silence that, to her, had become uneasy.

A smile twitched at the corners of his hard mouth. "I'll tell the rental agency you said so." He slid the key in the ignition and started the engine.

"It isn't yours, then?" Somehow she hadn't expected that answer.

"Not this one." Which indicated that he owned one. As he turned the car into the street, his gaze skipped to her. "I always dreamed of owning a Jaguar. As soon as I could afford it, it was one of the first things I bought. Now it's stored in a garage somewhere." He seemed incredibly indifferent to the fact.

Jessica stared. She couldn't help it. "You do know where it's stored, don't you?"

"In Louisville, I think." His attention was on the traffic. His reply was so absently given that Jessica had to believe he wasn't certain of its location and wasn't bothered that he didn't know. "That sounded arrogant, didn't it?" Brodie shot her a brief, self-mocking glance. "I travel a lot and it hasn't been practical to have my personal car wherever I am for a very long time."

"How did your travels bring you to Chattanooga after all these years?" Jessica questioned. "You never did mention why you came back."

"It was a combination of circumstances," Brodie said, which told her absolutely nothing. "Mostly it's a sentimental journey to see where it all began." Again she was the cynosure of his blue eyes. "You find that hard to believe, don't you, Jessica?" he said, seemingly with the ability to read her mind. "But it's difficult to know where you are if you've forgotten where you came from."

"So you're taking a trip into the past, so to speak." She thought she understood. At the same time, she was also discovering that Brodie was a complicated man with many facets.

"Tonight's journey brings me here." He swung the long car into the partially lighted parking lot of a restaurant. "Have you eaten here before?"

Here turned out to be a nondescript building with a pink neon sign spelling out the word RESTAURANT. It was a busy place, as evidenced by the numerous other vehicles parked in the lot and the crowded tables visible through the windows.

"I'm not sure," Jessica admitted.

"Not surprising." His remark seemed to be a sardonic comment on her more prosperous background. The engine was turned off, but Brodie made no attempt to get out of the car. Instead he gazed at the building, alive with sounds and people. "When I was a boy, my father brought me here every Friday, payday. It was a weekly treat, the one night we ate out. As I grew older, it was a place to hang out with my friends. I checked earlier this afternoon to see if it was still in business, but I can't vouch for the food. Want to try it?" His look held a hint of challenge.

Jessica wondered if he thought she was going to say that the place wasn't good enough for her. If he did, he didn't know her very well.

"Why not? All those people can't be wrong." She glanced at the filled tables inside.

Brodie opened his door and stepped out. Jessica didn't wait for him to walk around the car and open her door. She did it herself instead and joined him at the front of the car, to walk to the restaurant entrance.

"I have another confession to make," Brodie said as they wound their way through the tables to an empty booth against the wall.

"What's that?" Jessica slid onto the bench seat.

He sat opposite her. "This is also where I brought my dates, especially the more beautiful ones, so I could show off in front of the guys." He was smiling as he answered, a teasing glint in his eyes.

But she didn't return the smile. "Is this where you would have brought Jordanna if she'd agreed to go out with you?"

"More than likely." Brodie nodded, his gaze narrowing fractionally.

"Are you fulfilling a fantasy, bringing me here as a stand-in for my sister?"

"Probably," he admitted.

Jessica was certain the truth was more positive than his answer. A waitress brought them menus, and Jessica opened hers and began studying it. The fare was varied: sandwiches to salads to full-course meals, breakfasts and desserts. She hadn't made up her mind when the waitress returned.

"Have you decided?" Brodie asked.

"Not yet." She didn't glance up from the menu. "Go ahead and order."

"As I remember, the most popular item on the menu was a hamburger, french fries and a malt. I'll have that. Coffee instead of the malt," he told the waitress.

Jessica closed the menu. "I'll have the same, with the malt, chocolate."

When the waitress moved away, Brodie said, "You didn't have to order that."

"I happen to like hamburgers and french fries," she defended her choice.

"I'll remember times when I had to wait for my

date to order so I would know whether I could afford to have anything. It was always a nightmare wondering if some girl was going to order an expensive steak and if I had enough money to pay for it." His mouth quirked into a dry half smile. "At sixteen, I don't know what Chateaubriand was, let alone how to pronounce it." He picked up a small placard advertising a pricey new beer.

"Designer suds," he said dismissively.

"A restaurant like this is the ideal place to advertise a new beer," Jessica pointed out.

"Oh? Do you handle accounts like that at your uncle's agency?"

Jessica sensed an implication that her job wasn't quite real. "Uncle Ralph doesn't practice nepotism, if that's what you're thinking," she told him firmly. "True, he did offer me the job because I was his niece, but if I'm not any good, he isn't going to keep me." "No executive would be successful if without that attitude." Brodie neither admitted nor denied that her correction was justified as he repeated his question. "What do you do?"

"I handle the older, more established accounts so I can gain experience before attempting to solicit new accounts," she said, and resented the way he made her feel so defensive.

"Your uncle is missing a bet. If you came into my office with a proposal, I would have difficulty looking at you and turning it down."

His look was suddenly very male and very suggestive. Jessica flamed under it and changed the subject to hide the hot confusion rushing through her.

"What do you do, Brodie? You didn't say earlier."

"I take things that are broken or rundown, repair them and make them run smoothly again."

She knew there was more to it than that.

"What kind of things?" she asked curiously.

"Companies, mostly manufacturing firms."

"So now you own a whole string of successful companies," Jessica concluded.

"No. I buy controlling interest in a faltering company, make it successful again, then sell it for a profit." "What did you do? Go back to school and get an MBA?"

"No. A long time ago I learned that ninety percent of everything you need to know in life is common sense. The other ten percent I could buy." Brodie studied her for a long moment. "I never really had the patience for school. You learned all the subjects and no one taught you how to apply them in life."

"Is that why you quit?" Jessica wanted to know.

"I quit because I thought I was smart. Later, I didn't go back because I didn't want to find out how ignorant I was. Over the years, I've had to educate myself, but it wasn't easy," he stated.

Unwillingly, Jessica felt a glimmer of admiration. Nothing he had said resembled bragging or boasting, just a simple statement of facts. She suspected he was as hard on himself as he probably was with everyone else.

"How did you get started, buying companies and so on?"

"A guy in Knoxville needed some help in his welding shop, but he couldn't afford to pay me the going wage. He offered me a working partnership and I accepted. A year and a half later, a larger welding company bought us out. He stayed on to work for them. I took my money and bought into a repair shop where the same thing happened," Brodie explained with marked indifference. "The third time I realized I didn't need a partner and I didn't need to physically work myself. All I had to do was clean out the deadwood, hire skilled people and computerize the accounting."

"As simple as that," she said with skepticism.

"Yes, it's as simple as that," he agreed. The waitress stopped at the booth to serve their food. A slice of raw onion rested on a lettuce leaf beside the hamburger on her plate. Jessica glanced at it before adding mustard to her bun.

Brodie noticed her hesitating look. "Go ahead and have the onion. We can buy some breath mints when we leave."

She had never been with any man who was quite so straightforward. The bluntness of his manner flustered her, plus the fact that he seemed capable of reading her every thought. Jessica merely shook her head in refusal of his suggestion. After swallowing a bite of hamburger she sensed her frustration amused him and attempted to divert his attention.

"You mentioned earlier that you wanted to ask me about some of the old crowd. Who, for instance?" she questioned.

The people he named were ones she either knew or knew about. Jessica suspected he had deliberately chosen people he knew had been friends of either her brother or sister.

When they had finished their hamburgers, Brodie ordered another cup of coffee. Jessica stirred her malt with the straw.

As he turned his head, she studied the black sheen of his hair. Devil black, she had called it once. It contrasted sharply with the vivid blue of his eyes. His lean, hard features were marked by lines crowfooting from the corners of his eyes and grooves slashed into the tan skin on either side of his mouth. It was the compelling face of a self-confident man certain of his ability and his masculinity—two rare characteristics. His gaze lifted and he caught her staring at him. Jessica sipped her malt and tried not to react to the almost physical sensation of his look.

"Has the place changed much since you used to come here?" she asked to erase the silence.

"Not much." He glanced disinterestedly around the interior of the restaurant. "It's been repainted and they've moved the jukebox to a different wall and added video games. But it's basically the way I remember it."

"It must remind you of a lot of good times," she suggested.

"Yes." Brodie seemed momentarily absent, lost in his thoughts. Then he came back to the present. "It also reminds me of what I never want to go back to being." He took a drink of his coffee and leveled his gaze on her. "We never had much when I was a kid. Our furniture, our car, practically everything we ever owned was secondhand. I was determined that when I grew up, I was going to have the best," he stated.

"Do you have the best now?" Jessica had difficulty meeting his look.

"Not in everything, but I'm working on it." He grinned wolfishly. "Are you ready to leave?"

"Yes." She pushed her malt aside. It had thinned out to a milky consistency.

Outside in the car, Brodie started the engine. "Would you like to go for a short drive?"

Jessica was tempted to ask their destination but decided against it. The question would have mirrored her distrust, something she preferred to conceal.

"Sounds fine," she agreed instead.

Once they were in the mainstream of traffic, Brodie punched a tape into the CD player built into the dash. A delicate symphony of strings came from the concealed speakers. He cast her a sideways look.

"I hope you don't object to classical music. I've discovered it's soothing, though I don't pretend to understand the fine points of its composition."

"I don't mind. Leave it on."

It had been years since she had listened to a symphony orchestra, probably not since music class in school, but Jessica found that Brodie was right. The music was quieting and it eliminated the need for conversation—which was a recommendation in itself. She relaxed against the molded headrest of the cushioned passenger seat and listened, watching the blur of passing streetlights.

For a time she kept track of where they were until at some point she lost her sense of direction. It didn't seem really important that she know their whereabouts precisely. There were people and other cars around, homes and businesses. She supposed Brodie was simply taking a tour of the city by night. She closed her eyes for a serene moment, then opened them to study the upholstered ceiling of the car's interior.

The signal blinked in the car to indicate that he was turning onto another street, but Jessica didn't glance out of the window to see where they were going. She was intent on the intricacies of a piano solo coming from the stereo. The car turned again, this time onto a rough surface that bounced her back into an interest in her surroundings.

Brodie was stopping the car in a deserted lot. The nearest building seemed to be some kind of a warehouse. Beyond it, the night's darkness cast eerie shadows on more peculiar-looking objects.

Jessica looked back to the empty road. On the other side, a patch of moonlight glittered on water.

Immediately she cast a wary look in Brodie's direction. The darkness shadowed his face as well, not that she thought his expression would have told her anything. But she didn't need to see to feel his eyes watching her.

"Where are we?" she asked with an attempt at calm. "Is this the place where you used to park with your dates?"

"No, I couldn't afford the gasoline to drive this far." He turned and for a minute his profile was etched by the moonlight. "It would have been a good place, though, private, with the moon reflected in the lake."

"Lake?" Was that body of water Lake Chickamauga or the Tennessee River?

"Yes, Lake Chickamauga," Brodie confirmed.

"What are we doing here?" If he wasn't revisiting one of his old haunts, then what was his reason for coming here? Jessica felt her heartbeat accelerate in uncertain alarm.

"There's something I want to show you."

With that, he opened his car door and stepped outside. When his door closed, Jessica remained rooted to her seat.

She had no idea what he intended to show her and cared even less. Danger signals were ringing in her ears. She hated to admit she was frightened, but she was. After all, he was virtually a stranger. Her car door was opened and Brodie's hand was extended to help her out. She stared at it, swallowing hard.

"Come on," he urged.

"Where?"

His throaty chuckle did little to ease her mounting fear.

Chapter Four

"I'm glad you think it's funny," Jessica declared in a burst of irritation.

"Earlier you asked why I'd come back to Chattanooga. I told you only the major reason. I decided to show you the contributing factor. Do you want to see it?" It was a challenge.

All her instincts cried a refusal, but Jessica couldn't show cowardice. Reluctantly she placed her hand in his and stepped from the car.

They had walked several feet toward the darkened building when a voice called out, "The place is closed. You'll have to come back tomorrow during regular business hours."

"You're Art Mason, the security guard, aren't you?" Brodie questioned.

"Yeah?"

"I'm Brodie Hayes. I met you late this afternoon. I want to show the young lady around the place," he stated in a voice that expected his wishes to be granted.

"Sorry, Mr. Hayes," the voice answered immediately. "I didn't recognize you, what with it being so dark and all."

"That's one of the first changes I'm going to make, Mr. Mason," Brodie walked forward, his hand on her waist drawing Jessica along with him. "Better lighting at night means better security."

Changes? Had he bought the place? What was it? Jessica stole a glance at his face, but it told her nothing. She could only surmise that her guess was accurate.

A uniformed man in his fifties emerged from a shadow of the building. "That sure will be a welcome change, Mr. Hayes. As it is now, only a cat could see anything."

Keys rattled on a metal ring as he bent to unlock the front door. He opened it for them and touched the bill of his cap when Jessica walked past him.

"There's a light switch just inside the door on the left wall, Mr. Hayes," the guard instructed, and shone his flashlight inside.

Except for that stream of light, it was pitch-black inside the building. The squeezing pressure from Brodie's hand instructed Jessica to stand still, and she waited in the inky blackness until a click illuminated the interior, momentarily blinding her. Then he was by her side again, taking her arm.

"Thank you, Mr. Mason."

"When you leave, just honk your horn and I'll know to lock up," the man said, and closed the door.

A series of offices were in the front of the building, but Brodie bypassed them to lead Jessica down the hallway to the rear section. She looked around for something that would identify the business.

"Is this your new restoration project?" she asked.

"Officially it will be at nine o'clock tomorrow

morning when I sign the final purchase agreement," he told her.

"Forgive me for being so ignorant, but what is this place?"

"Have you heard of Janson Boats?" Brodie opened a door to a dark area. "Stay there a minute until I find the light switch," he added without giving her a chance to answer his first question.

Jessica waited. "Janson Boats?" She frowned while he disappeared into the shadows. "I think one of our clients was just talking about the company not too long ago. They manufacture houseboats, don't they?"

"That's right." A switch lit up a massive assembly room with large square-shaped boats in various stages of construction.

"The Janson family started it and sold out about five years ago," Jessica recalled aloud what she had heard. "Our client was a friend of the Jansons. He was saying they were lucky to get out when they did because the company has been steadily going downhill."

"Janson had a thriving business when he sold it. The new owners traded on the reputation he'd established. They began cutting corners, constructing inferior boats and charging higher prices. They siphoned every dime they could out of the company and into their own pockets. Now that they've skimmed off the cream, they've decided to unload the company and take what they can get."

Brodie was wandering through the assembly room. Jessica followed, picking her way through the debris scattered about the floor, dodging ladders and assorted equipment. The framework skeleton of a boat loomed beside them, and Brodie stopped to examine it.

"Do you know anything about building boats?"
She eyed him curiously.

"Not a single thing, except maybe the bow from
the stern," he admitted.

Jessica frowned. "Then how will you ever make
it a successful concern again?"

Brodie glanced over his shoulder at her and
smiled dryly. "That's the ten percent I can buy—
money for the man who knows how to build boats."

"But who will you hire?" She wasn't convinced
it was as easy as he was implying.

"When I heard the company was in trouble, I
asked around. It seems Janson isn't enjoying his
retirement. What's more, he's upset at the way his
name has been damaged by the company's business
practices. I talked to him yesterday and offered
him a position as president of Janson Boats, and
he accepted."

"Why?"

"Because he wants to work and he wants to see
the company become successful again," Brodie
explained with commendable patience.

"If that's true, then why didn't he buy the company? Didn't he have the money to buy it?" It
didn't make sense to Jessica that a man would go
to work for a company that he could own instead.

"Yes, Janson had the money to buy it. But he's
getting on in age and liked the idea that he had
a nest egg securely tucked away for his old age. He
didn't want to risk it in case he couldn't get the
company back on its feet again," Brodie explained,
as if it were all very logical.

"But you're risking it," she reminded him.

"I don't have anything to lose," he said with a
shrug.

"Your money," Jessica pointed out.

"I can afford the loss," he replied with a diffidence that hinted at just how successful he was.

Jessica fell silent while she absorbed that discovery. Brodie resumed his wandering inspection of the plant area. He was several yards ahead of her before she realized he had moved away. She hurried to catch up with him, unsure whether she could find her way out of this maze alone.

"This will make a very good publicity story for you," she commented.

"What?" He half turned, then agreed, "Yes, the news that Janson is taking over will be great publicity. That fact alone will increase business in the beginning."

"I wasn't thinking of Janson, although it would be good, too. I was referring to you," Jessica explained.

"Me." Brodie paused to measure her with look. "The boy from the wrong side of town comes home a success, is that how you see it? A Cinderella story, starring a guy?"

"Something like that," she admitted. "Is that wrong?"

"No, probably not, except that I'm not interested in publicity for myself." The pathway had widened, with much of the rubble cleared to one side, enabling them to walk together.

"Why not? It would open a lot of doors for you." Jessica wondered if he was still as eager to be accepted as he once had been.

"Doors that were closed to me before, you mean?" Brodie mocked. "No, thanks. I prefer to open my own doors in my own way."

"That's being stubborn."

"Yes, it is. But I won't be walking into places where I haven't knocked." Brodie pushed back the sleeve of his sweater to check the Rolex on his wrist. "It's getting late and I know you have to work in the morning. Would you like me to take you home now?"

Jessica glanced at her own watch, surprised to see it was much later than she realized. "Yes, please. I just hope you know how to get out of here."

"Through that door." He pointed to his right and Jessica realized they had made a full circle of the assembly room. She waited in the hallway while he switched off the light, and together they walked to the front entrance. The night watchman wasn't in sight as they closed the door and returned to the car. At the honk of the horn, he appeared and waved his flashlight beam at them before Brodie drove out of the lot onto the street.

The drive back to her apartment complex seemed to take little time, possibly because Jessica spent it thinking about the man behind the wheel and how much she had learned about him in one short evening. There was much more about him that attracted rather than repelled. Yet she still felt a wariness that she couldn't explain. Something cautioned her not to attempt to begin a relationship with him.

They were only a few blocks from her apartment when she felt the need to break the silence. "Do your parents still live here?"

"My father died ten years ago."

Ten years ago, Jessica thought. That was before Brodie achieved his success. She wondered if it bothered him that his father had never lived to see how far he had progressed, but decided the question was too personal.

"I didn't know. I'm sorry," she offered in sympathy.

"There isn't any reason why you should be. You didn't know him," Brodie stated in an unemotional tone.

"No, I didn't know him," Jessica admitted, and fell silent.

"There was something else you wanted to ask me, wasn't there?" He slid a sideways look at her. Jessica nibbled at her lower lip, but didn't answer. "You were wondering about my mother." She caught her breath, stunned that he had guessed so accurately. "I don't know where she is. She and my father were divorced when I was two. An attorney tried to locate her when my father died, but he couldn't find her."

There was absolutely no emotion in his voice, neither bitterness nor remorse that he had never known the woman who had given birth to him. The twinge of pity Jessica felt was wasted. Family had always played an integral part in her life, even now when her relatives lived at a distance. Brodie, obviously, hadn't missed what he had never known. The car slowed to a stop in front of her apartment building. It took Jessica several seconds to shake off her reverie. In that time Brodie had got out of the car and walked around to her door.

As she stepped out of the car, a whole new set of thoughts assailed her. The male hand at the small of her back alerted her to the fact that she would soon be telling Brodie good-night. At the conclusion of every date, with the exception of her first few as a teenager, it was expected that a kiss would be exchanged at the door, but her senses shied vigorously away from the image of his hard mouth pressed against hers.

Her heart was skipping beats when they reached her door. She made a project of searching through her bag for the key. Aware of his eyes watching her, she had the uncanny sensation that Brodie knew exactly what she was thinking, feeling and trying to avoid.

"Thank you for dinner." Her fingers closed around the key at the bottom of her bag. It struck her then that Brodie might expect her to invite him in for coffee. She had no intention of doing so and wondered how she could delicately avoid it if he suggested it.

"It was my pleasure." Brodie sounded as if he was silently laughing.

Jessica didn't look to see if he was. She removed the key from her bag. But before she could insert it in the lock, Brodie was reaching for it. The touch of his fingers was like scalding water. Jessica surrendered the key to him without resistance and took a step backward to avoid further contact while he unlocked the door.

The bolt clicked open. Jessica trembled when he straightened to face her and tried not to show it. She wondered if it was by design that he was between her and the safety of her apartment.

She held out her hand for the key. "Thank you again. And good luck in your new venture."

She attempted to slide between him and the door, hoping her movement would prompt him to step aside. He didn't. In consequence, she was uncomfortably close to him, and Brodie still hadn't returned the key.

Her gaze focused on the tiny stitches in the sleeve of his sweater while waiting for the key—but not for long. The hand with the key moved toward her. She followed it, expecting the key to be placed in her outstretched hand. Her hand was ignored as his continued in an upward motion that stopped with his forefinger at her chin, the key hidden inside his closed palm.

Forced to meet his gaze, Jessica felt a rushing heat sweep over her skin. One corner of his mouth was a fraction of an inch higher than the other, implying mockery.

"Are you wondering whether I intend to kiss you good-night?" His voice was a slow, lazy drawl, pitched low to lull her into a sense of false security.

How should she respond to that? Laugh it off? Deny that it had even occurred to her that he might kiss her? Or perhaps she should be cool and cutting. She wasn't able to make up her mind as to the best way to handle it. Her indecision gave Brodie command of the situation. Truthfully, he had been in charge of the evening from the beginning, and he didn't relinquish the position as it came to an end.

His tracing finger underlined the sensitive skin from her jaw to her chin and back, a tantalizing caress that sent the pulse in her neck throbbing at an incredible rate. Inside she was a quaking mass of jelly. Outside, there was the faintest quiver.

"I believe—" the finger of the hand with the key slowly worked its way down her neck to the vee neckline of her silk T-shirt, and Jessie was suddenly aware of how deeply it plunged in the front, "—you're frightened of me." She took a breath and lost it as she felt the cool metal of the key being slid inside the lacy cup of her brassiere and against the warmth of her breast. Her stomach was instantly twisted into knots.

"I believe," she began in a voice that was husky from the disturbed state of her nerves, "you're trying to frighten me."

His mouth twitched in a fleeting smile while she

silently congratulated herself for having the presence of mind not to reveal how much she was intimidated by his raw virility. It was a small victory, but she cherished it.

"Perhaps I am," Brodie conceded the possible truth in her statement. He was no longer touching her. The lack of actual physical contact didn't lessen the sexual tension that coursed through her nerves. "But a little fear is good," he added. "It sharpens the senses and sends adrenaline shooting through the veins. It can be very stimulating and exhilarating."

His words defined precisely what Jessica was feeling. She was frightened, but not too frightened to run. The fact made the situation doubly dangerous and placed more power in his hands.

"You can stop wondering, though." His heavily veiled look encompassed every feature of her face. "I'm not going to kiss you good-night." He turned the knob and pushed the door open, all without taking his eyes from her. Moving aside he added a promise, "Not this time."

Not until Jessica was inside her apartment with the door closed did she realize that he had implied that there would be another time. Yet he hadn't asked her for a date or even said he would call her. Perhaps because of the pressures of his business, he didn't know when he would be free.

She listened to the echo of his footsteps in the hallway. The curve of her breast tingled where his hand had made brief contact with it when he had slid the key inside her bra. She took the key and returned it to her bag, but that didn't erase the sensation.

A surge of irritation burned through her as she realized he had assumed she would accept a subsequent invitation from him. The only reason she had gone to dinner with him tonight was because she had trapped herself into agreeing. The next time she wouldn't let that happen. Admittedly, Brodie Hayes was a fascinating man, but that was all the more reason to stay away from him.

The next few days Jessica lived in constant anticipation of a telephone call from him, either at work or at home. Yet the weekend came and went without a word from Brodie. At first Jessica blamed the silence on whatever was involved in purchasing the boat manufacturing company. Then she had assumed that other business interests had taken him out of town.

By the middle of the following week, she was forced to consider that he might not be interested in seeing her again, regardless of what he had implied. That possibility became more logical when Jessica remembered he had admitted taking her to the restaurant where he had wanted to bring her sister. She discovered her ego was bruised. It was one thing to look forward to rejecting him, and quite another to be the one rejected.

While Jessica tried not to admit it, the experience had had an effect on her. She became irritable and defensive. Her patience with others grew short. She pretended that she had forgotten the entire incident, but it was forever nagging at the back of her mind.

There was a knock at the door of her private office. "Yes?" she answered in a voice sharper than she realized. Ann Morrow, the receptionist, walked in. "A guy from the printer's dropped this by for you." She handed Jessica a bulky manilla envelope.

"He said you'd told him you wanted to go over the proofs as soon as he had them ready."

With a sigh Jessica unfastened the flap. "Do you suppose I'm experienced enough to check copy?" As far as she was concerned, it was something anyone who could read could do, and she found it very boring.

"I wouldn't let it get you down just because Mr. Dane isn't going to let you handle that new account you brought in," Ann insisted.

Jessica raised a dark blond eyebrow and stared at the receptionist. "What new account?" she demanded.

"How many are there, for heaven's sake?" Ann laughed. Before Jessica could reply that she didn't know, she was interrupted by the ring of the telephone in the reception room. "Oops, I'd better get that."

Jessica watched her leave, overcome for a minute by curiosity. Then she shrugged. Ann must have got her information confused. She knew nothing about a new client. It must have been someone else in the office who had solicited the new account. In any event, her uncle hadn't mentioned anything about it to her yet, but she generally heard about new accounts in a roundabout way. She took the proof copies out of the envelope and began checking them. The first glaring error fairly leaped off the page at her as she noted that the wrong size of type had been used. Farther down the same page the wrong style of type had been set.

The instructions had been very clear and it annoyed Jessica that they had been so blatantly ignored. She raced through the rest of it and found three more mistakes, minor ones. As far as she was concerned, they were marks of shoddy workmanship.

Bundling the corrected copy back into its envelope, she called the printing company, told them what she thought of the quality of their work, and instructed them to have someone return immediately for the proofs. Much of her annoyance had been vented in the phone call, but a trace of it was still shimmering in the green of her eyes when she entered the outer office.

"A man from the printing company is coming to pick this up," she informed Ann as she tossed the envelope on her desk.

"At lunchtime? But I'll be gone," Ann protested.

Jessica glanced at her watch. It was eleven-thirty. "I didn't realize what time it was," she apologized with irritation at her oversight. "Just leave it on your desk, then."

As she turned, the door to her uncle's office opened and Brodie Hayes walked out. His blue eyes lighted on her immediately and a half smile curved his mouth while she tried to get her breath back. Again he was dressed in a dark suit and tie that emphasized his good looks and gave the impression of a prosperous businessman.

It was a full second before Jessica became aware of the stranger who was with him as well as her uncle. Ann's comment about a new client clicked in her mind. Had she meant Brodie?

"Hello, Jessica," Brodie greeted her, but didn't give her an opportunity to answer. "I don't believe you've met Mr. Janson."

Jessica managed a smile as she stepped forward. Janson was the man who had agreed to take over the presidency of the boat company he had once owned. He was a sparely built man with bushy eyebrows and a mass of iron gray hair. The harshness of his features was softened when he smiled, as he was doing now. Jessica had the feeling he was a very honest, trustworthy man.

"It's a pleasure to meet you, Miss Thorne." The man shook her hand and cast a glance sideways at Brodie. "I can certainly see why Mr. Hayes found you so persuasive?"

"Persuasive?" She was confused, and a glance at Brodie only added to it.

"There's no need to be modest, Jessica." The unsettling blue eyes were fixed on her. "Mr. Janson has already added his endorsement to your suggestions."

"My suggestions?" She was beginning to feel like an echo.

"Yes, and they were very good, too," her uncle inserted. "The campaign you outlined to Mr. Hayes will be just the thing to rebuild the reputation of the company. Janson back at the helm," Ralph Dane said as if quoting a line from an advertisement.

Nothing was making any sense to her. She didn't know what they were talking about. She had made no suggestions for a campaign nor even suggested that Brodie should use this firm. But before she could correct the impression, Brodie was speaking.

"You can handle everything from here, Cal," he told Janson, and turned to her uncle. "It was a pleasure meeting you, Mr. Dane. While you two have lunch, I hope you don't mind if I take your niece out for an early lunch of our own."

"I certainly don't," her uncle smiled broadly.

"But—" Jessica began.

"Where's your coat?" Brodie interrupted.

"In my office." There was more she would have said, but his hand was already on her elbow directing her there.

Chapter Five

Brodie ushered Jessica into her office and closed the door. She turned to face him, his bland expression telling her absolutely nothing.

"Would you mind explaining what's going on?" Her hands were on her hips in challenge.

"Over lunch. Where's your coat?" he repeated his earlier question, then noticed the coat hanging on a wall hook.

Jessica was much too confused to object when he helped her into it and handed her shoulder bag to her. He was guiding her to the outer office before Jessica realized how readily she was falling in with his plans. She pulled her arm free of his hold.

"What are you doing?" she demanded.

"I'm taking you to lunch," he responded.

"I never said I'd go with you."

Brodie tipped his head to an inquiring angle. "Will you?"

"I have no intention of going anywhere with

you." Jessica set her handbag on the chair and started to slip out of her coat.

"The same way you had no intention of providing me with your address." His hands were on her shoulders, as if to help her off with the coat.

Something in his voice made her pause. "What are you talking about?" She feigned ignorance.

"I'm talking about the last time you accepted my invitation to dinner, knowing that I didn't know where you lived and doubting that I would find out." His hands remained on her shoulders, his closeness a tangible thing.

Jessica's back was to him, but the warmth of his hands seemed to burn through the coat to her skin. "You knew!" The murmur was halfway between an accusation and an admission.

"Yes, I knew."

"Why did you bother to find out where I lived when you guessed what I did?" She lifted her head to a proudly defensive angle, refusing to feel guilty for her act.

"I invited you to dinner. You accepted. I always do what I say I'm going to do and I expect the same from others." With one hand, Brodie turned her around and slipped his other hand inside her coat to rest on the curve of her waist.

The floor seemed to rock beneath her feet. Tipping her head back to look at his handsome face, Jessica was reminded again that Brodie got what he wanted, one way or another. Resistance seemed futile.

"Shall we have lunch?" he asked, as if suggesting it for the first time.

All she had to do was refuse. Since he had revealed his knowledge of her previous deception, she felt trapped. She was honor bound to go with him. Reluctantly she nodded agreement.

Brodie stepped away and held the door to the outer office open for her. Flipping her blond hair free of the coat collar, Jessica swept past him. She paused at the receptionist's desk, trying to ignore the imposing man accompanying her.

"If anyone calls, I've gone to lunch. Be sure to leave that envelope for the printer," she instructed. "I'll be back around one o'clock."

"Maybe," Brodie inserted.

Before Jessica could contradict him, he was ushering her outside. The last thing that registered was the faintly envious gleam in the receptionist's eyes. Silently she acknowledged that Brodie was capable of turning heads. He had caught her attention when they had both been waiting at the crosswalk. Because he had seemed familiar, she had continued to stare at him that time, but it had definitely been his commanding male presence that had first drawn her eye. So it really wasn't so surprising that Ann had been drawn by it, too.

"I thought we'd have lunch at the railway station," Brodie said as he helped Jessica into his car parked at the curb. "Is that all right?"

"Fine," she agreed with an indifferent air that said she didn't care where they lunched.

There was no further attempt at conversation as Brodie negotiated the luxury car through the city traffic and onto the street where the renovated railroad station of the Chattanooga Choo-Choo was located.

"I suppose you've eaten here many times before," Brodie commented after they had parked the car in the lot and entered the station remodeled to house assorted shops and restaurants.

"Not recently," she replied coolly.

"I hope you don't mind coming here." He led her to the high-ceilinged restaurant. "I've never been here before—I couldn't afford it."

It was an offhand statement, without apology, that instantly reminded Jessica of his background. Yet he handled his new status with the ease of one who had been accustomed to having everything he wanted all his life. She was forced to remember that it hadn't always been so. Brodie had fought his way to the top and shouldn't be underestimated.

The tables in the restaurant were nearly all taken, mostly by tourists. But within minutes, Brodie had persuaded the hostess to find them a table at the window with a view of the gardens. The sun glared through the skylight. Jessica had just opened her menu when the waiter appeared.

"Two glasses of white wine, please. We'll order later." Brodie set his menu aside.

"I do have to be back by one," Jessica stated.

"It won't hurt if you're late," he insisted with infuriating complacency.

She gritted her teeth for an instant. "I know you believe that because my employer is also my uncle, I can come and go as I please, but that doesn't happen to be true. I have work to do, work that I'm paid to do."

"Your uncle isn't going to object if you take a longer lunch today." He paused as the waiter brought their wine.

"Especially since you're with me. After all, I'm a new client and my account with your uncle's firm promises to be very large."

"That's another thing," Jessica seized on that. "What was all that nonsense about me persuading you to bring the Janson account to us? I had nothing to do with it.''

"Don't be naive, Jessica." His mouth curved above the rim of the wine glass. "You had everything to do with it. You're the reason, the only reason, I ordered Janson to have Dane handle the advertising.''

Jessica swallowed, his bluntness throwing her again. "Why me?" God, she didn't know why she asked that question. She'd give anything to have it back.

"Because you have blond hair and beautiful green eyes. Because you're a woman I want to get to know . . . very well." The slight hesitation was designed to underline the last two words. Their message was unmistakable. Jessica felt the blood rush hotly through her veins. His observant blue eyes noted her reaction. "Hasn't a man ever made a play for you before?" Brodie asked bluntly.

"Of course." She tried to shrug away his question with a worldliness she didn't feel at the moment. Self-consciously, she fingered the stem of her wine glass.

"And?" he prompted.

"And what?" Jessica tried to appear nonchalant.

"And what would you do if I tried to?"

A table separated them. Yet the way he was looking at her made her feel he was making love to her in his mind. She could almost feel the caress of his hands, and it awakened a sensual hunger that had nothing to do with food.

"I guess you'll have to wait and find out." She clung to her air of bravado, despite the fact that she was so vulnerable.

"I'll look forward to it. But don't worry." He smiled lazily.

"I'm not going to rush you."

"Am I supposed to be grateful that you warned me?" she retorted.

"Do you consider it a warning?" He quirked an eyebrow thoughtfully. "I thought it was a promise."

"We'd better order." Jessica picked up her menu, finding she was no match for him in this battle of innuendoes.

"You've eaten here before." Brodie didn't object to her suggestion. "What would you recommend?"

"Since I'm not familiar with your tastes, I can't help you." She refused to look up from the menu.

"But you know my tastes. I want only the best. Nothing less will do." His disconcerting blue gaze was leveled at her, and she sensed that he wasn't referring to food.

"My definition of that might differ from yours. You'll have to choose for yourself," she insisted. "I'm going to have the chef's salad."

Brodie motioned the waited to their table, gave him Jessica's order and his own for a rare steak. As raw as she felt, she thought his choice was somehow fitting. It was even more nerve-racking to know that he was aware of what he was doing to her.

"Don't you like the wine?" Brodie asked.

Jessica had yet to take a sip of it. "I generally don't have anything to drink during the day, except water."

"But this is a special occasion."

"Why?"

"Because we're here together, you and I." He took a drink from his glass and set it down. "I was beginning to think there would always be an appointment, a telephone call to make, something to prevent me from seeing you again."

"Really?" she murmured.

"Do you mean you didn't expect to hear from me before today?" His question was faintly taunting.

"I didn't think about you at all," Jessica lied.

"Did you really believe I wouldn't be back to claim a good-night kiss?" His gaze slid to her lips and Jessica had to fight an impulse to moisten them.

"Isn't there something else we can discuss?" she demanded in irritation while her fingers nervously traced a circle around the rim of her wine glass.

"How about the weather?" Brodie asked.

"I don't care what it is. The weather or the cost of a loaf of bread, it makes no difference," Jessica breathed out impatiently.

"Then stop playing with the wine glass like that." Her hand jerked from the glass as if it had suddenly caught fire. She folded her hands in her lap and struggled to regain her momentary loss of poise. Fortunately, their waiter chose that moment to arrive with their meal, which smoothed over Jessica's sensation of inadequacy.

Yet it was a relief when each had finished and Brodie signaled the waiter for their check. She, who had thought herself so experienced, had discovered that she didn't know how to handle this man. Brodie was in control, directing events, conversations and feelings.

As they left the restaurant, Jessica started toward the exit to the parking lot, but the pressure of Brodie's hand forestalled her.

"You still have plenty of time to get back to the office. Why don't we wander through the shops?" he suggested smoothly.

She hesitated. The trouble was he was right. It was well before one o'clock yet. Still she attempted to wiggle out of it.

"They just have the usual assortment of things," she said, shrugging.

He raised an eyebrow. "A woman who doesn't care to browse? That's rare."

He made it sound like a compliment. Out of sheer perversity, Jessica turned into the entrance of the first shop, determined to look at every single item. If he got bored, that was just his tough luck.

After a short time, it wasn't difficult to pretend an interest in the various items. Jessica was aware of Brodie strolling along behind her, pausing when she stopped to inspect something that had caught her eye, but she did a credible job of ignoring him.

A pair of candlesticks carved out of oak particularly attracted her attention. The workmanship in the set was flawless.

"They're beautiful, aren't they?" she admired them aloud, holding one to examine the intricate carving on the base more closely.

"Yes, they are," Brodie agreed.

A few minutes later Jessica moved on to several shelves of pottery. Within seconds, she sensed there was something wrong. She turned around and found she was alone; Brodie was no longer with her. She glanced around the shop and saw him walking away from the cash register, carrying a package. A furrow of puzzled curiosity drew her brows together as he approached her.

"For you." Brodie offered her the package and added the explanation, "The candlesticks you liked."

Her gaze jumped from the package to his chiseled features. "But I didn't mean that I wanted you to buy them for me."

"I know you didn't." He forced the package into her hand. "But I wanted you to have them." Jessica unfastened the clasp of her bag and, with one hand, tried to find her wallet. "I'll pay for them."

His hand curved along the side of her neck, his thumb forcing her chin up. "Didn't your parents teach you how to accept a present graciously?" he chided. "You smile very prettily and say 'thank you.' "

He touched her without a trace of self-consciousness. It was done with such ease, naturally, as if he was long accustomed to treating her so familiarly. The sensations his touch created were not familiar to Jessica.

"My parents did teach me not to take candy from strangers," she offered in defense, fighting the breathlessness that changed her voice.

His intensely blue gaze commanded that she look at him. "But we won't be strangers for long, Jessica."

It became easier to surrender than struggle against a superior force. "Thank you. They're beautiful," she accepted the gift with stiff gratitude.

"Now the smile," Brodie prodded. Only when she gave it to him did he take his hand away from the slender curve in her throat. "Shall we go look at the model train display?"

"Yes," Jessica agreed readily with his suggestion. Although the pressure of his hand had been in no way threatening, the sensation of danger faded when it was taken away. Her heart continued to beat at an uneven tempo, but she didn't feel quite as weak as she had a minute before.

Leaving the gift shop, they walked outside onto the platform of the old train depot to the store with the model train display. The display, which occupied almost an entire room, was a scale model of Chattanooga, complete with train, tracks, tunnels, bridges and detailed structures to scale. Miniature trees forested a replica of Lookout Mountain. Houses had clotheslines and there were women hanging clothes.

As the model trains, passenger cars and locomotives raced around the tracks, barely missing each other at switching stations and crossings, there was always something new to see. It captured the imagination of young and old alike. "It's fascinating, isn't it?" Jessica watched the precise timing that miraculously avoided any crashes of locomotives. "Justin had a model train set up in his room. Nothing as large as this, of course. His was built on a wooden table. Whenever he had it running, he used to let me come in and watch. He always insisted I was too young to operate it."

"When you were old enough, I bet you were more interested in boys, boy bands, and talking about boys than model trains," Brodie concluded.

"Something like that," she admitted.

A child's voice echoed clearly through the room. "Can I have that, daddy?" His arm swept out to indicate the entire display.

"We don't have a room large enough for it," the man holding him answered. "But maybe Santa can bring you one train for Christmas. Is that all right?"

"Will it make smoke like that one?" the boy pointed.

"Yes, it'll make smoke," the father agreed.

"That's okay, then. Santa can bring me that." The boy accepted the compromise offer.

A smile tugged at the corners of Jessica's mouth. "I'll bet every child that sees this wants a train for Christmas." She glanced up at Brodie through the sweep of her lashes, idly curious. "Did Santa ever bring you a train for Christmas, one that blows smoke?"

"No, I never did get a train." He shook his head briefly, his black hair gleaming. "But there were a lot of Christmases that Santa didn't make it to our house. I'm not sure whether it was because we were too poor or because I was a bad boy."

Rather than comment on his background, Jessica chose a facetious remark. "Santa always knows who's been good or bad."

"He certainly knows that I didn't make my father's life any easier." His hands were braced on the railing that cordoned off the display. "My father used to work for the railroad."

"He did?" Jessica was glad he had changed the subject. The memory of her brother saying that Brodie was no good was still very clear in her mind.

"Yes. He was hurt in a derailment when I was about five and ended up partially disabled. He never was able to get enough part-time work to combine with his pension to give us enough to live on, and he was too damned proud to go on welfare, so we went without a lot of things."

"What was your father like?" She tried to visualize an older version of Brodie, but had difficulty picturing a disabled man when Brodie was so vital and robust.

"Stubborn, proud. The one thing he couldn't tolerate was failure. In the end, he was a broken man." His gaze narrowed on the miniature tracks of the display. "He couldn't work at the job he loved—the railroad. His wife had run out on him. His son brought him pain instead of hope."

"I'm sorry, Brodie." This time Jessica wasn't offering empty words. "He would have been proud of you today."

"Yes." Brodie straightened from the rail, his action indicating that he was ready to leave the model-train display. "But it didn't work out that way."

She marveled that he could accept it so calmly, but he'd had more time to adjust to it. He'd had to put the remorse behind him and carry on with his life, while she was just tasting the bitter pangs of disappointment on his behalf for the first time.

They wandered outside again, onto the platform. The locomotive of the famed Chattanooga Choo-Choo waited on Track 29 of the 1905 Terminal Station. A collection of dining cars and sleeping parlor cars occupied other tracks within the center.

"Have you ever eaten in one of the dining cars?" Brodie asked when Jessica slowed her steps for a closer look at one.

"No." She smiled wryly. "Isn't that typical? No one takes advantage of attractions in their own hometown."

"True," he agreed.

"Anyway, I've never been able to get reservations on the night I wanted to go." She shrugged at the thwarted opportunities.

"We'll have to correct this oversight, since I've never dined there, either. I'll make dinner reservations here some evening when I'm in town."

He was taking her acceptance for granted, something Jessica couldn't allow. "As long as I happen to be free the same evening."

"Of course," he said with a look that expressed confidence that she would be available.

They continued to stroll along the platform. As they approached a group of tourists occupying much of the platform, Brodie's hand moved to a spot between Jessica's shoulders to guide her through the throng. The vaguely possessive touch sent quivers down her spine, especially when his hand slid downward to the back of her waist.

"I understand the parlor cars are actually rented out. Couples can spend the night in them," Brodie commented.

"That's true. I've seen pictures of the interior. They're beautiful—Victorian furniture, brass beds." Jessica told him.

"When I make our dinner reservations, maybe I should reserve us a sleeping car." His sideways glance inspected her face. Jessica felt it grow warm. "No, thank you."

"Does the thought of making love embarrass you?" Again his candor unnerved her. "Or don't you talk about things like that?"

She didn't want to answer either question. She was on treacherous footing and the sooner she reached solid ground, the better off she would be.

"It must be time for me to get back to the office," she offered desperately.

Brodie glanced at his watch and mocked, "So it is. Always the conscientious employee, aren't you?"

"I earn my salary." She refused to sound righteous.

They turned and started back for the parking lot. "And do you work Saturdays as well?"

"No, the office is closed on Saturdays." Her steps quickened.

"That doesn't mean you don't work. Officially, the office may be closed, but there still may be work to do," he reasoned.

"So far I haven't had to work on Saturday," was the only answer Jessica could give.

"What do you do, then? Play tennis? Golf? Swim?"

"It depends."

"What will you be doing this Saturday?" Brodie asked.

"I don't have anything special planned." Immediately Jessica realized she had fallen into another one of his traps.

"In that case, we can plan something together," he decided.

"If you have in mind that sleeping car . . ." she began with rising indignation.

"Actually what I had in mind is a tour of some of Chattanooga's attractions. A day spent sightseeing. Is that innocent enough for you?" A wicked light glinted in his eyes.

"I suppose so." Again it was an invitation that left her without grounds to refuse. Part of her didn't want to refuse, either.

"Good. I'll pick you up at your apartment at ten Saturday morning." It was all settled.

Chapter Six

Saturday morning was flooded with sunshine, without a cloud in the crystal-blue sky. The white flowers of the dogwood blossomed in the green hills. The air was filled with mating calls from the trilling song of birds to the chattering cries of squirrels.

Jessica stood on the narrow balcony of her apartment to watch and listen. A loose-fitting silk blouse of olive green, its color a shade darker than her eyes, was belted at the waist over a pair of white Levis. A long, chunky chain of gold hung around her neck.

It was a warm, coatless day, certainly not the kind of day one wanted to spend indoors. But of course she wasn't. Jessica glanced at the gold watch on her wrist—one minute before ten. As if on cue, the doorbell rang.

Her heart gave a sudden leap of excitement and she paused until it had resumed its normal rate. It was essential to keep both feet on the ground today. It would never do to be carried away by spring fever, a malady she was susceptible to.

The doorbell rang a second time as she turned the knob and opened the door wide. Her heart became lodged in her throat at the sight of Brodie, despite her effort to keep it firmly in its place. He seemed so potently male standing there.

A white shirt stretched across his wide shoulders to taper to his waist, the long sleeves rolled halfway up his forearms, the top three buttons unfastened. A pair of faded denims hugged his hips and emphasized the length of his legs. But it was the impression of so much tanned, hard flesh that was causing the most havoc with her senses.

"Hello." His greeting had a velvet quality to it. "This is for you—a rose for a Thorne, if you'll forgive an overworked sentiment."

Until Brodie offered it to her, Jessica hadn't noticed the single red rose in his hand. Her fingers curled around the stem to take it from him, the carnelian red petals in full bloom.

"It's beautiful," she murmured inadequately. "Thank you."

"Are you ready?"

"Yes. Just give me a moment to put this in a vase."

She hurried into the kitchen, took a bud vase from the cupboard, and partially filled it with water. Standing the rose stem in the vase, she carried it into the living room and set it next to the mantel clock where the polished grain of the wood would show off the rich red of the flower.

Brodie watched it all from inside the doorway, commenting when Jessica joined him, "If I'd known you were going to go to all that trouble, I would have brought you a bouquet."

"It was no trouble."

In the hallway, Brodie waited while she locked the door.

"Have you had breakfast?"

"Toast and coffee." Generally she ate a hearty breakfast, but she didn't want to dwell on why she hadn't been hungry this morning.

"Good. I didn't have time to eat, either. Instead of lunch, let's have a late breakfast," he suggested.

"Very well," she agreed.

Considering her lack of appetite earlier, Jessica was surprised to discover she was almost ravenous when the waitress set a plate of bacon, eggs, grits and biscuits in front of her. Brodie's meal was similarly huge. Neither had difficulty finishing it all.

"Had enough? Want something more?" he asked.

"More than enough," she declared with a decisive nod. "I'm going to need to exercise to work it off."

"That can be arranged." There was a smile in his voice as he lifted the coffee cup to his mouth. Draining all but the dregs, he set the cup down. "Let's go."

At her nod of agreement, he paid for breakfast and they left. Outside in the car, he started the engine but didn't put it in gear, turning an inquiring look at her.

"Where would you like to start our tour?"

Jessica had no preference. "You're the driver—you choose."

A pleasantly wicked look stole over his face. "Maybe I'll choose the sleeping car at the Train Station in order to provide you with that exercise you said you needed."

This time his suggestive comment did not completely shatter her poise. "That isn't the kind of exercise I had in mind," she answered with commendable calm.

"What did you have in mind? Something more tame and less stimulating, like walking?" Brodie mocked.

He directed his gaze at her lips to watch them form the words of her answer. The action tested the strength of her composure. It held.

"Yes, like walking."

"In that case, we'll start our tour at the top by beginning at Lookout Mountain." Brodie shifted the car into gear and finally looked away from her.

The mountain towered at the edge of the city like a sentinel. Access to the top was by a road that twisted and curved its way up the slope. As they neared the entrance to Rock City, one of the more popular tourist attractions atop Lookout Mountain, Brodie glanced at Jessica.

"I never thought about it, but it probably would have been quicker to take the Incline," he said.

"I prefer driving to the top. That railway is too steep for me." The one and only time Jessica had ridden it, it had seemed to go straight up the mountain, so steep was the slope.

"Do heights bother you?" Brodie eyed her curiously.

"Yes." She didn't lie about the phobia she had of high places.

Although he didn't comment, she had the sensation that Brodie stored the information away. He parked the car in the lot opposite Rock City Gardens and they walked across the street to the entrance, a building that didn't attempt to compete with the natural splendor that lay beyond it.

A trail wound its way through ageless rock formations, majestic and massive. Trees grew where it seemed impossible that they could root. There was a springtime explosion of flowers that filled the air with their delicate scents. The myriad sights, sounds and smells demanded a leisurely pace.

Jessica lingered at the balancing rock to study its seeming defiance of gravity. "It's been so long since I was here that I'd forgotten how unique this place is." She glanced at Brodie, remembering his previous comments about the deprivation of his childhood. "Have you ever been here before?"

"My father brought me here a couple of times when I was small. The last time I was here, though, I was thrown out." His mouth quirked at the memory.

"Why? What did you do?"

"I didn't have enough money to get in, so I snuck in without paying. Unfortunately—or fortunately, depending on your point of view, I was caught."

As they continued along the trail past the balancing rock, his hand seemed to automatically seek hers. The grip of his hand was strong and firm. Jessica doubted that she could have pulled her hand free of it—not that she wanted to. She discovered that she liked this sensation of being linked to him. She was content to enjoy the feeling rather than question the wisdom of it.

Without referring to her fear of heights, Brodie guided her away from the swinging bridge that spanned a chasm in the park and chose the more solid alternative of the stone bridge instead.

At Lovers' Leap, Jessica gravitated unconsciously toward the Eagles' Nest, a man-made aperture that jutted out from the rock face of the mountain. The view was spectacular from the observation point. The air was perfectly clear except for a thin band of haze on the distant Great Smokey Mountains. The vivid green of the land contrasted with the sharp blue of the sky, a combination of colors only nature could make.

At the foot of the mountain was Chattanooga. Close to that was the Civil War battlefield of Chickamauga where the South had won its last major victory. But it was the far horizon that stunned the imagination. Here was a view of seven states. Directly south were the rolling landscapes of Georgia and Alabama. Then, looking north, South Carolina, North Carolina, Virginia, and finally Tennessee and Kentucky could be seen.

So wrapped up was she in the sprawling vistas, Jessica wasn't aware of how close she was to the edge until she accidentally looked down. A cold chill ran through her bones, freezing her heartbeat for a terrifying second.

An arm circled her shoulders and turned her away from the edge. Her heart started beating again and she darted a grateful look at Brodie. His smile was gentle but fleeting. Once they were away from the edge and back on the trail through the park, he took his arm from her shoulders, but made no attempt to hold her hand.

"Quite a view, wasn't it?" he offered in idle conversation.

"In every direction except down." Her attempt at laughter wavered from her throat.

"I wondered how long it would take before you realized where you were standing." There wasn't a trace of sympathy in his voice, only faint amusement.

Jessica felt suddenly defensive. "Everyone has a weakness. What's yours?"

Brodie stopped and looked her over, his direct

gaze lingering on her honey-colored hair before meeting her eyes. "Women with blond hair and green eyes."

Over his shoulder there was the sparkling silver ribbon of a waterfall, but Jessica didn't notice it or the fellow sightseers scattered along the trail. She was aware of nothing but the man in front of her and the sudden tightness that had gripped her throat.

"Is that right?" She tried to make it a breezy retort, but it came out breathless.

"Yes." Relentlessly he held her gaze. "I read somewhere that a gentleman shouldn't kiss a lady until the third date. Counting lunch, this is the third time we've been out together, Green Eyes. I don't remember if it said when a gentleman is entitled to claim his kiss, but . . ." His hand molded itself to the curve of her neck, his long fingers sliding into the silky length of her hair at the back of her neck. His other hand cupped the side of her face, lifting her chin with his thumb. "I'm not going to wait any longer."

His mouth made a slow, unhurried descent to her lips. There was ample time to protest, but Jessica didn't utter a sound. The curiosity to discover his kiss was overpowering. As the distance lessened, her eyes slowly closed.

Then his mouth was warmly covering hers, its touch firm and experienced. At its persuasive movement on her lips, the tension of anticipation eased and Jessica responded to the kiss. Her hands spread over his rib cage for support, feeling his hard flesh through the thin material of his shirt. The arching of her spine enabled the rest of her body to lean closer to his male length. Resistance melted as a slow burning fire spread through her veins.

The pressure of the kiss was ended, but he didn't move his mouth from her lips. "I've been wanting to do that for a long time," he murmured against their softness.

Jessica found herself wishing that he hadn't waited so long. In the next second, that thought was banished under the driving possession of his mouth. The pressure at the back of her neck lifted her on tiptoes. She felt drawn to the edge of a precipice, the ground quaking beneath her feet, creating shudders within her.

"Don't look down. Just hold onto me," Brodie muttered thickly as if he knew exactly what she was feeling.

In blind obedience, her hands curved around to his muscled back, fingers curling into the material of his shirt stretched taut by the flexing muscles. The biting hold of his hands on her head and neck caused pain, but Jessica didn't object to it. An inner voice told her that if Brodie ever let her go, she would never recover from the fall.

Gradually she became aware that he was letting her down slowly. The ground beneath her feet became solid. She was no longer balanced on the edge of her toes, but was standing squarely. In another few seconds the warmth of his mouth was no longer on hers. Before his hands left her face, they smoothed her hair. Reluctantly she opened her eyes, hoping she didn't look as dazed as she felt.

Brodie was glancing around them, his attention only returning to her face when he sensed her eyes were on him. A smoldering light was visible through the banked blue fire of his gaze.

"We have an audience." His comment implied that he would not have stopped otherwise.

Jessica felt no embarrassment at the announcement. "Oh, well," she murmured.

Brodie didn't respond to that. By silent mutual consent, they continued along the trail through the rock garden to its end. From there, their tour included Ruby Falls, the Chickamauga battlefield, and very late in the afternoon, a stop for sandwiches.

Not once did either of them allude to the kiss by the waterfall. Yet Jessica was aware that what had begun as a reluctant attraction to a charismatic man had become something physical. The slightest touch of him vividly recalled the more intimate contact. There was a part of her that didn't regret the change.

When Brodie stopped the car in front of the apartment building, she had the feeling that the afternoon had ended too soon. As he took the key from the ignition, his comment seemed to echo her thought.

"I wish I'd had that second cup of coffee the waitress offered back at the restaurant." He stepped out of the car and walked around to her side.

"If you like, I can make some coffee," Jessica offered.

There was a mocking twinkle in his eye that gave him a roguish look as he closed the door after she had climbed out. "I thought you'd never ask!"

Inside her apartment, she motioned toward the living room. "Make yourself comfortable while I fix the coffee."

She continued on to the kitchen, fighting a sudden attack of nerves. After she had rinsed out the glass pot, she turned to find Brodie had followed her into the kitchen.

"I never have figured out how I'm supposed to make myself comfortable sitting alone in a strange room," he explained his presence in the kitchen.

"I know what you mean," Jessica laughed. "I always end up sitting on the edge of the chair waiting for the other person to come back. It's awkward."

However many times she had felt that way, she had never once admitted it to the host or hostess. Yet Brodie had, with casual frankness.

Measuring the fresh-ground coffee into the filter, she slipped it into its place in the coffee maker. Brodie watched, his arms crossed in front of him, one hip leaning against the kitchen counter. Jessica filled a plastic container with the proper amount of water and poured it into the coffee maker. She flipped the brew switch to the on position.

"It won't be long," she promised him.

Brodie was standing in front of the cupboard where the plastic water container belonged. As she approached, Jessica had the sensation that all of him was watching her—not just his eyes, but his other senses were observing her, as well. She found herself wishing that she had had time to freshen her lipstick, brush her hair to a silken texture, dab on some perfume behind her ears.

As she reached past him to put the container in the cupboard Brodie straightened to avoid the door. "It doesn't matter about the coffee."

Jessica stared at him. "Why didn't you say so before I made it?"

"We both know it was just an excuse. An excuse so you could invite me in and an excuse for me to accept." Brodie sliced through any attempt at pretense. "You'll pour me a cup and I'll drink it." He reached out to span her waist with his hands and pull her closer to him. "But this is why we're here."

She flattened her hands against his chest in a weak attempt at protest even as she lifted her head to accept his kiss. It was hard and demanding, parting her lips to deepen the passion that sprang between them like a living flame. Her hands slid around his neck, her fingers seeking the sensual thickness of his black hair.

His own were molding her back and hips, crushing her softer flesh to the unyielding contours of his body. The heady scent of his masculine cologne, the intimate taste of his mouth, the thudding of his heart against hers—they all combined to dominate her senses. Jessica realized that she was losing control, not just of her flesh, but of her will, too.

It was much too soon. She couldn't surrender to someone she barely knew. She twisted away from the possession of his kiss only to quiver with desire as Brodie nibbled at the sensitive skin of her neck. Her muscles tensed an instant before she pushed herself out of his embrace, but he didn't pursue when she took a shaky step away.

Jessica avoided his gaze. "I just remembered I have some cake in the refrigerator." She realized that she was probably babbling like an idiot, but she couldn't endure the sudden silence. She started toward the refrigerator. "It's bought cake, but it's really very good. Would you like a piece with your coffee?"

When she would have opened the door to get the cake, Brodie's hand was there to close it and turn her around. Jessica took a step backward, bumping into the refrigerator, the smooth finish cool against her shoulders. Brodie leaned a hand on the refrigerator near her head.

"No, I would not like any cake." He slowly enunciated each word.

Without touching any other part of her, he bent his head to kiss her. He displayed a hunger for her lips, tasting them, eating them, and arousing her appetite for his all over again. Their mouths strained for each other, but their bodies made no other contact.

Finally Brodie stopped and straightened while Jessica leaned weakly against the refrigerator, her pulse thudding in her ears. He reached out to trace her features with his fingers, his thumb outlining the curve of her mouth. His other hand drew a line from the point of her chin to the hollow of her throat. Then both slid to her shoulders, massaging her flesh, and Jessica shuddered at the wave of intense erotic longing that rushed through her.

"Don't tremble," Brodie ordered softly. The sound of his voice proved almost as provocative as the upheaval his hands were causing. "I'm not going to make love to you, Jessica. I don't have time to do it properly."

"You don't?" Was she relieved or disappointed? She was so incapable of coherent thought that she didn't know.

"No, I don't have time. I have to leave." He pulled her away from the refrigerator, kissed her hard and swiftly, then let her go. "The coffee's done. Pour me a cup."

He walked to the dinette table and sat in one of the chairs, while Jessica tried to gather her scattered senses. It seemed unjust that he would destroy her this way, then announce that he had to leave. Irritation helped to steady her hand as she filled two mugs with coffee.

"Are you sure you have time to drink this?" An acid ring crept into her question.

Amusement glittered as he detected the tone. "I wouldn't have asked you to pour if I thought I didn't."

"I wouldn't want to make you late for an appointment." Jessica set one mug on the table in front of him.

His hand closed around her wrist to take the other coffee cup from her hand and set it on the table beside his. Before she could guess his intention, Brodie was turning her around to sit her on his lap.

"You've already made me late." He took a sexy nibble of her earlobe. One large hand held both of hers prisoner in her lap. Jessica was disturbingly aware of the muscular solidity of his thighs beneath her. "My plane is waiting at the airport."

She realized that when he said he was leaving, he had meant leaving town. "Where are you going?"

"Nashville." He adjusted the collar of her blouse, then let the tip of his finger explore the shadowy cleft. "I have to be there by seven-thirty. I was supposed to be there at noon today, but I was able to postpone the meeting until tonight, just so I could spend today with you."

"I . . ." Jessica didn't know what to say. "I didn't know."

"Maybe now you'll understand just how determined I am to have you." Brodie regarded her steadily, his blue eyes unwavering.

She wasn't sure how he meant that, but at the moment it didn't seem important. "When will you be coming back?" "Sometime next week." His hand moved down to rub her thigh. "I don't know when—I'll have to call you."

He was taking it for granted that she wanted to hear from him again. Jessica didn't mind, because it was suddenly and unexpectedly vital that she did.

"My telephone number isn't listed."

"I already have it," Brodie said.

"How did you get it?" She frowned.

"When I was here the other night, I memorized it from the telephone in the living room." He flashed her a mocking smile.

She should have been angry that he had taken such liberties, but she wasn't. It was impossible to feel anything but the power of the attraction he held for her. There was a growing sense of alarm that she was giving in to him too easily, but even that had difficulty making itself heard.

His gaze focused on her mouth. "I think the coffee is the only thing around here that's getting cold." Unceremoniously, he kissed her before lifting her to her feet. "I'd better drink it and be on my way."

Jessica pushed a handful of hair away from her face and reached for her own cup. The coffee was lukewarm against her lips. She remained standing while Brodie drained his mug. Rising from the chair, he touched her cheek briefly.

"I'll call you."

"Yes." Jessica didn't walk him to the door. Brodie found his own way out of the apartment.

Chapter Seven

By Sunday night Jessica had almost convinced herself that she had succumbed to some temporary kind of madness. She had been kissed passionately before, had believed herself in love before, but her complete abandonment of control with Brodie had bordered on insanity.

Curled on the sofa, with her feet tucked beneath her, she closed the book she was holding. She hadn't read a single word in the past hour, and it was useless to pretend she would. It was equally useless to sit in the apartment. Maybe she should call her cousin Barbara Dane, her uncle's daughter, to see if she'd like to go to a movie. Anything with Tom Cruise, or Josh Hartnett would do.

As she reached for the telephone sitting on the end table by the sofa, it rang. Her hand jerked back in surprise, then she picked up the receiver, wondering if Barbara had had the same idea.

"Hello?"

"I have a long-distance telephone call for Ms.

Jessica Thorne,'' the nasal voice of a hotel operator responded.

"Speaking." Her mind was racing. The only person it could be was . . .

"Hello, Green Eyes."

It was Brodie. Her heart did a somersault. "I thought you said you were going to call one day next week," she accused, but she couldn't stop the thrill of delight that tingled through her.

"I said I'd make it back to town one day next week, but I didn't say I wouldn't call you in between," Brodie corrected. "What's the matter? Did I catch you at a bad time? Are you entertaining some other guy?"

"It so happens I'm alone." Her answer was snappish, a defensive mechanism as she wondered if Brodie thought she made a habit of behaving with all her dates as she had with him.

"All alone on a Sunday night?" He seemed to mock her solitude.

"I have to work in the morning," she reminded him.

"I forgot how conscientious you are. That's why you're having a quiet evening alone, isn't it?"

"Exactly why did you call?" Jessica demanded. "If it was just to make fun of me—"

"It's much more simple than that," Brodie interrupted. "I wanted to hear your voice."

Did he mean that? Jessica gasped back a sob as she realized that she desperately wanted him to mean it. He must have heard the strangled sound.

"Jessica?" His voice was crisp and inquiring.

"Yes?" Her tone was more subdued than it had been.

"I . . ." There was a pause and she could hear

some background noises. "There's someone at the door. I'll have to let you go."

"All right. Goodbye, Brodie."

"Jessica . . . I'll call you." He sounded impatient, tired. Then there was only the hum of the dial tone as the connection was broken.

Slowly Jessica replaced the receiver on its cradle and hugged her arms around her stomach. She wished she understood him. She wished she knew whether she could trust him.

Monday, Tuesday, Wednesday went by while she waited for the promised phone call from Brodie. It didn't come. Jessica wondered whether her sharpness on Sunday had made him change his mind about seeing her again.

"One day next week," he had said. There weren't many days of the week left. Jessica stared resentfully at the office phone, its presence interrupting her concentration with a reminder of Brodie. It was probably a case of out of sight, out of mind, and she should be glad of it.

The interoffice line buzzed. Jessica punched the button to the receptionist's desk and picked up the telephone. "Yes, Ann." She acknowledged the call. "What is it?"

"There's a Mr. Hayes on line one. Isn't he—"

But Jessica was already picking up Brodie's call. "Hello, Brodie." She hoped she didn't sound as eager as she felt.

"Hello, Jessica. I'm between meetings so I only have a couple of minutes." He sounded very brisk and coolly businesslike. "We can have dinner this evening."

"Tonight?" Jessica was all too irritatingly aware

of the fact that he hadn't asked whether she had other plans.

"I'll come by your apartment at seven-thirty."

"I—"

"Sorry, Green Eyes, I have to run. See you tonight."

The line went dead. Jessica held the receiver away from her ear, glaring at it, impotent with the fury of being taken for granted. Her fingers were white from gripping the receiver.

"Jess?" The door to her office opened and her uncle, Ralph Dane, stuck his head inside. "Ann tells me that's Brodie Hayes on the phone. Tell him I'd like to talk to him for a few minutes."

"He already hung up," she told him stiffly, and proceeded to do the same herself.

"Already?" A dark brow lifted in surprise. "That was a short conversation. Why did he call?"

"To tell me that I was having dinner with him tonight." Jessica bristled, unconsciously emphasizing the fact that she had been told and not asked.

Ralph Dane had been married many years and raised three daughters. He recognized the indignant look on Jessica's face and its cause. There was an attempt to hide a smile.

"Forgot to ask, did he?" His tone was sympathetic, but Jessica suspected that his sympathies were with Brodie.

"I'm beginning to suspect that Brodie Hayes never asks. He takes, commands, or presumes," she snapped.

"Don't be too hard on him, Jessie," her uncle attempted to mollify her. "At least you're assured that he wants to be with you and not someone else."

"Am I supposed to be grateful?" But she wasn't

as sharp in her criticism as she had been a minute ago. There was consolation in knowing that Brodie wanted to be with her. "He could have pretended to observe the niceties of asking."

"You have to understand," Ralph Dane cautioned, "a man as successful as Hayes travels in a cutthroat circle. You have to be harder, tougher and stronger than the next man or he's going to step on you. There isn't much time for observing the niceties."

"Perhaps not," Jessica conceded, and remembered, also, that his upbringing probably hadn't taught him perfect manners.

"Tell him when you see him tonight that I'd like to talk to him about a couple of proposals Janson has made. I think he should know about them before I go ahead." The moment of family conversation had passed and her uncle was once again all business.

"I'll tell him," she promised.

By quarter past seven, she managed to rationalize away most of her irritation at Brodie's presumptuous behavior. Just enough of it lingered to put a combative sparkle in her eyes. She would have dinner with him, but she wasn't going to fall in his arms when he walked through the door.

The bell rang. Her pulse thundered erratically before she could bring it under control. Then, taking a deep, calming breath, she smoothed her palm over the white silk of her dress and walked to the door.

"You're early," she said as she opened the door to Brodie. "You said you'd be here at seven-thirty and it's only a quarter after."

The glitter in his eye welcomed her into his arms, but Jessica turned away, refusing the invitation she read in his look. She swept into the living room, leaving him to close the door.

"Is it a crime to be early?" he challenged.

"I'm not ready yet." Which was a lie. She had been ready twenty minutes ago.

"Jessica?" His voice commanded and she obeyed by turning to face him. He made a thorough, disturbing study of her. "You look perfect to me."

All her senses were reacting to him, dangerously handsome in his dark evening suit. "Thank you," she stiffly acknowledged his heady compliment, "but my lipstick—"

"Needs messing up." He caught her hand and pulled her into his arms.

She tried to keep her lips rigid under the slow exploration of his mouth, but a fiery glow of pleasure soon had them softening as her body relaxed in his hold. When Brodie lifted his head, he viewed her through the thick screen of his lashes.

"That's better," he declared.

Her gaze slid to his mouth and the smear of sensual color. "You have lipstick on you now," she informed him, and moved out of his arms, clinging to the poise his kiss had all but shattered.

Brodie reached into his pocket for a handkerchief and proceeded to wipe away the telltale smear. "What's the matter, Jessica?"

"Nothing," she said.

"Yes, there is. You're upset about something," he insisted.

Jessica knew nothing remained hidden from those piercing blue eyes for long. "What if I told you I'd made other plans for tonight?" she challenged.

His gaze narrowed on her face, his look suddenly cutting and ruthlessly cold. "Have you?"

"It's a fine time to ask now, isn't it?" She laughed in brittle mockery.

Brodie caught her by the shoulders. Her dress was sleeveless and the minute his hands touched her, they began to lightly rub her soft flesh. "If you'd told me—" he began with an attempt at patience.

"If you'd asked me," Jessica retorted, "I would have."

He expelled an angry breath. "How much time do we have before he shows up?"

Her eyes widened in hurt astonishment. He actually believed she was going out with someone else and he wasn't even jealous. Jessica didn't know whether to laugh or cry.

"All evening," she answered bitterly. "As it happens, I didn't have any plans for tonight, but you could have had the courtesy to ask." She glared at the knot of his tie. "I don't like being taken for granted, and I won't be at your beck and call!"

He forced her chin up, amusement glittering in his blue eyes. "I don't take you for granted, Green Eyes. At least, not consciously," he qualified his statement.

"I . . . I hope you don't." Jessica found it hard to stay angry.

Brodie reached inside his jacket. "Here, I bought you this." When his hand came out, it was holding a small narrow case. Jessica took it from him hesitantly, then lifted the lid. On a bed of black velvet was a delicate, spun-gold chain with a single, sparkling blue diamond.

"It's beautiful," she murmured, and felt her stomach twist into a sickening knot. She closed the lid and handed it back to him. "I can't accept it."

"Why not?" A dark eyebrow swept up in an arrogant, impatient line. "I bought it for you."

"It's much too expensive," said Jessica, fighting the waves of nausea. "I can't accept it."

"You're used to expensive things. Should I have bought you some cheap piece of costume jewelry and risked offending you?" Brodie demanded.

She lifted her head, her chin quivering with an abundance of pride. "At least I wouldn't feel as if you're trying to buy me."

"Buy you!" Brodie flared, and controlled his temper with effort. "I was not attempting to buy you."

"Do you make a habit of buying diamond necklaces for whatever girl you happen to be dating?" Jessica retorted.

"No, I don't make a habit of it," he snarled. "I buy gifts only for people who are special to me. The motive is simple: I want to give them pleasure. That's all I get out of it, and that's all I expect to get out of it."

Perhaps he hadn't been trying to buy her affection. Jessica began to doubt the conclusion she had reached. She searched the tempered steel of his eyes.

"Then you shouldn't buy such expensive gifts and people wouldn't misinterpret your reasons," she backed down from her accusation.

"The cost is relative. I can afford this necklace." He lifted the case in his hand. "When I was fifteen, spending five dollars on a girl was major. Now I can afford to spend a lot more." He studied her for a long second. "I want you to have this necklace, Jessica. Will you accept it?" She hesitated. "What good is money," he argued, "if you can't spend it on people you care about?"

His logic was irrefutable. Reluctantly she held out her hand for the case. "It was very thoughtful of you, Brodie." She recited her acceptance of it as if she was a child being prompted to say the right things. "It's beautiful. Thank you."

"Jessica," he sighed her name.

She lifted her gaze. Her green eyes shone brightly with pride. A muscle flexed in his jaw where tanned skin was stretched taut. His hands closed over her shoulders, their hold firm but not gentle.

"I gave you that neckless with feeling," he said in a growling underbreath. "Why can't you put some feeling in accepting it?"

"I tried." Her answer was stiff as her body.

"You damned sure haven't tried hard enough." He hauled her against his chest. "It can be done without words."

His fingers wound into a handful of honey gold hair and forced her head back. The iron band of his arm crushed her ribs, denying her breath, while his mouth brutally smothered her lips. Jessica was caught in the dangerous whirlpool of his savage aggression.

She had angered him, aroused latent instincts from his childhood where survival and power went to the strongest. Despite the violence of his possession, her hammering heart was reacting to the indomitable force of his virility. She trembled at its power.

The sensuality of his kiss changed from punishment to passion. The iron bars of his imprisoning embrace became gloved in velvet, firm hands stroking her skin. Jessica experienced the exquisite joy of being mastered and responded to it. Then Brodie dragged his mouth from her lips to the pleasure spot behind her earlobe.

"We don't have much time," he said in a groaning mutter, his breath hot and disturbing against her skin. "Do you want the necklace, Jessica?"

"Yes." She wanted anything from him—his anger, his kiss, his love.

It was a devastating discovery and she closed her eyes to hide it from him when he lifted his head. Her own was still tipped back, held there gently by the male fingers twined in her hair.

"Will you wear it tonight? Here?" His mouth located the hollow at the base of her throat.

"Yes," Jessica agreed, inhaling the earthy smell of him.

Brodie unwrapped his arms from around her and took the case from her hand. Snapping open the lid, he removed the necklace and Jessica watched the sparkle of the diamond come toward her. Obligingly, she lifted the thick hair at the back of her head so Brodie could fasten the gold chain. Her skin tingled at the feather-light touch of his fingers.

When he took his hands away, she fingered the chain and the hard diamond nestled against her throat. Brodie turned her around so she could see herself in the wall mirror, but Jessica barely glanced at her own reflection before her eyes were drawn, to his. He stood behind her, so tall and darkly compelling.

"It's beautiful," she told him. "I do like it."

"Do you?" The wry slant of his mouth seemed to mock her statement. "I much prefer your actions to your words. They're more convincing."

The sweep of his inspecting gaze made Jessica aware of her mussed hair and her mouth kissed free of any lipstick. She hardly resembled the poised, sophisticated woman Brodie had seen on his arrival.

"You'd better go and fix yourself or the others will be guessing why we're late," Brodie taunted.

"The others?" Jessica echoed.

"Yes, that's my bad news for tonight. We won't be dining alone." He moved away from the mirror and Jessica turned to watch him. "We're going to Janson's for dinner."

"You said others. That sounds like more than two." He shrugged.

"I image there'll be a dozen in all—Janson, his attorney, mine, my accountant, Janson's son."

"Sounds like a board meeting," Jessica commented.

"In a sense, it is." His mouth quirked. "Janson has been hounding me to come to his house for dinner, meet his wife, his family. There were a few details to iron out regarding the company. I combined business with a social obligation so I can have both of them out of the way at the same time."

"Actually, you're ridding yourself of three obligations. You forgot me." Jessica smiled, but there was disappointment in knowing they would not be alone tonight.

"You're not an obligation, Jessica." He eyed her steadily, a faint grimness in his look. "When all this came up, I refused to deprive myself of the pleasure of seeing you again. I wanted to be with you . . . in the company of others if it couldn't be alone."

A searing pleasure coursed through her, sweetening the taste of disappointment. "I . . ." The admission Jessica had been about to make suddenly made her tongue-tied, so she changed her response. "I'll only be a few minutes."

With her makeup freshened, her hair brushed into its style, and a silk shawl around her shoulders, she left the apartment with Brodie. On the way to the Janson home she remembered to relay her uncle's message, which drew a muttered exclamation of impatience from Brodie followed by silence.

The Janson home was a massive two-storey structure with a porticoed entrance. Their host was at the door to welcome them and inform them that they were the last to arrive. As they were led into a formal living room, Jessica discovered she was nervous over the prospect of meeting Brodie's close associates.

Brodie made the introductions. Jessica shook hands with Drew Mitchell, a lean good-looking man who was Brodie's legal adviser, and his wife, Marian. Next was a balding man with black-rimmed glasses and a perpetually serious expression—Cliff Hadley, Brodie's financial consultant. After that was Janson's attorney, a smooth Southern gentleman named Lee Cantrel. His wife, Rachel, was an acquaintance of Jessica's, and several years older than she was. Finally there were young Cal Janson and his wife, Sue, and their hostess, Emily Janson.

When the introductions were completed, Cal Janson slapped Brodie on the shoulder. "It's time for a drink. I know you're a bourbon man, Brodie. How about the little lady here?"

"Chardonnay, please," Jessica ordered, knowing the older gentleman would be shocked if she asked for anything stronger.

Almost immediately the gathering separated into two groups: male and female. Brodie was off in the corner of the room with the men and Jessica was drawn into the circle of women.

"How are your parents?" Emily Janson inquired.

"The community was so sorry to lose them when they sold their home and retired to Florida."

"They wanted to be near their grandchildren," Jessica explained politely.

"Of course, the climate there is wonderful. Cal and I usually spend a month or two there in the winter, but I could never persuade him to leave these Tennessee hills permanently."

The inconsequential chatter began, with Emily Janson as the perfect hostess, drawing each of the women into the conversation and leaving no one out. A short time later the dinner was served. Jessica found herself seated on the opposite side and at the opposite end of the table from Brodie.

She remembered, with irony, his comment that he hadn't wanted to deprive himself of the pleasure of seeing her. That was about all he was doing. Her gaze slid down the table to him. He was listening intently to something his attorney was saying in low tones. Jessica watched him rub his forehead, concentrating on the spot between his dark brows. But he didn't glance her way. She hadn't noticed him looking at her, so he hadn't been "seeing" much of her, either.

"How is Jordanna?" Rachel Cantrel inquired, sitting opposite Jessica at the long, formal dining table. "Are she and Tom still getting along together, or has the honeymoon finally ended?"

"Jordanna and Tom are very happy," Jessica answered calmly, but she was fiercely aware that the mention of her sister's name had drawn Brodie's attention when her presence hadn't.

The meal became an ordeal, the excellently prepared food tasting like chalk to Jessica. If her hostess noticed her lack of appetite, Emily Janson was too polite to comment it. After dinner, it was back into the living room for coffee and liqueurs. Again the men secluded themselves on one side of the room, embroiled in a business discussion, while the women sat on the opposite side.

Jessica sat on the plush sofa, a china cup and saucer balanced in her hand. From the sofa she could watch the men. Brodie rarely did any of the talking, his bland expression revealing none of his thoughts. Two or three times she noticed him briefly rub that one spot on his forehead. The gesture seemed to indicate that something serious was troubling him.

"Have you known Brodie long?" a voice inquired beside her.

Aware that she had been caught staring at him, Jessica turned to the woman seated on the sofa beside her. It was Marian Mitchell, the wife of Brodie's attorney.

"No, not very long," she admitted, and shifted the subject to the other woman. "Are you from here?"

"Gracious, no," the woman laughed. "We live in Richmond—or we do when we're there, which is seldom. Since Drew started working with Brodie our home has become some place we *used* to live."

"How long has your husband worked for Brodie?"

"He's started his sixth year. I stopped counting how many airports we'd been in a long time ago or which hotels we'd stayed at." But Marian Mitchell didn't seem to be complaining.

"Don't you mind?" Jessica was curious.

"Drew loves working for Brodie. He enjoys the excitement, the feeling of never knowing what's going to happen next. The first three months I stayed home and saw Drew for a total of forty-eight hours. Our phone bill rivaled the National Debt!

I decided that I had a choice of living the life of a widow or packing my clothes and going along. I've never regretted my decision to travel with him."

"Excuse me," Sue Janson interrupted their conversation.

"It was very nice meeting both of you."

"Are you leaving?" Marian glanced up in surprise.

"Yes, we promised the sitter we would have her home by eleven, and it's after ten now," the young woman explained.

She said her goodbyes and entered the circle of men. It was several minutes before she was able to persuade her husband that they had to leave.

His departure made little impression on the other men, except as an unwanted interruption to their discussion. Emily Janson brought more fresh coffee.

Chapter Eight

It was after eleven. The four women had run out of small talk, but the men showed no signs of letting up. Jessica was convinced they had forgotten they were in the room.

Marian Mitchell smothered a yawn with her hand and glanced at Jessica, Rachel Cantrel and their hostess. "This meeting will last until the wee hours of the morning—I've been through this before. Excuse me."

She walked to her husband, whispered something in his ear, and waited. Drew cast her an apologetic smile, then engaged in a hurried discussion with the others. Some sort of decision must have been reached, because Brodie separated himself from the group and walked over to where Jessica was seated.

He held out his hand for her to join him and nodded politely to the other two women. "Would you excuse us for a moment?"

"Of course," Emily Janson said with a smile.

Jessica's hand felt cold in the warm clasp of his

as he led her into the large foyer. There was an absent look about him that said, even though he was with her, his thoughts were elsewhere. In the entry hall, he stopped.

"Drew is phoning for a cab to take Marian back to the hotel. I know you're tired and have to be at work in the morning. I don't know what time this meeting will break up, so I've asked Drew to arrange for the cab to take you home after it's dropped Marian at their hotel," Brodie informed her in crisply businesslike tones.

"That's very thoughtful of you," said Jessica, trying not to be offended that he was arranging to dispose of her like an inconvenience.

The touch of dryness in her voice narrowed his gaze. "I had no idea this was going to come up when I asked you to come with me this evening."

"I know that," she admitted. "And I know it must be very important to you."

"I'd take you home myself, but—"

"I understand, Brodie," Jessica interrupted.

His gaze flickered impatiently toward the living room. They still were in full view of the others, although their conversation couldn't be overhead.

"Do you?" he growled.

His hand closed roughly on her arm as he pushed her away from the living room doorway. Seconds later she was backed up against a bare wall. Brodie leaned against her, an arm resting against the wall above her head, a hand cupping the side of her face. The crushing imprint of his body left her in no doubt of his true desire at the moment. "Do you understand that all I want to do is make love to you?" Brodie demanded before his mouth captured her lips.

Jessica was only allowed to answer by returning

the frustrated ardor of his kiss. Her hands explored his jaw and the column of his throat, nails digging into his shoulders. He rained angry kisses on her nose, cheek and ears.

"The problems aren't just mine," he explained, his voice muffled by her hair. "If they were, I'd say to hell with them. But those men in there have invested their time and talent in this project. I can't tell them to wait until I feel like handling the situation."

"I understand," she repeated, and she did, more fully this time.

"Hey, Brodie? Where are you?" Drew Mitchell called from the living room.

Brodie levered himself away from the wall and Jessica. A mask of control slipped over his features, changing his image from one of a passionate lover to a cool, poker-faced gambler. His indifferent blue gaze flicked to Jessica as if to be certain she was regaining control of herself. She had straightened from the wall. Brodie turned to the doorway.

"Out here, Drew."

The lean, brown-haired man rounded the corner. "Jessica's with you—good." He nodded. "The cab will be here in five minutes."

"Thanks, Drew." Brodie glanced at Jessica, his look still impersonal. "Will you be all right?"

She wondered what he would do if she said no. "Of course." She smiled, a tremulous action by a mouth that was still afire from his kiss.

There was barely time to say her goodbyes and thank her hosts for the evening before the taxi arrived. She waited while Drew kissed Marian. Brodie was already in the living room so they exchanged no tender farewell.

As the taxi pulled out of the driveway, Jessica

leaned back in her seat and sighed, staring out the window into the blackness of the night.

"You'll get used to it," Marian said.

"Beg your pardon?" Jessica glanced at her companion.

"You'll get used to evenings ending like this if you continue seeing Brodie," the other woman explained.

"Oh." Jessica couldn't think of anything else to reply.

"Like prices, all of Brodie's plans are subject to change without notice. Which means our plans, too. It's their way of life . . . Brodie's and now Drew's."

"Doesn't it bother you?" she repeated the question she had asked Marian earlier.

"If you love a man, you learn to accept the way he is and don't try to change him."

Jessica had a feeling that the comment was meant as advice. "Yes, that's true," she agreed.

"Brodie is quite a man, all man. Who knows? Maybe if I'd met him before Drew, I might have fallen for him." The woman was joking. Jessica sensed that Marian was very much in love with her husband. She had only made the comment to invite Jessica to confide in her. But Jessica wasn't sure enough of her own feelings to do that yet.

"Have you met Brodie's other girlfriends?" she asked instead.

"Girlfriends—that's the operative word." Marian seemed to consider the question. "I've seen him with other women, but he's never made a point of bringing them along for a social evening. I think I would have to say no, I haven't met his other girlfriends. You're the first. Brodie generally keeps his private life private."

"I see." Jessica hadn't doubted for an instant that there were other women in his life, but it was heartening to hear Marian say that she was the first she'd met socially.

The cab whisked into the hotel entrance. Marian stepped out of the rear seat with a friendly goodbye, and Jessica continued the journey alone to her apartment complex.

At the office the next morning, a dozen red roses were delivered to her. The message written on the attached card had been simple. "I'm sorry. B."

All day long she expected him to call. That night she sat by the telephone, but it didn't make a sound. Saturday morning, there was a curt message on her voicemail. "Had to fly out of town. Be back next week."

Jessica was beginning to discover what Marian had gone through when Drew was away so much. Not that she knew precisely. After all, Marian had been married to him at the time, whereas her own relationship with Brodie was tenuous at best.

On Wednesday night, the telephone was ringing impatiently when Jessica arrived at her apartment from work. She fumbled for the key and, in her haste, couldn't get it to turn the lock. An agonizing number of seconds went by before she could open the door and race to answer the phone.

"Hello?" Her greeting to the unknown caller was eager and rushed.

"I missed you at the office. I called, but the receptionist said you'd just left." Brodie didn't bother with a greeting.

It didn't matter. Just the sound of his voice sent a thrill of happiness through her veins. "I just got home," Jessica admitted.

"After the last time, I thought I'd better call first

to see if you'd made any plans for tonight." Brodie
was dryly mocking.

"None," she told him shamelessly.

"I'll be over."

"When?" But the line was dead.

Jessica hung up the phone and glanced around
the apartment. She hurriedly picked up the maga-
zines scattered about, plumped the pillows and
emptied the ashtrays. Then it was into her bedroom, out of her clothes and under the shower.

Once out of the shower, she slipped into her
short, Japanese-style robe. A shower cap had kept
her hair dry. She brushed it until it glistened like
gold, then began applying new makeup.

As she pressed a tissue to her mouth, blotting
her lipstick, the doorbell rang. Jessica stared at her
reflection in the mirror. It couldn't be Brodie, not
yet. She wasn't dressed. There was nothing to do
but answer the door. Wrapping the velour robe
more tightly around her, she secured it closed with
the sash, tying it in a double knot. Then she hurried
to answer the second ring of the doorbell.

"I would have been here sooner, but I stopped
to buy dinner." Brodie indicated the bag of grocer-
ies in his arm. His disconcerting blue gaze swept
her from head to foot, noting the bare skin of her
legs from her knees down and the robe fastened
only by the tie around her waist. "I should have
been here sooner," he corrected himself with a
suggestive look that sent Jessica's pulse rocketing
into space.

"I didn't expect you so soon." She moved out
of his way when Brodie walked in. His lack of inhibi-
tion never ceased to remind Jessica of the abundance of hers. She closed the door behind him.

"You can put the bag in the kitchen. It will only take me a few minutes to get dressed."

"Why bother?" In the short time it had taken her to shut the door, Brodie had set the grocery bag on the nearest flat surface and was blocking her path.

"Brodie, please!" Jessica held up a hand to stave off his advance.

He used the obstacle to pull her into his arms. She strained against his hold, twisting her head to elude his mouth. But Brodie seemed to take pleasure in intimately investigating every inch of her exposed shoulder. The action sent delicious shivers of gooseflesh over her skin, all the way down until her toes curled. Weak with desire, Jessica let him capture her mouth, only to find his kiss more potent.

She shuddered as his hands slid inside her robe and caressed the round breasts that swelled to his touch, rosy nipples turning hard under his teasing fingers. When it seemed there was no turning back from the flames she sensed Brodie's withdrawal. The front of her robe was drawn closed and a last, hard kiss was planted on her lips. Then he was holding her away from him.

"There's a bottle of bourbon in the bag. Would you fix me a drink?" he asked huskily. "I'm going to need it."

Jessica opened her eyes slowly, hardly daring to believe that he meant it to end this soon. She wasn't even sure if she wanted him to stop now.

"I promised not to rush you, Green Eyes, so don't look at me like that unless you mean it." The smoldering light in his eyes told her it wasn't an idle warning.

"I . . ." Jessica wavered, "I'll fix you a drink."

Brodie walked to the bag, handed her the bottle from it, then picked it up and followed her into the kitchen. "I thought we'd have dinner here tonight—it's the one place I can be sure there'll be no interruptions. Drew might guess I'm here, but since your number isn't listed he can't get hold of me." He set the bag on the counter while Jessica took a glass from the cupboard, "I hope you like steak."

His talking had given her time to settle her senses. She wondered if it had been deliberate on Brodie's part. There was so much about him that she was only just beginning to understand. He wanted her, but he was waiting until she could come to him with no regrets. His control of his emotions was frightening, as frightening as her lack of it.

"Yes, I like steak," she answered him.

"Show me where everything is." Brodie began unpacking the bag. "I'll do the cooking while you get some clothes on." He arched her a mocking look. "Imagine what your parents would think if they knew you were entertaining a man in your robe!"

Jessica ignored that. "Do you want your bourbon straight?"

"A splash of water and a couple of ice cubes will do."

She added two cubes of ice from the refrigerator and set the drink on the counter beside him. Unconsciously her hand moved to hold the gaping front of her robe together.

"It will only take me a couple of minutes to change. Have your drink. I'll take care of the cooking when I get back."

"I'll cook," Brodie insisted. "I'm very good.

Don't forget I've led the life of a bachelor almost since I learned how to walk.''

As it turned out, he was an excellent cook. The steaks were done to perfection, the new potatoes were steamed to lose none of their flavor. The sauce for the asparagus spears was creamier than Jessica had ever been able to make hers. Dessert was fresh strawberries.

Not only had the meal been superb, but so had the company and the conversation. They had talked about everything, argued over politics, agreed on musical tastes, had a few favorite authors in common. Over coffee, the subject had shifted to his business and the two men who worked so closely with him—his attorney and financial advisor—both of whom Jessica had met the previous week.

"Drew has practically become my right arm." Brodie swirled the half an inch of coffee left in his cup. "He's a very valuable man. I don't know how I got as far as I did without him."

The candlelight flickered and waned. The dancing flames drew Jessica's attention to the carved candleholders in the center of the table, the ones Brodie had bought for her. It seemed appropriate that they should be used for the first time with him.

"I think Drew has a great deal of respect and admiration for you, too," she commented.

"Why do you say that?" Their eyes met over the diminishing candles.

"Marian told me how much he enjoys his work, which has to mean that he enjoys working with you. That kind of feeling only comes when you respect and admire the other person. Besides—"

she smiled, "—he has to love his work or he wouldn't put up with the schedule you keep!"

"It gets hectic," Brodie admitted with a wry twist to his mouth. "You lose track of time and cities. All airports look alike."

Jessica noticed his cup was empty. "More coffee?"

"Please." He handed it to her in its saucer.

"Why haven't you ever married, Brodie?" she asked curiously, rising from the table to refill his cup.

"Who says I'm not?"

His reply hit her in the stomach. Shaken, she let go of the cup and saucer, which shattered on the floor. She clutched the back of her chair for support. Until that moment, it had never occurred to her that he might be married. Marian had said she'd seen him with other women, but she'd also said that he kept his private life private.

"You've broken the cup." Brodie rose from his chair and stooped to pick up the pieces.

Jessica stared at him. His hair gleamed blue-black in the candlelight. The white of his shirt stretched across his broad, muscled shoulders and back.

When he straightened to hand her the broken pieces, she found her voice, "Are you?"

"Am I what?" A black brow arched in deliberate ignorance.

"Are you married?"

"Are you afraid you might be on the verge of having an affair with a married man?" He noted the ashen color of her complexion, her eyes as green and round as the unbroken saucer. "It wouldn't be right for a woman like you to become involved in a triangle like that, would it?"

Her fingers dug into the wooden back of the chair. "Answer me, Brodie! Don't play games."

"As it happens—" when she didn't take the pieces from him, he set them on the table, "—I'm not married. Does that make you feel better?"

"Is that the truth?" Jessica continued to eye him warily, swallowing at the tightness in her throat.

"Don't you believe me?" he taunted softly.

"I don't know what to believe." She turned away, angry and frightened and uncertain. She crossed her arms, rubbing her hands over her elbows.

Silently Brodie came up behind her, his large hands closing around the soft flesh of her upper arms. "You can believe this." He kissed her neck.

Jessica lifted her shoulder to shrug him off, but he moved to the other side. She tried to twist away. Instead she was turned into his arms.

"And you can believe this." His mouth brushed her lips before she could turn them away.

"Stop it!" She kept her head lowered to one side, but she didn't struggle.

"You're hurt and confused, aren't you?" His voice held amusement.

"Yes, damn you!" Jessica hissed.

The heat from his body was burning her skin, the muskiness of his male scent like a drug to her senses. She was aware how tantalizingly close his mouth was. All of these things stirred her blood.

"You're trembling," Brodie accused softly, "but not from anger. I can see that pulse beating in your throat. I make you feel things that you're not sure you should feel, especially with a married man. But if this is sinning, Green Eyes, imagine what heaven must be."

"Stop playing this bizarre game!" She closed her

eyes for a second, then opened them to give him a sideways glance. "Are you married or not?"

"I've already answered that question. Why should I repeat myself if you didn't believe me the first time?" he challenged with an arrogant shrug. "I can't prove it. I don't carry around a piece of paper that says I'm unmarried, do you?"

"Of course not," Jessica answered impatiently.

"Then why should I believe that you're not married? Maybe you have a jealous husband lurking in some corner waiting to surprise us when we climb into bed, mmm?" He tucked a finger under her chin and turned it to face him, a wicked light dancing in his eyes.

"I don't think it's funny!" She flashed him an angry look.

"Neither do I. I hope to die in bed, but not by the hands of your husband," Brodie mocked.

"Stop it! You know I don't have a husband, jealous or otherwise," she snapped.

"What about me?" Brodie tilted his head to one side. "Look at me and tell me you think I have a wife tucked away somewhere."

Jessica lifted her gaze, but it faltered under his piercing stare, so sharply blue. She shook her head. "I can't."

"Then if I ask you to have dinner with me Saturday night, you'll accept?" He phrased it as a question.

The breath she released was a sign of surrender, unwilling but inevitable. "Yes, I'll accept," Jessica nodded.

"With feeling, Green Eyes," Brodie demanded. Defiance flared as she looked up. "Damn you—"

She heard his throaty chuckle of triumph before his mouth descended on her vulnerable lips, parted in speech. They stayed that way under his direction. His hands moved to her hips, molding them tighter to his thighs. Her fingers, spread across his chest, slipped inside his shirt to tangle themselves in the froth of black hair.

"I have to leave, Jessica," he finally muttered against her mouth.

"Now?" Her breath was shaky, her lips trembling against the solid outline of his warm mouth. She couldn't believe he meant it.

"Yes, now." But his mouth refused to leave the corner of hers. "My plane is waiting for me."

"Again?" It came out in a moan of protest.

"I only flew in here to be with you tonight because I couldn't stay away a second longer."

Jessica could feel the disturbed pattern of his heartbeat. Not very different from her own. "I'm glad you did," she admitted.

His hands reached up to grip her shoulders and push her away from him. "If I leave now, I'll have just enough time to take a cold shower before we take off." He studied the glazed look of passion in her eyes. "Unless you want me to shower here . . . with you."

She hesitated, wavering between the yes of her flesh and the no of her mind. There was a cynical slant to his mouth. "One of these days you aren't going to have to think before you answer, Jessica." He let go of her. "Saturday. Eight o'clock."

"Yes."

Chapter Nine

Saturday couldn't arrive too quickly for Jessica. She fluctuated between walking on air and dragging herself through the pits of depression. She spent half of her paycheck on a beige pantsuit that looked more like a pair of silk pajamas, then worried how she would eat.

Marian's comment about Brodie's constantly changing plans had her listening for the ring of the phone. Pessimistically, she expected him to cancel their date.

Saturday night arrived and she was ready at seven. The mantel clock ticked away each second, all thirty-six hundred of them. This time Brodie didn't arrive early. He didn't arrive on time, either.

One minute after eight, Jessica began pacing the floor. She began imagining the reasons he might be delayed. Business, traffic, plane trouble. She glanced toward the TV, wondering morbidly if there had been a crash.

Five minutes later she reached for the phone and the doorbell rang. She raced to the door and swung it open wide. Then she couldn't move, because Brodie was alive and unharmed.

"Don't you ever check first to see who's outside?" he smiled.

"I knew it was you." One jacketed arm curved around her waist while the other pushed the door shut. Jessica's fingers slid along his lapel toward his neck. His hands locked behind her back, arching her to his length. The contact with his hard, muscled body seemed suddenly very intimate. The lines deepened around his mouth, suggesting that he knew exactly the upheaval he was causing to her fluttering heart and weakening knees.

"One of these days you're going to open that door to a stranger," Brodie warned. "You need a peephole installed."

"The apartment manager has been promising one," Jessica pointed out.

While she looked up to his face, Brodie looked down to hers. The peephole was the farthest thing from her mind, but it was impossible to read what was written in his eyes. All she knew was that it was doing crazy things to her, like making her feel that she was wearing nothing beneath her pantsuit with its lacy, ribboned neckline, and she knew very well that she was.

"You're wearing the necklace I gave you," Brodie observed, but Jessica had the distinct feeling that his gaze was focused lower than the diamond at her throat.

"Yes." She felt out of breath and tried to control the rapid rise and fall of her breasts.

"No earrings. Is that an invitation to nibble?" He bent his head to gently take her earlobe between his teeth. The warmth of his breath stirred all sorts of fires.

"I didn't have a pair that looked right." Desire throbbed in her voice.

It was a short side trip from her ear to her lips, but Brodie seemed to make it in record time. His mouth moved slowly, not ending the kiss until he had investigated each curve and line of her lips.

"We can correct that," he said.

"Correct what?" What had been wrong? Jessica's quivering lips had found nothing wrong with the kiss. The only thing unsatisfactory about it was that it had ended.

Without answering, he reached into his inside pocket, his sleeved arm brushing across the front of her breasts. When he drew his hand out, it was holding a small square box. With a deft flick of his fingers, he snapped the lid open and a pair of diamond stud earrings winked out at her, the brilliant gems as large as the solitaire of her necklace.

A cold chill ran down her spine, the same as before. She shook her head in a mute, negative rush of feeling. Her throat seemed to close.

"Brodie, don't give them to me," she managed finally.

"It's a shame to break up a matched set, don't you think?"

His arm at her waist made no attempt to hold her when she turned to walk away. "You'd better get used to accepting gifts from me, Jessica, because you're going to get a lot from me. I'll never come to your door empty-handed."

Jessica glanced over her shoulder, her green eyes rounded and appealing in their confusion. His rough, compelling features were drawn in such grim lines. Why did he have to bring presents, she wondered. Because he had once come empty-handed to her sister's door and been turned away?

Didn't he realize that for her all he had to offer was his heart? Perhaps he did. Perhaps he was giving her presents because he couldn't give her what she really wanted.

She controlled a shudder and managed a stiff, surrendering smile. "In that case, I'd better start learning to accept it now." But she wasn't referring to the gift.

When he walked over, Jessica removed the earrings from their jeweler's case and moved to the mirror to put them on. This time Brodie's reflection didn't join hers in the mirror and she faced him to receive his approval.

"How do they look?" Her brightness was forced.

"Beautiful." His response lacked emotion. Standing there, with his feet slightly apart and a hand thrust into his pants pocket, he resembled a model out of the latest men's fashion magazine. His rugged countenance was sternly masculine and forbidding in its expression of indifference.

Something inside Jessica shivered. "Are we ready to go?"

Over dinner, the atmosphere changed. Her apprehensions were temporarily forgotten under the spell of Brodie's charm. Again he became the companionable escort. They talked and laughed and discussed any subject. Not once was Jessica subjected to any of his mocking taunts. They seemed to come only when the air, or his thoughts, were heavy with passion.

It was nearly midnight when they paused at the door of her apartment. Brodie took the key from her and inserted it into the lock.

"Are you going to pretend to invite me in for coffee?" He pushed open the door and waited.

"Are you going to pretend to come in for coffee?" Jessica countered.

"Of course." His arm curved around her waist to guide her inside.

Closing the door, Brodie returned the key to her. Jessica dropped it in her bag and started toward the kitchen, but he caught her hand to stop her.

"Where are you going?"

"To put the coffee on."

"Pretend it's already on and we're waiting for it to be made." He kept a firm hold on her hand, drawing her with him as he walked to the sofa.

He sat down and pulled her onto his lap. He wasted no more time on talk or preliminaries, his mouth unerringly finding hers in the dimness of the room. Her arms wound around his neck as she returned the slow-burning fire of his kiss.

All her nerves and senses were vibrantly alive and glowing under the golden heat of his kiss. Its warmth melted her inhibitions and a languorous passion was stealing through her bones.

His hand slid under the silky hem of her top to reach her bare skin, setting her flesh on fire. With unhurried progress, his touch moved to the confining material of her bra. His fingers circled inside to cup the swelling roundness of her breast. A gasping sigh of sweet pleasure was muffled by his possessing kiss.

She was forced backward, onto the cushions of the sofa. Brodie followed her down, his length stretching partially on and beside her. His hands were stroking and molding her hips and thighs, arousing and satisfying the desire to fit her to every bruising contour of his body. A primitive need ached through her, a throbbing to have the expertise of his lovemaking brought to consummation.

"I want you, Green Eyes." Brodie nuzzled her neck, his voice thickened to a husky level. "For God's sake, don't say no!"

Jessica breathed in sharply, but it wasn't his request that was affecting her. His mouth had brushed her ear and she felt the cold metal of the diamond studs, precious gold and brilliant gems, so very expensive.

With a sudden twist she rolled away from him, stumbling upright to take a shaky step away from the sofa. She was hot with shame over the step she had almost taken.

"I can't," she choked the denial. Her trembling fingers fought their way through the thickness of her blond hair to an earring. They made her feel like a mistress who had been rewarded in advance for pleasure to be given. "I . . . I feel as if I've been bought."

His hands swung her violently around, sending the earring flying from her fingers. "Dammit, Jessica!" Brodie exploded with a fury that took her breath away. "We've been through that before!" Nothing masked the fiery blast of rage in his eyes. "I . . . I know," Jessica stammered through her shock, intimidated by this profound display of emotion when she had almost believed him incapable of feeling anything deeply.

"The jewelry was a gift!" he snarled. "Not payment for services!"

"I know." Her head bobbed in admission of what he had previously told her.

Brodie released his bruising hold of her shoulders with an obvious disdain. His body was rigid with anger as he stalked to where the earring lay, a sparkling treasure in the threads of the carpet. He picked it up and held it out to her.

"Here," he challenged, his tone icy.

Hesitantly, Jessica reached out and took it from his hand. She stared at the diamond, believing him and knowing she had accused him unjustly. Her conscience, her own sense of guilt, had caused the words.

"I'm sorry." She whispered the words, her head lowered, blond hair swinging forward to conceal her colorless cheeks.

He lifted her chin. "We'll have dinner next week. I don't know which night—I'll have to call you."

All she had to do was tell him not to bother and she knew she would never see him again. "Yes," she agreed, because the thought of not seeing him again was worse than the gifts she was loath to accept.

Holding her chin, Brodie pressed a cool kiss on her mouth. "Good night."

She murmured an answer as he walked to the door. He paused to send her one last look, his expression unreadable. Then the door was closing behind him.

During the next month Jessica saw Brodie at least once a week, sometimes twice. Always he brought a gift, a jade bracelet one time, a cashmere sweater another. Jessica never made any protest, accepting them and concealing, she hoped, the heaviness of her heart.

The sky outside the glass doors of her balcony was ink black. A crash of lightning illuminated trees whipped by the wind. The violent burst of light was followed by a roar of thunder that rumbled to shake the ground and rattle the glass in the windows. Rain lashed the panes, driven by a savage wind.

Jessica hugged her arms and turned her back on the fury of the spring storm. Brodie had called this afternoon to say he would see her tonight, but the rampaging weather was changing that. Incoming planes would be rerouted to other airports. He hadn't called her yet, but Jessica was sure he would when he landed safely elsewhere.

The doorbell rang. For a minute she stared at it in disbelief. Hesitantly she moved forward to answer it, opened it a crack, then swung it wide when she recognized Brodie. The dampness of his hair made it blacker still. His suit jacket was almost drenched by the rain.

"You didn't land in this weather!" Jessica protested.

Thunder rumbled. "It was a helluva flight, but it takes more than an act of God to keep me away from you," Brodie stated.

As he walked into the apartment, she saw how haggard he looked. The last two times she had seen him, she had noticed he seemed tired. Tonight, exhaustion had carved deep lines in his face, even dulling the sharpness of his eyes.

"Your jacket's wet. You'd better take it off." She stepped behind him to help him with it.

"Your present is in the inside pocket," he told her when she draped the sodden garment over a chair back.

Her hand hesitated on the damp material. "I'll get it in a minute." She glanced over her shoulder to see him tiredly rub the back of his neck. "How about a drink?"

"Sounds good."

The storm had broken shortly after six o'clock.

Jessica had been so certain that Brodie wouldn't be able to make it that she hadn't bothered to dress. She was wearing the tight-fitting brushed denims and red chambray blouse that she'd put on after work. The storm, her clothes and his tiredness convinced her that the place to have dinner was in her apartment.

As she fixed his bourbon and water, Brodie called from the living room. "Do you mind if I use your phone? I have to get hold of Drew."

"Go ahead," she answered.

When she returned to the living room, Brodie was seated on the sofa. He was leaning forward, his elbows on his knees, holding the telephone receiver with one hand and rubbing his forehead with the other. Jessica set the drink on the table beside him and his mouth quirked briefly in thanks. His attention was instantly back to the phone.

"Hello, Drew. It's Brodie,"

The line crackled. Then his attorney's voice came through so clearly that Jessica could hear it. "Brodie! Where the hell are you? I've been trying to reach you for the last two hours."

"I'm in Chattanooga."

"Chattanooga?" The stunned response echoed into the room "That's the fifth or sixth time you've made an unscheduled stopover there. Listen, if you have to keep holding Janson's hand, maybe we have the wrong man for the job. What the hell's the problem this time?"

Brodie leaned against the sofa back and attempted to loosen the knot of his tie. Jessica reached over and did it for him, unfastening the top three buttons of his shirt.

"I'm not here to see Janson."

"Then what are you doing there?" In the pregnant pause that followed Drew's question, Brodie glanced at Jessica. She wondered if he would respond to that invasion of his privacy. But the need didn't arise as Drew guessed, "You're there to see Jessica, that blonde you took to Janson's place. Brodie, I know I'm butting my nose in where it doesn't belong. You're as human as the next man. If you have to keep making these stops in Chattanooga, rearrange things. You're beating yourself to death with this schedule."

"That's my problem, not yours." There was just enough snap in his voice to terminate that discussion. "I went over those figures Cliff gave me on the food-processing plant in Memphis, and they told me nothing. I'll be there in the morning. Have Cliff meet me at the airport with something more than what I have. And fax a backup to the office."

"What time?"

"What time am I supposed to meet the banker in Nashville?" Brodie countered.

"Nine, I think. Yes, nine o'clock."

"Okay, change it. Have Cliff fly to Nashville. Take the earliest flight. That way I can go over everything with him en route to Memphis. Anything else?

"It can wait until I see you tomorrow," Drew answered.

"All right, see you then." Brodie hung up.

"He's right, you know," Jessica said. "You are working too hard." She reached out to lightly trace the deep groove near his mouth with her fingertips. "Can't you meet on-line or something?"

"I can't give people hell on-line the way I can in person." He caught her hand and pulled her over. Then with a reprimanding slap on her rump, he pushed her away. "Go and open your present."

Jessica walked over to the chair where his jacket was. "I thought we'd have dinner here tonight instead of going out, is that all right?" It was easier to talk about something else while she was opening the package she didn't want.

"Perfect." His hooded gaze watched her strip away the paper.

"How hungry are you?" Her mind raced through the contents of her cupboards, trying to plan a menu.

"Ravenous. I don't think I've eaten since yesterday."

"How could you forget something like that?" she laughed, and tried to ignore the box in her hand.

"It's easy. I could have had something on the plane tonight, but I knew I'd be having dinner with you, so I waited."

There was no way to delay opening the box any longer. Inside was a 14-karat gold compact with the letter *J* etched on it, the initial punctuated with a diamond.

"It's beautiful." Jessica admired it for the necessary minute, then walked over to kiss him. "Thank you." She tasted the bourbon on his mouth. "Is the drink all right?" she said, changing the subject as quickly as she could.

"Very good. And very thoughtful."

"Just trying to show a little old-fashioned Tennessee hospitality." She smiled. "You sit back and enjoy your drink. I'll start dinner."

Her choice of menu was limited by the food and the amount of it on hand. It turned out to be more Italian in origin than Tennessean, with a salad, spaghetti and meat sauce, and warmed bread. But it was quick and hot and stuck to the ribs. Afterward

Jessica cleared the table but left the dirty dishes in the sink to join Brodie in the living room.

"Would you like another cup of coffee?" she asked.

"Not particularly." Seated on the sofa, he was looking at her in a most disturbing way. "Drink, dinner, more coffee—are you trying to impress me?"

Outside the thunder and lightning were competing for honors in a violent contest. Jessica was indifferent to the battle. It was happening on the periphery and had little to do with them.

"Come here," Brodie ordered, and lazily watched her cross the room to stand in front of him.

Pulled onto his lap, Jessica met his kiss halfway, her lips parting almost instantly to know the full possession of his mouth, sensual and stimulating. His hands tugged her blouse free of her waistband and began unfastening the buttons.

Abandoning herself to the heady oblivion of his kiss, she could only think of the pleasure her flesh would feel at his touch. His fingers entered the shadowy valley between her breasts.

His mouth curved against her lips. "Must have been a man who invented bras that hook in front."

In the next second, her breasts were freed. Brodie's mouth burned its way down her throat to celebrate their release. Her fingers curled into the springy thickness of his black hair, her hands pressing his head to her. A sweet ecstasy claimed her at his intimate caresses. Eventually his mouth returned to her throat and neck, taking sensuous little nibbles of her skin.

"Isn't this better than coffee?" Brodie whispered when she couldn't hold back a tiny moan of desire.

"Much better," she whispered back.

"Now if you're really intent on showing me your hospitality, you'd offer me a place to sleep." He teased her mouth, making it tremble for his kiss.

"I do have—" she tried to end the tantalizing brush of his lips, but he continued to elude her, "—a spare bedroom."

"If I stayed, you know I wouldn't sleep there."

His hand was at her waist and the snap of her jeans gave way to his probing fingers. The telephone rang at the same instant. Jessica jumped guiltily at the sound. She heard Brodie's muffled curse as she leaned over to reach the telephone on the end table beside the sofa.

"Hello?" Jessica avoided glancing at Brodie as she answered the phone.

"Is Brodie there? Let me speak to him," an unfamiliar male voice requested.

Covering the mouthpiece with her hand, Jessica looked questioningly at Brodie. "It's for you." There was a disconcerting darkness to his pupils, ringed with clear blue. His mouth thinned grimly. "Find out who it is."

She took her hand away from the telephone. "Who's calling, please?"

"Tell him it's Jim. I just got an update on the weather," the voice answered.

Jessica covered the receiver again and relayed the answer. "It's a man named Jim. Something about the weather."

"I'll take it." Brodie took the receiver from her hand and helped her off his lap. "Yeah, Jim. What's the word?"

Jessica couldn't hear the reply as she turned away from Brodie to fasten her bra and button her blouse. There was a shaking awareness of how much she wanted Brodie to make love to her. At the moment, the desire was drifting into the past tense under the brilliant light of uncertainty. She guessed that he had only to touch her again and the light would go out.

"Okay, Jim, I'll be there." Brodie hesitated a minute, then replaced the receiver.

"Who is Jim?" Jessica asked, pushing her hair away from her face.

His gaze flickered over her buttoned blouse front. "My pilot. Radar shows this storm cell should be out of the area in about a half an hour. There's another one approaching that should arrive in an hour, possibly an hour and a half. If we expect to take off tonight, it has to be soon."

"Your pilot? You mean you have your own plane?" Jessica stared.

"A Lear jet."

"A Lear jet?" She laughed in astonishment. "I thought . . . I guess I thought you were flying in and out on a commercial line . . . or a charter. I didn't realize you owned your own jet, complete with a crew."

"I'll take you for a ride in it some day," he promised, faintly amused by her reaction. "I'll have to leave. I'll probably be back next Tuesday." He rose from the couch.

Jessica looked up. "I'll be waiting."

Brodie curved a hand around the back of her head and bent down to kiss her. It was brief and unsatisfying for both of them. When he straightened, she reached out for him, but he was already striding toward the door.

Chapter Ten

On Tuesday, a meeting at the office made Jessica late returning to her apartment. She hurried along the corridor, hoping she'd have time to shower and relax before Brodie came. At the door, she blew a strand of hair from out of her eyes and inserted the key in the lock.

But the door wasn't locked. Jessica was positive she had locked it this morning when she had left. Cautiously she pushed the door open and glanced inside. The first thing she noticed was the aroma of roast beef. She frowned. Was Brodie here? Had he arrived earlier and persuaded the manager to let him in?

Walking inside, she closed the door. "Hello?" she called. A young woman stuck her blond head around the corner of the kitchen, "Well, it's about time you got home."

"Jordanna!" Jessica stared at her sister. "What are you doing here?"

"Surprise!" was the laughing response. "Tom and I are on vacation. Mom and dad volunteered to look after the children. So here we are, two weeks all to ourselves!''

Before Jessica could recover from the shock, she was being hugged by her older sister. ''But what are you doing here?''

''We're on our way to Memphis to see Justin, then on to New Orleans to spend time with Tom's parents. We decided to spend the night here with you. It will give us a chance to visit. Hey, we haven't seen you since Christmas,'' her sister declared, stepping back to take a look at her. ''You seem different, changed.'' Green eyes, a shade brighter than Jessica's, glittered with knowledge. ''Must be a man.''

Jessica's mouth became dry. ''There is someone,'' she admitted reluctantly.

''You'll have to tell me all about him. Come in the kitchen with me.'' Jordanna took hold of her hand and pulled her toward the room. ''I was just going to add some carrots and potatoes to the roast.''

''I . . . I was going to take a shower. It's been a long day and—''

''Tom's using it now.'' Her sister unknowingly cut off that avenue of escape. Cleaned carrots and potatoes were sitting in a colander in the sink. When Jessica reached for them, her sister protested, ''Pour yourself a cup of coffee and sit down. I'll take care of dinner.''

Jessica did as she was told and watched Jordanna open the oven door, releasing a new wave of cooking smells. It was the first time she had really looked at her sister in years. Motherhood and maturity had affected her figure, which was still trim but now bordered on the voluptuous. Her hair was rinsed to a platinum shade and cut short to frame her attractive oval face and draw attention to her unusual green eyes. Fresh and outgoing, her personality was one of Jordanna's greatest assets. Jessica felt her heart sinking.

"How are the kids?" she heard herself ask.

"Fine. Julie has to wear braces on her teeth, which infuriates her. I can remember . . ."

But Jessica didn't bother to listen to the rest. She was wondering where Brodie was and whether there was any way she could get in touch with him to let him know that she couldn't go out with him tonight. Somehow she had to prevent him from coming, but she didn't stop to consider her motive. He had never given her a cell phone number, and she had never asked.

"Jessica, did you hear me?"

Startled, she looked up. "I'm sorry. I guess I was daydreaming. What did you say?"

"It doesn't matter," Jordanna laughed, a pleasant, warm sound. "Who is this new man in your life? Anyone I know?"

"He'd better not be," a familiar voice declared from the doorway as Tom Radford walked into the kitchen, saving Jessica from answering the question. She hadn't mentioned Brodie to any of her family except her uncle. She wasn't sure what their reaction would be, especially her sister's. "Hello, Jessica. You look more beautiful each time I see you," Tom greeted her.

"I think that's because she's in love," Jordanna teased.

"I do believe she's blushing," Tom observed, joining his wife to gang up on Jessica. Deliberately she ignored both remarks. "It's good to see you again, Tom," she greeted her brother-in-law, a tall, good-looking man with brown hair and a few extra

inches around his waistline. "Even if I wasn't
expecting you. When I discovered the door
unlocked I almost called the police. I thought
someone had broken into my apartment," Jessica
lied.

"It was Jordanna's idea. I wanted to call to let
you know we were coming, but she thought it would
be more fun to surprise you," he explained.

"It certainly was a surprise," she admitted. "Does
Justin know you're coming?"

Jordanna explained that they were going to surprise her brother, too. Then Tom related their
plans for New Orleans, the sight-seeing they were
going to do, and the relatives they were going to
visit. Jessica felt the minutes ticking away, yet she
still wasn't able to think of a way to contact Brodie.

"Do you have any bay leaves, Jessica?" Her sister
was opening cupboard doors, looking for spices.

"The one on the left side of the sink," Jessica
directed.

But Jordanna paused at the adjoining cupboard.
"There's a bottle of bourbon here. Can you believe
that, Tom? My baby sister has liquor in her cabinets!"

"I've grown up, Jordanna," she responded
patiently.

"You certainly have," Tom agreed, "And there's
absolutely nothing wrong with good bourbon. Fix
me a drink, wife," he ordered.

"How're mom and dad?" Jessica asked to change
the subject.

"Fine. Tom took dad out golfing with him in
January, and now dad has the bug. He has his own
set of golf clubs and he's talking about buying a
golf cart," Jordanna answered as she opened more
cupboards until she found the glasses.

Jessica's nerves were stretched to the breaking point as she listened to her sister tell about the seat cushions their mother was needlepointing for the dining room set. It all seemed so unimportant.

The doorbell rang. Jessica's heart leaped into her throat.

"I'll get it," she mumbled, and had to fight her trembling knees to make it into the living room.

This time she didn't open the door wide to Brodie. She opened it a foot and blocked his entrance. Her complexion was pallid, her breathing shallow. She had difficulty meeting his curiously inquiring gaze.

"Something's come up, Brodie. I'm afraid I can't go out with you tonight," Jessica rushed, keeping her voice low.

A frown darkened his rough features. "What is it? What's wrong?" His hand came up to push at the door. For a minute, she tried to hold it before realizing she was no match for his strength.

"Nothing's wrong. It's just that I have some unexpected company," she explained as he stepped inside the doorway. "I would have let you know, but I—"

"Jessica, do you have any mushrooms?" Jordanna walked into the living room and stopped abruptly.

Brodie's gaze swung to her, his expression slowly lightening into a smile of recognition. Jessica watched the transformation and felt sick inside.

"Jordanna! It doesn't seem possible, but you're more beautiful than I remembered," he said. His voice was husky and caressing.

"Brodie?" Jordanna stared at him uncertainly. Her head tipped to the side. "Brodie Hayes? It can't be!"

"But it is." He walked forward to take her hand and carry it palm upward to his lips, a gesture that came as naturally as shaking hands. "After all these years, I thought you would have forgotten me."

Jessica watched the pleased smile that spread over her sister's face at Brodie's open display of admiration. There was no sign of nervousness or feelings of intimidation. In fact, Jordanna looked quite attracted to him.

"I haven't forgotten you," Jordanna assured him. Neither of them appeared to notice Jessica standing several feet away, excluded from their reunion. "How have you been? Where have you been? What have you been doing?" She seemed possessed by a sudden need to know everything about him.

"Jordanna, I found the mushrooms for you." Tom walked around the corner and stopped when he saw his wife with a strange man. "Hello." He didn't look at all upset, not even by the fact that Brodie was still holding Jordanna's hand.

"Did you ever meet my husband, Tom?" Jordanna asked with absolute unconcern. "Tom, this is Brodie Hayes. My husband, Tom Radford."

"I don't believe we've met." Brodie released Jordanna's hand to shake Tom's. "Hello, Tom."

"I take it you're an old friend of Jordanna's," he said, smiling.

"That's right." He cast a look sideways at Jordanna. "I tried very hard to make it more than friendship, but she already had you in her sights at the time."

Jessica wanted to scream and stamp her feet and tell them all that Brodie was here to see her. The trouble was he had lost interest in her the minute he'd seen Jordanna. It was the very thing she had feared all along, only she had refused to face it.

"What are you doing here?" Jordanna asked curiously.

But it was Tom who put two and two together. "Are you the mysterious man in Jessica's life?" he joked.

"Oh!" Jordanna clasped a hand over her mouth in surprise. "Are you dating Jessica?"

"Yes, as a matter of fact, we were supposed to have dinner together tonight." For the first time since he'd seen Jordanna, Brodie glanced behind him to Jessica. It seemed like an invitation to join the circle. She walked stiffly forward, pride refusing to let the hurt show through. "Only now she tells me it's off."

"Jessica, you don't have to cancel your date just because we're here." Tom frowned.

"But you're only going to be here tonight. When else would I have a chance to talk to you?" Jessica rigidly defended her action.

"We never meant to upset your plans, Jessica," her sister apologized. "Stay for dinner, Brodie. I have a roast in the oven. There's plenty for all of us."

"No!" Jessica spoke without thinking how it sounded. She was conscious of Brodie's piercing gaze narrowing on her. With difficulty, she met it. "I know how busy your schedule is. I'm sure there's some place you have to be other than here."

"I took Drew's advice and rearranged my schedule so it wouldn't be so crowded," he told her. "There isn't any place I have to be until tomorrow afternoon."

"Well, I'm sure there are papers or financial

statements you need to go over,'' Jessica tried to find a reason for him to leave.

"A man can't work all the time,'' Tom pointed out. "Stay for dinner, Brodie.''

"Seems you're outnumbered, Jessica,'' said Brodie, measuring her with a cool look. "That's two invitations for dinner.''

"You're welcome to stay, of course,'' she lied. She wanted him far away from here . . . and from her sister. "I just thought you might have something more important to do.''

"Not a thing, I'm glad you want me to stay.'' A muscle jumped in his jaw as he uttered the last statement in a faintly sarcastic tone.

"How did the two of you meet?'' Jordanna asked, missing the charged look that passed between Brodie and her sister.

"I picked her up on a street corner about two months ago.'' Brodie phrased it so it was deliberately suggestive. When he saw the fire flash in Jessica's eyes, he smiled. "We bumped into each other quite by accident. When I first saw her I thought it was you, Jordanna. It was only after a few minutes that I realized the resemblance was superficial.''

Jessica wanted to die—that he should actually admit he had mistaken her for her sister. It seemed the final humiliation.

"Excuse me,'' she murmured. "I think I'd better check on the dinner.''

She retreated into the kitchen. Jordanna, despite her earlier protestations that she would fix it, stayed in the living room with Brodie and Tom. She could hear them talking and laughing. Jealousy seethed through her veins.

The roast was out of the oven when Jordanna finally wandered in to help her. Jessica barely glanced at her as she took a meat platter from the cupboard to put the roast on. At that moment, she was trying very hard not to hate her sister.

"The table is already set," Jessica told her. "You can get a bowl down for the potatoes and carrots."

If Jordanna noticed her waspish tone, she ignored it. "Brodie has certainly done well for himself, hasn't he?" she murmured as if speaking her thoughts aloud.

"Yes. Do you want to make the gravy or shall I?" Jessica didn't want to discuss Brodie with her sister.

"I will. Where's the flour?" Jordanna asked, and opened the cupboard Jessica pointed to. "He's really a very attractive man."

"You didn't think so way back when," Jessica reminded her. She didn't give her sister a chance to reply as she carried the platter of meat to the table in the dining room. "Will you carve the roast, Tom?" she requested, and avoided looking at Brodie.

The meal was a miserable ordeal, listening to Jordanna and Brodie talking about the past. Tom had been a part of it, so he joined in the conversation. Jessica hadn't, and she wasn't a part of the dinner conversation, either. She was the fifth wheel and felt it all the way to her bones. She served the dinner, cleared the plates, brought the dessert and coffee, and was as ignored as a servant.

"It hardly seems that long ago, Brodie," Jordanna sighed, as she took the photographs she had shown him of her children and put them back in her purse. "Yet I have two children who aren't that much younger than we were when you came to my house wanting me to go for a ride with you."

"Yes, and you turned me down flat." Brodie recalled dryly. "I was the boy from the wrong side of town. It isn't surprising that you didn't want anything to do with me."

"I don't know." Jordanna seemed to consider the thought. "Where you came from didn't have much to do with it. If I hadn't already met Tom, I probably would have accepted your invitation."

Jessica didn't want to hear this. She rose abruptly from the table. "Excuse me. I think I'll wash the dishes."

"We can do them later, Jessica," Jordanna protested.

"I'd rather do them now," Jessica insisted tightly. "It's getting late and I—"

"Jessica's right. It is getting late," Brodie said. "I've intruded on your family gathering long enough. It's time I was leaving." He rose from the table and glanced pointedly at Jessica.

Courtesy demanded that she offer, "I'll see you to the door."

"Thank you." There was dry mockery in his voice. He took hold of her arm as if he expected her to change her mind and was determined that she would follow through with her offer. Jessica stood rigid in his grasp while Brodie said goodnight to her sister and brother-in-law.

There was an electric quality to the air when they reached the door despite Brodie's attempt to smooth things over. He reached in his pocket and took out a long, thin case. "Here. I didn't have a chance to give it to you earlier," he said.

Jessica took the inevitable gift. She longed to throw it in his face or tell him to give it to Jordanna, but this late in the evening, she was well schooled in controlling her emotions.

"It's a strand of pearls," Brodie told her when she didn't open it.

"I'll open it later. Thank you." A poor replica of a smile curved her stiff mouth.

His jaw hardened, his nostrils flaring in anger. Then his gaze flicked to the adjoining room and the couple who were doing their best to ignore the two at the door.

"I'll call you," he said, and it sounded like a threat. Jessica briefly inclined her head, but Brodie wasn't looking. He was opening the door and walking out, closing it behind him much too quietly. Jessica shuddered and turned away.

"Has he left already?" Jordanna asked the obvious, "What's that in your hand? A present?"

"Yes." Jessica stared at it. Her fingers were as white as the beautiful paper it was wrapped in.

"Well, open it. Don't you want to see what it is?" her sister urged, coming into the living room to join her. To make a negative reply would have invited questions Jessica didn't want to answer. Unwillingly she tore the paper off and opened the box.

"Pearls!" Jordanna exclaimed. "They're beautiful!"

"Is it some special occasion or something?" Tom asked.

"No, no special occasion." Jessica looked at the perfect strand of matched pearls, but couldn't bring herself to touch them. "Brodie just does this."

"Lucky you." Her sister smiled, then turned to her husband to scold him playfully, "How come you never bought me presents like that when we were dating?"

"I didn't want to spoil you. Besides—" Tom glanced at the pearls, his look assessing, "—I wasn't rolling in money the way he is."

After that, Jessica was besieged by questions about Brodie, some of which she dodged, others she answered. It was a relief when the hour grew late enough that she could escape them to the isolation of her room. The bed was inviting, but sleep was far away.

In the morning, Jessica was able to pretend that she was sorry to see her sister go. She even managed to lie that she wished Jordanna could stay longer.

An hour after Jordanna and Tom had left for Memphis, Jessica was at the office, tormented by the hell of being jealous of her own sister; so nervous that nothing she did went right. By ten-thirty that morning she was bent over her desk, her face buried in her hands. Her computer screen was frozen, she'd lost all her unsaved work, and the tech guy was out sick.

She was sure she was losing her sanity and wondered how she would get through the rest of the day.

The door to her office opened and Brodie walked in, tall and vigorous while she felt small and beaten. She stared at him, half afraid she was having hallucinations.

"What are you doing here?" she breathed.

"I came to take you to lunch," he said, matter-of-factly.

"But you said last night that you had an appointment at noon. Next time, call me. Or e-mail me."

"We're flying to Nashville for lunch. I promised you a ride in my jet, remember?" An eyebrow lifted, arrogant and mocking, yet his look was compelling.

"But I can't—"

"Yes, you can," Brodie interrupted her protest. "I've already spoken to your uncle, and he has no objection if you take a few hours off. Don't forget the lucrative advertising account of Janson Boats. Get your handbag. We don't have much time."

Jessica was swept into the maelstrom of his commanding presence. Before she could think, she was hustled out of the office, into his waiting car, and was halfway to the airport. By then it was too late. She stared at the clasped hands in her lap and wondered what kind of fool she was.

"I guess Tom and Jordanna left early this morning."

"Yes, they did," she acknowledged stiffly.

He shot her a piercing glance. "Why were you so anxious to get rid of me last night, Jessica?"

She started guiltily. "Don't be ridiculous! I wasn't anxious to get rid of you," she lied. "I know the way you drive yourself. I thought you'd be better off resting than listening to a lot of boring family conversation."

"I wasn't bored."

Jessica swallowed at the pain that knifed through her. No, Jordanna didn't bore him. Her sister never had. She felt his glance and knew she had to make some response.

"I'm glad," she murmured as he parked in front of an airplane hangar. The sleek private jet was waiting on the concrete apron.

There were hurried introductions of Jessica to the pilot, Jim Kent, and the copilot, Frank Murphy, before she was hustled aboard.

The interior of the aircraft was not fitted out for passenger seating, but instead resembled a den with two lightweight desks mounted to the floor, some comfortable-looking chairs and a divan. Brodie helped her to buckle herself into one of the chairs.

"Ever flown in a Lear jet?" He took a seat near her.

The plane was rolling down the runway. Jessica could feel the acceleration of the powerful jet engines.

"Sure. Millions of times."

He grinned.

"It's very practical. There's work space for myself and Cliff or Drew. There's a shower in the wash-room." He continued to talk to her as the plane roared into the air. "I can nap on the divan or hand out drinks and snacks if I want to play flight attendant."

Jessica glanced at him. "Are you trying to impress me?"

"Are you impressed?" Brodie countered, his mouth quirking.

"Yes," she admitted.

"Good."

"How long will it take to get to Nashville?"

"It's a short flight. By the time we take off, climb to the designated altitude, and level off, Jim starts his descent." He was eyeing her with an intent yet rather sly look.

"There isn't enough time to earn a Mile High pin." "What's that?" she asked blankly. "That, Green Eyes," Brodie unfastened his seat belt and straightened to tower beside her, "is awarded to couples who've made love a mile above ground."

His low, throaty laugh said that he had noted the agitated movement of her breasts. His hand cupped the back of her head, turning her face up. There was a blinding brilliance of his gaze on her. Then he was kissing her long and hard, melting her resistance with his hot mouth.

Jessica responded, convinced she was without

pride where Brodie was concerned. When he straightened, she felt light-headed and shaken.

"Want anything to drink?" he offered. "Coffee? Tea?" *Or you*, she thought naughtily.

"Nothing," she refused.

While he got himself some coffee, she sat quietly in her chair. She found herself wondering how many women had received a Mile High pin from him. Her stomach churned in a sickening knot.

A rental car was waiting at the Nashville airport, where they lunched with some stranger. Afterward Brodie drove her back to the airport and put her on his jet alone to be flown back to Chattanooga.

"I'll call you next week," he told her as he kissed her goodbye.

She would be waiting. She had the feeling she would always be waiting.

Chapter Eleven

Brodie didn't call. A week later he drove the sleek Jaguar up to the curb of her apartment building just as Jessica was arriving home from work. He honked the horn to call her over and left the engine running.

"Same car. They reserve it for me. Shall we go for a ride?" he asked.

"All right. Give me a couple of minutes to change."

"There's nothing wrong with what you're wearing." His gaze swept over the short skirt and beige wrap top she had on.

"But I—"

"Are you looking for compliments?" He grinned boyishly.

"No," Jessica said.

"Then climb in," he ordered. When she was in the passenger seat and the door was closed, Brodie shifted the car into gear and turned it onto the street. His gaze rested on her briefly. "Are you upset with me for not calling?"

"I . . . no," she admitted. As long as she saw him, it didn't seem to matter whether she knew in advance or not. And that was the shameless truth.

As if he knew what the admission had cost her in pride, Brodie took hold of her hand, linking his fingers with hers and carried the back of her hand to his mouth. Her hand remained in the warm clasp of his as he drove through the city streets. Jessica leaned against the seat, turning her head to study his profile. She felt she had been more than amply rewarded for telling the truth.

"Had a rough week?" He didn't look tired, at least not as tired as he had that other time he had visited.

"Not any more than usual." Brodie slowed the car to make a sharp turn onto a tree-lined road.

"Where are we going?" Jessica glanced around, noticing that they had seemed to leave the city behind.

"I forgot. Your present is in the glove compartment," he said. Hiding her displeasure, Jessica opened the compartment. There was an envelope inside with her name on it. She hesitated. Surely he wouldn't be so crude as to give her money? "Go on, open it," Brodie prodded.

Grudgingly she took it out and lifted up the flap. There was a key inside. Her gaze flew to Brodie as she held it up. "What's this for?"

He merely smiled, made another turn, and slowed the car to a stop. As he switched off the engine he glanced to her.

"Why don't you try it on that door?" he suggested, and nodded in the direction behind her.

Jessica turned. They were parked in the driveway of a sprawling house nestled on the crest of a hill. A thousand questions spun through her mind, but a second look at Brodie told her he would provide the answers when he felt it was time.

She climbed out of the car and waited for Brodie to join her. Together they followed the curving sidewalk to the front door. The key in her hand turned the lock. She glanced at Brodie's enigmatic expression and opened the door.

A few steps inside, she entered a completely furnished living room with a beamed ceiling. The starkness of the off-white walls and terrazzo floors was relieved by the subtle colors of contemporary pieces. The fireplace was framed by a luxurious sofa facing two easy chairs.

In the opposite corner of the room was a sweeping curved sofa in leather with overstuffed armchairs flanking it. Unusual lamps on matching end tables completed the arrangement. Despite the expensive elegance, every corner invited Jessica to sit down and relax.

But Brodie's hand at her elbow was guiding her to the formal dining room where a pastel carpet accented the velvet of the chairs. The dining room credenza held a beautiful china set and figurines. Natural silk draperies hung at the windows.

From there it was on to a spacious U-shaped kitchen with tiled counters. Antique copper pieces decorated the wall. The room was complete with a breakfast nook—a cozy sitting room filled with white wicker.

Backtracking, Brodie showed her the den with its wall of books and handmade brick fireplace. A thick area rug complemented the plaid sofa and easy chairs, and an antique walnut desk dominated one side of the room.

The two guest bedrooms were skipped over as Brodie led her to the master bedroom. The king-size bed was covered with a white quilt, and white brocade upholstered two small armchairs arranged with a low table between them.

"What do you think?" Brodie finally broke the silence that had been between them.

"What can I say?" Jessica lifted her hands, at a loss for words. "It's beautiful!"

"Beautiful enough to live in?" he challenged. Jessica stared, hardly daring to believe what he was saying. Brodie continued before she could respond, "It's close to town yet far enough away to give us some privacy." Her heart sang at what followed. "I figure you'll want to keep working, although I'd much rather have you here waiting for me."

Jessica was so full of happiness she couldn't speak. But it didn't seem necessary. Somehow she found herself in his arms, her hands around his neck to bring his head down to hers. Their lips met in a fiery kiss that fused them together as she was lifted higher and higher on a cloud of sweet joy. She clung to him, her life, her love. The dizzying climb was too much and she had to stop to catch her breath. She buried her face against his chest, feeling the roughness of his kisses on her hair. She was afraid she was going to do something silly like cry.

"Would it be very selfish of me," she murmured against his shirt, "to ask you to take a week off so we can have a honeymoon?"

Brodie became very still, his muscles tensing. "What honeymoon? What are you talking about, Jessica?" His hands gripped her shoulders to hold her away from him.

The smile faded from her lips as she stared at the puzzled frown on his face. "Didn't you . . .

didn't you just propose to me?" Her voice died to a whisper as she saw the answer in his face.

"No." The denial was flat and decisive. "I can't marry you, Jessica." Letting her go, he walked several feet into the master bedroom and stopped, looking around. She felt drained and lifeless. The descent to earth had been too rapid.

"Why?" Her voice cracked and she tried to control it. "Do you already have a wife? Won't she give you a divorce? Is she sick or an invalid?" Now her voice sounded brittle, devoid of feeling.

"I have no wife," Brodie answered curtly. "Marriage is out of the question."

"I see." Jessica thought she did see. Jordanna was the woman he wanted. If he couldn't marry her, he wasn't marrying anyone. "You want me to be your mistress."

"If you want to put it that way, yes." He blew out a long breath with the words.

"Why bother with the house, then?" Her poise was wearing thin, but it was holding. "Why not just ask me to quit my job and fly around the country with you?"

"Like a groupie?"

"Sort of. Your own private—"

"I'm not going to get into a debate with you over definitions, Jessica," Brodie warned.

Her gaze fell beneath the icy blast of his. She studied the intricate pattern of the Oriental rug, as if searching for something but not knowing what.

"Have you made these convenient arrangements in other cities?" she questioned stiffly. "Memphis? Nashville?"

"No," he denied that, coming to stand in front of her. "I admit that I've had other women. But you're the only woman I want on more than a casual basis."

"Will I . . . have to share you or something?" Jessica faltered on the question although her voice remained cool.

His gaze bored into her. "You haven't shared me with anyone almost since the day we met. Which is why I can't wait any longer. We either begin now or we stop." A silence ensued that Jessica couldn't break. Finally Brodie turned away. "I'm going to the basement to see if they've installed the new furnace. Look around some more. If you don't like the place, we'll find another." He walked out of the room.

Jessica stared at the empty doorway. It had been an ultimatum he had issued. And he had assumed she would stay. But was he wrong? If he hadn't put it in such black and white terms, if he had made love to her instead, she wouldn't be going through all this soul-searching now. It would be an accomplished fact.

The question wasn't whether she loved him, but rather, could she leave him? A surge of despair sent her into the room. She paused at the bed, her fingertips touching the white quilted coverlet. This would be the bed they would share, the room where they would wake up together.

She wandered to the long closet. Their clothes would hang inside. She slid open the louvered doors and found the closet wasn't completely empty. A single hanger held a lacy negligee. The store tags were still on it to show it was brand new, and another hanger held a matching robe.

There was something premeditated about it hanging there, as if Brodie had never expected them to leave the house tonight. Perhaps if she had opened the refrigerator or cupboards in the kitchen, she would have found them stocked with food.

The house was all furnished, waiting to be occupied. Jessica knew she could fill it with love, maybe only with her love. She closed her eyes and pictured Brodie. Opening them, she took the lacy negligee from the closet and laid it on the bed. Mechanically she stripped off her clothes and hung them in the closet. When the delicate material slid over her body, she walked to the mirror and used the hair brush from the vanity set to fluff her hair.

At the sound of Brodie's footsteps in the hallway, she turned. A tremor ran through her limbs, but she was motionless when he appeared in the doorway. Brodie stopped, his muscled chest expanding in a breath he held, and stared. His eyes darkened as they made a slow, raking sweep of her.

Just as slowly, he walked to stand in front of her, looking down, not touching her, not making a move toward her. Jessica felt her breathing become shallow, her heartbeat become rapid and erratic. His control was supreme. She realized he was waiting for her to speak and make the first move.

Hesitantly she rested her hands on his waist and felt his muscles constrict. Swaying toward him, she wondered if she had the voice to speak.

"I want to live with you, Brodie." It came out trembling and low, but it was said.

His arms moved, but not to hold her. His hands found the bow that fastened the silly nothing robe covering the frothy gown. Brodie untied and pushed it off her shoulders, down her arms where it slid off to fall to the floor.

Jessica was shivering, her bare feet as cold as ice, when Brodie swung her into his arms. He held her easily, as if she weighed no more than a feather. The bulging muscles of his arms formed an iron-hard cradle. His gaze never left her face as he carried her to the bed and laid her gently down. He followed her down, stretching beside her, his hand cupping the side of her neck to feel the pulse that throbbed wildly there.

"I'll make you happy, Jessica." He smoothed the blond hair from her throat and kissed her there.

Yes, she thought, temporarily he would make her ecstatically happy. Her hands slid inside the collar of his shirt. He tugged it out of his pants and dispensed with the last few buttons, giving her free access to his warm, hard flesh.

His caressing hands explored her shoulders and arms and the hollows of her throat, ignoring the intimate areas covered by her flimsy negligee as his mouth ignored the taste of her lips. Jessica begged him with her hands and lips and her body to make love to her.

"There's no need to rush, Green Eyes," he told her. "We've got all the time in the world now. And I'm going to use every damned minute of it."

Finally he came to her lips, covering them with a possessive kiss that gave her back a measure of reassurance. Jessica strained closer to his length, trying to absorb some of the strength he had in such abundance.

"Maybe I will take a few days off," Brodie nuzzled her ear. "I'm going to enjoy teaching you how to please me as much as I'm going to enjoy pleasing you."

A tiny sob came from her throat, born not out of desire but of pain, a pain of the heart. She tried to respond to his kisses, to unleash the love that consumed her.

How many times he had wakened the same feelings in her! But this time something was wrong. The purity of her emotion was gone. What once she had given freely, she now held back, protecting and shielding.

"Green Eyes," he had called her. Was it really his pet name for her? Or did it belong to Jordanna? How many times would he hold her in his arms while she wondered if he was making love to her or pretending she was Jordanna? In the end, these doubts would destroy her love for him, and they would destroy her.

"No." It was the first word she had muttered since the agreement. It came out choked and broken. Brodie paid no attention to the negative sound until Jessica repeated it more forcefully, "No!" and began to struggle.

"What's the matter? he frowned. "Have I hurt you? How?" He had levered himself on his elbows above her. His shirt hung open, revealing tanned skin and curling dark chest hair that vee-ed to his stomach. Jessica closed her eyes, because she couldn't look at him without loving him.

"I—can't," she cried softly. "I can't go through with it!" She attempted to roll away.

"No!" Brodie's anger exploded. His arm caught her waist and tossed her back onto the mattress beside him. His legs covered hers to hold her there, pinning her with his weight. "You can't go this far and stop! My God, do you think I'm made of ice!" Imprisoning her arms, he spread-eagled them above her head.

Jessica stopped struggling. She kept her head averted, burying a cheek in the coverlet. Her breasts were rising and falling with her deep, panicked breaths. Her eyes were tightly closed, one tear squeezing through her lashes.

"I can't, Brodie," she whispered. "I tried, but I can't."

And she waited for a violent physical response, knowing she had brought it on with her actions and prepared to pay for the mistake. She could hear Brodie's heavy breathing, troubled by passion and anger. She waited for the punishment of his mouth, aware of the pressing heat of his body holding her down.

Instead she felt his weight ease from her. The creak of the bed springs was followed by the sound of his feet on the floor. Swallowing convulsively, she opened her eyes and slowly wrapped her arms across her breasts, barely covered by the revealing garment. Brodie stood beside the bed watching her movements and noting the fear in her eyes.

His mouth had thinned into a tense line, his features harshly condemning. Blue steel was in his gaze. Lust had gone from his expression, to be replaced by contempt.

Jessica dragged herself up, sliding to the opposite side of the bed. "I'm sorry, Brodie." He would never know how sorry she was.

"That's it, then." His voice was clipped and final. "It's over."

With heavy steps, she walked to the closet and took out her clothes. She hugged them to the thinness of her gown. The pain inside her was so intense, she wanted to die.

"Will you take me home, please?" she whispered.

There was a long silence. She thought for a minute he wasn't going to answer, then it came. "Five minutes." It was a harsh, savage answer. "Be dressed and in the car." He issued the last command as he was striding from the room.

Jessica was dressed in less than that. She paused at the door to wipe the single tear from her cheek, then hurried outside to the waiting car. The engine was running as she slid into the passenger seat.

Brodie never looked at her as he reversed out of the driveway. The envelope that had contained the key was still lying on the seat near her. Jessica slipped the key inside and returned the envelope to the glove compartment. She would never have a need for it.

She glanced at Brodie. His profile was almost savagely expressionless. Not once during the drive to her apartment did his gaze stray to her. It was as if he was the only one in the car. When he stopped in front of her building, Jessica hesitated, wanting to say something, but his hands remained on the steering wheel, the car idling. He stared straight ahead.

Finally Jessica opened the car door and climbed out. She had barely closed the door before Brodie was driving away. He had meant it. It was over and he had just cut her out of his life, ignoring her as if she didn't exist.

Chapter Twelve

With her arms hugging her knees, Jessica rocked gently on the sofa. It had been three weeks since Brodie had let her out in front of her apartment; three painful, heartrending weeks. She had lost weight and the dark shadows beneath her eyes revealed her incapacity for sleep.

Over and over again she went over the events. What had she hoped to gain? Had she thought if she denied Brodie the act of love that he would want her so badly he would offer marriage? If that had been her subconscious plan, it had backfired with agonizing consequences.

The telephone rang, and Jessica covered her ears with her hands. There wasn't anyone she wanted to talk to. She'd had more than enough advice to last her a lifetime. Between the receptionist, Ann, issuing platitudes and her uncle using anger to try to snap her out of her depression, she had been besieged with pearls of wisdom. They weren't any more comforting than the impersonal strand of pearls Brodie had given her. Everyone she knew had made some comment until she longed to lock herself in the apartment and never come out.

The telephone was insistent, ringing shrilly on the table beside the sofa. Jessica ignored it for as long as she could, then on the seventh ring, she reached for the receiver.

"Hello." Her voice was dull and lifeless. No one answered her, but she sensed there was someone on the other end of the line. "Hello?" she demanded with irritation.

"Who is that?" a voice snapped.

"It's Jessica Thor—" Then the quick, harsh voice heard so briefly, gripped her heart. "Brodie?" she whispered, clutching the receiver with both hands as if to hold onto him and never let him go.

"Sorry. I dialed this number by mistake." The voice never acknowledged his identity, but Jessica knew him just as she would know her own name.

"Brodie, please!" But the buzz of the dial tone was the only thing to hear her plea.

For long minutes she held onto the receiver. Hanging it up seemed to mean breaking some vital link. One tear rolled from her eye, followed by a second and a third. When she put the phone down, an ocean of salty tears was drowning her cheeks. It was the first time she had truly cried. A stray tear here and there didn't really count. It took her all night to make up for the omission.

Perspiration stung her eyes. The cotton blouse she wore clung to her sticky skin. Summer had arrived in earnest, complete with heat and humidity. She used a folder as a fan, trying to stir the dead air of her closed-in office, but its relief was only temporary.

Impatiently she rose from her desk and walked into the reception area. "Ann, I can't stand much more of this. When is that man going to come and fix the air conditioner? That office is like a furnace!"

"He promised to be here by noon," the receptionist answered.

Jessica glanced at her watch. "He isn't late, is he?" she retorted sarcastically. "It's twenty to twelve."

"Do you suppose I should call him again?" Ann cast an uncertain glance at Jessica.

"Yes, you call him and you tell him that if he isn't over here by noon, he—" Her voice had grown steadily louder as her impatience had given way to anger.

A male voice interrupted, "He'd better be here this afternoon." Her threat was finished by her uncle. "You're getting a little hot under the collar, aren't you, Jessie?" Her uncle laughed at his little joke.

"Very funny!" Jessica snapped, not at all amused.

"Where's your sense of humor, Jessie?" he admonished with a clicking tongue.

"It melted—in my office. I'm going to have the art department make a sign to hang on the door, identifying it for what it really is—a sweatbox," she insisted, and Ralph Dane laughed, which didn't improve her temper. "It's all very well for you to laugh. You have an enormous electric fan in your office."

"Naturally. It's my company," he smiled.

Suddenly Jessica was very close to tears. "Well, you can take your company and your fan and your sweatbox and you can—"

"Careful, careful, my dear." He was instantly at

her side, his voice soothing her, a comforting arm curving around her shoulders. "I diagnose a severe case of heat exhaustion. My recommendation is that you have lunch in a cool, air-conditioned restaurant, preferably in the company of some handsome, distinguished man—namely me."

Jessica had succeeded in blinking back the tears and swallowing the anger. Now she laughed, somewhat tremulously. "If you think I'm going to refuse, you're wrong, I have a witness to that invitation, so you can't back out."

"I wouldn't dream of it." Her uncle turned to the receptionist. "If anyone wants to know where I am, tell them I'm lunching with a beautiful blonde. Unless my wife calls. Tell her I'm lunching with Jessie."

"Let me get my bag." Jessica dashed into her office and was out just as quickly.

Linking arms with her uncle, she walked out of the door with him. On the street, he guided her to his car and helped her into the passenger seat.

"Where would you like to go?" he asked, sliding behind the wheel.

"I don't care, just as long as it's air-conditioned." Jessica rolled down the window to let the wind blow over her face until the car's AC kicked in.

"I'm really proud of you, Jessica."

Both his statement and his use of her full name drew her attention from the passing scenery. "You are? I don't recall doing anything spectacular in the past week to earn such praise."

"I wasn't referring to the office. I meant that I'm proud of the way you managed to pull yourself together. A couple of months ago I would have sworn you were headed for a breakdown," her uncle said.

Intense pain flashed across her face. She looked quickly out of the window, pressing a hand to her mouth to hide her trembling chin. Any unexpected reference to Brodie could crack her thin, protective shell.

"Time has a way of healing things," she lied. The wound was still bleeding.

"I know that's what people say, but we both know it isn't entirely true. I was rough on you a few times, but I was really only doing it for your own good. I apologize if you thought I was being heartless."

"I know you were, and I appreciated all your attempts," Jessica assured him, although she remembered one that had been particularly painful.

Looking back, she could see that she had failed miserably at her job the two months after she and Brodie had broken up. One morning her uncle had summoned her to his office and told her that she was to patch up whatever quarrel she'd had with Brodie. Since she had never given him the reason they had parted, she had been paralyzed by his order. When she had stared at him dumbstruck, he had changed his statement. He had told her that she had two choices—either patch things up or accept that it was over.

It was a painful memory, but it had proved to be the best advice she had received. It drummed in her mind every time she found herself dissolving in self-pity. She still hurt, but she had learned to live with it and conceal it from others.

"Here we are," her uncle announced.

Jessica pulled herself out of her recollections to see their destination. God, no, her heart cried in pain. It was the Terminal Station where Brodie had taken her for lunch. Her first impulse was to ask her uncle to take her elsewhere, but common sense overruled it. She couldn't keep avoiding places simply because she had been there with Brodie.

Hadn't she learned to walk the sidewalks and stop wondering when and if she would ever see him? Hadn't she learned not to look at the drivers of every expensive car, wondering if Brodie was in town?

Still her legs were shaking when she climbed out of the car and walked with her uncle to the renovated railroad station and the restaurant inside. Her smile to the hostess was tense as they were led through the tables to an empty one.

"Ralph!" a voice called to her uncle. "Hello, how are you?"

A man rose from a table near the window to greet them. It took Jessica only a second to recognize the bushy-browed man as Cal Janson. She had arranged to be busy the rare times he had stopped at the office on business. Mostly someone from the company went to see him.

"Hello, Cal. How's business?" Her uncle's hand was engulfed in a vigorous handshake.

"Fine, fine," Cal Janson replied, and turned his attention to her. "Jessica, you're looking more beautiful every time I see you." He clasped her hand warmly in both of his.

"Thank you." Inside she was praying frantically, *Please God, please, don't let him mention Brodie!*

"You make me wish I were ten years younger—well, maybe twenty," Cal winked at her uncle when he made the correction. "I was going to suggest to Brodie that the two of you come over to dinner tonight." It took all of Jessica's control not to blanch at his statement. It meant that Brodie was in town, and she didn't want to know that. "Since you're here, I'll extend the invitation to you first. Emily and I would love to have you."

"Thank you, but I'm afraid that isn't possible." Jessica was trying very hard to find a tactful way of telling Janson that she was no longer seeing Brodie.

He misunderstood her gentle wording. "That's why I'm asking you first. Brodie is very much his own master. I understand very well that he wants you all to himself, but if anyone can persuade him to accept the invitation, you can."

"But—"

"Here he comes now. We'll both go to work on him," Cal Janson declared, casting her a conspiratorial smile before directing his attention behind her.

Her heart stopped beating and her face drained of color as she pivoted. It was Brodie, purposefully winding his way through the tables to the windows. Tall, imposing, turning heads, he was more sternly handsome than she remembered. Devil-black hair, tanned skin stretched across cheekbones and jaw, the tense line of his mouth, those piercing cold eyes, and that wolflike grace of movement, all struck her like a body blow and took away her breath.

She wasn't ready to see him again. She wasn't prepared. Why did he have to show up just when she was beginning to put her life back together? She wanted to run, but she couldn't tear her eyes away from him.

What was he thinking right now? What was he feeling? She searched his compelling features for a sign of reaction. There wasn't anything, just hard, cold stone. Surely he had seen her? He was looking right at her. Pain constricted her chest as Jessica realized he was looking *through* her.

"Hello, Brodie," Cal Janson greeted him. "Look who I ran into—"

"Hello, Cal." Brodie walked past her as if she weren't even there. "Sorry we're late. We were held up on the ground in Baltimore."

"I haven't been waiting long." Cal Janson darted a puzzled glance from Brodie to Jessica, her green eyes rounded with hurt, still staring at Brodie in disbelief. "I was just saying to Jessica that—"

"Drew and I had a chance to go over the latest balance sheet on the flight here," Brodie interrupted again. Jessica was only dimly conscious of the second man accompanying Brodie. Shock was still quaking through her as Brodie sat down at the table Janson had been given. He was ignoring the reference to her, treating her as if she didn't exist. "I didn't like the production figures. What's the problem? Are you having labor trouble?"

She was unaware of the frowning looks of confusion Brodie was receiving from both Drew and Cal Janson. Neither did she notice the indignant expression on her uncle's face. Hurt, humiliation and anger were all violently swelling up inside her. She wouldn't be snubbed this way.

Instinct and the desire to strike back directed her action. A glass of ice water was sitting on the table. Jessica picked it up and emptied it in Brodie's face. She didn't wait to see the results. Spinning away, she heard the muffled swearing and the gasps from onlookers. The only thing she wanted to do was get away from him as far and as fast as she could. Her legs carried her swiftly over the winding path through the tables to the exit. Heads turned at the hastiness of her retreat, voices murmuring curiously.

The end of the long tunnel of pain and humiliation didn't seem very far away until a steel hand clamped itself on her arm and pulled her away. Just as savagely, it yanked her around and Jessica found herself facing Brodie. Moisture was beaded on his features, taut with rage. His brutal grip was tight enough to bruise her arm.

"Let me go!" she hissed.

"Shut up!" His lip curled in a snarl, baring teeth in a wolflike display of anger.

Jessica strained against his hold, but didn't struggle, "Let me go or I'll have the manager call the police," she threatened in a treacherously low voice. Part of her couldn't help cowering from the savage fury in his eyes.

His answer was to jerk her on tiptoe and silence her with the sensual force of his mouth. It deadened not only her voice but her will to fight. Her mind was all messed up by the sensations crowding in. She couldn't feel anything but the tautness of his muscled thighs and the solidness of his chest and the hard punishment of his mouth.

In the next second Brodie ended the kiss as abruptly as he had started it. Bereft, Jessica waited for whatever was to come next. Turning her, he pushed her toward the exit, not relinquishing his hold. They were nearly there when he was stopped.

"Brodie, for God's sake, what are you doing?" Drew was there, his face darkened with angry concern.

"Butt out!" Brodie snarled, and tried to shoulder his way past the attorney, but Drew was having none of it.

"Dammit, what's got into you? You deserved that ice water. My God, you can't treat people like that!" Drew flashed a worried look at Jessica. "Let go of her!"

"I said get out of my way!"

"Get out," Drew repeated, anger flashing in his eyes. "How far out do you want me to get? Maybe completely? Do you want my resignation? Is that what you've been pushing me to these past few months?"

"Listen, Drew, I don't give a damn." This time Brodie physically pushed him out of the way and pulled Jessica along with him out the door.

"Where are we going?" Jessica was practically running in order to keep up with his long strides.

Her demand was met with the same response as previous ones, "Shut up!"

He continued to drag her along to the car. Opening the door, he pushed her inside and slammed it shut, Jessica rubbed her arm where his hard grip had bruised the flesh. Already the red marks had a bluish tinge to them. Excitement was mixed with fear at the way he had manhandled her into coming with him.

Intimidated by his rage now under slender control, Jessica sat quietly in her seat as Brodie drove out of the parking lot. She didn't reissue the question regarding their destination. Soon she guessed where it would be—her apartment.

Parked in front of the building, Brodie walked around to the passenger door, opened it and hauled her out without giving her a chance to step out on her own. Jessica bit her lip to check a protest of her treatment and let him push her inside. At the door, he ripped the key out of her hand, unlocked the door and shoved her inside.

With familiar ground beneath her feet, Jessica took a stand, facing him, a scant three feet separating them. "What comes next, Brodie? Rape?" Bravado trembled in her challenge.

His jaw tightened ominously. He turned away, combing his fingers through his hair in a savage motion. "Damn you, Jessica," he muttered.

"Damn me?" An incredulous laugh ended in a sob. "Damn you for ignoring me as if I wasn't even there!" The look in his eyes told her she should be terrified, but she couldn't bring herself to be afraid of him. "You know what I've been considering," Brodie said almost thoughtfully "I'd be better off dead."

"Why?" Her overwhelming emotions would only permit the one word. "I've tried to forget you, crush all the memories, block out the smell and taste and feel of you, but I can't. The harder I try, the stronger they get, until—damn you!" he cursed. "And damn my memory for tormenting me with wanting you!"

His mouth came down hard and angry on her lips, punishing their softness. Behind the brutal possession, Jessica felt the pent-up agony of desire, the needing and wanting that she felt just as intensely. It was to this that she responded as his arms crushed her to his length. Jessica clung to him, shaken by the fierceness of his desire.

"Is it really me you want?" she whispered.

"My God," Brodie breathed savagely. "There hasn't been anyone else since I met you. You've stolen my potency as well as my heart."

"What!" She tried to struggle away. His rough embrace had her senses clamoring so loudly that she couldn't hear her own thoughts. It was suddenly very necessary to be able to think and assimilate words.

He caught her face in his hands, holding it still, the blazing fire of his eyes smoldering over her features. "You're a heartless bitch. You won't give back my heart, my love or my manhood."

"Brodie, do you love me?" Her voice throbbed. "Do you really love me?"

"Don't pretend you didn't know!" he jeered. "I spent more hours in the air just to see you than I ever did on any project. A man doesn't do that for mere lust."

"But I thought—Jordanna . . ." Jessica was so confused that she didn't know what she thought.

"Your sister?" Brodie frowned as if incredulous that Jordanna had anything to do with their discussion.

"I thought you only wanted me because of her," she offered lamely.

"You mean because I was infatuated with her a long time ago?" he demanded.

"You did say I reminded you of her," Jessica said defensively. "When you . . . that evening she was here, you hardly took your eyes off of her," she accused.

"That night I was so painfully conscious that you didn't want me there, I don't know where I was looking. If it was at Jordanna, I was probably trying to discover what I ever saw in her," Brodie retorted angrily before a frown of confusion flickered across his forehead. "Were you jealous that night?"

"Insanely jealous," she admitted with a faint laugh.

"My God!" he breathed. "And I thought . . . you believed I wasn't good enough to associate with your family."

"Brodie, no!" Jessica denied it vehemently, her fingers curving tightly over his wrists. "How could you possibly think that?"

His mouth twisted in a self-deprecating smile.

"A lingering inferiority complex of the boy from the wrong side of town.

"As for Jordanna, yeah, I was interested in dating you because of her. The prospect of going to bed with you satisfied a longing to avenge that previous rejection by a Thorne. But after the third or fourth time I saw you, the sensations you were arousing in me had nothing to do with vengeance."

Of its own volition, her body molded itself to the hard length of his, her heart thrilling to his declaration. "I love you, Brodie," she responded, trembling with the depth of her emotion.

His arms encircled her in an iron band of love that crushed her to him, as if he was intent on defying the physical restrictions of their bodies to bring her closer to him still. His mouth moved roughly over her hair, kissing and caressing.

"If you love me, why did you put us through this hell?" Brodie demanded, his voice echoing the shudder that racked through him. "Why did you refuse to come to me?"

"Because . . . I think I hoped if I wouldn't let you make love to me, you'd marry me," Jessica admitted. "I wanted to be your wife, Brodie. I wanted to share your life, not just your bed."

"You'll get your wish," he told her at last. "If that's the only way I can have you, then I'll marry you."

"Why, Brodie?" She drew her head away from his gaze in confusion at his face. "Why don't you *want* to marry me?"

"Because—just look around you. You have everything. You've always had everything—clothes, the finest schools, a beautiful home. Everything you've ever wanted." Impatience darkened his eyes.

"Money? That's your reason?" Jessica frowned.

"What difference should that make to you? You're wealthy and successful. As a matter of fact, you were intent on keeping me in a style I wasn't accustomed to."

"Yes, I have money today," he snapped. "But I'm not a blind fool. I can't expect to come up a winner every time I roll the dice. I could lose everything I have tomorrow."

"Money doesn't mean anything to me. I don't care whether you have any or not. I love you," she argued.

"Noble words," Brodie said with contempt. "But you don't know what it can be like to have nothing. When that day of cold reality comes, you'll find that love isn't enough."

"It is!" Jessica searched for a way to prove to him that it was true. "It isn't everything, but it's enough. These past few months we've been apart, I've had all those expensive gifts you gave me, but they didn't mean anything because I didn't have you. You said it yourself, Brodie—what good is money if you can't share it with someone you care about? Without money, at least you know that love is real. And—"

She would have continued, but Brodie was convinced. He silenced her in a most satisfying way.

SAVAGE LAND

Chapter One

Another bolt of lightning flamed out of the dark, rolling clouds, followed by a heart-pounding clap of thunder. Colleen McGuire's pulse raced as she involuntarily cringed in her seat. Her large hazel eyes remained fixed on the windshield where the wipers were vainly attempting to wash away the sheets of rain descending from the menacing clouds. Apprehensively she glanced at her brother behind the wheel.

"Danny, don't you think we should stop?" Fear made her voice tremble in spite of her effort to control it.

"Just where would you suggest, Coley?" he snapped, not taking his attention from the emptiness in front of them. "If we stop now, we probably won't get this old clunker started again."

"We should have listened to that man back at the garage," Coley murmured as a fresh torrent of water pummeled down on their car.

"That was thirty miles back, and it was only sprinkling then!" Danny flashed at her. Tension from the strain of creeping along the winding Texas road made him unnaturally sharp. "How was I supposed to know it would be like this?"

"But he said it was raining bad in the mountains, that the road could flood. And those signs we've been seeing," Coley persisted. At her words, a highway sign was illuminated by the car's headlights: FLOOD HAZARD—RISING WATER AT LOW CROSSINGS. A sickening moan escaped her lips. "Oh, Danny, there's another!"

"Coley, will you stop carrying on about a little rain and thunder! Aren't you ever going to grow out of that childish fear?" her brother retorted. His knuckles were white from gripping the steering wheel as if his life depended on him not letting it go. With determination, he added, "We're going to make it. Don't you worry."

A forced smile appeared on Coley's mouth as she gulped down her fears and turned to look out her side window. She chewed nervously on a fingernail while watching the jagged forks of lightning turn the hills and mountains around them into towering monsters. Her reflection in the window glass dimly mirrored her oval face with its fine, arched brows and large hazel eyes that had, if it was possible, grown wider with her anxiety. Her wispy brown hair was as indistinct in the reflection as it was in life, limply hanging below her small ears. And yet there was a childlike charm about her that was oddly appealing and a promise of unusual beauty at maturity.

The old Chevy slowed slightly while water swirled around its wheels. It was another water crossing. The color washed out of Coley's face as she turned her head from the sickening rush of the stream. Numbly she watched her brother's try to drive feeling the current tugging at the car, trying to sweep it off the road. Coley felt herself stiffen with Danny as they slowly edged their way between two poles midway in the crossing. The water was above the hubcaps and inching under the door before they finally made it to the other side. Coley could see the relief on her brother's face when they reached solid ground again.

"What were those poles there for?" She forced herself to speak to stem the rising panic within her, knowing her brother was beginning to worry, too. When he failed to answer her immediately, she repeated the question.

"High water markers," he replied grimly. His young face was beginning to show the strain of the constant demands on his driving ability. He glanced worriedly over at his sister before returning to the road. "I'm sure we don't have too much farther to go."

Despite his attempt to reassure her, his growing apprehension increased her fear. Danny was ten months younger than she, but he had always taken the part of older brother, watching over and protecting Coley even now when she was almost twenty.

"I wish we would have let Aunt Wilhelmina know we were coming." Coley ruefully surveyed the lonely stretch ahead where shadowy canyons met the road. "At least someone would know we were here. Why didn't you let me write and tell her we were coming?"

A cynical laugh slipped out of Danny's drawn lips. But he couldn't voice his feelings because he knew his soft-hearted sister didn't realize that people often extended offers of help with no intentions of having them accepted. Never having met Aunt Wilhelmina, he had deliberately not notified her for fear that she would retract her invitation for them to come live with her.

He glanced over at Coley huddled on the passenger seat, flinching at each crash of lightning. Silently he studied her long-limbed body and the cheap flowered print dress she wore before turning back to stare out the rain-coated windshield. *What a hell of a life she's had,* he thought, not considering that his had been the same. The first time that he had recognized and understood the abuse they had received at the hands of their father was during one of his drunks, when Danny had done his best to shield his sister and to protect her if he could. Sober, their father had been a wonderful man, but he hadn't been sober very often. There had been a subconscious relief when he had finally been killed in a car wreck—the result of drunken driving.

But for Danny and Coley in the first years of their teens, the hardships had just begun. Their mother's health began to deteriorate and within a year she was an invalid with asthma and other respiratory illnesses. It was shortly after that that a stubborn pride and hardened bitterness grew in Danny. Not because of the little luxuries they were deprived of, nor the constant part-time jobs that he took to earn enough money to keep them going, but for the clucking tongues of neighbors who continuously deplored their lack of supervision while offering empty promises of help at the same time. The alternative had been foster care, but he'd had no intention of letting that happen.

Their mother had refused to let either of them leave school, which Danny supposed he should be grateful for. But since both he and Coley had to rush away as soon as the last bell rang, he to go to work and Coley to look after their mother, there had never been any time for sports, or school dances, or friends. As far as he was concerned, it didn't matter, all that much, but Coley should have had something in her life besides housework, cooking and nursing.

"Why do you suppose Momma never mentioned Aunt Wilhelmina?" A frown creased Coley's wide forehead, unknowingly interrupting Danny's musings.

"I don't know," Danny shrugged. "I'm just glad she had an aunt."

"Aren't you just a little scared? Coming out here and presenting yourself to a complete stranger who didn't even know we existed until you wrote her that letter telling her that Mom had died."

Coley had never been around other people much and strangers tended to make her shy and withdrawn. Her quiet ways usually made people forget she was there, which increased her reserve. Almost hypnotized by the back-and-forth sweep of the wipers, she remembered the day she had been helping Danny go through their mother's trunk about a week after the funeral. She hadn't quite understood his excitement at finding that letter at the bottom of a pile of old photographs. With painstaking care he had written this unknown relative, saying a silent prayer that she hadn't died already. When the reply and invitation came just a week ago, Danny had walked into the restaurant where Coley worked as a waitress and, with a jubilant air of satisfaction, told her to quit. He'd hated her working there and the off-color remarks his naive sister was subjected to. He didn't like the idea that Coley, should have to serve people who weren't fit to serve her. His conviction had deepened when he had caught Carl making a pass at Coley.

Another roll of thunder reverberated out of the hills, drawing a terrified gasp from Coley. Glancing over at her tightly clasped yet trembling fists, Danny fortified his confidence in his decision.

"We have to forget everything we've left behind," he said. "This is our chance to start a whole new life, to make something of ourselves with nobody around to tell us we can't do it."

"But we could have done that in San Antone," she replied, gazing earnestly at her brother. "With me working, we would have had enough money to get a nicer apartment, and I could have gotten a better job. And you had so many friends there."

"I couldn't stand you working in that place," he declared vehemently. "And the thought of you marrying one of those guys and having a bunch of brats running around makes me sick. No, when you marry, it's not going to be someone like Carl."

A shudder quaked through Coley as the memory swept through her. How she had tried to forget that night when Carl had taken her home, saying that Danny was going to be late. She had tried to be polite despite her inner revulsion, because he was Danny's friend. She could still remember the way his dark eyes had raked over her as he unlocked the apartment door and barred her entry with a tanned arm. She'd stood numbly silent, a crimson blush covering her face. She could still hear his mocking laugh as he teased her about her unkissed lips before drawing her to him. She had tried to push herself away from him, but he had only laughed and forced her face to his. The naked lust in his face had terrified her, but she had been helpless against his animal strength. The opportune arrival of Danny and his strident yell broke the one-sided embrace. In a tightly controlled temper, her brother ordered Carl out, but not before he had winked cockily at Coley.

A fresh onslaught of rain stirred Coley out of her reverie. Silently she watched the headlight beams pick out another water crossing ahead of them. The angry black flood swirled menacingly before them as she felt Danny change gears in anticipation. The crossing markers showed water churning just below the three-foot mark.

"Danny, it's too deep!" she cried. "We'll never make it across!" Her brother's face was ashen as they inched their way through the water. Her breathing stopped while the swift current swayed the back end. They were almost on the other side when the motor died. Gasping, Coley turned her terrified eyes to Danny and watched him vainly attempt to start it again. It was no use. In a fit of anger, Danny jerked the key out of the ignition and looked at Coley sitting petrified on the opposite side of the car.

"I'm sorry, Coley," he muttered. "We'll have to leave the car. Let me get out my side first." Rolling down his window, Danny squirmed out the narrow opening into the swirling dark waters. Coley watched him make his way through the driving rain around to her side. Storms had always terrified her and being stranded in one of such violence was her worst nightmare. Bravely she crawled through her window to Danny's waiting arms.

"I can walk," she protested faintly when Danny continued carrying her until they were out of the stream. Watching the rain stream down his troubled face as he stood her up, she added, "I'm all right, Danny. I can make it."

He smiled tenderly at her for just a moment before searching for shelter from the storm. His gaze stopped at the faint outline of a plateau with an overhanging section of rock.

Pointing towards it, he instructed, "Do you see that place where the rocks jut out over that high area? Go there and wait for me. I saw a trail back on the other side and it might lead to a house and help."

"No, Danny, let me come with you," Coley cried. "I'm not a child, I can make it."

"No sense in both of us getting soaked," he replied. "I'll come back for you as soon as I can."

He didn't give her any further opportunity to protest, but immediately waded into the swollen waters of the crossing. Coley stretched out her arm to him, then drew it back to cover her mouth as she watched him disappear into the flooding waters. He was swimming now as a glimpse of his white face appeared to her in the midst of another flash of lightning. The swift, churning current dragged him downstream, but she saw him reach the other side and struggle on to the bank. Gratefully, Coley saw him wave that he was okay and cup his hands to call to her, but his voice was carried away by the thunder. He was probably reassuring her that he would be back, and she waved in answer. Then he was gone, swallowed up in the blackness of the land.

Silently she stood watching the empty road until a bolt of lightning crashed again to the ground, jolting her out of her immobility. Conscious of her sodden dress and the chilling cold creeping into her bones, Coley struck out for the shelter Danny had pointed out to her. It looked farther away now than it did before and she cast a rueful glance down at her sandals as she set out. Determined not to lose her way, she picked out landmarks, a yucca plant here, farther on a willow, all in a straight line with her destination. Her long legs doggedly trudged on, one foot in front of the other, despite the slippery, muddy ground.

Four times Coley stopped and wiped the rain from her face to peer through the sheets of water at her goal. Panting now, her teeth chattering from the cold, she pushed on until she reached the bottom of the hill. The slope up was a lot steeper than it had looked. With water oozing out of the spongy ground, she knew she would have to crawl up the hill. Coley gazed back forlornly to the road, but her vision was obscured twenty feet around her by the rain. She couldn't even see the top of the hill except when the lightning illuminated the sky with its eerie glare. Sighing her despair, she turned to the hill.

If only she could have gone with Danny—but she knew she would never have made it across. She couldn't swim.

The slick-soled sandals were no use on the slimy hill, reducing Coley to clawing her way with her hands and pushing herself up with her knees. Her pantyhose were in shreds and her best dress stained with mud. Her breath came in panicky sobs as she fought to keep herself from sliding back. She was almost at the top. Gasping for breath, she dug her long fingers into the ground to pull herself closer.

A hand grabbed hold of her arm, another caught her under the opposite shoulder and she was on top! A faint laugh escaped between her gasps as Coley swiped a muddy hand through her hair to get it out of her face. *Danny made it. He's already here,* she thought with relief.

"Oh, Danny!" she sobbed aloud, just as a silver-gold fork of lightning stabbed a nearby hill. The words froze in her throat. Standing before her was a tall, dark form with a cape billowing about him, a hat pulled low on his face, but not so low that Coley couldn't see the short stubble of a dark beard and the haunting hollows of his eyes during that brief flash. Behind him loomed a shiny black horse, his head tossing and his hooves pawing viciously at the ground.

Recovering her wits, Coley managed to stammer, "My brother went . . . our car . . ."

"I saw it," was the abrupt reply. His voice was deep and sharp. Coley watched in petrified silence as the stranger swung into the saddle. Was he going to leave her? Nudging the prancing horse over beside her, he lowered an arm to her. Frightened, she started to step back.

"Come on!" Impatience growled through his words. "We can't stay in the rain all night." He didn't really expect her to get on that horse, she thought. She'd never been on a horse in her life! But common sense had moved her hand into his and she was effortlessly swung up in front of him.

"W-where are we going?" stuttered Coley as he tucked the front of his rain slicker, that she had thought was a cape, around her to afford her as much protection as was possible from the down-pour.

"There's an old line shack on the other side of the hill," he replied, an arm holding her slight, boyish figure closely to him. He nudged his horse into a walk. Despite the strength of his arm, Coley, so high off the ground, felt rather precariously perched, especially with the rolling motion of the horse's shoulders.

The warmth of the stranger's body slowly seeped into her, though she shivered helplessly in her wet dress. His broad shoulders dwarfed her with their immensity and her drenched brown hair felt the occasional brush of hair from his unshaven chin. Coley's heart pounded wildly at the closeness of the forbidding stranger, compounded by the violent storm that turned the most innocent objects into sinister shapes. The splintering crashes of lightning, the death drums of the thunder and the rhythmic clopping of the horse's hooves were the only sounds to accompany the rainfall.

"What—what are you doing out here?" Coley finally asked, almost unnerved by the quietness of her rescuer.

"Looking for dumb animals." His reply was sarcastic and sharp.

A spark of indignation flamed briefly in Coley before she asserted, "My brother went to get help. He'll be back soon with someone to help him pull the car out and get it started."

"Not in this weather he won't," his voice growled just above her ear. "Besides, I saw your car floating away just before I saw you. The water's too high now for any kind of traveling, so wherever your brother went, he's stranded for the night the same as we are."

Despite his gruff voice, Coley recognized an unmistakable kindness and considered her companion in a new light. She started to speak again, but stopped when the looming outline of a small building appeared before them. Halting his mount in front of the gloomy shack, the man lowered Coley to the ground before he dismounted, nestling her under the crook of his arm, his slicker over her head. He half carried her beneath the overhang where he stopped and put a shoulder to the swollen door. It swung open, yawning its blackness in their faces. Hesitantly, Coley followed the impatient beckoning of his hand into the void. Her bright, wondering eyes peered uselessly around as she clutched her arms tightly around her while the stranger walked directly to his left.

The scrape of a match gave birth to a light, which flickered dimly for a moment inside the chimney of a lantern before spreading its cheerful rays to all but the darkest corners of the room. Coley watched numbly as the lantern was carried over to rest near the center of the room. Without wasting a motion, the stranger knelt before the fireplace and after the first crackle of flame devouring paper, began adding wood from a nearby box. As soon as it was going, he turned to a makeshift bed near the fire, pulled off a blanket and tossed it to the girl shivering before him.

"Get those wet things off and wrap yourself in this," he ordered before walking to the door.

"Where are you going?" Coley gasped, touching his arm almost involuntarily.

The light moving over shadows on his face revealed features previously hidden and her eyes widened as she saw the jagged scar across his left cheek. Startled, her gaze flew to his eyes to find two piercing blue diamonds now gleaming down on her coldly. As if in a trance, she noted his anger before the grim mouth opened to reply to her question. She swiftly withdrew her hand from his arm, knowing her expression must mirror her surprise and horror.

"I'm going to take care of the horse," he snapped.

"I'm sorry," Coley murmured, ashamed of having let him see her shock at his disfigurement, but the door had already slammed shut.

Glumly Coley turned back toward the fire, idly fiddling with the blanket. That was a rotten way to pay him back for helping, even if it was unintentional. If what he said was true and Danny hadn't been able to get back, she would have spent a miserable night out in that storm. Now there was the warmth of a fire and a roof overhead, such as it was. With a shudder, Coley glanced around the dismal room.

She slipped off her wet sandals and placed them by the hearth to dry. The zipper of her flowered dress refused to budge at first and it took a while to fight her way out of the clinging garment. Carefully she placed it on the back of a chair near the fire. Now that the car was gone it was all the clothing she had. The remnants of her shredded hose she peeled off rather sadly, using the more substantial portions to wipe the mud from her slender legs before tossing the ruined hose into the fire. Shivering with the cold, Coley gathered the blanket around her and moved closer to the fire's heat. Little rivulets of water trickled from the curling strands of her hair onto her face, where she impatiently brushed them away.

A crash of lightning accompanied the opening of the door as the tall stranger stomped in. He removed his hat with an impatient movement of his hand before shaking free of the slicker. Timidly, Coley watched him hang them on a hook inside the door. His hair was black and straight, the sides and back long and plastered against his neck by the rain. In a stifling silence he walked to the hearth, and then unbuttoned the top of his shirt before pulling it over his head. The naked expanse hypnotized Coley as she stared at the bronze back tapering from wide shoulders to a narrow waist. When he turned his chest with its cloud of dark hair towards her, she gulped and clutched the blanket a little tighter. But his eyes flicked over her to the chair where her forlorn flowered dress lay. He glared at her with fury.

"I told you to take your clothes off, and I meant all of them!"

Coley managed a stiff, negative shake of her head while her body attempted to shrink inside the blanket. Her eyes widened in fear as he took a step towards her. Her gaze was riveted to the scar on his face, its white jagged line resembling a lightning bolt across several days' growth of dark stubble. He stopped. His mouth was drawn into a grim line and his teeth clenched tightly, flexing the muscles in his lower jaw.

"I've seen female undergarments before, if that's what's worrying you," he murmured, his voice soft and almost gentle, but the diamond-like quality in his eyes revealed the hidden hardness of his tone. His upper lip curled slightly as he added, "And if it's the other thing that's worrying you, I prefer my women with grown-up curves. I leave children alone."

He didn't seem to expect a reply from Coley as he walked to the far side of the room, taking the lantern with him. She watched him hang it on a hook near a makeshift cupboard.

"I'll see if I can find us something to eat while you finish undressing," he said, and turned his head to look at her. "You hungry?"

Coley nodded hesitantly, never taking her eyes off the stranger. He continued to stare at her across the room before remarking very quietly, "I won't watch."

With that he turned back to the cupboards and began opening doors. Coley studied his back for a moment before standing. She glanced around her for a moment seeking some place to change, out of sight if possible. Finally she maneuvered the chair her dress was on over to the bed. There she used the blanket to make a screen behind which she could undress. The sounds of water being pumped assured her that he was occupied for the moment. Quickly she pulled the slip over her head, letting it drop to the floor while she worked at the hooks on her bra. Finished, she searched for an inconspicuous place to dry them before putting them on the open chair with a sigh. Shivering now from her nakedness and the cold, she hurriedly wrapped the blanket around her.

"Got some hot coffee here whenever you're ready," the man offered.

Coley shuffled across the room, aware that two spots of red were staining her cheeks.

"I'll have some, thank you," she said, coming to a halt a few feet from the stove.

He looked down over his shoulder at her bare feet before raising his gaze to her button nose and hazel eyes. His eyes were like a mirror, showing nothing of their owner's emotions, but reflecting Coley's attempt to hide her embarrassment.

"I'm nineteen," Coley declared, sensing a need to defend her status of womanhood.

"Really?" He nodded, turning to pour the strong, black coffee into a metal cup. "The food will be ready shortly."

"Can I help with anything?" Coley asked, stung by his offhand manner at her previous statement.

When an eyebrow raised over a blue eye, she added, "I can cook."

"Wearing that blanket, you'd be more of a hindrance than a help." The sharp tone dismissed her offer. Slightly hurt by the unqualified rejection even though he had a point, Coley shuffled over to the table and sat in one of the chairs where she sipped her coffee in silence. A few minutes later a brown hand placed a plate heaped with beans, fried Spam and whole tomatoes before her. Coley murmured a polite thank-you without looking at her companion before picking up her fork to eat.

"Not exactly gourmet food, but it's hot," was the reply as the man sat down in the chair to her left.

It was a struggle eating with one hand holding the blanket around her while the other attempted to get the food to her mouth without the blanket slipping. It was a slow process that her rescuer seemed not to see, his attention never leaving his plate. Finally, covering a white shoulder for the fifteenth time, Coley pushed the plate away, her hunger sated and her discomfort growing.

He glanced up at the scrape of the plate. "More coffee?"

Coley shook her head. She watched silently as he cleaned his plate and rose to pour a cup for himself.

"Is there a ranch house near here that my brother could have reached?" Coley asked, watching the muscles of his bare arm as he stirred sugar in his cup.

"The Simpson place is about three miles from the crossing. I'm sure he made it to there." His glance at her was inquisitive with a slight hint of arrogance about it. "Just where were you going?"

"To stay with our aunt," Coley answered, adding in a smaller voice, as she lowered her gaze to a crack in the wooden table, "Danny said she doesn't live very far from here—on a ranch."

"What's the name of the ranch or your aunt? I might know her." He sat his metal cup on the table and fixed his compelling eyes on her.

Nervous under the demanding gaze, Coley stammered, "Her-her n-name is Wilhelmina G-Granger and she lives at the Slash S." Tension filled the air as the stranger's eyes narrowed at her words. "Is that far from here?"

"She expecting you?" he asked as if he knew the reply would be negative.

"She invited us," Coley skirted his question as best she could without lying. "Do you know her?"

"Yes." He pushed his chair from the table and stood up. "You must be getting cold. Go over by the fire and I'll wash up."

"Does she live nearby?" Coley persisted, not wanting the conversation to end now that she had found someone who knew her aunt.

"Yes. You're on the Slash S ranch now."

"You work for her." A degree of relief was in her voice.

"No, her brother-in-law, Ben, owns the ranch. You might say I work for him." His words emerged slowly and concisely through tightly compressed lips. His calculating gaze seemed to be daring her to ask any more.

Coley sat quietly huddling in her chair and solemnly watched him as he gathered the dishes. She started to shiver again, but whether it was from the cold or the oppressive atmosphere that had suddenly engulfed her, she couldn't tell. Silently she rose from her chair and shuffled morosely to the fireplace on the other side of the room. She stared into the flickering flames, trying to shake the feeling that she and Danny had jumped from one bad situation into another. Had it been the reticence of the stranger or the bitterness and suppressed anger in his voice that had made her feel this way? Or was it her imagination running away with her because of the thunderstorm outside and the vicious scar on his cheek? If only Danny were here!

A movement behind her roused Coley out of her contemplation. She turned to see her companion remove the mattress from the bed. She studied his rough-hewn features, wondering again at the apprehension that was growing inside of her at the prospect of meeting her aunt.

"Sleep in front of the fire tonight. You'll be warmer." the man said, placing the flimsy mattress behind her.

"Where will you sleep?" Coley asked, submissively lowering herself to her makeshift bed to sit cross-legged on it.

"In a chair," he replied, poking the fire and adding another log to it. "I've slept in worse places."

"Do you know my aunt very well?" Coley blurted out, the tension building inside her at her unknown destination and its occupants. "We've never met her before and I was wondering what she was like."

"Sometimes it's wise to find out for yourself. Other people's opinions aren't always right," he answered cryptically.

"But—" Coley began.

"I suppose I should at least know the name of

the girl I'm spending the night with," he commented, but without a teasing smile on his face.

Coley blushed furiously.

"Colleen McGuire, but Danny calls me Coley," she replied. Gathering courage, she continued, "I'm sorry about the way I looked when I saw your scar. You see," she hurried as his expression changed, "I was already frightened by the thunder and lightning when you found me. And you seemed so angry that I was a little scared of you, too. I guess seeing the scar just took me by surprise." His face had become a mask, with blank blue eyes. "It really doesn't look that bad, sort of like a badge of courage," Coley suggested, trying desperately to undo the damage she was doing by bringing the subject up. But the cynical smile that appeared confirmed her failure. Hanging her head, she stared down at her hands. "I'm sorry. I shouldn't have said anything."

"It's all right, Coley." He hesitated over her name. "Beats the Bible phrase I usually hear."

"The mark of Cain," Coley whispered hoarsely, wishing she could take back the words the minute she had uttered them. He stared at her quietly before rising from his chair to extinguish the lantern. In the semi-darkness the flames from the fireplace danced eerily on his face, accenting his brooding look.

"You mean your brother . . ." Coley began, the chill of his words creeping up her back.

"We'd better get some sleep. We've done too much talking already." His voice was bland and unrevealing. Confused and uneasy, Coley stretched out on the mattress, cradling her head on one arm as she stared into the fire. Raising her head, she looked up at the man in the chair, his head resting against the back and his eyes closed. Sensing her gaze, he opened his eyes and looked down at her.

"What's the matter?" he asked, not changing his position.

"I don't know your name," Coley answered, an apprehensive but subdued expression on her face.

"Jason." He added with the barest ghost of a smile, "My friends call me Jase. Good night, Coley."

"Good night, Jase."

Chapter Two

The horse lifted his feet high as he picked his way down the slope. Coley swayed with the gentle rocking motion, her slender body in unison with the man in the saddle. The horse's coat, that had glistened so blackly in last night's rain, now gleamed blood-red in the morning sunlight. On the road below them was a car with two figures watching their approach. Coley recognized one as her brother and figured that the other was the rancher whose help Danny had sought.

Although Coley was relieved to see her brother, the apprehension she had felt last night hadn't eased with the morning light. Jason—Jase—had been even less communicative this morning than he had last night, nodding only a hello when he had entered the cabin to find her dressed and drinking the tea he had left for her. He had informed her that the horse was saddled and he was ready to take her to her brother. And that had been the sum total of the conversation for the last fifteen minutes.

There had been so many questions Coley had wanted to ask him, about her aunt, the ranch and everything. But his tight lips and withdrawn look very clearly closed the door on any conversation. Very soon now she would be finding all the answers herself, but the chill shuddering through her told her she wasn't going to like them.

It was a very serious-faced Danny who helped Coley down from the horse. His anxious eyes examined her stained dress and uncombed hair for any telltale signs of trouble that he should know about.

"Are you all right, Coley?" When she nodded a yes, he added, "Are you sure?"

"I'm fine," she assured him.

"I tried to get back last night, but the water was too high. I nearly went crazy thinking about you out there in the storm all night. I should have taken you with me somehow," he said worriedly.

"I was all right. There's a cabin on the other side of the rise and I—we spent the night there," Coley replied, her face reddening slightly with her words. She glanced self-consciously over to where Jase stood talking with the other man.

"Mr. Simpson told me about it, but I couldn't help thinking that you might not find it," Danny answered, following her gaze to the man she had ridden in with. His eyes narrowed on her face. "He treated you all right, didn't he?"

"Yes, I was frightened at first, that's all," she replied, avoiding Danny's searching eyes for fear they would find the doubt that troubled her. "He works at the ranch for Aunt Wilhelmina's brother-in-law. She doesn't own the ranch, Danny."

"I know." The grim tone of his words did little to boost Coley's confidence. "I got our clothes and

all out of the car. It was swept downstream by the
water last night.''

"Will it still run?"

"I have to get it towed and checked out. Even
then . . ." His voice trailed off expressively. He
looked at his sister's face, reading the anxiety written there. If Aunt Wilhelmina couldn't or wouldn't
take them in, they had no money and now, no
transportation. "Don't worry, Coley, everything'll
be all right, I promise you."

"But, Danny, what if . . ."

"If you two are ready to go, we'll leave now," the
man who had been talking with Jase interrupted.

"Of course, Mr. Simpson," Danny answered,
leading Coley to the car where the two men were
standing.

Two hard blue eyes studied her brother thoroughly as Danny introduced his sister to the
rancher. But, other than the sharpness of the gaze,
the expression was bland when Danny turned to
Jase. Danny didn't miss the noticeable scar under
the beard growth before he noted the other man's
piercing eyes, but this time there was no reaction
from Jase, the mask securely on his face.

"Thank you, sir, for taking care of my sister,"
Danny said, extending his hand.

Jase accepted it and merely nodded his acknowl-
edgment, before gathering the reins and mounting
his horse. His face was now hidden in the shadows
of his hat brim as he lifted his hand in an indifferent
good-bye and trotted his horse away from the
group. Coley stared after him.

"Ahh," Simpson sounded as though he was trying to rid his mouth of a bad taste. "He's a cold
one." Danny glanced at the rancher suspiciously,

as if hoping for an explanation of the remark, but receiving only, "Come on. Let's go."

Silently, brother and sister slid into the front seat with him. The closing of the door seemed to echo the closing of the last door of escape for the two. From here on they were committed to whatever lay ahead.

The morning sun came through the dotted swiss curtains, warming the curled, sleeping figure half out and half under the chenille bedspread. Outside, birds were trilling in the morning breeze, their faint calls awakening Coley as her eyelids lifted slowly from their heavy burden of sleep. She blinked bewilderedly at her unfamiliar surroundings. Then yesterday's memory drifted back. She pulled herself into a sitting position, then bent her legs so that her slender arms could hug her knees. All the despair from yesterday came echoing back as her sad eyes gazed forlornly at the rose-flowered wallpaper.

All her misgivings had loomed larger during that silent ride to the Slash S ranch house. Had it been Danny's moodiness or the skeleton-faced Simpson's ominous silence that first made Coley aware that some of her fears might come true? She knew that Danny had found out something that had shaken his confidence when all her arguments had failed. If only that stranger had told her more . . .

When they had come to a stop in front of the big, two-storey house, gleaming whitely through the leaves of the large oak trees, Coley's heart involuntarily leaped with joy at the serene picture. But that was before Mr. Simpson spoke.

"Sorry, boy," he'd said, "looks like the old man

is sittin' on the porch. Much as I hate to, I'd better go up with you.''

Coley had started to ask Danny what Mr. Simpson was talking about, but he'd already opened the door and stepped out of the car. Barely able to stem her rising panic, Coley followed him, brushing vainly at the stained spots on her dress and trying to force the wayward strands of her brown hair into some semblance of order.

Coley leaned forward and chewed on a fingernail without relaxing her hold around her legs as she remembered meeting the man that Simpson had referred to as the ''old man.'' The wheelchair he was sitting in had drawn her attention first, but when Mr. Simpson had introduced him as Ben Savage, Coley had looked at the man. He was an eagle, though age had made him a gray eagle, but an eagle all the same. His keen gray-blue eyes had inspected them thoroughly from beneath bushy eyebrows. His head was covered with an abundance of white hair streaked with grey. Only the sallow color of his skin and the way it hung so loosely on his face and neck betrayed the state of his health.

Mr. Simpson had explained to him that Danny and Coley were Wilhelmina's nephew and niece and had come for a visit. He'd also told him about their car and implied that both had spent the night at his ranch. Coley had been too awed by her prospective host to correct Mr. Simpson. Ben Savage had watched them carefully while the rancher was talking, taking in the mud stains on Coley's dress and their general appearance of something less than prosperity. He had said not one word of greeting to them. His words echoed back in their hopelessness to Coley.

''Hm. Hoped I'd seen the last of sponging relatives," he had said, smiling slightly maliciously when Danny bristled. "But since I haven't, she's out back in her rose garden." The directness of his gaze had silenced any reply from Danny. "I'll be talking to you two tomorrow." Then he had turned his wheelchair and left them with his unvoiced threat hanging over them.

A silvery white head peeped around Coley's bedroom door.

"Are you awake now, dear? You looked so exhausted last night that I told myself to let you sleep as late as you wanted to in the morning."

"Oh, Aunt Willy, is it very late?" Coley asked with a note of alarm as she hopped out of bed. "I don't want Uncle Ben to think that I sleep late all the time." Coley and Danny had been given definite instructions by Aunt Willy: that they were to refer to Mr. Savage as Uncle Ben, even though there was no blood relation. Coley couldn't think of anyone less like an uncle.

"Oh, fiddle what Ben thinks," Wilhelmina stated as she set a stack of clothes down on Coley's dresser. Coley marveled again at the tall woman's erect posture. "Maggie washed up some of your clothes." She opened and closed drawers briskly. "Colleen, honey, I'm sorry to tell you this, but that muddy river water just about ruined everything. Just look at this skirt—or worse, this blouse!" With a horrified expression she held up a faded navy skirt and a very worn white blouse before placing them in drawers. "We'll just have to go on a shopping expedition," she went on cheerfully. "I haven't been on one in ages."

Coley walked over to the mirror, picked up a

brush and began pulling it through her hair. She was too embarrassed to correct her aunt about the state of her clothes. Wilhelmina Granger walked over to stand behind Coley, her taller frame enabling her to see over Coley's head into the mirror. She took the brush from Coley, her bracelets jingling, and began expertly brushing here and fluffing there.

"Your hair needs a good styling, too," she remarked to Coley's red-faced reflection in the mirror. "Now, don't you go getting all upset about it. If your dear mother, Rosalie, were here you know she would have seen that your hair was properly cut."

Coley nodded silently, hanging her head so that her aunt couldn't see the moistening eyes. How could she tell her that she'd never had her hair done by a professional? "Colleen, listen to me," Wilhelmina Granger turned the girl towards her and lifted her chin gently with the tip of a polished fingernail. Coley looked up at the generous red mouth, the pink-blushed cheeks, the bright, jeweled glasses that winged over her aunt's blue eyes. "I know sometimes I'm a silly old lady who's a little absent-minded now and then. The good Lord didn't see fit to give George and me any children, but now he's given me you and Daniel. Forgive me if I get too interfering or sentimental, because, you see, you mean very much to me."

"Oh, Aunt Willy!" Coley smiled gratefully through her tears.

"Well," Aunt Wilhelmina inelegantly sniffed back her tears, "We'd better stop this or we'll both be crying. You'd better hurry up and get dressed. Maggie's got breakfast ready downstairs. Hurry up, now."

She smiled as she pushed Coley toward the bed before walking out the door in rhythm with the jangling of her bracelets. Coley clasped her arms about her excitedly. It was a glorious feeling to be wanted, absolutely glorious! Hurriedly she slipped off her night clothes and began dressing.

Coley trailed her hand down the banister of the open staircase. Her eyes roved contentedly through the hallway below her as she slowly made her way down the steps. Her sandaled foot was on the last step when one of the doors in the hall opened and a slender, dark-haired man emerged.

"And you tell Jase I want a full accounting of his absence," came the gravelly voice of Ben Savage from inside the room. "It's about time he learned that nobody disappears from this ranch for three days without me knowing about it and knowing where they are and what they're doing."

"Yes, sir," the man replied with a deferential nod of his head before closing the door. But his expression when he turned towards Coley was anything but respectful.

Coley noted the thin face, the sleek black hair, the black, snapping eyes, the fine winged brows and the thin lips with their almost insolent curl. When he saw Coley, his mouth immediately changed its expression to a smile, although she saw his eyes narrow before becoming a part of the widening smile.

"Well, good morning. You must be Colleen." He extended his arm, an even golden brown color from the rolled-up short sleeve down to his long fingers. "Aunt Willy told me all about you."

Coley shyly accepted his hand, slightly intimidated by his practiced charm. "How do you do."

"I can tell she forgot to tell you about me. That's just like her," he grinned to show a flashy expanse of white teeth, "I'm Tony Gordon, the old man's nephew."

Coley glanced apprehensively at the closed door. "He's full of the devil today." Tony grimaced playfully as he followed her glance. "Where were you going, the dining room?"

She nodded.

"I'll show you the way. I won't be able to stay, though I imagine Aunt Willy will be there. I've got to go find Jase and then I'm supposed to meet your brother and show him around," he stated cheerfully, taking her elbow and guiding her down the hallway. "Did Danny talk to Mr. Savage this morning?" "He was going out as I was coming in."

"I hope Danny didn't say anything to upset him," she murmured.

"Knowing Uncle Ben, I doubt if he got the chance," Tony laughed. He turned his young face towards her a happy-go-lucky glint in his dark eyes. "Hey, your turn is coming."

"I'm supposed to talk to him this morning," Coley replied. Some of her earlier good spirits deserted her as they reached the sun-filled dining room.

"And the condemned ate a hearty breakfast," Tony teased, pulling out a chair for Coley at the table.

"Tony, stop that," reprimanded the silver-haired woman already seated.

"I was only joking, Auntie." But this joke had stolen Coley's appetite.

"Pay no attention to him, Colleen." Aunt Wilhelmina began passing dishes to Coley with her nervous, busy hands. "Run along, Anthony. Daniel is waiting for you outside."

Tony waved a cheerful good-bye to Coley, who could barely manage a smile in return. She nibbled at her toast and pushed her scrambled eggs around on the yellow-flowered china plate while her aunt chattered in her blithe, ebullient way.

"Colleen dear, you've hardly eaten a thing." Her aunt's red lips were pursed poutily. "We'll never cover those bones sticking out through that blouse."

"I'm sorry, but I'm just not very hungry," Coley replied apologetically. "I've always been skinny anyway. I've never been able to gain weight."

"You'll be grateful for that one day." The older woman sipped her coffee. "And I bet lots of fashion models would love to have your natural figure."

"But they have faces to go with them," Coley said, forcing a lightness into her voice to hide the inner hurt.

"You aren't unattractive, Colleen," Aunt Willy stated kindly. "A little plain, perhaps, but that can be changed. Now, if you really are done with your breakfast, Benjamin wanted to see you privately in his study." Aunt Wilhelmina rose from the table, smoothing her skirt with her hands. The rings on her fingers flashed brilliantly in the sunshine. "And don't you let Anthony's teasing upset you."

"No, Aunt Willy." Coley stood resolutely.

If only she could forget Tony's teasing. If only she didn't feel as if she were going to an inquisition with herself as the victim. Her long legs moved slowly down the hall to the study. Why did she have to be so afraid of everybody and everything? Danny had always been there to get her out of tough spots, but this time he wasn't there and she was on her own. She just couldn't go into that room knowing how that old man in the wheelchair would mock her.

That was it. He was in a wheelchair; he was a sick man like her mother had been. Many times during the years that Coley had nursed her mother, the distress had become more than her mother could bear and she had been irritable and snappy. Uncle Ben must have the same problem. And her mother hadn't liked Coley to change things, clinging steadfastly to the familiar. That would explain why Uncle Ben resented her and Danny being there, disrupting his household. She had never been frightened of her mother, so why should she be frightened of Ben?

A bright light now gleamed in her eyes as she rapped lightly on the study door.

"Come in, come in," was the gruff reply.

Coley stepped into the oppressive study. The maroon drapes were closed, shutting out the morning light while the dark paneling added to the gloom. She glanced at the gray-haired man behind the desk. He didn't look very sick.

"Would you like me to turn on a light?" Coley asked timidly.

"What's the matter? Can't you see?" he growled.

"It's a little dark in here."

"It's plumb foolish to have the electricity on during the day. A waste of money! The sun's plenty of light," his tone reproached her sharply. Coley glanced over at the closed curtains, wondering if she should say anything more. "Perhaps I could open the curtains?" she suggested hesitantly.

"Persistent little snip, aren't you?" Coley swallowed nervously, waiting for him to speak again, not trusting her voice not to tremble. "Think it'll improve my sunny disposition, do you?" His eyes squinted threateningly at her, a glint of humor lurking at the corners. "Very well, open them, if it makes you happy."

Gratefully Coley walked over to the window and pulled the cord to the maroon curtains, allowing the sunlight to tumble in.

"Satisfied?" he snorted. He waved a bony hand towards the chair in front of his desk. "Come over here and sit down, now that I can see you."

Coley did as she was told and managed to sit quietly under his disconcerting stare. She rather liked his sarcastic humor. It made him a little more human and gave her a little more courage.

"There's not much to you," he said disparagingly. "Can't you do anything with that hair of yours? It looks like you forgot to brush it."

His blue-gray eyes saw her look at his own bushy hair. "I don't like back talk, so you might remember that," he said severely. "Now, let's get down to business. There's no such thing as a freeloader on this ranch. Everybody pulls his weight or leaves." He paused to allow his words to sink in. "What are you good for?"

"I can cook and clean," Coley answered, "and I took computer classes in school, but I'm not very good."

"We got a housekeeper and the house isn't big enough for two. Don't need any damn computer. What else?"

"I nursed my mother for several years."

"I don't need any nursemaid!" he bellowed, raising himself in the wheelchair.

"No, I didn't mean . . . I mean . . ." Coley stam-

mered. She leaned forward, her smooth forehead
drawn together in an anxious frown.

"Get out of here! Go on!" Ben shouted, running
a gnarled hand through his grizzled hair.

"I'm sorry." Coley's round eyes began to mist
with tears. "I just don't know how to do many
things."

"I'll find something for you to do," he growled.
"Now, get out of here. I've heard enough of your
prattle. Your aunt will be wanting you anyway."

Coley rose numbly from the chair. Through the
shimmer of tears, she saw Ben's hand plucking
nervously at the chair handle. She ruined everything. She should have known how sensitive the
poor old man would be about his handicap. Why
couldn't she have been more tactful? Twice now
since coming here, she had referred to two people's afflictions, first Jason's and now Uncle Ben's.
When would she learn to keep her big mouth shut?

When she reached the study door, Coley turned
back towards her uncle, seeking the words to undo
the damage. The forlorn picture of the invalid
staring blankly out of the sun-filled window hushed
her words, and she silently closed the door behind
her.

An hour later she wandered out into the shaded
backyard where her aunt was busily at work among
her roses. Coley watched indifferently, noting the
gloved hands and the sure clipping of the scissors.
Her aunt's floppy straw hat picturesquely framed
her silver-white hair while protecting her complexion from the steady rays of the sun. Coley approached her aunt slowly, trying to phrase the
words that would explain her unsuccessful meeting
with Uncle Ben.

"Colleen, I wondered where you were," her

aunt's voice sang out. "I was pruning my roses. Don't you just love roses? They never cease to delight me. The buds are so fragile and delicate, and the full blooms are so rich and velvety. But the fragrance is like a heady wine, sweet and tantalizing." She turned, expecting a reply from Coley. But Coley hadn't been following her aunt's words. She was wrapped up in her worries about Ben Savage. "What's the matter, dear? Didn't your talk with Benjamin go well?"

Coley shook her head glumly.

"Let's go over here and sit down," Aunt Wilhelmina said, pulling off a glove and placing a hand on Coley's shoulder. She guided her towards some lawn chairs under a spreading oak. "You can tell me all about it."

Slowly Coley began her story, stuttering for the words, then rushing incoherently when she couldn't find them. She ended in a burst of tears.

"There, there," comforted her aunt. "I probably should have mentioned to you how touchy he is about his paralysis. He didn't mean anything by it. I'm sure he was sorry for his temper afterwards. He likes to think of himself as independent, so the least reference to the fact that there's something he can't do for himself sends him into a rage. He knows you aren't the kind of person to mean anything by it."

"I hope so, Aunt Willy," sobbed Coley, twisting her hands nervously in her lap. She looked earnestly in her aunt's face. "I tried to tell him I was sorry."

"It's best not to say anything. Pretend that everything went well and forget that burst of temper of his."

"But it happened!"

"Of course, but bringing it up won't make you or Benjamin feel any better about it, now will it?" reasoned Aunt Willy.

"No," Coley agreed, wiping the tears from her cheeks and smiling into the jeweled eyeglasses.

"I have an idea. Benjamin always likes some tea before dinner. Why don't you go to the kitchen and have Maggie fix a pot? Then you can take it to him as a sort of peace offering."

"All right."

"Put a cold cloth on those eyes of yours first," instructed Aunt Willy, rising as Coley did. "Otherwise he'll know you cried a river and feel twice as guilty."

"Yes, Aunt Willy," Coley called back, already hurrying back towards the white house. Entering the back door into the kitchen, she spied the housekeeper cleaning some vegetables over the sink. Quickly she walked over to the thin, middle-aged woman. "Aunt Willy suggested I see if you could fix a pot of tea for Uncle Ben."

"I've already got it brewin' on the stove and the tray is sittin' on the table," the woman answered tersely, the rhythmic strokes of the brush unbroken by the conversation. " 'Twill be ready in a jiffy."

"I'll take it in to him as soon as I clean up," Coley replied, a little awed by the businesslike housekeeper.

The cold, wet washcloth felt good against her face. After a few applications, the redness left and the swelling was down. Coley's cheeks looked quite pale, so she rubbed them a little to bring a touch of pink to the surface. She really felt much better. Quickly she hung the towel and washcloth on the rack and hurried back to the kitchen. The flowered teapot was now sitting on the tray with the cup and saucer.

"If you'd like me to come back and help you, I will," she offered as she picked up the tray.

"Been doin' everything by myself for eight years, I guess I can do it for eight more," Maggie retorted, her back to Coley.

Feeling she had already put her foot in her mouth once today, Coley left without saying anything else. She hummed happily as she walked down the hallway towards her uncle's study. At least she could let Ben know that she held no hard feelings towards him. A few steps from the open door she heard someone talking.

"We only lost four head to the flood." It was Jase with Ben.

"You could have sent out one of the hands to find that out," Ben said irritably.

"I needed the air."

Coley stopped short of the doorway, sensing a hostility in the conversation.

"I see. And I thought maybe you'd left for good." There was a trace of sarcasm in the invalid's words.

"You should have learned by now I'll never leave," Jase's voice raised to emphasize the last word. "As long as there's an inch of land left that's Savage land, I'll be here. You might as well get used to that fact."

Curiosity drove Coley to the doorway to view the tall, broad-shouldered man leaning on the desk towards the old man in the wheelchair. The bitterness and hatred etched on their faces stunned her.

"You should have left! No murderer will ever get one grain of dirt on this ranch!" Ben cried.

"Then you'd better throw me off." Coley watched, appalled, as anger twisted Ben's face at

Jase's words. "But you can't—and furthermore, you wouldn't if you could," Jase went on sarcastically. "Because you need me. Your precious Tony would destroy everything you've worked for in a week. You need me!"

In a fit of frustration, Ben wheeled his chair away from Jase to stop with his eyes on Coley. At Ben's startled expression, Jase turned, too. It took but an instant for him to assess the horrified and incredulous expression on her face before he turned away towards the window.

"I brought your tea, Uncle Ben." Coley's small voice was followed by a heavy silence.

"Bring it in, girl," he instructed gruffly.

She practically ran into the room, the tea cup rattling in its saucer in protest. All the while her mind raced. Was Jase going to speak to her? Would he tell Uncle Ben they'd spent the night together during the storm? What would she say if Uncle Ben introduced them? But Ben had no such intention.

"Thank you," he said as she set the tray down on his desk. "You can go now."

She nodded and turned towards Jase. He still hadn't shaved, though now the beard almost covered the scar, but nothing covered the ice-blue eyes that challenged her. She hesitated only momentarily, drawn to him in spite of her fear, just as she had been that night, before she rushed out of the room.

Chapter Three

Coley stared out her bedroom window, stalling for time. She had come upstairs to dress for dinner. Aunt Willy had told her it had been the custom for many years to dress for the evening meal. It was easy enough, Aunt Willy said, to sit down in work clothes, bolt your food and finish the evening in a state of apathy, but dressing up made you feel like a new person and the evening became a special time. It all sounded very grand to Coley if she could just shake off the uneasy feeling she had.

On the surface everything was just the way she had always dreamed a home would be. The house was roomy and comfortable. Aunt Willy was sweet and caring. Even Ben was likeable in spite of his gruffness. But underneath was a foreboding of the hidden things she didn't know; things that could destroy her precarious sense of security. And Jase was the key to it all, the man who had rescued her in the storm, who, even though he frightened her a little, had made her feel safe and protected.

She stared down at the bold flowers splashed on

the material of her dress. The mud stains were all gone now, thanks to Maggie. It was her best dress, but Coley knew it didn't measure up to Aunt Willy's expensive tastes. It was just a cheap dress, different from her others only because she bought it and it wasn't someone's hand-me-down. She glanced out the window again. Her morose expression lifted as she recognized her brother walking through the yard gate. She rushed quickly out of the room and down the stairs to be at the door when her brother entered.

"Danny!" she cried happily. "I've been watching for you to come."

"Hi!" He wrapped an arm around her shoulders and continued towards the stairs. "What have you been doing all day?"

"What have you been doing all day?" Coley countered. "You were gone before I got up and I missed you for lunch."

"Can't you tell what I've been doing?" he smiled. "Smell."

"Whew!" she exclaimed, inhaling deeply next to his shoulder.

"I've been cleaning the barns." He grimaced playfully at her before scooting her on ahead of him up the last step.

"Oh, poor Danny," Coley laughed. She swung his hand happily as they walked down the hall to his bedroom. "Thank heaven, we're supposed to dress for dinner or Aunt Willy would never allow you at the table. Did you know about that—dressing for dinner, I mean?"

"Yeah, Tony told me about it." He unbuttoned his shirt to take it off. "Now tell me what you've been doing."

"Nothing."

"Nothing? Did you go in and talk to the old man?" His brown eyes watched her reaction carefully.

"Yes, I did," Coley answered, seating herself on his bed. But her thoughts weren't on her meeting with him, but on the conversation she had overheard between Ben and Jase.

"How did it go?"

"All right, except he doesn't know what to do with me." She plucked nervously at the chenille bedspread.

"Don't worry about that. I told him I'd take care of paying for your keep." He rolled his shirt into a ball and tossed it in the hamper. He smiled over at her. "Of course, he assured me that I would."

Coley smiled in understanding. "What did you think of him, Danny?"

He paused before answering. "I like him. I mean, he's rough and says what he thinks, but I like him."

"So do I."

"When I was out there cleaning the barn, I thought about how he can't even get out there to see if I'm doing my job. He's got to be hard or everything he's worked for will crumble away. Do you know what I mean, Coley?" She nodded. "I don't feel sorry for him. You can't pity a man like that even if he is an invalid. I said as much to Tony, but he just laughed. I don't think he understood what I meant."

Jase's words rushed back to Coley. "Your precious Tony would destroy everything you've worked for in a week." She sat silently on the bed, debating whether she should tell Danny the things she had overheard.

"Come on," her brother said, taking hold of her hand and pulling her off the bed. "You'd better clear out. I've got to shower and change. I'll meet you downstairs.''

"Okay.'' She left the room meekly, not yet willing to put her thoughts into words.

"Colleen! Oh, there you are,'' said her aunt, standing at the bottom of the stairs. "Would you help Maggie set the table? I haven't got the flowers done yet or I'd give her a hand. I didn't realize it was so close to dinner time.''

"I don't mind,'' Coley answered, skipping on down the steps.

"Is your brother ready yet?'' At Coley's negative shake, Aunt Willy pursed her lips nervously. "Well, it never takes men long to get ready,'' she mused, and bustled Coley into the dining room. "The silverware is in the china cabinet over there. The rest of the things Maggie has in the kitchen.''

Coley glanced around at the six plates resting on the white tablecloth. "Is Maggie eating with us tonight?''

"Oh, no, dear. She says that hopping up and down is bad for her digestion, so she eats later.''

"Who's the extra plate for?'' Coley asked. "Oh, didn't I tell you? Benjamin's grandson will be here for dinner this evening. Now really, you must hurry. The men will be coming in shortly and the table won't be ready.'' Coley placed the silver around the table, filled the glasses with iced water, and brought in the necessary salt, pepper, butter, sugar and cream containers from the kitchen. Danny entered the room as Aunt Wilhelmina was putting the finishing touches on the centerpiece and Coley was ticking off on her fingers the various items on the table.

"Is dinner ready?'' Danny asked, stretching and patting his stomach hungrily.

"Mmm," Aunt Willy answered absently, stepping back to admire her handiwork. "We'll be sitting down soon. My, but you look nice, Daniel."

Coley glowed at the praise for her brother. He looked like a different man, especially with his fresh-scrubbed face, and the touch of gel in his immaculately combed hair. A murmur of voices sounded from the hallway.

"That will be the men coming." Aunt Willy adjusted the strand of pearls around her neck and patted the silver waves that wouldn't think of being out of place.

Coley and Danny turned to the arched doorway expectantly. Ben wheeled in first, his grizzled hair still bushily denying any efforts to style it.

"I hope dinner's ready by now, Willy," he grunted.

"Of course it is, Benjamin. We always eat at this time," Aunt Willy admonished, accompanying her brother-in-law to his place at the head of the table. Tony followed his uncle into the room, smiling at Danny and slapping him on the back.

"How are you feeling? The old muscles tightening up yet?"

"Some," Danny smiled, his head cocking inquiringly at the man now standing in the doorway. He glanced at Tony and added, "I guess I'm not used to it yet."

"You will be," Tony nodded with a mock grimace. Turning towards the doorway, he said, "I don't think you've met our new guests, Jase."

Coley stood transfixed, staring at the man in the doorway. His beard was gone, revealing the strong cheekbones and sharp jawline. The scar wasn't as visible against the tan of his cheeks as it had been. His straight black hair was still too long and his icy blue eyes hadn't lost their brilliance. He looked younger, in his early thirties. His clothes were different, per Aunt Willy's orders. He seemed so distinguished, so commanding and slightly ruthless. He was walking forward. Coley dimly heard Aunt Willy making the introductions, catching the words only half-consciously.

"—my sister's daughter's children. Colleen, Daniel, this is your Uncle Ben's grandson, Jason Savage."

Jase held out his hand to Danny. "I understand you got caught in one of our floods," he said.

Danny cocked his head bewilderedly, then with dawning comprehension, he took Jason's hand and replied, "We're lucky we were able to get to the Simpson ranch."

Jason turned to Coley. "I'm happy to meet you."

Coley awkwardly placed her hand in his warm, firm handshake. She couldn't speak. She just swallowed and nodded.

"Did you want me to start servin' dinner now, Mr. Savage?" Maggie asked from the kitchen doorway.

"Of course," Ben scowled. "I'm not sitting here for my health. Providing that you're finished with all of your polite amenities, Willy."

"I believe we're ready to sit down, Maggie," Aunt Wilhelmina agreed with a stately nod. "Remember, Benjamin, quarrelling at the table is bad for the digestion."

Jase had pulled out the chair on his grandfather's left for Coley before walking around the table to sit at Wilhelmina's left. Coley glanced hesitantly at her brother beside her, but he frowned at her slightly to signal silence. She clinched her hands tightly in her lap, watching the dishes pass from Uncle Ben to Tony on to Jase and Aunt Willy.

She tried to act as nonchalant as everyone else, to assume the indifferent mask that Jase wore, but it was impossible for her. She jumped every time Ben grumbled a sentence, expecting each time that the arguing would start, and a little more tense each that it didn't.

"What did you do today, Coley?" Tony asked, flashing his white teeth at her from across the table.

"I helped Aunt Willy in the garden," stammered Coley, almost dropping her fork as she spoke. She felt her cheeks flush as Jase glanced at her.

"Well, now—what did Uncle Ben decide for you to do around here?" Tony grinned, eyeing his uncle mischievously.

Coley averted her eyes to her plate and waited breathlessly for him to answer. Not for anything would she let Tony know how badly her interview had turned out.

"She's worthless for anything but ornamentation," replied Ben, scowling at her through his bristly brows. "The way she looks a sight now means she ain't much good for that either. Willy, you're going to have to get something done about her hair. It's always sticking out all over."

"Like yours, Uncle?" Tony teased.

"Don't be insolent!" Ben glared at his nephew. Looking back at his sister-in-law, he continued, waving a fork in the air as he did so. "Get her some decent clothes, too. Next time she comes to dinner I want her dressed for it and not looking like a ragamuffin."

Shame and humiliation welled up inside Coley. She blinked desperately, aware of Jason's stare. Coley glanced quickly at her brother. The back of his neck was turning red, but his mouth had clamped shut on his anger. For Danny, this was their last chance and they must make a home here at any cost, even their pride.

"Benjamin, shame on you?" Willy scolded. "You're so tactless sometimes. I'd already planned to take Colleen shopping tomorrow. Most of her clothes were lost or damaged in the flood."

"I'm sure Colleen'll enjoy the shopping trip," Jase said, sending a small smile of assurance in Coley's direction.

"Of course she will. All women do." Aunt Willy stretched her red mouth into a playful, conspiratorial smile.

"Yes, it'll be fun." Coley's words trembled only a little, but she knew it was enough to betray her.

"Nonsense!" snorted Ben. "You females just like to spend money." He reached over and laid a gnarled hand on Coley's arm. "But you be sure to pick out something nice for dinner tomorrow. I'll expect to see a pretty little lady sitting next to me."

His words touched Coley as she sensed that he was, in his own way, apologizing for his rudeness. She felt Danny relax a little, too.

"Maggie!" Ben bellowed. When she finally poked her head around the door, he said, "We'll be having our coffee on the porch." As the chairs scraped the polished wood floor, Ben turned to Coley. "Well, are you going to help me or not?" She nodded slightly and stepped behind the wheelchair to lead the entourage out to the porch. As she maneuvered the chair through the screen door and on to the porch, Coley heard the lowered voice of her aunt speaking.

"You are coming out with us for a little while, aren't you, Jason?"

"No." His voice was clipped and hard.

"But, Jason—" her aunt began plaintively.

Coley glanced at the other three on the porch. Danny and Tony were talking and Ben was staring out into the sunset. Only Coley's ears were straining to hear the conversation inside. "It's no use," Jase said sharply. "Leave Ben and me alone. There's nothing you can say or do that can change the past. We don't like each other and that's that."

Coley's eyes mirrored the confusion and pain on Willy's face as she stepped through the screen door onto the porch. Her aunt glanced beseechingly at Ben, but he was staring into the distance at the crimson glow above the hills. Coley watched the flustered woman and saw her shoulders straighten and the sagging chin lift, before her aunt seated herself next to Ben, regaining her grace and dignity. Coley remained in the shadows apart from the group, noticing that her aunt's hands trembled ever so slightly as she poured the coffee. When the same hands were done with their task and one went to its owner's throat to click the beads together nervously, Coley knew she could watch no more. She slipped unnoticed off the porch into the yard.

Silently, not wanting to be seen or stopped, Coley followed the evening path of shadows to the back of the house. At last out of sight, she slowed her steps and began wandering aimlessly among the stately oaks. Her thoughts became jumbled and incoherent. Flashes of her night spent with Jase came searing back, but mixed up with the never-ceasing echo of Ben's ringing "Murderer!"

She looked bewilderedly up to the evening sky with its smattering of stars. Once again, ominous rolling clouds were splintered by forks of lightning . . . before they were blocked out by the vision of a jagged white scar against black stubble and her own taunting words, "Mark of Cain." Her lids closed tightly over her hazel eyes trying to shut out the pictures she was seeing.

What had happened that could cause such hatred between grandfather and grandson? Why hadn't Jase told her that night that he was the grandson of the owner? Why had he let her think he only worked on the ranch? He must have known she would find out.

Danny had had such high hopes for them. Her generous mouth turned up slightly with affection for her brother. He had wanted a family and a home for her. She had both and now wanted desperately to belong, but this family was torn apart by hate and mistrust. A sickening feeling knotted itself in the pit of her stomach at the thought of the enmity between Jase and Uncle Ben. Coley, who hated any disagreement, who couldn't cope with bitter words from people she cared about, shuddered in fear. Jase couldn't be a murderer, she told herself. If he really was, he would be in prison. Somewhere there were answers, a solution. That was what she must find.

Suddenly, amid the shrilling cries of the cicadas and crickets, Coley heard the rasp of a match being struck behind her. Her spine tingled in apprehension as she turned towards the sound and murmured hoarsely, "Who's there?"

Without answering, a figure stepped out of the shadows, extinguishing the match as he did so. The light of the quarter moon illuminated the blue shirt and then the face of the figure. Jase walked slowly towards her, the gentle glow of a lit cigar in his hand.

"Hello, Coley," he murmured very politely. "It's a lovely night for strolling through Aunt Willy's rose garden, isn't it?"

Her body tensed as he stopped beside her, barely controlling a wild desire to flee. His blue eyes challenged her, but only briefly as she turned away from his gaze. Did he know or had he guessed that she had overheard him talking to Aunt Willy? Did he think she had expected to find him out here?

"I needed some fresh air and I was too restless to sit on the porch with the others," Coley explained breathlessly. She glanced up at him hesitantly and had the peculiar feeling that those piercing eyes saw right through her.

"I see," he replied grimly, "Did you enjoy the evening meal?"

Coley knew he wasn't referring to the food and lowered her head to stare at the ground rather than reply.

"We do things in our own way. Guess you noticed that. Well, I'm sure you'll be like the rest of us in no time," he mocked.

"Are you really Ben's grandson?"

"Yes." His smile as he answered was cynical, with a bitter twist to the corners of his mouth. "You find that hard to believe, don't you?" She nodded silently. A large, callused hand gripped her elbow and they began walking as if he couldn't bear to stand in one place. "You overheard a few things today in Ben's study, didn't you?"

"Yes," Coley answered, acutely conscious of the burning restlessness of the man beside her.

"That was unfortunate," he stated, taking a puff from the cigar before hurling it into the night.

"I don't really understand," Coley said, glancing hesitantly at his masked face. "Why do you . . . dislike each other so? What happened?"

His short laugh was embittered and angry. "That's a long story that has been told too many times. It's better that you don't know. You're incapable of taking sides and you would be torn apart like Aunt Willy is. Let it be."

"How?" Coley asked. Her eyes grew rounder in her effort to understand. For a moment she thought she saw a reflection of pain that she felt there in the recesses of his glance. But he turned away.

"You can't be a murderer!" Her protest was vehement, though spoken softly.

"Think so?" It was a question and not a statement, but it held a soul-deep note of sadness that drew an involuntary sigh of pain from Coley.

"Looks like your dress survived the storm," he observed, his hand still guiding them as they walked aimlessly among the fragrant roses.

"Sort of," Coley replied quietly. She was grateful for the change of subject and yet wishing Jase would talk about the other. "It still is a pretty awful dress."

"No, no, it isn't." Jason's voice was almost gentle with a bit of the reassurance that he had attempted to give her at the dinner table tonight. "But I'm sure you'll find another one you'll like better when you're shopping tomorrow."

From the near side of the house came shouts of laughter and splashes of water followed by more boyish cries. She glanced questioningly at him.

"Tony and your brother must be swimming. Would you like to go and see?"

She nodded agreement and they turned towards the house. The bright lights at the pool blinked through the thick branches of the oaks, lighting their way to the pool and sundeck surrounding it. Coley and Jase stood on the extreme outer edge of the sundeck, out of reach of the exuberant sheets of water that sprayed from the hands of the two swimmers. Coley watched the wet, gleaming bodies of her brother and Tony enviously as they cooled off in the water. She felt Jason's eyes on her and smiled up at him briefly before turning back to the pool.

"Hey, Coley!" Danny cried, waving an arm at her. "I wondered where you were."

"Go and change," Tony ordered, his dark hair glistening blackly in the lights. His white teeth flashed brightly. "Come on in. The water's fine."

"I can't," Coley called back, a shy smile lighting her face. "I don't have a swimsuit."

"Who cares?" hooted Tony, pulling himself on to the sundeck amidst another flood of water. He laughed at her blush. "Willy can fix you up with something. Come on in."

"No, thanks," Coley smiled. A wistful look crept into her eyes as Tony jackknifed into the water near Danny.

"Do you know how?" Jase asked astutely.

"No." Coley's voice was soft and shy. "I've never learned."

"Would you like to?"

"Of course," she replied. Her eyes glowed with the hint of a long-held dream shining through. "It always looks so graceful."

"If you'd like, I'll teach you," Jase offered, staring out into the pool at the shimmering lights on the water.

"Would you really?" Coley exclaimed excitedly. "I mean if it's not too much trouble."

"I wouldn't have offered otherwise." He gazed into her happy face. "Be sure to have Aunt Willy buy you a suit when you go shopping tomorrow."

"Oh, I will," Coley cried delightedly. "When can we start?"

"Day after tomorrow," he answered. "I always take a morning swim at six, if you can get up that early."

She glanced up at him, expecting to see a teasing glint in his eyes, but his expression was just as undefinable as it always was. "I'll be there," she promised solemnly, as if she were taking an oath.

"Fine. Good night, Coley," Jase said with a polite nod to her.

"Good night, Jase," Coley answered as he walked from her towards the house. She watched his tall figure for a moment, hugging her delight to her, before she turned back to the two swimmers in the pool. Soon she would be like them, confident and fearless. Very soon.

Coley chewed nervously on her fingernail as the two women studied her reflection in the mirror of the beauty salon. She felt small and insignificant as her aunt plucked at a strand of Coley's hair and discussed it with the stylist, Gloria. The hair stylist nodded an agreement with something that Aunt Willy had said and then stepped behind Coley's chair to draw the hair back from her face, turning and tilting her head this way and that, like a manne- quin. A comb appeared from nowhere and began parting her hair.

"Okay, gorgeous," she said to Coley, swinging the chair away from the mirror, "let's get down to business."

Somehow Coley managed a weak smile of agreement before she was whisked out of the chair and placed in the hands of an assistant who was given explicit instructions for the type of shampoo, rinse and conditioner. It seemed to Coley that she had barely relaxed under the brisk, vigorous fingertips when a towel was wrapped around her head and she was bustled back to the stylist. Her hair was combed out and sectioned, before the scissors began snipping away. Out of the corner of her eye, she watched strands of hair falling to the floor in a precise rhythm. Then deft hands began putting rollers in her hair as Coley stared into the mirror.

She submitted numbly to the strong hand of the stylist as she was led to a row of dryers where she was stuck under one of the hoods and left. Her head felt strangely heavy and cumbersome. Never had she ever been in a hair salon. Any cutting or trimming that had to be done in the past had been done by her mother or one of their neighbors. But now here she was, in a salon filled with immaculately dressed women walking in and out, their hair gorgeous and sophisticated. She couldn't suppress a little thrill that maybe she would look a little bit like that. The steady rush of hot air that had flushed her cheeks stopped and soon Gloria was beside her, bustling her off to another chair, this time with an array of cosmetics spread out before it.

Again Aunt Wilhelmina was beside the stylist, only this time her silver hair was in rollers too, outlining the heavily madeup face like a comical hat. Gloria was holding Coley's arm while she tested various sheer foundations with her skin. Brisk instructions were given to Coley while the selected base was applied to her face, but Coley was too excited to really listen. Next came the eyeshadow, a rich shade of olive green that brought out the green flecks in her hazel eyes, then the mascara which darkened her lashes and further enhanced her eyes, and finally a pale peach lipstick was applied.

Then she was off, back to the chair where she had started, and the rollers were being taken from her hair. Coley gasped with pleasure as she saw her formerly limp, mouse brown hair bounce and curl about her face with a golden-brown sheen to it.

"Now I've used a color rinse to bring out the blond highlights in her hair," Gloria was saying to Willy. "But it won't be necessary once she's out in the sun, because it'll bleach out on its own."

All the time the stylist was talking, a brush was vigorously going through Coley's hair. It was replaced by a comb and the styling began. With miraculous flips of the wrist, feathers of hair curled here and there, changing from wayward wisps to flattering waves. Her reflection showed a new face—a delicate and attractive face with an awed expression transparently obvious in the rounded eyes.

"Aunt Willy, is that really me?" Coley exclaimed, half fearfully.

"Yes, dear," her aunt answered, her red lips smiling widely. "Gloria, it's perfect, absolutely perfect. You're a remarkable woman!"

"So are you, Mrs. Granger," the stylist replied, basking unashamedly in the praise. Gloria whisked away the plastic cape from around Coley's shoulders and applied a cloud of styling mist to finish her creation. "You, little lady, are very beautiful. You deserve to be proud."

"Thank you, thank you so much," Coley answered breathlessly, not wanting to take her eyes off her reflection in the mirror.

How long it took for Aunt Willy to be combed out, Coley had no way of knowing. She was too enchanted with her new self to care. To Coley, in no time at all they were walking out the door of the salon and Aunt Willy was chattering about which shops they were going to and what clothes Coley would need. And Coley was swept into another breathless whirl. It didn't matter what she tried on, sexy suits, party dresses, short sets, jeans— she looked gorgeous in everything. Once when she heard Aunt Willy tell the sales clerk they wanted three more pairs of jeans and to show them some knit tops, Coley couldn't help feeling a twinge of guilt.

"Aunt Willy, this is going to cost too much money," she whispered.

"Now don't worry about such things, Colleen," admonished her aunt. "You need the clothes and I'm enjoying every minute of it."

Coley was too. Never had she ever dreamed she could look as pretty as her reflection kept telling her she was. Each time she looked in the mirror she would reverently put a hand to touch her hair, the feathery, wavy strands that looked so carelessly windblown and free. But when she tried on the short, whipped-cream-colored dress with a touch of lace around the neckline and a pair of matching low heels, she stood in front of the dressing mirror in a trance. She felt beautiful, really and truly beautiful . . . for the first time in her life.

"That is your color!" Aunt Willy exclaimed. Her bracelets jingled loudly as she clapped her hands together in appreciation. "Oh," she called to the sales clerk, "please bring me that chiffon party dress, the yellow one on the mannequin."

"Yes, ma'am," the woman replied.

"Aunt Willy, I don't really need another dress.

This one is perfect," Coley finally managed to speak.

"Nonsense. That's a perfectly good dress, but you're going to need a party dress. You should have several of them, but we don't have a very big selection to choose from here. One or two will have to do for now." With her usual efficiency, Willy took charge of getting the chiffon dress on Coley.

Aunt Willy was right. Coley looked and felt like a fairy princess in the dress. It floated in soft butter-cup folds around her, softening the slenderness of her body into an ethereal ray of sunshine, all golden and airy. "And now, accessories," her aunt murmured. "We'll pick those out as soon as you change, Colleen. I think we've got everything you're going to need for a while."

"Aunt Willy," Coley called hesitantly as her aunt started to turn away.

"Yes, dear?"

"I—I don't have a swimsuit," she stammered.

"Oh, good gracious! I completely forgot about it," Aunt Willy exclaimed. "Of course you must have one. I guess I didn't think about you swimming."

"I don't know how yet," Coley answered, flushing in embarrassment.

"You don't? Who is going to teach you? Daniel?"

"No," Coley replied, hesitating a little over her next words, unsure of how her aunt would react. "Jase said he would teach me. If that's all right with you."

"Of course it's all right," Aunt Willy replied. But her blue eyes were narrowed by the frown on her forehead. "Jason is going to teach you?"

"Yes, Aunt Willy," Coley replied.

"That's strange," said Aunt Willy, more making a comment to herself than talking to Coley, "We'll have the clerk find something for us in a swimsuit."

That evening Coley rapped lightly on her brother's door. She was wearing the whipped-cream dress with the lace around the neckline. She had been admiring her reflection for the last hour. Even though she realized how vain she was acting she was enchanted with herself. When she had heard Danny leave the shower and return to his room, she had raced across the hall so that he would be the first one to see the new Coley.

"Danny, it's me! Open up," she whispered.

As the door was swung open by her bare-chested brother, still vigorously drying his hair with a towel, she twirled happily into the room.

"Coley!" Danny's voice was as dumbstruck as she had expected it to be. "Is that really you?"

"I'm beautiful, Danny!" Her words ended in a joyous laugh as she danced around his room. "You should see all the wonderful clothes Aunt Willy bought me. And my hair . . . don't you love it!"

"My sister, Cinderella!" Danny laughed, pride glowing on his face. "May I have the privilege of escorting Your Highness to dinner this evening?"

He bowed low before her, his towel flung in front of him like a cape. She laughed and curtsied.

"I would be delighted, sir."

"Then you'd better get out of here so I can get dressed," he said, turning his towel into a whip.

She laughed again and danced out of the room. A few minutes later he was at her door, offering her his arm down the stairs. Coley felt like a princess making her grand entrance down a winding stair-

case. The new pride and assurance gave a previously hidden dignity and grace to her slender
body. When Danny opened the door to the dining
room for her, she walked unhesitatingly into the
room, totally conscious of the pleasing picture she
made. Her hazel eyes gleamed brightly at the group
already seated at the table. Tony rose immediately
from his chair, the stunned surprise showing on
his face. Her gaze softened as she looked at the
agreeable smile on Ben's face as he looked at her.

"Aunt Willy," Tony exclaimed, walking around
the table to stand in front of Coley, "you're a fairy
godmother!"

Coley's eyes turned to Jase, expecting to hear an
echo of Tony's words or at least, the unspoken
praise that was in Ben's eyes, but the mask was
there, more firmly in place than ever. Her expression flickered briefly in hurt and confusion before
taking Tony's arm with a smile. If she had looked at
her aunt, Coley would have seen an equally puzzled
face studying Jase very intensely.

The meal was just a continuation of a fantasy for
Coley, a dream that had long been dreamed. Tony
fairly danced attendance on her, flattering her with
his words and eyes. Even the gnarled man in the
wheelchair went out of his way to be chivalrous
towards her. And the few times she glanced into
her brother's eyes, the glow of pride was there for
everyone to see. Except for Jason's silence, everything was complete.

When they finally all withdrew to the veranda,
Coley was pleased and surprised to see Jase join
them. She took a seat on the bright wicker settee,
feeling deliciously flirty with Danny on one side of
her and Tony on the other and Jase smoking one
of his slender cigars in the chair next to them.

Coley tilted her head towards Tony, a newfound confidence in her smile. His brown arm rested lightly behind her shoulders while his dark eyes snapped messages to her.

"Were you really surprised over how I changed?" Coley asked, knowingly seeking a compliment, but too full of her own glory not to want it voiced by another.

"You knocked me cold when you walked into that room, Coley," he affirmed, his gaze roving over her face while drinking in her loveliness. "It really was like seeing Cinderella at the ball, complete with Aunt Willy as fairy godmother. And I got to play Prince Charming, stunned into adoring speechlessness." Coley's laugh drifted over the porch, intoxicated by his easy praise.

"I felt like a princess today," Coley said softly, almost in fear of breaking the spell of enchantment that surrounded her. She gazed unconsciously at Jase as she spoke. "Just as if the clock would strike any moment and I would be changed back into that sad person I used to see in the mirror. Do I look different to you, Jase?"

He, of all people, must see the change from the bedraggled girl he had rescued to this innocently sophisticated young woman. Her eyes gleamed brightly in the dim light as she waited in anticipation for his answer. He had to agree, the change was too dramatic.

"You don't look like a princess at all to me," he replied. His voice was brittle and in the dim light, Coley was hurt to see his controlled anger. "Tony's mistaken."

Coley gasped uncontrollably at the censure in his voice. His eyes sought her out.

"You remind me of one of Aunt Willy's roses,"

he said. His gaze softened ever so slightly, although his expression never changed. "One of her pale yellow rosebuds, filled with the purity of innocence and just beginning to open into a full bloom." His soft yet distinct words echoed into a deepening silence on the porch. Coley's eyes misted brightly at the praise, so unqualified and so full of a promise to her as she matured.

"So words still come easily to your lips, huh?" The gravelly voice of Benjamin Savage sliced into the silence. Jase didn't answer the sarcastic question as he stubbed his cigar out in the ashtray on the table beside him.

"If you'll excuse me," he murmured, rising and nodding towards his aunt as he spoke.

Coley watched as he descended the veranda steps into the night. His walk was slow and his posture erect. Coley turned to her uncle to protest, but was silenced by a sharp nudge from Danny.

Chapter Four

Coley watched the long, gleaming form slicing effortlessly through the water, shimmering a pale blue in the morning sun. She was late, she knew, for her lesson, but the graceful, rhythmic strokes of the muscular arms fascinated her with their precision. Would she ever get over her own fears and be able to swim like that? Coley wondered.

This morning would mark her fifth lesson and she still shivered apprehensively at entering the pool. Only the deep desire to learn drove her on, making her overcome the quaking of her body. It wasn't so bad now as it had been that first morning when Jase had had to practically help her into the water.

Coley had been surprised at his patience with her. He had taken her step by step, until she understood. He took the fundamentals slowly, persuading her to immerse her head in the water and blow bubbles, letting her hold on to the side of the pool as she kicked her feet with a scissorlike movement and instructing her in the arm movements that he was now doing so effortlessly.

He reached the opposite end of the pool and stopped, shaking the water from his black hair with a twist of his head. Holding on to the edge of the pool with one hand, he waved a greeting to her with his free hand.

"Oversleep?" he asked as Coley walked shyly to the edge of the pool.

She nodded sheepishly before shrugging off her terry cloth robe to reveal a Lycra tank top and matching bikini bottom with bright yellow flowers. Coley hurried into the shallow end, just a little embarrassed by her scanty attire. Jase swam slowly down to her end of the pool, stopping a few feet from her and letting his feet settle to the bottom as his chest and head raised out of the water. His hands carelessly swept the water from his face and the hair from his forehead before coming to rest on his hips.

"We'll practice some more floating today," he said, his blue eyes abstractedly taking in her appearance. He moved away from her in the water and instructed, "Float over to me on your stomach and remember to keep your head in the water."

Taking a deep breath, Coley allowed herself to slide into the water, her arms outstretched and reaching for the solid, reassuring hands of her handsome teacher. Within a few seconds that seemed like minutes, she felt two hands catching hold of hers and lifting her upwards. She wiped the water from her face and looked to him for approval. As usual, there was nothing but the mask.

"Okay, let's do it again."

Twice more she floated slowly towards him, and twice more after that with the accompaniment of the scissorlike motion of her legs.

"All right," said Jase, looking expectantly at

Coley, "we're going to learn the backfloat now. It's easy. Just relax like you did before and I'll hold you up." Obediently Coley turned her back to him and supported herself on his arms. But as the water swirled around her face and over her head, she sputtered and gripped his arm in panic.

"It's all right. Come on, lean back now," his patient voice instructed. Again she leaned into his arms, unconsciously stiffening her body as she did so. "Relax. Don't tighten up."

Shutting her eyes to close out her inner fear, Coley surrendered herself to the firm hands supporting her shoulders and her back until the buoyancy of the water claimed and soothed her. It wasn't so hard, she thought to herself, as the little waves lapped around her body. She actually felt serene and at peace floating like this in the water. Unknowingly, a blissful smile had curled her generous mouth.

"You're enjoying it, aren't you?" Jase asked, his knowing tone answering his own question.

"It's so peaceful," Coley breathed, her voice tinged with the mystification that she felt. She opened her eyes to look up at him, seeing with pleasure that his own eyes were almost smiling back at her.

"You're not afraid any more," Jase replied as Coley closed her eyes again. "Now move your hands to propel yourself through the water." When she began to move her arms away from her sides and sink, he quickly repeated himself, holding her up in the water with his hands. "Just your hands. Just move them a little bit."

This time she just moved her hands back and forth and thrilled as she felt her body being pushed along by her own movement. She sighed dreamily, relaxing now in the comfortable motion of the water.

"I really am going to learn how to swim, aren't I, Jase?" she asked, opening her eyes to look into his face. But it wasn't there! Suddenly she missed the pressure of his hands on her back. In terror she turned her head swiftly to see him treading water just a few feet away from her. And then everything went wrong. Her long legs tumbled over themselves in a desperate effort to find the bottom that wasn't there. Her arms began flailing as she panicked, the water swirling around her head.

"Jase!" she gurgled, striking out desperately towards him. She saw him moving towards her as she tried to make her arms move in the synchronized rhythm that he had shown her. Then she was in his arms, being pulled towards the edge of the pool, coughing and spluttering as she went. When they had reached safety, her arms remained clasped around his shoulders, her body trembling and shivering with fright.

"You're all right now," Jase said, his arm remaining firmly around her bare waist. "You did fine. You actually swam to me."

"I . . . I did?" she stuttered, her terrified eyes gazing into his as she huddled closer to him, grateful for the broad, tanned chest to lean on. "Why d-did you let go of me?"

"Because you didn't need me. You were floating all by yourself and I was in the way," he answered patiently, smiling comfortingly into her face.

"I really did?" Coley asked, warming to his praise, in spite of her previous scare.

"Yes, you did." His smile was so gentle and unexpected that she could only stare at his lips, growing slowly more conscious of the few inches that separated them and the suddenly burning touch of his hand on her bare midriff. His head began to bend towards hers as her eyes remained hypnotized by his mouth.

"What have we here? An early morning rendezvous?" came a teasing voice from poolside.

Almost roughly Jase pushed Coley away from him, yet not letting her go, as they both turned towards the mocking face of Tony.

"I was just giving Coley a swimming lesson," Jase retorted sharply at Tony's raised eyebrows. "She panicked in the deep water."

"And Daddy was going to kiss her little fears away," Tony finished in mock baby talk. Color rose high in Coley's cheeks as she left the protection of Jason's arm and edged her way along the side of the pool to the shallow end. The scar on his cheek stood out whitely as Jase glowered at Tony before moving after the retreating Coley.

"If that's the way you teach swimming," Tony said, "I'd like to stand in for you one of these days, cousin."

He grinned widely at the pair before striding off jauntily towards the ranch yard, whistling as he went. Coley watched him leave, wondering how she could look Jason in the face after what almost happened. She knew he was standing just a few feet from her in the shallow water, his piercing blue eyes watching her.

"Had enough for today?" His voice rang harshly in her ears as she nodded her assent.

He was waiting by the ladder, one arm gripping the rung and the other resting impatiently on his waist. She longed to run past him, but the water around her legs reduced her pace to an ungainly waddle. Coley kept her head lowered, hiding as best she could the red flush on her cheeks and the tears in her eyes as she groped blindly for the ladder. As his hand gripped her arm to steady her when she stumbled on one of the rungs, she almost ripped it away from him in her shame.

Somehow she made it one of the lounge chairs and began drying herself off with whatever dignity she had left. She silently wished he would grab his towel and leave as he usually did. This time he hovered above her like a hawk over his kill. She tried to ignore him. She had to, she couldn't face him, not in the state she was in.

His hand reached out and imprisoned her, turning her face upward to his. She could feel him studying her intently, but Coley couldn't look him in the eye. Just as suddenly as he had grabbed her, he let her go, walking a few paces to her right where his towel lay. Again she felt his eyes on her.

"I told you you were too sensitive," Jase said briskly. "If you're going to last around here, you're going to have to toughen up."

Then he was gone. She clutched the towel tightly around her shoulders, hugging it close to her. He was right, she was too sensitive. It was a silly thing to get so upset. Tony's teasing had embarrassed her so, not the thought that Jase might have been going to kiss her. But she didn't even know if that was what he was going to do. Suddenly Coley realized how much she had wanted him to. Momentarily stunned by her discovery, she stared blankly into the pool.

She had always shied away from any close contact with the opposite sex, especially after that repulsive episode with Carl, but a few minutes ago when Jase had held her, it had seemed almost instinctive. In that one brief moment when his head had begun to bend towards hers, Coley had actually felt that it was natural and right. Was that where her shame came from, from her own bold desire and from his catching her in that vulnerable moment?

Visibly subdued, she made her way into the house and up the stairs into her room, her mind conscious of only this confusing revelation.

She spent the rest of the morning trailing after her aunt as Willy made her daily rounds in her rose garden. If the older woman noticed Coley's inattention to her conversation, she made no mention of it. The whole family was present for lunch, a rare occurrence, since one or several were usually out on another section of the ranch. Somehow Coley managed a small smile when she looked at Jase, her round eyes expressing an apology for her conduct that she was too shy to put into words. With a barely perceptible nod, Jase accepted it.

Danny's expression was a little grim when he sat down beside her while Tony winked at her from across the table. Coley fought for composure although she was aware that there were two bright dots of color on her cheeks.

"How goes the swimming lessons?" Tony asked with a malicious twinkle in his eye. Danny stabbed at a pea on his plate.

"Very well," Coley replied, accepting a dish from Ben with just the slightest tremor. "I'll be as good as you and Danny soon."

"Well, when you get to the advanced level, why don't you let me take over for Jase?" Tony leered at her, flashing his white teeth at her in a knowing smile. "I'm an excellent teacher."

His barely disguised innuendo flooded her cheeks as she concentrated her attention on her plate. She glanced briefly at Jase, meeting the full force of the piercing gaze. He was waiting for her reply, too. She mustn't let Tony's teasing get her. She had to show Jase that she was tough enough to take it.

"Really, Tony?" she replied as coolly as she could. "I never would have guessed that you were experienced at anything besides talking."

Tony's head jerked back at her words as he glanced over at Jase. He missed the sly smile that Coley saw before it was quickly suppressed by a studied concentration on the steak he was slicing. She could have almost giggled with her delight, but she turned instead to her brother, anxious for a change of subject.

"What have you been doing this morning?" she asked.

"Taking care of a mare that just foaled," Danny answered, a hard glint in his eye as he looked at his sister. "It's a late foal and we've been keepin' a close eye on it." He couldn't keep the pride from sneaking in his voice.

"Wow!" Coley exclaimed, captured by the excitement of birth. Turning excitedly to Ben, she asked, "Can I go down and see it?"

"Of course. Danny can take you down after lunch," Ben smiled good-humouredly.

"Will you, Danny?" Her eyes gleamed.

"Sure. But you'll have to change into some jeans. Those shorts aren't exactly the thing for a barn," Danny stated.

"Right away," Coley cried happily, pushing her chair away from the table. "May I be excused, please?"

"You haven't had your dessert yet, Colleen," admonished Aunt Willy.

"I'm not hungry. I'll have it later," Coley called,

already at the doorway. She started to leave the room, then ducked her head back in. "You be sure and wait for me, Danny."

"I will." His voice sounded disgruntled, but there was a pleased expression on his face as she returned his smile and bounced out of the room.

Coley raced up the steps into her room, creating a small whirlwind when she got there as she rummaged through her drawers for her jeans and a top. She changed in record time, then stopped in front of the mirror to touch up her hair briefly with a comb and add a hint of the peach lipstick. She wrinkled her button nose at her reflection and dashed out of the room.

She arrived breathless at the bottom of the stairs and hurried to her brother, who was waiting only slightly impatiently at the door. With a cheery "I'm ready" from Coley they left the house.

Coley managed to slow her anxious feet to the sedate pace her brother was taking. She flashed a happy smile at his somber expression, taking his arm with eagerness.

"What are you so serious about?" she asked, hugging his arm like a child.

"What happened at the pool this morning?" His question was so unexpected that Coley couldn't suppress a little gasp. She had no trouble now slowing her previously bouncy steps to match his.

"You talked to Tony, I suppose," Coley replied, knowing immediately who'd told him.

"He said he saw you and Jason in a clinch." His words came out slowly through gritted teeth, but there was concern and speculation in his eyes when he glanced at his sister.

"That's not the way it was," Coley replied, going on to explain about her scare in the deep end of the pool and Jason's rescue. "I was just hanging on to him because I was frightened. And that's when Tony came along."

"So that's all there was to it," Danny breathed, his relief plain to see.

"Well—" Coley drawled, desperately seeking the words that would explain her confused feelings. She had always confided in her brother and she needed to again. He had always been able to put things right. "Not exactly. You see, Danny," she rushed, "afterwards I got this feeling that I would have liked him to kiss me. I don't really understand it. That's why I got so embarrassed at Tony's teasing, because I wanted it to happen." She paused briefly. "I've never felt like that, especially after Carl . . ." Her words drifted away in silence.

"Coley, there are some things you don't know about Jase." Danny spoke hesitantly.

"I overheard Jase and Uncle Ben arguing one day shortly after we came here." Coley spoke very low so that Danny had to bend his head to hear. "Uncle Ben called him a murderer. That's what you're talking about, isn't it?"

Danny studied her very intently before answering. "Yes, that's what I'm talking about. I've heard things, stories, I don't know how much is true, but either way, he's thirteen years older than you. He's . . . I don't know, only I don't want you getting too close to him or you're going get hurt."

That was the second time she'd been warned off, the first time by Jase himself, Coley thought as they reached the stables. Did she seem so much like a child to everybody that they couldn't trust her to judge the facts?

As they walked down the roofed breezeway and past the stalls, Coley looked around her. She had been so engrossed in her conversation with her brother that she hadn't noticed her surroundings. This was the first time she had ventured in the actual ranch yard and she studied the various buildings and corrals with interest. Several hundred yards away she noticed a large barn surrounded by heavy reinforced fencing. She could barely make out the gray shapes within the fences.

"What's over there?" She directed Danny's attention to the distant corrals.

"In those enclosures? Brahma cattle," he answered. "They raise them for rodeo stock. I understand Jase had been doing some experimental breeding with them, too. They put up with the hot weather and insects better than the Herefords and Angus. They're awful touchy, though, so don't you go hanging around those corrals. They didn't build those fences like that for nothing."

Coley shuddered, remembering pictures she had seen of rodeo bulls tossing riders and clowns around. No, she wouldn't be going near them.

"Here's the new mother," Danny crooned, stopping beside the open foaling pen at the south end of the stable. He reached out and laid a reassuring hand on the shiny brown neck of the mare. He took hold of his shy sister and drew her up beside him see the spindly-legged colt sprawled exhaustedly on the hay. "Here's the Johnny-come-lately."

As if the mare knew that Danny was showing off her foal, she turned her head and nickered to the sleeping colt. He raised his too-large head in answer and then attempted to get his long legs in the correct position to get him on his feet. After several awkward attempts that brought quiet laughter from Coley, he made it and stood staring at them, swishing his whiskbroom of a tail arrogantly.

"He's all head, ears and legs," Coley laughed, delighted with the little colt.

"He'll grow into all three," Danny promised, scratching the mare's forelock as she nuzzled him for her share of attention.

Coley tried coaxing the colt over to her, but he just shook his blazed face at her and dashed, as best he could, to the protection of his mother's flank.

"Coley, do you like it here?" Danny asked unexpectedly, turning an anxious face to her. "I mean, do you want to stay? I don't really get to be with you very much and if you're unhappy . . ." "Oh, no, I like it here," she said quickly. "Aunt Willy is so good to me that I feel guilty about not being able to pay my way. But, Danny, I wish you wouldn't work so hard. You're always off in the barns or stables somewhere."

"You know something, I like it. It's all so interesting that it doesn't seem like work," Danny replied earnestly. "Can you imagine that, a city boy like me? But there's so much you have to know to be able to operate a ranch successfully, especially one of this size. Do you want to see some of the other horses?" he asked as if suddenly self-conscious of his enthusiasm.

"Yes," Coley replied, following Danny as he walked away from the pen.

When they reached an adjacent corral, Coley climbed on to the top of the fence beside Danny, barely concealing her dismay as the horses within trotted over to them.

"They won't hurt you," Danny said as a bold sorrel horse butted his arm playfully. "They just want some attention."

Hesitantly Coley placed a careful hand on the

head of a small bay and made a haphazard job of scratching his head as she had seen Danny do. As another horse moved in, making Coley feel like she was being surrounded, she scooted closer to Danny. The new horse, a blaze-faced chestnut, nuzzled her arm.

"His nose is so soft," Coley exclaimed, turning her hand palm upwards as the horse investigated it. "It feels like velvet."

She gradually grew more confident, not jumping every time one made a move that she wasn't prepared for, until she was laughing along with Danny at the spats of jealousy that took place between the horses. They were so engrossed in the little byplays that they failed to hear Jase ride up behind them.

"Why don't you take your sister out for a ride?" he said to Danny, almost startling Coley off her perch. Danny looked at his sister before making a rueful noise that very plainly said "forget it."

"I'd love to," Coley murmured wistfully, "but. . ."

"I know, you don't know how to ride." Jase laughed, a warm delicious laugh that tingled through Coley. "Do you want to learn?"

"Sure," said Coley, slipping off the fence, followed by her brother.

"Danny could teach you," Jase suggested.

"Oh, no, not me," Danny cried, begging off with grim determination. "I've been through that before. She'll last about as long as it takes to saddle a horse and then she'll give up."

"Do you want to learn?" Jase repeated, his blue-diamond eyes challenging her.

"Of course," Coley asserted, indignant and a little put out by her brother's lack of faith in her.

"Grady!" Jase called, turning in his saddle to

hail a ranch hand leading a white-faced roan out of the stables. "Bring Misty over here! Miss McGuire needs a gentle mount, so you'll have find another one for this afternoon."

"I didn't m-mean now exactly," Coley stuttered as Jase stepped down off his blood-bay stallion. Jase accepted the reins from the rider and turned to Coley.

"What's wrong with now?" His eyes twinkled although the deadpan expression on his face didn't change.

"He's got you now," Danny hooted, overcome with brotherly glee at his sister's predicament.

"Nothing, except I promised Aunt Willy . . ." Coley began, searching wildly for some way out of the trap that her big mouth had got her into.

"There isn't anything that Aunt Willy would want you to do that couldn't be put off," Jase interrupted. Then he turned to the roan and stroked its neck. "She just doesn't like you, Misty."

"Oh, she's fine. I mean, she's . . . there's nothing wrong with her. It's just. . ."

"You'd better tell her yourself, because I don't think she believes me," said Jase, shaking his head in mock despair.

Feeling like an utter fool, Coley stepped over towards the horse. Unwillingly she stared into the liquid brown eyes of the roan that blinked so trustingly back at her. As if on cue, the horse stepped forward and nuzzled Coley's shoulder until she placed a reluctant hand on its head and began stroking it.

"Misty likes you," Jase commented, while Danny stood back, silently shaking with ill-concealed humor. "Just a few turns around the corral wouldn't do any harm."

"Oh, all right," Coley agreed, slightly ashamed of her reluctance. She turned a glowering look on her brother. "But I don't need an audience."

"I'll take my cue," Danny grinned, and moved off towards the stables with a wave and a dubious "good luck" to Jase.

"Okay. Now what?" Coley asked. Her anger was bolstering her courage.

"Come over here to the left side of the horse," Jase instructed, taking her by the hand as he spoke.

"Do you have to get on from the left?" stalled Coley.

"It's best. That's the side the horse is used to seeing a rider approach from. If you come from the other side he won't be expecting you and might spook," he explained patiently.

"I thought a horse wouldn't let you get on him except from the one side."

"No, that's not true. In fact, the Indians mounted their ponies on the opposite side," Jase smiled. "That peculiar quirk of theirs saved a cavalry patrol from ambush once."

"Really?" Coley asked, interested in spite of herself.

"Two patrols were supposed to link up at a designated point. The scout from one patrol spotted the second patrol waiting for them. He was just going to report to his commanding officer that he had sighted the other patrol when he saw one of the so-called soldiers mount his horse—from the wrong side. He realized immediately that Indians must have wiped out the other patrol, stolen their uniforms and were waiting to ambush his patrol," Jase concluded. He stared at her rapt face. "But that little story isn't getting you on this horse, and that's what we're supposed be doing."

Coley grinned at him shyly, and surprisingly he returned the smile. He threw the reins over the roan's head and turned back to Coley.

"Step over here," he said, indicating a place on the ground at the horse's side. "Place your right hand on the saddle horn and with your left hand grip the reins and rest your hand on the horse's neck." He guided her hands through the moves. "You always want to shorten the inside rein just a little so that the horse's head turns towards you. Never turn your back to the horse. Keep him in sight so that you know what he's doing. We have a few that take a playful nip here and there, or shy away when you try to mount." He glanced at her make sure she was taking it all in. "All right, now place your left foot in the stirrup." Coley did as she was told, although her balance was not too good. Luckily the roan wasn't a big horse and Coley was fairly tall.

"Okay, now pull yourself in the saddle," Jase finished. It was a simple instruction, but not easy to carry out, as Coley soon discovered. She got halfway up, only to lose her balance and slip to the ground. She glanced at Jase and tried again. This time she got her leg over the saddle, straddling it awkwardly for a second before receiving a shove from Jase that slipped her into the seat. She sat very still, her left hand clutching the saddle horn as well as her right, and stared at the ground so very far below her. If Jase noticed her panic, he made no mention of it. He stepped to the roan's head, took hold of the reins under the chin while still retaining a hold on his own horse's reins and began walking. His voice was matter-of-fact when he began speaking again.

"I'll lead you over to the corral so you can get

used to the movement of the horse," he said. "All you have to do is relax, don't hold your body too rigid and follow the motion of the horse."

Coley stared at a point between the horse's ears and tried to do as she was told. It sounded so easy. Jase stopped at the corral gate, opened it, and led them all in, closing the gate behind them. He swung easily into his saddle and reined his horse over beside Coley. He reached over and removed Coley's hands from the saddle horn, his eyes twinkling as she swallowed nervously. He placed the reins in her left hand and instructed her to let her other arm fall to her side. Against her better judgment, she did as she was told.

He showed her how to lay the reins against the side of the horse's neck to get him to turn, the proper length of rein from the horse's mouth to her hands, and, most important as far as Coley was concerned, how to stop him.

"We'll walk around the corral now. Just squeeze your legs and heels a bit." He waited until she did it before starting his own horse out.

After several plodding rounds, Coley felt quite good. She even relaxed a little. Of course, the ground wasn't quite as far away now, or at least it didn't seem to be.

"Do you want to try a trot?" Jase asked. She nodded confidently. "Do the same as before, squeeze your legs."

She did. Her horse began a lazy semblance of a trot while Coley bounced all over the saddle and nearly off. Instinctively she pulled her horse back into a walk. Her hazel eyes were very round when she looked over to Jase.

"This time, sit well back in the saddle so you don't get the motion of both the front and back legs of the horse. Don't move against the motion, ride with it. Try it again," he said.

She'd gone too far to quit now, Coley thought, and resolutely tightened her legs against the horse's sides and off they went. She really tried to do as he said and succeeded to a certain extent, but she still bounced, although not quite as much. Around and around the corral they went, Jase holding back his bay to stay alongside the slow, shuffling roan.

"Let's canter now," he ordered, and held back again until Coley had urged her horse to the faster pace. "That's easy!" Coley exclaimed delightedly as Jase rode alongside. The rhythmic, rocking motion was such a snap after the bouncing, jarring trot. "This is fun!"

He pulled his horse into the center of the corral and stopped, watching her circle several times before he called to her that that was all for today. She pulled the roan up and turned him into the center towards Jase.

"You've had enough for today. Any more riding and you'll be stiff as a board." He smiled, and Coley smiled back. "I'll tell the boys that Misty is yours. You can ride her whenever you like, but only in the corral for the next week or so until you get used to it."

"Thanks," Coley cried, rubbing the side of the roan's neck happily. She slid out of the saddle to the ground, leading her new mount over to the fence with Jase following suit. "I never thought I could ride. I always got so frightened. But you didn't give me a chance to get scared."

"That was the general idea," he replied, leaning against a fence post.

"Still, I want to thank you. You've taught me to

swim. Though I don't know how yet, I know I'm going to learn. And now you've taught me to ride," Coley trailed off breathlessly. Then she glanced over at him with a sudden stab of guilt. "I'm sorry about the way I behaved this morning. At the pool, I mean."

"Nothing happened at the pool this morning," Jase said coldly, turning his head to Coley where her gaze subsequently rested on his scar. "Except in Tony's imagination."

"I didn't mean that," said Coley, lowering her head to watch her boot scuff the dirt of the corral. "I meant that I didn't mean to make things more difficult for you."

"How could you do that?" he asked, eyeing her speculatively.

"Well," Coley's face was red now as she struggled over the words, "I know you're in some sort of awkward position here on the ranch. I don't know why, only that it's something about your brother, and I don't want to do anything that would make things harder for you." She searched his inscrutable face for some sign of understanding. "You've been so good to me, teaching me things and all, that I don't want to get you in trouble over it."

"I won't," Jase answered, staring down at her with a grim expression on his face. Seeing the anxious eyes dwelling on him, he smiled. "So don't worry about me, buttercup." Coley laughed and walked in step with him as he started towards the corral gate.

"You know, you're really a very good teacher," she smiled up at him. "I can just see you teaching your sons and daughters." Her imagination painted bright pictures as she spoke, of dark-haired little boys with blue eyes.

"There won't be any!" His voice was cold and hard. The biting tone brought Coley to a complete halt as she stared into his blazing eyes. "Because there won't be any wife."

"Why not?" Coley asked. Her eyes grew round and just a trifle fearful at the anger in his face. "I have nothing to offer a wife. Not a home, not a future, not an inheritance for children. Nothing!" Jase exclaimed bitterly.

Coley stared at his cheek where the jagged scar seemed to be throbbing with the rapid pulse of his temper. His hand reached up and touched the scar lightly with his fingertips. "I have this for my wife," he mocked. "The mark of Cain." And he was gone while Coley stood silently, wincing from the backlash of his words.

Chapter Five

Coley paddled idly in the water, enjoying the refreshing coolness of the pool in the afternoon sun. She could swim now, after a fashion, thanks to a week of intensive lessons from Jase. Of course, she had been restricted, like a child, to the shallow end of the pool whenever she swam alone. She could handle Misty pretty well now, too, but there again he wouldn't let her ride alone except in the corral. She grimaced disgustedly.

He treated her so differently. He had become distant and aloof since that first riding lesson. It was as if she was a total stranger. And all because of her big mouth, Coley thought. He had left yesterday to go into San Antone for something or other and she hadn't even known he was gone until she asked where he was at the dinner table last night. He could have said good-bye at least.

Depressed and hurt, Coley climbed out of the pool and began briskly rubbing her long legs and arms. She was too sensitive. How many times had Jase told her that? Well, he was too *in*sensitive!

"Hi, golden girl," said Tony, walking up behind Coley and tousling her wet hair. "What are you doing out here all by yourself? Don't you know two's company?"

"Aunt Willy and Uncle Ben are resting, Danny's out tinkering with his car, and Jase is gone. I was too hot to sit around sticking to chairs," Coley remarked lightly. "Where were you?"

"Would you believe I was looking for you?" Tony asked, taking the towel from Coley and drying off her back. At her mocking glance, he continued, "It's true, I figured you'd probably be down riding your little merry-go-round."

He handed Coley the towel back, his hand touching the golden tan of her shoulders.

"It was too hot for riding," she replied, ignoring his jibe. "What did you want to see me for?"

"Danny needs a part for his car and I volunteered to go into town for it. I wondered if you wanted to ride along."

"I'd like to," Coley smiled, then flushed under the penetrating inspection of his black eyes. "Give me a minute to change."

"Not too long, princess," Tony called after the rapidly departing Coley. When she was out of earshot, he added quietly, "I'd like you all to myself."

Coley changed quickly, spent a few minutes touching up her makeup, and another few minutes arranging her now sun-streaked hair into flattering waves around her face. Skipping down the stairs to meet Tony, she reflected over his increasing attentiveness. Ever since the day he had discovered her in Jason's arms in the pool, he had been watching her with a certain gleam in his eyes that had made her aware of him as more than just Ben's nephew. "The golden pumpkin awaits you in the drive, Cinderella," Tony teased, taking her arm possessively as she walked out the door on to the porch. She smiled at him coyly as he opened the door of the gold Firebird and helped her inside. She was suddenly bursting with confidence again over her new looks, enjoying the compliments Tony's eyes kept sending.

The trip into town hardly seemed to take any time at all, what with the lively conversation that Tony kept up as he teased Coley into bursts of laughter with his outrageous remarks. She was so involved with her first active participation in flirting that she was only half conscious of the reckless speed he drove at. All too soon Tony pulled up in front of the store and hopped out, promising to be back in a sec. Coley leaned back and gazed dreamily out of the window. She had just begun to wonder idly where Jase was and what he was doing when Tony opened the car door and tossed a package in the back seat before sliding in behind the wheel.

"Told you I wouldn't be long," he said, turning the key in the ignition and maneuvering the car into the street. "Let's go to the drive-in and get a mug of cold, cold root beer, huh?"

"Sounds retro," said Coley. "Sure, let's go."

"What were you thinking about a minute ago?" Tony asked, after they had parked in a stall and he had given their order to one of the waitresses. "Besides that we live in a time warp around here."

"When?"

"When I got in the car. You were all dreamy-eyed. Am I expecting too much to think that you just might have been thinking of me?" He gazed at her intently, though his lips were curved in a brilliant smile.

"Conceited," Coley teased. "Actually I was wondering about Jase."

"Jase?" His narrow forehead creased into a scowl as he spat out the name in disbelief. "What were you thinking about him for?" Surprised by his nearly bitter tone, Coley stuttered in reply, "I . . . I knew he went to . . . to San Antone and I w-was just wondering where he was. Danny and I used to live there, that's all."

"I'd forgotten," Tony replied, as near an apology as he was capable of. He glanced at his watch. "I imagine he's lying beside some pool with some babe in a bikini."

"Does he have a girlfriend?" Coley asked, her spirits sinking with the picture that Tony had conjured in her mind.

"I imagine he has several," Tony answered slyly, "but not the kind you'd bring home to mother. You didn't think he was some kind of a monk, did you, Coley?"

"No, of course not," she replied, but with just enough uncertainty in her voice to make Tony chuckle maliciously.

"Coley, sometimes you're so naive that I just can't believe it." At the quick rising of color in her cheeks, he reached over and held her hand. "My sweet little Cinderella, not everyone is as inexperienced and pure as you are." His voice grew husky as he continued, "You just don't know how beautiful and tempting you are."

The intensity of his look frightened her and she was glad when the waitress arrived with their drinks and Tony was forced to let go of her hands. As she accepted the frosty mug from him, she turned ever so slightly in her seat until she was resting against the door and had placed more distance between them.

"Did I embarrass you, princess?" Tony mocked, his arm nonchalantly over the back of the seat.

"Of course not," Coley replied indignantly, now that she had recovered some of her composure. "I don't see why you all seem to want to wrap me up in a package marked Fragile. I am almost twenty." Quickly the picture flashed in her mind of the night when she had asserted her womanhood to Jase and met his indifferent glance.

"Are you accusing me of doing that?" Tony mocked.

"Yes. You're just like all the rest," she replied, enjoying the surge of righteous anger. "You treat me like a child who has to have decisions made for her."

"Now how do we do that?" Tony tilted his head and studied her with interest.

"Just look at all this secrecy about Jase," Coley told him, leaning forward as she tried to make Tony understand. "Everyone knows what happened—about his scar and his brother, I mean. Everybody but me. Every time I ask someone they just pat me on the head and tell me to run along like a good little girl."

Tony laughed lightly at her indignant words, but his eyes were narrowed and glittering. "What could it possibly accomplish for someone to tell you that? It's water under the bridge, so to speak."

"Then how come Danny knows?" she flared.

"Maybe you're right, princess." His expression grew serious as he studied her before he turned to stare out the front of the car. "You're one of the family now. You should know what happened."

"Will you tell me, Tony?" Coley asked breathlessly.

He didn't answer her for a minute, just stared at her somberly.

"I don't really know where to begin." He frowned slightly and swirled the root beer in his mug. "Rick, his brother, was two years older than Jase. He was quite a guy." Tony smiled briefly. "I think you would have liked him, Coley. He was kinda crazy, always ready to do anything, try anything. Just the opposite of Jase. But Rick was Uncle Ben's favorite. It didn't matter what Rick wanted to do or where he wanted to go, it was okay with Ben. Anyway, one night Rick came home late. He'd been to a party and he'd been drinking pretty heavily."

Tony paused and glanced over at Coley. He seemed to hesitate. "Nobody knows for sure what happened from then on. We do know Rick went into the pen with Satan, that big Brahma bull we've got out there. Rick was forever teasing him, jumping in and out of the pen like a rodeo clown. He wasn't so lucky that night. The booze had affected his reflexes and the bull got him. Jase said he heard the commotion and came out. He eventually got Rick out of the pen, but not before Satan had gored Rick and slashed Jason's cheek with his horns.

"Uncle Ben wasn't paralyzed then. I saw him sitting on the ground holding Rick in his arms, tears streaming down his face. I'll never forget the sight of him crying like a baby. I don't know where Jase was, calling an ambulance, I guess. Rick was still conscious." Tony's voice became strained. Coley huddled in the sunshine beating through the window, shivering in spite of the warmth. "He was delirious. He kept screaming for Jase, crying, 'He's going to get me . . . don't just stand there, help me!' I guess he kept that up all the way to the hospital, with the old man breaking up beside him and Jase just sitting stone-faced through the whole thing. Rick died on the operating table.

"There was an inquest after his death," Tony went on. "During his testimony, Jase said that he couldn't have got Rick out of the pen any quicker than he did. That was when Ben went to pieces, shouting that Jase was a liar and a murderer, that he'd let his brother die because he knew Rick would inherit the ranch. He swore that Jase had deliberately stayed outside the pen and watched his brother being gored to death. Jase never said a word, he just let the old man rage on until he told Jase that he would carry the mark of Cain for the rest of his life. Then he walked out and the old man collapsed with a stroke. He's been in a wheelchair ever since."

A pregnant silence followed the conclusion of Tony's words that not even the outside noises of the drive-in seemed to penetrate. Finally Tony looked over at the white face beside him.

"Now you know. Aren't you glad?" His voice was bitter as he looked around impatiently for the attendant to pick up the tray.

Coley didn't reply. She didn't speak the rest of the way home. She just sat and stared out the window at the blur of the scenery. When they finally reached the ranch house, she crawled out of the car and hurtled straight for her room where she lay on the bed, staring numbly at the bright flowers on the wall.

* * *

The lone horse and rider stood silently within the corral, both gazing over the rails at the distant, shimmering hills. The horse whinnied forlornly. Coley sighed in agreement while rubbing her horse's neck affectionately.

"I know. I wish we could go riding out there, but you know what Jase said, Misty," she concluded with a wistful but resigned expression on her face. She had been in a melancholy mood since Tony had told her the story of Rick's death three days ago. Jase was back from his trip to San Antone, but Coley had been reluctant to be alone with him. Not that Tony's story had outright damned Jase. She still instinctively trusted him, but she recognized that there was a slightly ruthless side to his nature.

"Hey, little princess, want to take that rocking horse of yours for a ride?"

Coley turned around in the saddle to see Tony astride a prancing chestnut horse at the corral gate. She reined her horse around and trotted it over to him.

"I'm not supposed to go out of the corral. Besides, aren't you supposed to be working?" she asked. For some reason, despite her earlier desire for a ride in the country, she didn't really want to go with Tony.

"Another one of Jase's commands?" he said with a sarcastic curl of his upper lip. "Or don't you think you'd be safe with me?"

"Why would I think a thing like that?" Coley protested, feeling a twinge of guilt. "Jase just didn't want me going out by myself. And if you're going to be working, I don't want to be in the way."

"You won't be," Tony remarked as he reached down and unlatched the gate. With difficulty, he maneuvered his high-spirited mount into a position to swing the gate open. "Jase wants me to check the well up on the north range. It's another one of his fool's errands, so you might as well keep me company." Tony grimaced, reining his horse over to Coley's side.

"Why do you say that?"

"With all the rain we've had, there's more than enough water for the horses up there," he grumbled, "but he's sending me anyway."

Coley wasn't in the mood to take part in any discussion about Jase, so she nudged her horse into a canter. Tony's jumping chestnut was soon alongside. She flinched as she watched him saw at the reins, his horse's mouth opened wide.

"Misty and I were just wishing we could go out riding," she remarked, trying to turn her attention away from the flecks of blood that dotted the saliva foaming around the horse's mouth.

"Then I'm glad Jase dreamed up this little chore for me. I'm getting my wish to be with you and you're getting yours to go riding." He smiled broadly while his eyes roamed over her face in open admiration.

Coley's cheeks flushed at his words. Tony seemed pleased by her reaction and turned his attention to the rolling landscape with a satisfied smile curling the corners of his mouth. Coley glanced around with interest. It was her first venture out onto the ranch proper since her dismal trek the night of the storm. The tranquil beauty of the hills and distant mountains seemed far removed from the sinister and ominous shapes the lightning had revealed.

They rode several miles with only subdued exclamations from Coley at the sight of the giant yucca plants, their stalks rounded with clusters of blossoms. Occasionally Tony would catch her attention to point out the white rumps of antelopes bounding away at their approach. When he finally slowed his horse to a walk, it was a wide-eyed and breathless rider that reined in beside him, her eyes dancing with pleasure and delight.

"Oh, that was so much fun!" Coley exclaimed. "You're so lucky to be able to ride all over."

"I'm enjoying it today, but most days it's a bore," he replied, reining his horse into a ravine. "What do you see right now?" The sides of the ravine sloped away to reveal a canyon meadow with a thin ribbon of sparkling water slicing it in two. On the rich dark grasses grazed a herd of horses. At the entrance to the canyon, the two riders halted. A frolicsome colt kicked his heels and dashed in whickering panic to the safety of his mother's side at their appearance.

"We have one of the best studs in the state. His ancestry, on both sides, traces directly back to Old Sorrel, one of the founding sires of the Quarter Horse breed. Those are Sun God's colts and fillies out there with one of our herd stallions. You can bet they'd fetch a high price in any auction," Tony told her, his eyes never leaving the herd before them.

Coley studied the foals as they peeped around their mothers' sides while the bolder ones skirmished playfully with each other. Each one seemed a replica of the other, from their red-gold coats to their flaxen mane and tails down to the white stockings on their feet and the blaze on their faces.

"They all look alike."

"That's what makes Sun God such a valuable stallion. He breeds true, just like Old Sorrel did,"

Tony explained, "Old Sorrel was born and raised down on the famous King Ranch near Alice, Texas."

"You're very lucky to know so much about all this." Coley glanced at him briefly before turning back to the herd. "How long have you lived here?"

"I came here seven years ago, after my father died. I was sixteen then," said Tony, lightly touching a spur to his horse's flank as they moved out together at a walk. "My mother was Ben's baby sister. If you can picture a female version of Ben, that was my mother." His smile as he glanced over at Coley was scornful. "Poor Dad, he worked here on the ranch for Ben. He figured by marrying Ben's sister he'd have it made. Of course, he didn't know Ben too well. He threw them both off the ranch. I came along a few years later. From the time I can remember, Mom was a regular shrew, constantly reminding Dad of all the things she'd had, and it was all his fault that we lived in such squalor. I was twelve when she flew into her final rage and her heart burst under the constant strain. And Dad, who only wanted an easy life, spent fifteen years of hell with her. But he never stopped trying. He got involved smuggling drugs across the border and was fatally wounded in a gun battle with Treasury agents. Even on his deathbed, his last words were that this ranch was my heritage and for me to claim my share. Since I was a minor, the court declared Ben my guardian and I came here. Not a happy story, is it?" Tony smiled grimly at Coley, his dark eyes studying her face intently. At the short, negative shake of her head, he added, "But from what Danny's told me, yours isn't pretty either. We're a lot alike, Coley."

A lump in her throat prevented her from replying. Poor, proud Tony, she thought. He always seemed so carefree, teasing her and constantly attempting to charm her into gaining more self-confidence and his life had been harder than her own. How mean of her to think badly of him when he teased her. He was trying to help her fit in, to be a part of the family. She blinked hastily at the tears forming in her eyes. It wouldn't do for Tony to see her pity.

She didn't notice the calculating gleam in his eye as he studied her face.

"Look at this view, Coley," he directed, sweeping a hand around him.

She looked around her in surprise. During their slow ride around the herd, they had climbed the crest of the canyon. Spread out below them were the coppery forms of the horses peacefully grazing on the canyon floor. Shimmering in the distance were the tiny toy buildings of the ranchyard. Behind them were the craggy hills and mountains. Dark splotches of cattle dotted the pastures between the ranch house and the canyon.

"As far as the eye can see is Slash S rangeland," Tony said calmly but forcefully. "All told, over sixty square miles, valued, with livestock and all, in the millions. And now it looks like one day it will all be mine." He turned once again to Coley. "You know, Ben's grown very fond of you these few short weeks you've been here. He told Willy your gentle ways hid a lot of determination and pride." Coley's eyes were captured by the forcefulness of his gaze. "I feel I have to warn you Jase realizes that Ben likes you. He's not above using you as a tool to get it. He constantly tries to make me look bad, gives me menial tasks, like today, then implies to Ben that I can't be trusted. He wants this ranch, Coley, any way he can get it."

On that ominous note Tony stopped, turning a grim face towards the hills. Jase's words came echoing back to Coley. *Tony would destroy everything you worked for in a week.*

Very hesitantly Coley spoke. "But if what you told me the other day is true, about Rick's death, isn't the ranch rightly his?" There was a long silence during which it seemed Tony was choosing his words carefully before he answered.

"Nobody saw what happened. We know only what Jase told us and what Rick screamed while he was conscious but delirious. Rick was very clear when he begged Jase not to stand there . . . to help him."

"What if someone else were there?"

His gaze sharpened as he studied her face. "You mean what if the sight of three thousand pounds of charging Brahma bull momentarily froze Jase? What if the horror inside the corral stopped him?" Tony asked, his complexion paling under his tan.

"Is that what you believe?" Coley asked breathlessly, half afraid to hear his answer.

"It's possible. That's what Ben believes," Tony answered calmly, lifting his shoulders briefly in an almost indifferent shrug. "That and the fact that Jase wanted the ranch, which will now, quite likely, be mine." Suddenly he smiled at her, his thin lips curling back to reveal a large expanse of white teeth. "How did we get on such a morbid subject when we both were enjoying the ride? *Quién sabe,* huh? I'll tell you what, you stay here and watch the colts play while I ride over the hill and check the pump on that water well."

Coley nodded a quick agreement. She needed

time to be alone, to think about Tony's new revelations. She smiled and waved in return as his horse danced down the hill. Her eyes followed him until he was out of sight. With a barely repressed sigh, Coley dismounted, leading her horse part way down the crest to a grassy, level spot where she let loose of the reins to allow Misty to graze. She stretched out on the incline, leaning back to gaze up at the vivid blue sky.

How strange that she had never guessed that Tony's occasional brashness had come from an unhappy childhood. She remembered often seeing those same lines of bitterness and discontent etched on Danny's face before they had come here. In some ways, the circumstances of Tony's early life had been like theirs, except that he never had known a mother's love and possibly not even a father's.

She wished they had not talked about Jase. So many things Tony had said seemed logical, though in direct conflict with her emotions. She had recognized the flash of ruthlessness occasionally revealed in Jase's face. Perhaps there was cruelty there as well. Coley rolled over quickly on her side as if to turn her back on such thoughts.

A movement several feet away caught her attention. Misty's front hoof was entangled in one of the trailing reins, causing her to stumble. Coley leapt quickly to her feet.

"Oh, Misty, I'm sorry!" she cried, rushing over to pat the roan's neck soothingly. "I should have realized you'd trip over the reins. Here, I'll tie them around the saddle horn." Finishing her task, she stepped back to watch her horse lower its head to the tender mountain grasses, unencumbered by loose reins. A questioning whinny rang from the canyon floor. The roan's head raised and her ears pricked alertly as she stared down. Her sides heaved briefly in an answering whicker.

"Have you got a friend down there, Misty?" Coley asked, studying the numerous horses, trying to determine which one had called to her horse.

Misty whinnied again, then started down the slope at an eager trot.

"Where are you going?" Coley cried. "Come back here! Misty!"

She hopped and slid down the steep incline to the canyon floor, vainly attempting to catch up with her unheeding horse. She was barely halfway down when Misty reached the bottom and cantered towards the herd.

"Misty! Misty!" Coley called, trying desperately to run after her horse and still maintain her balance. Her feet failed to keep up with her gathering momentum and she landed ignominiously on her rump. She rolled and slid to the bottom, scraping and bruising her arms and hands as she tried to stop her fall. Out of breath and painfully sore, she struggled to her feet and hobbled stiffly after her roan. But Misty had reached the herd. There was a brief flurry of movement before the curious mares encircled the saddled but riderless horse and she was hidden from Coley's view.

"Oh, Misty, how could you do this to me!" Coley exclaimed disgustedly, flowing down to a disgruntled, toe-scuffling walk.

From the grove of trees that lined the opposite canyon walls came an odd shrill sound followed almost immediately by a thundering of hooves. Coley glanced up quickly from her morose study of the ground to see a coppery red horse charging around the herd towards her. While the mares and colts scurried together, the sorrel horse slowed to a dancing halt between Coley and the herd. With long, powerful strides he paced back and forth in front of her, his flaxen tail held high, flowing out behind him like a banner going into battle. Coley paused, then chided herself for the momentary recurrence of her fear of horses. She clapped her hands loudly and stepped boldly forward.

"Shoo, horse shoo!" she yelled, flapping her arms wildly, hoping to send him scurrying off.

His shrill, piercing scream sent her hands rushing to cover her ears as he lowered his head, snorting loudly and stamping the ground. Coley realized with growing terror that he wasn't a bit afraid of her and had no intention of allowing her to approach the herd he was protecting. She glanced around her hopelessly. All the trees of any size were on the opposite side of the canyon. Ahead of her and slightly to her right was a huge boulder where, if she could make it and scramble up it, she would be out of reach of her angry antagonist. Now she had to decide whether to try for it, stand her ground or retreat. The last two made her more vulnerable if he decided she posed a threat wherever she was. That only left the first, to try for the rock.

Taking a deep breath, Coley tried to still the trembling in her legs. They felt like two sticks of jelly. The horse was tossing his head, shaking it from side to side. Now, she thought, now! And she was off, the ground shuddering beneath her as the pounding of the horse's hooves told her that he was giving chase.

She was at the rock! She'd made it! Scrambling, clawing, inwardly cursing the slick soles of her cowboy boots, she dragged herself to the top. The angry screams and clicking teeth below her underscored the fine line separating defeat from her victory. Coley tucked her legs beneath her as she clung tightly to the pointed top of her precarious perch. Below danced the sorrel, rearing in a tantrum.

"Help!" Her voice was barely a squeak. She swallowed hard and tried again. "Help!"

Tony wasn't far away. Surely he'd hear her.

"Help! Tony, help!"

The enraged stallion circled the boulder, his fiery eyes never leaving his quarry. She watched the slope she had just come down, fervently hoping to see Tony appear on the crest.

"To-o-ne-ee!" she screamed at the top of her lungs, before breaking off into a hastily stifled sob. She mustn't panic. The horse couldn't reach her and Tony would be along soon. She just had to keep her head. "Take deep breaths," she ordered herself. "Relax. Enjoy the view." Now all she had to do was wait. She glanced down at the horse, trying to be calm, but she couldn't suppress a shudder at the sight of its menacing teeth.

A muffled sound of hoofbeats reached her ears, but they seemed to be coming from the opposite side of the canyon, from the hill that was its wall. Seconds later a horse and rider appeared on the crest above the grove of trees. The horse pranced impatiently against the backdrop of blue sky, as Coley, holding her breath, stared at the rider. Even at this distance she recognized the calm way he sat so surely astride the dancing red horse, moving with his mount as if they were one. It was Jase.

"Jase! Jase!" Coley screamed, waving an arm frantically at him. What if he didn't see her?

The horrifying thought numbed her throat as

she rose precariously to her feet trying to balance herself astride the pointed rock.

"Here! Here! I'm over here!" she yelled. Again she waved her arm wildly.

Suddenly the slick soles could no longer maintain their hold and she slipped. A short cry escaped her lips as she clutched madly at the smooth boulder, trying to check her fall. She felt her blouse rip as a corner snagged on a small outcropping. Quickly she grabbed at the small hold. Straining every muscle in her slender arms, she managed to stop her slide. Without wasting a glance to see where the stallion was, because she could almost feel the heat of his breath, she began to scale the rock again. A glancing blow of a hoof struck the sole of her boot, adding impetus to her scramble to safety. Completely winded, she reached the top, tears streaming down her cheeks from fright.

Her hazel eyes lifted to the hill where she had seen Jase, but he was gone. Suddenly she realized that pounding noise she was hearing wasn't her heart as she had first thought, but a horse. She turned to see Tony plummeting down the slope, yelling and spurring his horse, his arm swinging a coiled rope wildly.

Momentarily the stallion below paused, as if preparing to meet the attack, before he spun and raced whinnyingly towards the herd. In an almost synchronized movement, the whole herd turned as one and raced from the canyon, the copper sorrel nipping at the heels of the stragglers.

Tony slid his horse to a stop at the base of the rock where Coley was perched. He dismounted quickly to rush over to help her down. His face was as pale as hers, except that his expression was triumphant and hers was relieved.

"Are you all right?" he asked, smiling down at her broadly.

Coley nodded, not trusting her voice at the moment. She glanced once again at the hill where she had seen Jase. But still there was no sign of him. Had she imagined it? Tony was speaking again and she turned back to him, her hands resting on his arms.

"I was so afraid something would happen to you, too," he said, a tightness in his voice. "Where's your horse?"

"She ran out with the herd." Coley's voice trembled. She was still so shaken by her close call that she had difficulty concentrating, and speaking. "Oh, Tony, I'm so glad to see you!"

"You just lean back against the rock and relax. We'll worry about catching up with your horse later. Right now I'll take a look at those hands."

Coley did as she was ordered, wincing as he dabbed at the grazes in her hands with his handkerchief.

"They're just minor. We'll wash them good when we get back to the ranch," he said, his dark eyes returning to her face.

She glanced down at her hands in a daze. The ragged shreds of her torn blouse flipped outwards at a gentle stir of wind. Instantly her hands raised to hide her breasts, barely covered by her lacy bra. Her gaze lifted hesitantly to his, discomfortingly aware of her reddening face.

"It's nice to see a girl blush." Tony's eyes sparkled as he lightly touched her cheek with his hand. Then his expression changed to a rather lazy regard of her face, as his arms moved into position, one on each side of her.

"Isn't it usual for a damsel in distress to reward

her knight with a kiss?'' he asked huskily. His tanned face moved in closer to hers. ''Or haven't your lips ever touched a man's before?''

As his face lowered towards hers, the ugly picture of another such scene flashed before Coley. Before it had been Carl, now it was Tony, but the feeling of repulsion was the same.

''No!'' she shouted vehemently, squirming out of his grasp.

''I wasn't going to bite you!'' he exclaimed in stunned disbelief.

Instantly Coley was contrite.

''I'm sorry, Tony. I didn't mean to . . . I guess you startled me.'' The words came slowly through the invisible stranglehold of fear and tension around her throat.

''Of course,'' Tony agreed. His stiff expression relaxed slightly. ''We'd better get you home.''

He turned, gathered up the reins and mounted his horse.

''Here,'' he held out his hand to her. ''You can ride up front.''

Clutching the shredded edges of her blouse together as best she could with one hand, Coley placed the other in his. Rather ungracefully she hopped and was pulled on to the horse. Tony's arm encircled her waist, nearly bared by the torn blouse. She tried to quell the feeling of discomfort. After all, it was too far to walk home.

Chapter Six

Coley and Tony had ridden only twenty yards out of the ravine that led to the canyon when Jase appeared leading Coley's horse.

So she *had* seen him on the ridge.

His blue eyes were burning their brightest when they rested on Coley. His face darkened like a thundercloud, his scar a jagged white lightning bolt.

"I see Tony rescued you in one piece—or almost," he added, his glance flickering over Coley's blouse.

"It tore on the rock," she said quickly. A rush of warmth covered her face at his derisive and accusing glance.

"How convenient. Your horse has been trained to stay when the reins hang to the ground. It's called ground-hitching," Jase explained with sarcastic preciseness. "To tie the reins to the saddle horn is an open invitation for the horse to leave."

"Coley, you didn't!" hooted Tony. "Of all the greenhorn ..."

"That's enough!" Jase interrupted sharply.

Coley felt Tony stiffen behind her before slumping sullenly in the saddle.

"Was that pump working?"

"Yeah, it was," Tony snapped. "What were you doing? Riding over to check up on me?"

"Did you oil it?" Jase completely ignored Tony's question and Tony ignored his. "I said, did you oil it?" he repeated in a darkly ominous voice.

"No."

"Then go and do it. Coley, get down from there and put this on," he ordered, reaching behind his saddle to untie his ever-present rain slicker.

"You go and check on it!" Tony fumed. "I'm taking Coley back to the ranch."

"You'll do as you're told," Jase stated unequivocally.

Coley slid from the saddle and gratefully took the slicker from Jase's outstretched hand.

"You don't give all the orders around here," Tony sneered.

"But I gave this one!" Tony sat in the saddle, shaking with anger before digging the spurs into his horse and spinning him back in the direction of the canyon. Turning his head over his shoulder, he glared at Jase.

"My day will come," he said darkly.

"You and I both know what would happen to this ranch if it ever did. You'd sell it to the first bidder. That's why I'll never let it happen," Jase replied sharply. With a sharp crack of the reins on his horse's rump, Tony bounded away. Jase turned slowly to Coley, nearly drowning in the oversized rain slicker. She couldn't meet his gaze squarely, so she shuffled over to her horse.

"Do you need help getting on?" he asked flatly.

"I can manage," she replied, trying vainly to push back the sleeves so she could mount.

He set his horse off the minute she was in the saddle. His horse was naturally faster gaited than her roan, so the entire ride to the ranch yard was made with Coley trailing behind. The whole way, Coley kept thinking all she had to do was say, "Jase, why didn't you come down the hill to help me?" The words were so simple, why wouldn't they come out? But she knew the answer to that. Tony had implied very clearly that Jase had had cold feet on one other occasion. As much as she wished otherwise, Coley couldn't forget that. At the corral, she pulled her mount to a stop beside his blood bay.

"I'll have one of the boys take care of your horse. You go on up to the house and have Maggie take a look at your hands," Jase ordered before reining his horse towards the stables.

Coley watched him glumly before swinging out of the saddle on to the ground. She flipped the reins over the corral fence with a quick half-hitch, then hurried to the house. No one was in the hallway when she entered, so she went immediately upstairs. She rolled the raincoat up and buried her torn blouse in the wastebasket, replacing it with a fresh one. She didn't feel like going into the details of what had happened. Ashamed of her thoughts against Jase and unwilling to have them spread before anyone else, she chose to make as little of the incident as possible.

On her way downstairs she left the raincoat in Jase's room. It would save having to face him in private.

* * *

The following day Coley was walking Misty around the corral when Jase rode up. She was so deep in thought over yesterday's happenings that she didn't notice him at first.

"How are your hands?" he asked, leaning an arm on his saddle horn while studying her intently.

"They're okay," Coley replied as she glanced down at them absently. Her heart seemed to be pounding in her throat.

"Come on. We're going for a ride," Jase ordered. He bent down and swung open the corral gate. Coley trotted her roan over to his side and followed meekly, though apprehensively, as he led the way through the ranch yard into the pastures. She saw him glance at her curiously with a slightly bitter smile before he urged his horse into a canter.

Thank heaven she didn't have to talk to him yet. She didn't know what to say and she never was any good at talking about trivial things.

Gradually the landscape began to grow more and more familiar. With a mounting breathlessness and tension, Coley realized he was taking her back to the canyon. Sooner than she wanted, the ravine entrance appeared before them. But instead of heading towards it, Jase veered to the left. She glanced at him nervously, longing to ask where he was taking her, yet dreading to break the tense silence. In the next instant they were climbing the incline of the outer canyon wall, Coley following behind his ramrod-straight back.

At the top he reined his horse in and dismounted, indicating with a gesture that she should do the same. She complied reluctantly. She stood motionless as Jase led his horse across the crest to the inner canyon side. She watched him stop before glancing back at her. With a sigh she walked forward. As she drew even with him, her eyes never leaving his still figure, he called out sharply, "That's far enough!"

Coley stopped with a jerk, staring first ahead of her, then down. She felt the blood rush from her face. In front of her were the tops of the trees that lined this side of the canyon floor. But just two steps away was a sheer drop of over fifty feet. Then Jase was taking her arm and leading her away from the edge. Calmly he sat her down on the grassy crest, settling down himself two feet away.

Coley swallowed hard. She should say something. He had obviously known that she had wondered why he hadn't come down yesterday to help her. Despite Tony's implication that Jase was a coward, Coley hadn't accepted that, but she hadn't been able to come up with a logical explanation of why Jase didn't rescue her. Now she knew. He had fifty feet of reasons.

"I know I cleared up one question, but what else is bothering you?" Jase asked harshly. His blue eyes rested on her face, searching it relentlessly.

"Nothing," she replied, none too positively.

"Something happened when I was in San Antone, didn't it?" he went on.

Coley plucked a blade of grass nervously and twirled it in her fingers. She could feel his determination and she hesitated telling him the reason for her quietness.

"Coley." His voice was low and threatening.

"Tony took me into town last Saturday," she said finally, glancing at him briefly out of the corner of her eye.

"And?"

"And—" Coley paused. "And he told me how Rick died." She flinched as she saw Jason's dark head jerk back as if he'd been stuck.

"I see," he murmured as he leaned back on one elbow and stared at her with his diamond-sharp gaze.

"I asked him," she asserted. An anger grew within her at his withdrawal. "I'm grown up. Things don't have to be hidden from me as if I were a child."

"If you were grown up, Coley, you wouldn't have to keep reminding people." Jase smiled cynically. "Now that you know, what good has it done you?"

Coley shrugged.

"I don't know," she said finally, "but I do know that you couldn't be a coward any more than you could be a murderer."

"Coley, for God's sake, stop it!" Jase exclaimed angrily. "I'm not some knight in tarnished armor who needs a maiden to defend him!"

"You're not trying to make me believe that you could have saved Rick and didn't, are you?" Coley exclaimed. Painfully hurt by his anger, she jumped to her feet. "Because if you are, I'm not going to believe you! I know you're not like that!"

He rose and stood silently behind her. "Coley." He watched as her slender shoulders shook with her silent sobs. His hands reached forward and drew her into his arms until his chin rested on her sun-streaked curls. "It's true that I want this ranch more than anything in this world."

With a heartrending sob, she wrenched herself free of his arms and ran to her horse. She was in the saddle and jerking the roan's head around when Jase caught hold of the bridle. She stared down at him, unashamed of the tears that were streaming down her cheeks.

"I told you you'd only be hurt," Jase said quietly. His rugged features were set in a hard line and his eyes were bitter.

"Jason Savage, if you really believed all those things you said about yourself, you wouldn't be here now," Coley said through clenched teeth. "And if you really want this ranch as much as you say you do, then you wouldn't care whose feet you'd have to kiss to get it—or what you'd have to do to prove you didn't let your brother die. But you haven't done either one. So I think you're just too proud. Too proud to go to your grandfather and tell him how you grieve for your brother and how you wish you could have got there sooner, and . . . and . . ."

She couldn't finish. She burst out crying and ended by jerking the roan out of his grasp. Viciously Coley put a heel to the horse's flank and raced down the hill, seeing nothing except the tears in front of her eyes.

She was in the ranch yard unsaddling her horse when Jase finally trotted his horse in. He reined in beside her and watched silently as she fumbled with the cinch in a desperate attempt to ignore him.

"Well?" she finally said in exasperation, staring at him boldly.

"I was wondering if the thorns were still on my long-stemmed rose." His eyes gleamed down at her, bright and questioning.

"How poetic. Yes, they are," Coley replied

angrily, pulling the heavy western saddle off the roan and dropping it on the ground.

"You can go ahead and ride alone from now on, as long as you stay within sight of the ranch and don't go near the pens." He didn't need to spell out which pens; Coley knew he meant the Brahmas.

Only after he had turned his bay around and headed back out to the pastures did Coley stop to stare wistfully after him. At the dinner table that evening Jase and Ben began bickering about the advisability of moving a herd of stock cattle out of the south section. Jase felt they should wait and Ben said he wanted it done now. Of late, these dinner-table discussions had become heated as both were stubbornly against giving in to each other. Coley listened to the exchange quite indifferently until Jase happened to glance her way. He stopped almost in midsentence as he studied her smug I-told-you-so expression before flashing her an amused and intimate smile. Coley tingled under its bewitching warmth.

"Ben," Jase turned his smile to the gray-haired man at the head of the table, "if you think I should move them, I will. Would you pass me some more of Maggie's bread?"

His sudden acquiescence startled Ben, but did not mollify him in the slightest. He turned his scowling face towards Coley, who quickly lowered her gaze to her plate so that he wouldn't see the bubbly brightness on her face. Instead she quickly started a nonsensical conversation with her brother over an imaginary difficulty in bridling her horse. The meal ended with Coley in giggles over some of the ludicrous suggestions posed by Danny and Tony.

Uncle Ben refused to join them on the porch,

insisting that he had things to do in his study. Coley couldn't help thinking that he was doing some childish sulking. She joined Jase on the cushioned porch swing and listened to Danny as he used his persuasive tactics on Tony to help him work on his car's transmission. In the end Tony gave in, reluctantly, and followed Danny out into the yard, but not with the same amount of enthusiasm that Danny had. Coley leaned back on the swing and gazed at the crimson-kissed clouds of the sunset while listening to Jase talk to Aunt Willy about her very favorite subject, her roses.

"I was just mentioning to Colleen the other day that as soon as my tea roses bloom we should have a garden party," Aunt Willy chattered, only to be interrupted by the distant shrill of the telephone in the house. "My goodness, I wonder who that could be. Oh, I should have bought a cordless phone."

Coley watched with an amused smile as her aunt rose quickly from her chair, unceremoniously tugging at her creeping skirt before dashing into the house after the persistent ring. At the strike of a match beside her, Coley turned her head to watch him light his familiar cheroot. A black eyebrow raised inquiringly at her. For a minute Coley studied him, admiring the strong, rugged angles of his face, the arrogant boldness of his nose, the soft yet cynical curl of his lips, the smooth, tanned forehead and the arching brows over his brilliant ice-blue eyes. The scar across his cheek seemed natural, a part of him, no longer frightening and ugly. Then the smoke from his cigar drifted between them, blurring her vision, and she turned again towards the sunset.

"What pearl of wisdom are you thinking of

now?" he mocked lightly. "Or did you run out of them this afternoon?"

"I was right, you know," Coley replied, tilting her button nose upwards ever so slightly at his words. "It takes two to make an argument. You proved that tonight at the table."

"It wasn't really an argument, more like a difference of opinion," Jase answered.

"It was rather a loud difference, then," Coley said, accenting the word loud with a trace of censure, which earned her a quiet laugh from Jase.

"And you feel I did the right thing, agreeing to his decision?" he asked.

"Yes, I do. It's time you two stopped lashing out at each other, trying to draw first blood. He's an old man, Jase," Coley said earnestly. "And he's crippled. He should be pitied and comforted, not quarrelled with."

"He's a Savage," retorted Jase angrily, "and no Savage needs pity."

"All right, compassion then," Coley said quickly, feeling a little flare of temper herself. "As much as you love this ranch, you of all people should understand how frustrating it must be to be confined to a wheelchair and not be able to get out and see what's going on. I believe you and your grandfather are equally devoted to this land."

"The Slash S is Savage Land," Jase declared, rising abruptly to his feet to lean against the porch railing and stare out over the darkening land. "And as long as there's a Savage alive, I'll never stand by and watch it go to anyone else. I'll do anything to stop it."

The passionate outburst brought Coley to her feet, moving her towards the straight back and broad shoulders of the man at the rail. She stood silently beside him and laid a hand on the tanned arm that was gripping the wooden rail tensely. At her touch he turned and looked down at her.

"Do you really believe that Ben doesn't feel the same way about this land?" Coley asked. Her eyes were wide and anxious as she gazed up into his stern face.

Slowly he turned and placed his hands lightly on her shoulders. A softness returned to him as he looked at her.

"Coley, however right you may be," his voice was low and husky, "you can't wipe away years of suspicion and distrust with a few words. There are some wounds that take more than a kiss to make them better. They take time. So don't push us too fast." Very lightly he turned her around and gently pushed her towards the steps leading down on to the lawn. "Now, run along and find out what your brother and Tony are doing."

Reluctantly Coley stepped off the veranda, gazing back at Jase wistfully. He had lit another cigar and was watching the gray smoke drift lazily in the night air. She turned her head and directed her unwilling feet away from the porch and Jase. She felt no elation or triumph, just a curious sense of suffering, as if she had taken over part of his burden. But why was her heart beating so loudly and why she was trembling too? Why?

With an impatient hand, Coley wiped away the sweat on her forehead as she fed the last of an apple to her horse. The hot Texas sun had sapped the enjoyment out of her late afternoon ride, ending it much sooner than usual. Lethargically she patted the roan's head and moved away, her boots scuffing at the scorched ground as she walked.

She sighed dejectedly as she glanced around the yard. She had thought Jase would be back by now. He had left the morning after their talk on the porch to move the cattle out of the south section. Everything seemed so purposeless without him around, and in this heat, there wasn't anything to do. Briefly Coley considered taking a short swim in the pool, but rejected it just as quickly. It would take more energy to change than she possessed right now. She didn't feel like going up to the house; she was too restless to sit around. So she just maintained her aimless, wandering pace.

Her fingers trailed lazily on the top rail of the fence as she meandered around the corrals glancing disinterestedly at their occupants. In front of her were the reinforced fences marking the Brahma cattle enclosures. A little spark of curiosity directed her footsteps towards the pens and the heavy plank boards that hid them from her view. She stood on tiptoe to try to peer over the slats, but the fence was too tall. Putting her feet on the bottom slat, Coley hoisted herself up to rest her elbows on the top board.

The lone inhabitant was at the far end of the pen, but at the sound of Coley climbing on to the fence he had turned to face her. The heat waves shimmered eerily between them as the sun cast a ghostly sheen on his hide. The enormous size of the animal glued Coley to the fence, the grotesque hump on his shoulders and the loose, pendulous skin under his throat fascinating her into immobility. He took a step forward, then halted to stare at her. His large ears drooped alongside his large head, accenting the menacing curve of his demonic horns. But it was his eyes that held her, small and dark and not at all like the warm brown eyes she had always associated with cattle. No, these eyes were haughty and malevolent with an arrogantly sinister gleam. Coley felt a shiver crawl up her spine as comprehension dawned.

This was Satan! The bull that had killed Rick and scarred Jason! The color drained from her face as she stared at the bull with mounting fear. A nightmarish feeling washed over her, followed by a desire to flee while her legs remained fixed on the bottom rail. Her mouth was dry as she watched the Brahma lower his head and make one incisive furrow in the sunscorched earth with his large front hoof. She was too frightened to call out or to move. With an ever-growing terror she watched the signaling hoof ripping the earth in mounting fury.

Was this how Jase had felt? This terror that paralyzed the mind and body? Had he been able to swallow? Had Satan's strange magnetism frozen him until the horror of Rick's screams broke the trance?

Her fingers tightened their hold on the fence, her knuckles growing white with the fierceness of their grip. Coley's breath came in short, panting sobs as her eyes watched with horror the beginning movements of the bull's charge. In the next instant she was ripped from the fence, the piercing scream of agonizing fear at last torn from her throat. Her head was pushed against a solid chest wearing a dusty cotton shirt. The familiar scent of cigar smoke clinging to the fabric broke the hysterical cries. The rigid terror that had held her captive was gone and Coley collapsed in Jason's arms. She was safe. He had rescued her and the sobs of relief felt wonderful.

The circle of his arms nearly crushed her as he held her ever tighter to him, but Coley didn't care.

His own face was pressed against the top of her head and though he was speaking it was too muffled to understand. And then she was being slowly disentangled from his arms as Jase held her away from him. Her long fingers remained resting on his chest as she looked up into his face. It was as drained of color as hers had been and there was no mask to hide the slowly receding anxiety in his eyes.

"I was so frightened I couldn't move," Coley whispered as she leaned slightly towards him, wanting only to return to the shelter of his arms.

"You should have been," Jase replied huskily, giving her shoulders a sharp shake. "You were told to stay away from here."

Coley looked into his face now, her lips forming the words of explanation, but the icy-cold anger in his eyes smothered the words. He had withdrawn from her, back behind his mask.

"Jase, please, don't shut me out," she pleaded softly, blinking quickly to hold back the tears.

It was as if he hadn't even heard her speak. "I don't want to see you anywhere near these pens again," he said coldly, releasing her shoulders to stand towering above her. "There's an invisible line that runs from the house to the stables and don't let me ever find you off that path. If I do, you can consider anything outside of the house yard off limits. Do you understand?"

"Yes," Coley answered weakly. Her round eyes glanced away from the ice-blue hardness of his gaze. Just for a moment she thought he had softened towards her and she added, "I'm glad you're back."

"Go up to the house," Jase ordered sharply, and her shoulders sagged under the harshness of his tone. Slowly she turned and took a few steps in the direction of the house. She hesitated and then looked over her shoulder, trembling under the censure in his expression.

"That was Satan, wasn't it?" she said quietly. An almost imperceptible nod answered her, although Jase didn't utter a word. He just eyed her coldly and turned away towards the pens.

It was a long walk to the house and though the distance shortened with each step, Coley felt each step she took was widening the distance between her and Jase. She spent a miserable evening in the house despite Danny and Tony's attempts to cheer her up. Later Danny came to her room, but she couldn't bring herself to confide in him. Somehow the simple incident seemed so complicated that she didn't know how to explain it to him without him scoffing at her overactive imagination, so she said nothing.

The next three days were equally miserable as Coley made the picket fence around the house her prison walls. She had no wish to incur Jason's wrath following that imaginary line to the stables. She tried to busy herself helping Aunt Willy in her rose garden and when that failed, she would exhaust herself in the pool. But after sitting through the evening meal while Jase repeatedly ignored her and for the fourth time in a row excused himself from the table as soon as everyone was through to go heaven knew where, Coley felt she had reached the end of her tether. A restless despair consumed her as she sat on the porch with her Aunt Willy and Uncle Ben. From deep within the hills came the echoing rumbles of a distant storm, with faraway flashes of lightning.

"Looks like we'll have a summer storm on us before morning," Aunt Willy said. "I certainly hope it won't be too severe. The last one played havoc with my garden. You seem very upset tonight, Colleen dear. Is anything wrong?''

"No, Aunt Willy," she answered quickly. "I was just thinking maybe I'd go up to my room, take a quiet bath and get an early night. My nerves are a little on edge—from the storm, I suppose.''

Coley was grateful that her aunt accepted the explanation and she sped up the steps and into her room before any more questions were asked that she couldn't answer. The bath did little to soothe her. In fact the stifling humidity of the coming storm made Coley wish she had showered instead of soaking in a tub of scented bubbles and hot water. Pulling the covers to the foot of her bed, she laid her robe on a chair before leaning back on the sticky sheets to stare at the ceiling.

A blinding flash of light followed immediately by an explosion of thunder wakened Coley from her fitful sleep. Her heart was beating at a frantic pace as she sat up in the bed and waited in fear for the last echo of the thunder to roll away. Another bolt of lightning flashed outside her window and she quickly covered her ears with her hands and squinched her eyes shut until the next roll of thunder passed.

In the brief lull that followed she hopped from her bed, grabbing her robe as she went by the chair and out of her bedroom door. The darkness of the hallway stopped her as she fumbled for the light switch. Then her fingers stopped their search; she didn't want to waken the others. She groped in the darkness for the stair banister while the intermittent lightning eerily illuminated the interior of the darkened house.

Silently Coley inched down the stairway, flinching at each reverberating roll of thunder. Downstairs at last, she tiptoed through the hall, one hand trailing to rest at her throat where it could immediately reach her mouth and stifle any cry she might make that would awaken the rest of the house. The ominous darkness of the rooms beckoned her only to stop her with the sudden, blinding glare of lightning. The rain had just begun, its rapid pitter-pat echoing the swift tempo of her pulse. Behind her, the grandfather clock chimed the first hour, frightening her with its unexpectedness. She stumbled against the little table in the hallway and valiantly chased after the rocking vase of flowers all the way to the floor where it smashed with unnatural loudness in the silence.

"Who's there?" came a booming voice from an adjacent room. "Willy? Is that you?" The soft whir of turning wheels reached Coley, just before the beam of a flashlight. With a little smile of relief, she swallowed her fear before turning with trembling legs towards her uncle.

"It's me, Uncle Ben," she whispered softly, her voice still in tune with her shaking legs. "I knocked over the vase."

Obligingly, he shone the light down on to the scattered fragments as she swiftly gathered them up.

"What are you doing up?" he asked gruffly behind the glare of the flashlight.

"The storm woke me," Coley replied, placing the broken pieces in the wastebasket.

"Frightened, huh?" Ben snorted, wheeling his chair around, leaving her in blackness. An ominous clap of thunder sent her scurrying after him.

"Couldn't sleep myself." Inside his den, the gray-haired man steered his chair over to the curtains and closed them, shutting out the storm. Then wheeling his chair over to the desk, he laid the flashlight down and lit two candles.

"Electricity's out," he explained, glancing briefly at Coley's white face before maneuvering his wheelchair behind the desk. "Sit down, girl. Might as well relax and talk to me until this storm blows over."

She sat down in one of the larger cushioned chairs, although she couldn't relax, not with thunder still echoing outside. The flickering candlelight cast a softening glow on the leathery face across from her.

"My wife, rest her soul, used to pace from window to window every time there was a storm," Ben mused, gazing into the flame of the candle. In the wavering light, Coley saw the twinkle in his blue eyes as he glanced over at her. "So I guess you could say I have a knack for soothing frightened women during a storm."

"You miss her," Coley said, smiling back at him.

"Yes," Ben sighed. "She's been gone for—well, ten years now. Just shortly after our only child, our son, and his wife were killed in an auto crash, she died." A glimmer of pain flickered briefly on his face. "Willy's husband had passed on the year before, so she moved in with me. And the place hasn't been the same since. "It's strange how a bad storm can bring back good memories," he went on absently, his voice a little husky and nostalgic. He opened a drawer of the desk and took out a gilt-edged frame. He touched the face of it fondly before handing it over to Coley. "My wife," he said in explanation. His tone was almost reverent as he spoke. "That was taken a few months before she died."

It was a family portrait, with the woman seated in

the center smiling sadly out at Coley. The slender, faintly lined neck was holding erect a proud white head, but the suffering expression in her eyes reached out to Coley as if to explain that the will to live was gone. The woman's delicate hand was gripping her husband's tightly, a more robust Ben Savage than was seated before Coley now. His hair was quite dark in the picture and there weren't as many lines on his tanned face. Then Coley was drawn to the two men standing on either aide of the couple. One she easily recognized as Jase, his blue eyes warmly looking out at her. Naturally he looked much younger and the scar wasn't there, just the rugged good looks accented by the confident tilt of his head.

And the last person in the picture was Rick, his boyish, laughing face barely concealing the mischievous gleam in his eye. Coley recognized the resemblance to Jase, but Rick's face was softer and not just because of a lack of maturity. No, it was the openness, the love-of-life expression that separated them. Yes, Coley could see how everyone would be drawn to Rick. Reluctantly she handed the picture back to Ben, wishing she could study it a little longer.

Ben cradled it gently in his gnarled hands as he gazed at it fondly. His forehead furrowed slightly before he put it down on the desk.

"Tragedies always come in threes," he said softly, staring down at the picture. "I lost my grandson just five years ago."

"I know," Coley murmured. Ben glanced up at her sharply, his mind no longer drifting in memories but centered entirely on her. She squirmed uncomfortably under his gaze. "Tony told me."

"And Jase," Ben sneered, "what did he tell you?"

"He . . . he . . . told me to . . . to stay out of it," Coley stammered as her hands nervously twirled the tie of her robe.

"That's all?" Ben asked, and snorted when Coley nodded.

"But Uncle Ben, it was an accident. I'm sure it was an accident," she hurried, her words spilling over themselves in the urgency of speaking before Ben did.

"You two have been together an awful lot lately," Ben said with hawklike sharpness, inspecting the reddening of her cheeks.

"You aren't—"

"Of course not," Coley interrupted, not wanting to hear how he might have ended the sentence. "It's just that—well, I saw Satan the other day." She leaned forward earnestly. "And I was scared. I was so scared I couldn't move, I couldn't run, I couldn't scream. I couldn't do anything. Then Jase pulled me off the fence just before the bull charged." The old man's eyes flickered ominously. "So you see, Jase saved me."

"But how long did he stand there just as terrified as you? And what part did Jase play in those scratches on your hands a few days ago?" Ben asked astutely, and Coley paled at his words. Then, with an almost physical shake of his head, he seemed to throw off her words. "The storm's died down. You'd better go up to bed." As she opened her mouth to speak again, Ben raised his hand and she saw the weakness and tiredness etched vividly on his face. "And take that advice he gave you—stay out of it. I'm too old a dog to be learning new tricks and he's like the leopard that can't change its spots. Go to bed." Glumly, feeling she had some-how failed both Uncle Ben and Jase as well as herself, Coley accepted the flashlight and followed the beam out the door and into the hallway. She tiptoed up the stairs, grimacing at each betraying creak of the steps. She was almost to her room when she heard a door open beside her. She flashed the light on to Jason's face.

"What are you doing?" he asked.

"The electricity's out," Coley whispered as he reached out and directed the light out of his eyes.

"I know that," he answered softly. "I meant what were you doing up?"

"The storm woke me."

"I wondered if you would sleep through it," said Jase, the reaching circle of the flashlight beam outlining his faint smile. "Where have you been?"

"Downstairs," Coley replied hesitantly. "Uncle Ben was up, too, so I've been talking to him. Do you think the storm's over for the night?"

She asked the question quickly to stop the mask from stealing over his face, and succeeded. He said he thought it was. He took the flashlight from her hand and led her to her door. For the first time, Coley noticed he only had on a pair of jeans and she had to pass that broad expanse of bare chest to get to her room. Her heart beat wildly as she stared at the curly black cloud of hair on his chest and wondered absently what it would feel like to touch it. Then his arm was around her shoulders and pushing her into her room. As she turned back to him, he placed the flashlight in her hand, turning the light off as he did so.

"Good night, Coley," he said firmly, and closed the door, shutting her in and himself out.

Chapter Seven

Coley lightly trailed her finger along the outer edge of a burgundy red rose, reveling in the velvety softness of its petals. She swatted absently at a buzzing insect harassing the bare legs beneath her shorts. Glancing briefly down, she was reminded of Jason's comment that she was a "long-stemmed rose." That seemed such a long time ago. Now he treated her with a brotherly indulgence and indifference. Not even brotherly, really—he never got that personal. All in all, she sighed deeply, since the night of the storm almost a week ago, their relationship, if that was what it could be called, had reached an impasse.

It was frustrating, she thought, positively frustrating. In the past when they were together, although it hadn't been altogether satisfactory, at least he had been interested in her. Now he seemed to have patted her on the head and said run along, like a good little girl. Like a child, Coley thought angrily, taking out her temper on the rose stem and getting pricked in the process by one of the thorns. At her unwitting yelp of pain, Aunt Willy turned just as Coley put her finger to her mouth to soothe the pain.

"Coley, I told you to be careful of those thorns," Aunt Willy remonstrated lightly.

The silver-haired woman dabbed her face daintily with an embroidered handkerchief, bumping her broad straw hat askew as she did so.

"I'm so glad we have those big oaks to shade my roses from the afternoon sun. They'd just shrivel and dry up without them in this heat." Aunt Willy took the roses from Coley's arms and put them in her basket before walking on to another group of bushes. "It's so difficult to grow roses in the Southwest because of the intensity of the sun—did you know that, Colleen?" Without waiting for her to answer, Aunt Willy went on, enthralled by her very favorite subject. "But if you really want to see roses, my dear, I mean thousands and thousands of roses, you must go to Tyler, Texas. More than half of this nation's field-grown roses are produced there. Most people think of oil and oil wells when you mention Tyler, but they've been growing roses commercially there since the eighteen-seventies. It's a standing joke that if there's oil underneath a rosebush, the rose stays. I'm sure that's a bit of an exaggeration, but we Texans are prone to exaggerate." Aunt Willy laughed her tinkly laugh, but Coley knew that Aunt Willy was serious about flowers. "They have over five hundred different varieties. And all colors, from the whitest white to reds so dark that you wouldn't be able to spot them if they were floating in a pool of oil. George took me there several times in October when they have their festival. You really must go there some time and walk through Tyler Park downtown," Aunt

Willy urged with a wave of her pruners. "It's an experience you'll never forget." Coley nodded absently, not able to mount much enthusiasm for the thought. She was too wrapped up in her dilemma over Jase to get excited about roses. That dumb Savage pride ruined everything, she thought.

"You're awfully quiet. Is there anything wrong?" Aunt Willy asked as she took her gaze off her beloved roses long enough to see the disgruntled expression on Coley's face.

"Oh, it's this ridiculous feud between Jase and Uncle Ben," Coley grumbled.

"It isn't ridiculous, honey," Aunt Willy replied, her eyebrows raised at the unexpected subject. "There's more to it than that."

"I know what it's about," Coley answered a little sharply. "But Jase is Uncle Ben's grandson. He can't really believe that Jase would let his own brother die."

"Fear does strange things, Colleen. In some people, their adrenaline surges to such a point that they're capable of doing things beyond the range of their normal strength. Others are turned to stone. In one case we applaud and in the other, we condemn," Aunt Willy observed, picking up her pruners to give her attention to a rosy pink bloom.

"I can't believe Jase is a coward any more than I can believe he's a murderer," Coley retorted, disheartened by the depressing wisdom of her aunt's words.

"No one can really judge your inner self but God, Colleen," Aunt Willy said quietly, holding the now clipped bloom in her gloved hand. "Only outward, visible acts can be judged by man, and Rick's death was ruled accidental."

"Then why must Uncle Ben go on punishing Jase as if he'd done it with his own hand?" Coley cried.

"You mustn't get so worked up over this," Aunt Willy began.

"But how can I not when two people I've grown to love are—" Coley stopped, her cheeks flushed at her words and the scrutiny in her aunt's eyes.

"Listen, child, you shouldn't get too involved with Jase . . ."

"I am not a child," Coley muttered angrily. Staring at her aunt with almost unnatural boldness, she added. "I'm nineteen and I'll be twenty soon."

Aunt Willy fell silent at her words, busying herself momentarily with her roses as if contemplating Coley's statement. Coley stood beside her, quietly wishing her anger had not made her words so sharp. She had no wish to offend her aunt. She was just tired of everyone putting her down. If only she was good at something, instead of basically useless.

"What we really should do, Colleen," said Aunt Willy, breaking into Coley's thoughts, "is have that party I've been talking about. You can meet some young people, get involved with some of their activities." *So I won't have time to brood about Jase,* Coley thought to herself, and was instantly sorry for the injustice of it. Poor Aunt Willy was only trying to cheer her up and even though she couldn't summon up much enthusiasm, Coley at least managed to agree cheerfully enough so that her aunt was convinced it was a good idea.

Coley had to admit, gazing at her reflection in the mirror, that when her aunt made a decision she carried it through. The very afternoon she had mentioned the party to Coley, Aunt Willy had begun calling the various families in the area and within two days had a long list of acceptances for her spur-of-the-moment party.

Coley never realized her aunt could be so organized, because in the next two days she supervised not only the preparation of salads and desserts by Maggie, but also the placing of picnic tables and lights and all sorts of decorations around the sundeck by Danny and Tony. At the same time she scurried into town to pick out the accessories that she felt Coley needed to go with her new party dress. And with all that, the household never once seemed disrupted, a concession that Coley felt was for Uncle Ben. And now the evening was here. Coley's hair was freshly styled by the salon and her yellow gown was just as beautiful as she remembered.

The first car of arriving guests had slammed its doors just minutes earlier. Although she had hoped that Danny was still upstairs so that she could go down with him, Coley had no real anxiety at meeting so many strangers. A few months ago she would have been quaking at the thought. Still, she wasn't altogether excited about the party. It just didn't seem to matter somehow. As she smiled lightly at her reflection before leaving the room, her heart made one last wish that Jase would attend the party and not join in with Uncle Ben's declaration that he was going to shut himself in his room. Perhaps tonight, in this dress, Jase would see her as a woman. . . .

"There you are, Colleen dear," Aunt Willy trilled as Coley walked down the brick path towards the sundeck. "My, you do look lovely tonight. Ethel, this is my niece, my great-niece actually, but let's not discuss ages now." Aunt Willy laughed lightly as she drew Coley by the arm into the circle of people gathered around her. "This is Ethel Merrick, one of my dearest friends, her husband Bob, and her two girls, Rachel and Roberta."

Coley nodded pleasantly to the warm, sun-weathered faces of the couple and smiled at the two dark-haired girls, one a little older than herself and the other a little younger. But the long whirl of introductions had just begun, as more and more people began arriving and her mind began swimming with strange faces and names. There were the Hamiltons with a boy named Howard and a girl named Brenda; and the Rasmussens with five children, John, Joe, Janet, Judd and Jean; the Petersons; the Simpsons; the Johnsons; the Masons; and then she stopped trying to remember. There was just too many.

Gradually, as fewer and fewer people arrived, the separation into age groups began, slowly at first and then naturally until the families automatically split up as they arrived. Thanks to Danny and Tony, Coley found herself drawn into the circle of young adults and was soon laughing and talking with the rest of them. She was proud of the way Danny fitted in, as easily as he had made a place for himself on the ranch. One dark-haired girl that Coley couldn't remember being introduced to stared at her openly, which Coley thought in passing was rather rude, but she was too caught up in the happy crowd to wonder about it.

The dinner bell rang out wildly amidst the deafening chatter of voices, followed by the familiar "Come and get it!" which triggered mass confusion.

"I'll get your plate," Tony said, touching Coley's arm lightly as he turned to leave.

"No, you won't, I will." A blond boy who had been sitting across from Coley spoke up. She quickly tried to put a name with the face—Rex, Peter? No, that wasn't it.

"Hey, come on, Steve," another boy cried. Steve, that was it, Coley thought. "You're always grabbing the new girls. I'll get it!"

That was one of the Rasmussen boys, Coley thought with a gleam of satisfaction.

"You were getting my plate, remember, John Rasmussen?" a lively auburn-haired girl put in.

"Of course," John replied, a little disgruntled and red-faced. "But I can carry both of them."

"And three plates for yourself as well?" the girl retorted wickedly.

Coley laughed with the others and John joined in, but very faintly. The three walked off towards the long table of food, still arguing over who was going to bring back Coley's plate.

Coley turned to the auburn-haired girl and smiled ruefully. "They'll probably still be arguing on the way back and none of them will have my plate."

"I doubt that," the girl laughed. "There's too many willing hands around to take their place. Just you stay away from John. I try very hard to make everyone believe he's wearing my brand."

"I hope I didn't do anything that—" Coley began, rather embarrassed.

"Of course not. All the guys are interested in anyone new that comes this way," the girl replied with a bright smile, "Especially the ones that look as great as you do. By the way, my name's Jill Saunders."

"Mine's Coley—to my friends," Coley replied, accepting the freckled hand that reached out for hers.

"Freckles, the curse of red hair," the girl named Jill grumbled.

"But it makes me different from most of you golden girls."

At that moment the dark-haired girl who had earlier eyed Coley so oddly walked by again. She glanced at the two girls coldly. Unable to conceal her curiosity, Coley asked, "Who is that?"

"That's Tanya Ford. I can't exactly figure out what she's doing here. There isn't really anyone here her age, except . . . but there I go again, letting my catty tongue run away with me," Jill said, shrugging lightly, but Coley noticed the hint of red in the girl's cheeks. As she saw the questioning look in Coley's eyes, she added reluctantly, "You probably don't know it, but she dated Jason quite regularly before the accident. At least that's the way the gossip goes. I heard she dropped him when the scandal started, but I really don't know. It was before my time. Oh, here come the boys. Looks like Steve won out. Come and sit with us, Coley," Jill invited as the two boys minus Tony walked up to them, their arms laden with plates and drinks.

Coley nodded agreement. She even managed to smile and laugh as they walked towards the tables, but her mind was racing back to finish one of Jill's earlier sentences. *There isn't anyone here her age except Jase.* And she used to date him . . . maybe she wanted to again. For some reason, Coley's heart sank at the thought. She was glad for the food, because as long as they were eating she didn't have to talk. Of course, the food stuck in her throat a little as it went down, but it was better than trying to hide the tremor she felt sure her voice would hold.

She began searching the faces at the various tables. Now she almost hoped that Jase hadn't come. Then she saw him, seated just a couple of tables from them. He was frowning and it looked as if it was at her. The next moment he was nodding and smiling as if he had just seen her. A warm glow flooded over Coley as she smiled in return before turning back to her own little group.

Shortly after everyone finished eating, the young group began massing together again. Coley noted that her brother had attached himself to a rather quiet girl with long brown hair. She gazed at him so adoringly that Coley immediately admired the girl's taste. There was talk of video games and movies and finally someone suggested dancing. Tony followed up the suggestion by going into the house for a boombox and CDs.

"What do you say we go and freshen up while the boys move the tables?" Jill suggested, already moving towards the house. Several other girls joined them. Coley walked quietly beside Jill, who was busy chatting with her friends. She suddenly felt apart from them, a feeling of aloneness settling in on her. When they reached the house, she excused herself, saying her lipstick was in her room. She tripped lightly up the steps, waving to the girls that she would be right down as they paraded into her aunt's bedroom, which was serving as the ladies' boudoir for the evening. Reaching her room, she quickly touched up her lips with berry gloss before wandering idly over to her window to gaze into the darkening evening shadows at the party below.

A sudden flare of light drew her attention to the

arbor. Jase was there. At first she thought he was alone. Then she saw another figure step out of the shadows. It was too dark to identify the other person, but the voluptuous silhouette very clearly outlined a female figure. Coley knew instinctively that it had to be Tanya Ford. There was a sickening sensation at the pit of her stomach as she watched the woman move seductively closer to Jase.

When his arms moved to close around Tanya, Coley turned swiftly from the window. Her lips trembled as she inhaled with a deep sobbing breath. She couldn't go back to the party, not yet. In a few minutes, the girls downstairs would be looking for her. She couldn't stay here. With a sudden decision, she dashed from her room and down the steps, pausing at the bottom to glance towards Willy's room where laughter and chatter penetrated the walls. She started to hurry by, but was halted by Jason's name being spoken by one of the girls inside.

"I think he's cute. Well, not really cute, I suppose," one girl was saying. "More masculine. He positively oozes male."

"What about his scar?" another exclaimed breathlessly.

"It gives me a primitive thrill," the girl boasted airily.

"Not me," another girl said. "I keep thinking about his brother and how everybody said he killed him. He's always so aloof, looking at you the way he does with those eyes of his. He just freezes me."

"I think it's sexy, and dangerous, too," the first girl replied.

"Shush, girls, Coley will be coming down any minute. She'll hear you," Jill interrupted quickly.

With that Coley hurried out the side door. Evidently Tanya wasn't the only one who found Jase attractive. She skirted the more traveled routes, going towards the silent and unlit patio under the oak trees.

"On your way to a rendezvous already?" Jason's voice mocked her from the shadows. "Of course not." Startled by his sudden appearance, Coley couldn't keep the anger and hurt out of her voice. "At least, not the way you mean." Her heart was beating rapidly now as he joined her under a tree. "I saw you from my window," she added tautly as he failed to speak. "You were over by the arbor then."

"Uh-huh," he agreed. His gaze narrowed on her tense face. "Enjoying your party? It's another first for you, isn't it?"

"Yes. Everyone is so nice. They don't make me feel like a stranger at all," she replied, silently cursing her feelings of jealousy as she forced herself to look into his face.

"I'm glad—for you," said Jase, standing silently before her for a moment before reaching his hand out towards her. "Now Aunt Willy would kill me for this . . . I stole one of her roses."

Coley reached out and felt the velvety softness of rose petals in her hand. She moved it out to where some light filtered through the tree limbs to shine on the rose in her hand. It was a deep yellow rose in full bloom.

"A yellow rose for a yellow rose," he said quietly.

"It's beautiful, Jase," Coley whispered, blinking at the tears that were misting her eyes. She tried to banish the thought that Tanya had probably received an exotic red rose. "Thank you."

"Here," he removed the flower from her trembling hands. "I'll put it on for you."

Gently he pulled the rose's stem through the circle pin that adorned her dress until the bloom rested firmly against her chest. When his task was done, he smiled down at her and moved away as if lost in thought.

"You seemed to be having such a good time that I really didn't think you remembered I was around." His voice was light. "You have a lot of admirers."

"So do you," Coley remarked flippantly, and at the quizzical raise of his eyebrow, she added, "I overheard one of the girls talking about you just before I came out. She really thought you were something."

"Really?" said Jase with a cynical twist to his question.

"Yes, really," Coley said tartly. "Now let me see, how did she put it? Oh, yes, she said you were ultra masculine and gave her a primitive thrill. She said you were dangerously exciting or something like that."

Jase laughed without mirth. "Everyone's bound to be attractive to someone. I'd hate to have you consider me repulsive—I already know you don't," he added quickly before Coley could interrupt. "I believe the dancing's started. You'd better run along." He looked down at the impish grin on her face and smiled ruefully.

"Don't tell me, I know," he said with an amused resignation in his voice. "You can't dance, right?" At the short negative shake of her head, he added, "You want me to teach you. What if I told you I couldn't dance either?"

"Oh, you have to, Jase, otherwise who will teach me?" Coley cried. At his sudden smile, she added, "Besides, I want you to teach me."

The faint melody of a love song came lilting to them through the night air as Coley looked up at him expectantly. Jase moved slightly, the dim light shining on to the troubled expression on his face, highlighting the jagged scar on his cheek.

"You're better off having Tony teach you," he finally said sarcastically.

Coley didn't speak. She just stood there, looking pleadingly up at him.

"Tell me what to do," she begged when it looked as if it was going to turn into a staring contest.

Blithely she put her left hand on his shoulder and stepped close to him. Instinctively his right arm encircled her waist as the left took her other hand. His steps were simple and easy to follow and his hand on her back guided her movements until Coley felt as light as thistledown in his arms. Soon she ceased to concentrate on her feet as she realized with quiet joy that her head could rest quite snugly under his chin.

Gradually there was no gap between them and they moved as one until she finally laid her head against his chest and felt the gentle stirring of his breath on her hair. She no longer listened to the music, if it indeed was still playing. The rapid beating of her heart had long since closed out any melody the wind carried. His cheek brushed her hair as his arm tightened its hold around her waist. His steps came to a stop while Coley swayed ever so slightly in his arms, her head lifting inquiringly up to him.

"I really don't think you need any more lessons," Jase said. His voice was husky but firm as he looked down at her.

Coley wanted to protest when his hands gripped her shoulders to move her away, but the thorns on her rose had caught on his shirt, preventing them from separating without doing damage. Jase swore softly before reaching down to extricate himself, and she took the time to study his bent head bathed in the light filtering through the trees.

His straight black hair shone in the light and his brows were dark furrows above the lashes that rested against the tanned, square lines of his cheek. His jaw was resolute but she noticed a small muscle twitch that marked a loss of control of his emotions. The green flecks in her hazel eyes sparkled brightly as she looked at the soft curve of his lips, so masculine and yet so desirable.

She realized that the flower was no longer stuck to his shirt. His head raised and his mouth opened to speak, but no words came out as he stared down at her face, her eyes now raised to meet his.

Her hands slipped to his chest and then up around his neck as she moved ever nearer, until the initiative was taken from her and Jase was pulling her to him, his head bending to meet hers. Their lips met hesitantly at first, Coley's innocent and yet following her instinct, and his retrained and exploring.

A sensual shiver quaked through her body, releasing a long-held torrent of emotion that soon engulfed her as Jase crushed her trembling frame against his. His kiss was no longer seeking, but taking and consuming. His mouth left hers for a moment, remaining suspended above hers until with a groan, he recaptured it, demandingly and hungrily aroused by her response. Then he was pushing her away from him, his arms trembling but his grip like steel.

Coley looked up at him, her rapture mirrored in her eyes. She loved him. She must have been in love with him all along. That was why she had instinctively trusted him. Why his slightest word could depress or delight her. She loved him.

"Stop it!" His brows constricted momentarily as he looked down at her. Coley remained standing where he had placed her, just out of his arms, the fire he had started still glowing in her eyes. Jase turned away from her pleading expression, struggling for self-control.

"Dammit, Coley!" Jase swore angrily, staring out into the night's darkness.

"Jase, I . . ." she whispered.

"Don't say anything," he interrupted, his voice sharp and bitter. "Just go on back to the party."

"I don't want to."

"You forget, you're not my type." Coley inhaled sharply at his wounding words. Her face twisted briefly with pain before she retorted sharply, "That's right, you like curvy women. All grown up. Like Tanya."

"Yes, like Tanya," he asserted, gazing at her speculatively before the mask slipped into place. "You know how to dance now and do a few other things," he added cynically. "Go on. You don't need to comfort the family's black sheep any more."

"No, I don't suppose there's any reason to hang around here, is there?" Coley agreed bitterly, with the barest hint of pleading hope in the last two words.

"Not unless you're the kind that gets a thrill out of being with someone who's been accused of doing evil deeds. Perhaps you like to dance with danger. Is that it?" Jase asked scathingly. "Tell me about that conversation you overheard tonight. You didn't say what they said about my brother. I don't suppose they mentioned his death at all, did they?'' Coley blanched at his words, but didn't answer. Suddenly her face was caught by his hand and twisted fiercely up towards him. "Did they?''

"Yes, they did,'' she answered. The words were barely audible because of his tight grip. Tears blurred her vision.

"It doesn't matter."

"Ha!'' Jase snorted as he released his hold. "It doesn't matter! You've got to be the most optimistic Pollyanna I've ever met. What do you think would happen if the two of us walked back to that party together?'' When Coley managed to shake her head no, he took a deep breath before continuing, "Well, let me tell you. The first thing that you would notice would be the silence. The second thing would be the eyes, all staring at us, shocked and condemning. Your brother would probably demand to know my intentions and Aunt Willy would draw you aside to tut-tut about getting mixed up with me. If we were lucky, Ben wouldn't see us. Otherwise he'd probably raise out of his wheelchair to beat you personally for being so immoral, and he'd probably file a restraining order forbidding me to set foot on Savage land.''

The dam had burst and the tears were streaming down Coley's face now at the unbearable pain inside caused by the mocking contempt in his voice. Then anger seared through her as she trembled with rage.

Her voice was low but it vibrated loudly with her anger. "That's the only part you'd care about. Savage land!'' Contempt now laced her voice as she fairly spat out the words. "I've never known anyone who could care about a lot of dirt as much as you and your grandfather. You'd kill for this land!''

Jase towered over her, the blue of his eyes freezing her with its intensity. His head was turned at just the right angle for the scar to be the only part of his face illuminated by the light. Coley cringed as the full horror of her words and their unspeakable cruelty dawned on her.

"I didn't mean it, Jase, I swear I di—" she began, but he interrupted.

"You were absolutely right. Good night, Colleen." Finality was so clear in his words that Coley knew he might as well have said "Good-bye."

She stood silent, as immobile as the oak tree beside her, while Jase walked off into the darkness. A dry, hacking grief tore at her, knowing that nothing she could do or say would bring him back to her. There were no words she could call out to him that could erase the wretched words she had uttered.

Finally she picked up the rose that had fallen from her dress. The delicate petals were as torn and bruised as her own heart. He had once compared her with a yellow rose. He had even laughed about her thorns, but what did he think of them now? she wondered as a brief but hysterical laugh escaped her lips before she buried her head in her arms and leaned against the tree to cry. What had she done to him now?

Chapter Eight

A month, a whole month since the party, Coley thought, staring at herself in the mirror. But it was as fresh in her mind as if it were last night. Somehow she had pulled herself together that night and returned to the party. There had been nowhere else to go and her absence would have been too noticeable.

Punishment for her hasty words had begun that night. The festivities and laughing voices had taken on a nightmarish quality as she endured it all in a stupor. None of it had seemed to touch her. She couldn't even summon an objection to Tony's persistent attention. Perhaps because she couldn't take her eyes off Jase and dark-haired Tanya who clung to his arm, never taking her eyes off him either.

And now, a month later, Coley's sadness remained. But her reflection showed that it had taken its toll in the dullness of her eyes, the drawn lines around her mouth and the gradual loss of weight. Her appearance hadn't gone unnoticed.

Aunt Willy clucked over her, trying to find out what was troubling her. Tony had become affronted by her continued lack of response to his attentions. Ben had been the most understanding, filling her days with busy but undemanding tasks. The hours spent with him had been the most rewarding for Coley. She felt in some unmeasurable way she was giving something back to him for the comfort he gave her.

Only Jase ignored the change in her. His subtle revenge was unique. He would ride off in the morning, as if on a day's work, and not return for two or three days. But his reappearance was always coincided with Coley's time with his grandfather, so that she could witness their maliciously cruel word-slinging matches. Only when Jase was absent was there ever a peaceful meal. Their quarrelling and vicious jibes seemed to be the only conversation at the table.

It was as if there was no gentleness left in Jase. His face had turned to stone, the expression never changing, always cynical and mocking. His eyes were like an eagle's, harsh and piercing. Oh, yes, Coley thought, the name Savage suited him very well.

The burden of her guilt weighed heavily on her shoulders as she replaced the hairbrush on her dressing table. At least last night she had shown Jase that he had won. It had been during the evening meal amidst one of their bitter arguments that Coley had finally lost control of her emotions. The heated dispute over some petty thing had driven her to the point where she couldn't take any more. She had dropped her silverware with a clatter and tipped over her chair in her frantic desire to get away. She remembered that she had stopped at the doorway, halted by Aunt Willy's imperious call, to look back at Jase. He had raised a quieting hand to Willy.

"But she didn't even ask to be excused," Aunt Willy had protested.

Jase had given her a reproachful, silencing glance before turning back to Coley. He had stood there, looking arrogantly across the room with narrowed eyes. Then, with head bowed, Coley had raced out the door and up to her room, an ignominious exit but a desperate one.

Funny, when she looked in the mirror now, she didn't expect to see this youthful shell of a young woman looking back at her with haunted eyes. Cupid's arrow had struck so swiftly and left an open wound in her heart. And despite everything, she still loved Jase. There was the cruelty of the whole situation, that those few brief words of anger to the man she now loved could destroy the fire that had flamed shortly between them. Her great hopes of bringing peace to the family had resulted in a full-fledged war. How many more battles were left before the end came? And how could there ever be a victory for either side?

Coley glanced at the clock on her dressing table. It was time for Uncle Ben's morning tea. Lately it had become a ritual for Coley to bring him his tea, a welcome ritual for her because it filled her morning. She had grown to like the dark paneled study, drawing comfort from its stern interior. No longer did she desire to throw wide the curtains and let the sunshine in. She reveled in the gloom just as she once reveled in the light.

There was no need to hurry as she made her way slowly out the room and down the steps. Maggie would have the tray prepared. Nothing was demanded of Coley except to carry it into her uncle's den, occasionally to comment about the weather, and, after an hour or so, return the tray to the kitchen. It was just as well, she thought to herself. Her wounds were too fresh and painful for her mind to dwell on anything but Jase.

She picked up the tray sitting on the kitchen counter, nodded absently to the stern housekeeper and walked quietly towards the den. Entering the room without knocking, she placed the tray on the desk. She poured a cup for herself and Ben before settling herself in the huge leather armchair that cradled her deeper into the gloom.

"If these cattle prices hold, we'll have a real nice profit this year," Ben commented, without taking his gaze from the books he was studying. When Coley failed to reply, his hawklike eyes glanced at her above the steaming cup he brought to his lips. "Well, aren't you going to say anything?"

"What?" Coley asked in a dazed voice before remembering just what he had said. "Oh, yes, that'll be great."

"Your enthusiasm is overwhelming," the man replied with a rueful shake of his iron-gray head. He peered at her intently beneath his unruly eyebrows. "Not too long ago you would have made some comment giving credit to Jase. Have you finally learned some truth about that unscrupulous foreman of mine?"

"Uncle Ben, please!" Coley begged quietly, shifting uncomfortably in her chair at his deliberate lack of reference to Jase as his grandson. "Your tea's going to get cold if you don't drink it."

"Don't change the subject with me, young lady," Ben growled. "When I ask you a question I expect an answer."

"There's enough quarrelling around this house these days without you and me starting in." Coley raised the cup to her lips to hide the trembling of her chin.

"What's the matter, child? Did you honestly believe the sheep's clothing was real and there wasn't a wolf inside?" the old man snorted. "It's about time you saw Jason for what he is, an unspeakably cruel man who firmly believes the end justifies the means. But then, of course, he hasn't got the Slash S yet, has he?"

"That's like the pot calling the kettle black, isn't it?" Coley said bitterly, sitting her cup rather abruptly on the flat surface of the magazine table. "Jase wasn't responsible for anyone's death. So what kind of a grandfather does that make you, when you can sit there and tell me that you believe your own flesh and blood would allow his brother to die?"

"So you do have feelings," Ben said, leaning back in his wheelchair to allow Coley to see the satisfied smile on his face and the devilish gleam in his eyes. "I'd almost decided you were incapable of emotion. But last night when you ran out of the dining room like a chicken being chased by a hatchet, I decided that maybe there was some life in the old girl yet."

"This is the most sadistic family I've ever met!" Coley retorted. "I've never known anyone who could get so much pleasure out of engaging in vicious quarrels."

"Anger tends to loosen the tongue and let the truth flow out," Ben snapped, wheeling his chair out from behind the desk.

"No," Coley replied, shaking her head slowly.

"Anger is like a whip lashing out at old wounds to prevent them from healing."

"Forgive and forget, that's your motto, huh?"

"If you can't forgive, you can't forget and vice versa," Coley replied with far more calmness than she felt.

"And that's what you expect of me, isn't it?" Ben demanded suddenly, bending forward in his chair to scowl at Coley. "You expect me to forget that Jase stood by and let his own brother die because he knew that Rick would inherit this ranch, and now I should welcome him back with open arms."

"But he didn't do that," Coley cried, the hurt choking her throat.

"That's your heart speaking, not your head," Uncle Ben mocked cynically.

"Yes, yes, it is!" Coley announced, hopping agitatedly out of the chair to stand before him, her fists clenched in anger. "I love him. I love him so much that I wouldn't care if he had accidentally killed his brother. I would marry him tomorrow if he'd have me. If I thought for one minute that I could take him away from here, I'd do it. But no, you've got him so weighed down with the guilt over something he didn't do that he's sentenced himself to remaining in your prison. He could no more run away from you and your accusations than you could if you were in his place. Instead he's condemned himself to staying here with a grandfather who loathes him. How severe a punishment do you require? That bull out there took your one grandson's life and permanently scarred the other when he attempted to save his brother. And you're still busy getting revenge. I think you're despicable and hateful, and I don't see how anyone, least of all Jase, could care what you think. If it wasn't for him, I wouldn't stay another minute in this house!"

"Stop it!" Ben shouted, his face red with anger. "You don't even know what you're talking about. You weren't there when Rick was killed. You didn't lie there holding him in your arms while his very life flowed out of him! How can you stand there and judge me when you don't even know what happened that night?"

"I do know!" Coley was shaking with rage. "I know. I got a detailed account of what happened from Tony. He told me how Rick had gone into town and come home drunk. I know about how he used to play rodeo clown down in the bull pens. But that night his bravado had come from a bottle and his reflexes were nonexistent. It was Rick who caused his own death. Sure, his screams brought Jase, but where were the rest of you? Didn't you hear your own grandson? By the time Jase got there, Rick was doomed. But did your cowardly, murdering Jase wait for help? No, he jumped into the pen and had his face ripped open for the effort. So don't tell me that I don't know what happened."

Coley's anger blinded her from seeing the tinge of blue around Ben's lips, as he stared blankly up at her.

"But Rick said—" Ben's voice was faint and broken, "he kept crying out for Jase not to stand there, begging him to help. He died crying out for Jase."

"Of course he would call out for him—after all, he was his brother, wasn't he?" Coley cried bitterly.

"But why?" Uncle Ben began. His face grew ghostly white as he whispered, "If it wasn't Jase, who was standing there?"

"I really don't know," Coley answered sarcastically before turning away from him. "It was probably a figment of his imagination."

A convulsive jump from Ben's chair drew her attention back to him. Her hand leapt to her mouth as she stared at the white face of her unconscious uncle slumped in his chair. "Uncle Ben," she whispered, reaching out towards him, touching his arm hesitantly. "Uncle Ben!" she screamed.

She realized he must have had a heart attack or another stroke and dashed madly out of the room calling frantically for Maggie and Aunt Willy. The housekeeper came flying out of the kitchen to meet Coley in the hallway where she managed to explain with very little lucidity what had happened. Maggie ran back into the kitchen to the telephone extension, while Coley rushed back to the den.

Entering the room, she came to an abrupt halt. Ben wasn't in the wheelchair. It sat empty in front of her. A sound from the side of the room turned her horror-widened eyes from the chair. He was lying on the couch and Jase was standing over him, beating his chest with his fist.

"Jase, no!" Coley screamed, rushing over to throw herself on his back and tug ineffectually at him. "No, Jase, no! Don't kill him! Please, Jase, don't!" With tears streaming down her cheeks, she pulled at his arm, but he shrugged her off.

"Coley, stop it!" he shouted, turning an angry and anxious face towards her. "His heart stopped. I'm trying to save him!" She reached for a chair and collapsed with a sob, tears rolling down her cheeks as she watched his desperate attempts to save his grandfather. What if Uncle Ben died? It would be her fault. Oh, why had she quarreled with him?

"It's my fault, Jase," she whispered, glancing

beseechingly at the scarred face. "He's going to die, and it's my fault."

"Don't get hysterical on me," he reprimanded sharply, not taking his eyes off his grandfather's face as he continued pounding on the unconscious body. "Go and make sure the doctor's on his way."

Her head jerked back as if he had slapped her. But after all the things she had said to him, why had she expected sympathy from Jase? With shaking legs, she stumbled out, meeting Aunt Willy who was rushing into the room. Coley's pleading eyes as she glanced at her aunt must have communicated the gravity of the situation because the older woman hurried to the couch.

No one needed or wanted her. Coley continued her stumbling pace to her room, her vision obscured with tears, and flung herself on to the bed to sob out her shame.

She didn't know how long she had lain there when she heard the door of her room opening. Uncle Ben was dead. They were coming to tell her that Ben was dead. She shut her eyes, then opened them slowly to turn her head towards the footsteps that had come to a halt by her bed. A very weary and drawn Jase looked down at her, his eyes blank.

"He's dead, isn't he?" Coley cried, uttering the dreaded words for him. "And I killed him, I killed him!" she finished, collapsing once again on to the bed in tears.

She felt the shifting of the mattress as he sat down beside her and couldn't help cringing when she felt his hands grip her shoulders and pull her up to face him.

"He's going to make it, Coley," Jase said quietly, but firmly. "He's alive and he's going to make it."

Sudden happiness swept away Coley's pain as the

tears ceased to cloud her vision. She searched his face for the reassurances she needed.

"Oh, Jase, if he had died," Coley said brokenly, the horror fading away as the relief washed in, "I never could have forgiven myself."

"Don't think about it," Jase instructed, brushing away a teardrop on her cheek.

"But it would have been my fault," she insisted, attempting to explain the awful burden inside her. "We were arguing and I was accusing him of terrible things, and that's . . . that's when it happened." His eyes narrowed at her words and what little softness that had been in his face vanished.

"I don't have to ask what you were arguing about, do I?" he asked, rising from the bed as he spoke.

"It was about Rick," Coley admitted very quietly, bowing her head as she did.

"How many times have you been told to stay out of that?" His face was turned away from her as he spoke, but Coley could hear the bitterness in his voice.

"I couldn't and I can't, Jase," she stated. "And you know why."

"Well, you're going to have to." His gaze turned to her face. "Because the reason you thought you had doesn't exist."

"I know," she replied, lifting her trembling chin proudly as she looked back at him. "I've destroyed anything you might have felt for me. And this morning, my dumb inability to understand that you were trying to save Ben finished anything that might have remained. But that doesn't stop me from wanting to see you and your grandfather make peace. I don't think I'll ever be able to give that up."

"Right now all I want you to concentrate on is making sure that Ben gets better," Jase said, his expression unchanged by her words, as if they were raindrops washing down a brick wall. "And so help me God, if I ever find you discussing me with him, I'll . . ."

His threat was interrupted by a knocking on Coley's door. He glowered briefly at her before opening it. Danny was standing anxiously outside. He glanced at Coley before speaking to Jase.

"He wants to see you," said Danny. With a hesitant glance at his sister, he added, "and Coley, too."

Jase took Coley by the arm and escorted her grimly down the stairs to the hallway where a bespectacled and harassed-looking man stood waiting.

"He isn't doing that well, Jason," the doctor said. "I'd like to move him, but I think the journey would do him more harm than good. He's asking for you and the girl, but I only want you to go in for a few minutes. If he begins to get agitated, I want you to leave immediately."

"I thought . . ." Coley began. "You said he was going to be all right."

"I said he was alive," Jase corrected icily. "He'll make it. He's a Savage."

"He doesn't seem to care whether he makes it or not." The doctor glanced speculatively at Jase. "I sincerely hope you can change his mind."

A very frightened and subdued Coley accompanied Jase into the den and Uncle Ben's adjoining bedroom. She came to a halt beside Jase at the edge of the bed where Ben lay, the upper half of his body distorted by a portable plastic oxygen tent that encased it. She watched the massive chest rise and fall in its shallow breathing before her eyes moved up to the pale face, the shaggy brows accenting the hollows under his closed eyes. The iron-gray hair looked strangely silver and ethereal against the snow-white pillow as the head turned towards them and the eyelids opened to reveal two dull blue irises.

"Coley, my child," Ben whispered, a gnarled hand beckoning at her feebly to come closer and lessen the exertion of talking. "You're not to blame yourself for what happened." Coley nodded numbly, blinking valiantly to hold back the tears. "No matter what happens, you're not to blame, do you hear?"

"Yes, Uncle Ben," Coley answered hoarsely, and looked imploringly at Jase.

Ben was looking at him, too.

"I understand you saved my life," he whispered.

"I had to, Ben," Jase answered, his stony expression never changing. "I didn't know if you'd changed your will in my favor or not."

"Jase!" Coley gasped, staring up into his cold face before glancing, terrified, back at Ben. There was the briefest flicker of a smile on his face and his eyes sparkled brightly for a minute.

"You'll never own the Slash S," Ben whispered. Then with a smile, he feebly waved a hand at the pair. "Go away now. Let an old man die in peace."

"You're too mean to die this easy, Ben," Jase mocked.

Ben snorted slightly. "We'll talk later, son. I need to rest now."

"Yes, Ben," Jase replied. His voice was sharp and clear in the otherwise silent room. "We will talk later. I mean to have the Slash S."

He didn't wait for a reply from the stricken man, but immediately turned Coley around and marched her out of the room. His hand maintained a firm grip on her arm, keeping her by his side as he spoke again to the doctor, all the time refusing to meet Coley's wide, terrified eyes. She didn't hear what was said; she didn't care what was said. Why hadn't Jase comforted his grandfather? Why had he persisted in taunting him, Coley thought with a lump in her throat, quite possibly on his death-bed? She knew the attack had frightened Ben a great deal. It should have been the time for a recon-ciliation between the two, but instead Jase had made it another warring ground.

Her arm was released as his hand moved to her back and began guiding her towards the stairs and then up them to her room. Still she couldn't speak or protest. She was a pawn being moved about to suit the needs of her king. They entered her room where Jase quietly but firmly closed the door.

"Now, to get back to what we were talking about," he said. His mouth was drawn into a grim line.

"Jase, why did you do that?" Now that he was no longer touching her, she found the words to speak again. "Why did you say those things to him?"

"Why do you think?" Jase asked angrily, blue-white fire in his eyes.

"I don't know why. That's what I'm asking you," she retorted, hugging her arms about her in an attempt to ward off the chill his gaze was giving her. "He would have forgiven you. If you would have just asked, he would have forgiven you!"

"Maybe I didn't want his forgiveness. Maybe I didn't want to play a role in some deathbed scene," he said sharply. "No, I won't be a part of some last-minute reconciliation so that an old man can go to his Maker with a clean slate, one that he couldn't have lived with if he was still alive the next day."

"Fine! Stick that stupid old pride in the way if you want to," Coley shouted, her voice trembling with her emotions. Only to have her breath taken away as Jase grabbed her and pulled her towards him in anger. "Did you have to be so cruel to him, Jase?" she whispered. "Did you have to tell him the only reason you saved him was because you wanted the ranch? Couldn't you have spared him that?"

"No!" His fingers dug hard into her shoulders as he seemed to control the urge to shake her. "No! I had to make sure he lived. Hate can drive you on the same as love, and if hating me can bring him back from the clutches of death, then let him hate me. Let him live on it and thrive and sleep on it, but let him do it alive!"

He let her go, the violence of his release almost throwing her on the bed, before he stalked from the room. Within a few seconds Danny rushed in, his youthful face drawn and pinched as he gazed at his sister with anxious eyes. She was still standing, clutching the bedpost that had saved her from falling, the tears streaming unrestrained down an otherwise silent face. Seeing her brother, she reached up and wiped the tears off her face while she turned to walk to the window.

"What happened? What did he do?" Danny asked tensely.

"Nothing, Danny," Coley answered hoarsely. "It's me. It's what I've done . . . to him and to Uncle Ben."

"I don't understand." Danny walked over to her side trying desperately to read the expression on her face, but there was none.

"No, I know you don't," Coley replied, a little smile curving the corners of her mouth as if to show him that she was all right. "If you don't mind, Danny, I'd like to be alone."

Puzzled and still concerned, Danny gave in to her wishes and left his older sister alone in her room.

* * *

Within a week, Ben's condition had stabilized, as the doctor put it. In Coley's terms, it meant that he was out of danger and on the road to recovery, still weak but capable of blustering if the occasion demanded it. During that week, Jase had not so much as put one foot inside the invalid's door. Several times Coley had heard him asking Aunt Willy about Ben, but he never looked in for himself. And he usually had morning coffee with the nurse, an attractive woman in her late twenties. Yet never once did he ask Coley about Ben, even though he knew she spent a great deal of time with him, reading to him when he wanted her to, or just sitting and talking to him. Jase didn't value her opinion too highly, she decided. And she couldn't blame him. After all, hadn't she misjudged him often enough, once when he was physically trying to save Ben's life and again when he was trying to give him the will to live.

As for Ben, he was too proud to ask for his grandson, but Coley could tell that he was expecting Jase to come and see him. It just tore at her heart the way his eyes would light up when the door to his bedroom opened and how that light would go out when someone else walked in. If only Jase would come to visit him, Coley felt sure everything would be all right.

Coley patted Misty's neck before shooing the horse out into the paddock area. The early morning ride had been a good idea in one way, she did feel a little refreshed. She meandered slowly to the house. The doctor usually came in the mornings and she was completely superfluous with the nurse there. At least the ride had given her something to do between lunch and breakfast. In the afternoon she would sit with Ben and again for another hour or two in the evenings. In some small way she felt she was making up for bringing on the attack and being useful at the same time.

It was only mid-morning, but she would have plenty of time to shower and change before she went down to help Aunt Willy and Maggie with lunch. The sound of her boots on the wooden veranda floor seemed too loud in the already hot and languid stillness. Coley opened the door to the house and noticed that Maggie had already gone around pulling curtains and shades where the sun beat mercilessly against the windows. The darkness was almost refreshing after the brilliant Texas sun.

Farther down the hall came the echo of boots and the click of a door opening. Momentarily Coley hesitated at the bottom of the stairs. The doctor had probably come and gone already. Perhaps she should check to see how Ben was. She debated briefly, glancing down at her dusty boots and Levis before deciding that she would look in on him, if only for a moment. She knew how aggravated and on edge he was after a visit from the doctor. Aunt Willy always spent the mornings in her garden and Maggie would be busy with lunch. Then she remembered the sound of footsteps in the passageway. Possibly someone was there with him now, but she'd look in, just to be sure. As quietly as she could, Coley walked down the hallway to Ben's room.

The door to his study was open and Coley walked in, glancing hesitantly at the half-opened door that led to his bedroom. When she heard Ben's voice, Coley turned to leave. Someone was with him so there was no need to stay. Then she heard the other person speaking. It was Jase. Suddenly she had to know what they were saying and tiptoed closer.

". . . All right, don't sit down," came Uncle Ben's gruff voice, "if it pleases you to tower over a sick old man."

"You may be sick and you may be old, but you are a man, Ben, so don't seek sympathy with me," Jase replied quietly. "I thought I'd bring you up to date on the ranch."

"Well, I don't want to talk about the ranch right now. That surprises you, doesn't it?"

"Nothing surprises me."

"I wanted to talk to you about Coley." At Ben's words, Coley straightened, her body tense as her mind raced, trying to anticipate what he might be going to say about her.

"Coley?" Suspicion laced Jason's voice.

"Yes, Coley. She's fallen in love with you, you know?"

Her heart was beating so hard against her rib cage that she was sure its pounding could be heard in the other room.

"And you're wondering what my intentions towards her are?" Jase drawled. The indifference of his voice stabbed at Coley. "Isn't that my own personal business?"

"Maybe so," Ben replied mysteriously. "What I'm more curious about is your feelings towards her."

"Do you think I might be playing around with her?" Jase asked. "Well, I'm not. When she first came here, she was extremely shy and very young. She's grown up a lot."

There was a pause as Ben evidently waited for

Jase to continue. "I believe you're attracted to her," Ben declared finally. "Have you ever considered marrying her?"

"Before I answer any more of your questions, I think you'd better tell me what all this is leading to," Jase replied sharply.

Coley could hear the rustle of papers followed by a short silence.

"This is a deed to the Slash S made out to me," Jase finally said, his voice deceptively quiet and ominous. "I think you'd better start explaining."

"Fair enough. If you marry Coley, the ranch is yours. All it requires is my signature on the bottom and Willy's and Maggie's as witnesses." Coley bit down hard on her lip to keep from crying out. The humiliating discovery that she was being dangled in front of Jase as something else that could help him earn his forgiveness was choking at her throat.

"Why?" Jason's cold voice penetrated icily into the adjoining room.

Coley's eyes were clenched tightly shut, the tears forming tiny drops on her lashes before cascading down her cheeks.

"Why?" Ben echoed. "Because you want the ranch. And you obviously feel some affection towards her. Arranged marriages usually work out better that way."

"That's not what I mean. Besides, she's too young," Jase retorted with exasperation.

"She's a woman, make no mistake about that," the older man replied. "She might not be as filled out as some, but her feelings are as adult as they come."

"You haven't answered my question yet, Ben. Why are you doing this?"

"I've grown quite attached to Coley these past

few weeks," Ben replied, his voice gruff and a little defensive. "I'd like to see her get what she wants. She's a scrappy little fighter and I like that. For some reason, Lord only knows why, she wants you. And since it's within my power to see that she gets what she wants, I'm doing it."

Oh, Uncle Ben, Coley moaned silently. *Please don't do this. Please don't make the ranch a prize for Jase!*

Ben spoke quickly to cover the growing silence. "I'd never tell her, and you certainly wouldn't."

"No, I wouldn't," Jase agreed quietly as Coley stumbled out of the adjoining room into the hallway, her vision blinded by her tears.

She groped her way down the hall, until she finally leaned against the grandfather clock near the base of the stairs for support. She rested there, her mind racing with distorted thoughts. How often she had wished to find a way to stop the feuding between grandfather and grandson, and now she was to be the instrument to accomplish it. What an ironic twist of fate. Jase would finally get the ranch he always wanted, while she, Coley, would achieve her heart's desire: have peace in the family and to become Jason's wife. Yet what a price all three were paying. It was a short trip from Hell to Hades?

She had no idea how long she had stood there, her mind flitting from one thought to another in rhythm with the ticking clock. Suddenly she realized that anyone could walk into the hall and find her standing there. Her state of mind was too confused to explain to anyone what she was doing there or the conversation she had overheard. Quickly she hurried up the steps toward her room, but not before she heard footsteps in the hallway below her and Jason's voice calling out for Maggie and Aunt Willy to come to Ben's room.

Chapter Nine

Never had Coley thought she could feel so miserable. When finally the humiliation and pain had receded and the tears had stopped flowing, an overwhelming sadness had taken hold. Suddenly she felt sorry for herself—for all the things she had missed during her school years, of the times she had to stay home to nurse her mother and of her great dependency on others that had brought her to this ranch in the first place. She hated the world and the way it twisted people's lives until they were caught up in a web of deceit and greed. But most of all, she hated the burning desire within herself to hurt as she had been hurt. Yet it was there, smoldering in the green fire of her eyes as she made her way down the stairs for the evening meal.

She had pleaded a headache at lunch and remained in her room the entire afternoon. Even now the throbbing at her temples confirmed her excuse was only the smallest of a white lie. And the strain of the morning's eavesdropping was visible in her fever-bright eyes and pale complexion. No, no one would question the validity of her excuse as she entered the dining room.

"There you are, honey." Aunt Willy hurried to Coley's side to inquire solicitously after her headache. "I was afraid that you might want a tray sent up to you."

"No, it's much better this evening," Coley murmured quietly, half choking on her words as she saw Jase seated at the head of the table, the place usually occupied by Ben. *How appropriate,* she thought cynically.

"I think I got a little too much sun this morning," she added quickly, hurriedly, occupying Danny's chair to avoid being placed at her usual seat which would put her on Jason's left.

Ben was seated in his wheelchair at Jason's right, his bushy eyebrows drawn together into an iron-gray line as he gazed at Coley, silently demanding that she acknowledge the change in seating between himself and his grandson. But she couldn't bring herself to give him that satisfaction, nor could she meet Jason's grim look for fear he would see the emotions in the depths of her hazel eyes. Instead she smiled at her aunt and asked about her roses, knowing full well it would start a monologue that would cover any conversation for the next few minutes at least.

She couldn't have said what was served that evening. She tasted none of it, merely placed it in her mouth and nodded agreement to whatever her aunt was saying. When the main course was over, Maggie removed the plates and brought in the dessert. At that point, a very impatient Ben interrupted Aunt Willy's dissertation on an especially hard to control fungus that had attacked one of her plants.

"We'll be having our dessert on the porch, Maggie," Ben announced. "And bring some of that wine, too. It's time we did a little celebrating around here."

Coley's heart skipped a beat at his words. Suddenly she knew she couldn't bear to be there when he announced that he was turning the ranch over to Jase. She knew she didn't want to hear the hypocrisy of his words as he toasted the new owner. "If you'll excuse me," she said, rising abruptly from the table. Her voice had a little catch in it as she spoke, betraying her nervousness. "I think I'd like some fresh air. I'll join you later."

Her retreat into the hallway was followed by an angry exclamation from Ben, but Coley hurried through the door on to the veranda and farther out on to the lawn before anyone could call her back. Instinctively she sought refuge among the giant oaks that shaded the house from the purple-pink rays of the setting sun.

She leaned back against one of the huge trunks and closed her eyes as the irony of the situation occurred to her once again. How she was paying for all those times she had misjudged Jase! If only Jase could feel the hurt and disappointment that she felt. Opening her eyes, Coley knew she would not make his victory an easy one. She would not be the instrument that would give the Slash S to him.

She heard his footsteps as he approached. She knew he would come looking for her. How else could he live up to the terms of his agreement with his grandfather unless he did see her alone? Perhaps that hidden knowledge was what had led her to leave the table so abruptly. She knew he would have to seek her out and she had made him do it on her terms.

"There you are," said Jase, walking under the big oak tree to stand beside her. "Why did you leave the table so suddenly tonight?"

"I was restless . . . and I needed the air," Coley replied abruptly, moving out of the shadows and away from him. She jumped slightly as he laid a hand on her shoulder.

"Coley, I want to talk to you," he spoke firmly, causing her to clench her jaws to keep the pain in her heart from voicing itself.

"Please, we really don't have anything to talk about," she replied, shrugging her shoulder to remove his hand.

"We've all been under a strain this past week." His tone was sharp as if he was controlling his temper. "Something happened today that you might be interested in."

Coley ignored him completely and stepped out from under the tree and began walking through the waning light into the rose garden. She knew she was deliberately antagonizing him, but she didn't care. He was going to propose all right, but she was going to make it exceedingly difficult for him. She never realized how much she wanted to hurt him the way she had been hurt. She heard his quick steps as Jase overtook her. A malicious sparkle gleamed in her eyes as she realized how she was trying his patience.

"It looks as if we're going to have a full moon tonight." But his eyes were studying Coley's face.

"Yes, it does, doesn't it?" she agreed, looking up into the darkening heavens at the pale moon. How romantic." The light edge of sarcasm in her voice penetrated her airy words as he seized her arm roughly and pulled her around to face him.

"What's the matter with you, Coley?" he asked sharply. "Why are you so bitter?"

"Can't you guess? I had a very good teacher," Coley replied, staring into his face boldly.

Even though her heart was breaking apart, she could still derive pleasure watching the angry scowl cross his face as his fingers dug into her shoulders. He actually seemed surprised that she wasn't falling into his arms as she was supposed to.

"Come now, Jase. The cat got your tongue?" she asked mockingly.

"I could shake you till your teeth rattled!" His hold relaxed ever so slightly. "What kind of game are you playing? Or do you want me to throw you over my knee and spank you? You're acting like a child!"

"But Jase, you've told me repeatedly that I am a child." Coley attempted to turn out of his arms, but was brought up sharply as he twisted her back towards him.

"No more games, Coley. Out with it." His eyes blazed and his mouth was drawn into a grim and forbidding line.

"Don't you want to tell me how much you love and adore me and how you can hardly wait to marry me?" Coley asked with a pretend pout. Her eyes flashed as she spoke. "I was looking forward to that part."

"What are you talking about?" His voice barely veiled the growing anger as his eyes narrowed. "Where were you this morning?"

"Oh, Jase, the night is young and the roses are in bloom. Surely you can think of more romantic questions than that." Coley waved her hand airily at the night.

"How much did you hear?"

"Don't tell me I'm going to have to be the teacher tonight," she mocked, curling her long arms around his neck and inching closer to him as she raised her face to his.

Her lips touched his lightly and coolly, through her heart begged for one more minute in his embrace. The hands on her shoulders started to push her away and then dropped around her waist to draw her violently into his arms. She was crushed against his body, every curve melting and molding to him, until there seemed to be no longer two bodies but one. His mouth consumed and ravaged hers until there was only one ruling emotion in her, that of passionate, yielding love. Then he let her go, disentangling her hands from around his neck, setting her away from him as if the fire that had consumed her hadn't even touched him. For a moment her heart throbbed painfully as she yearned to feel his touch again, willing to submit to anything that would put her back under his spell, but that was before Coley's senses stopped reeling and her mind could once again rule. With difficulty she assumed a calm expression.

"That's how it's done," she mocked. "Now it's time for the pretty speeches." He would never know the pain those words were causing her.

"I don't think there's any need for speeches," Jase said, gazing down at her face indifferently. "You seem to have overheard at least a portion of a private conversation with Ben. I think it's only a matter of a yes or no from you. Although I would like an explanation of your bitterness."

"A simple yes or no!" Coley lashed out angrily.

"Oh, what an egotist you are! I refuse to be the way you get the title to this ranch. I refuse to be dangled above your head with a marriage license in my hand and a little note pinned on me that says 'Marry this girl and the ranch is yours.' I may be a poor relation, but I won't marry without love."

"And love isn't possible between you and me," Jase said coldly.

"Certainly not," Coley said angrily and with what little dignity she could muster. "I know Uncle Ben told you that I was in love with you, but that wasn't what I told him. I said I loved you, but then I also love Uncle Ben, Aunt Willy, and my brother, but I'm not about to marry any of them either. Don't misunderstand me, Jase. I want to see you and Ben make peace. Yes, I've been on your side, but Danny will tell you I'm a great one for rooting for the underdog."

"You really lay it on the line, don't you?" His expression hadn't changed since he had released her from his embrace. "And those tempestuous love scenes of ours—I take it they're practice sessions, like the riding and swimming lessons?"

"Well, if a person is going to learn, he might as well go to someone who has some experience, like you," Coley replied coolly. Her tingling body could attest to that. She glanced up at his rough-hewn face. "But desire doesn't last. Despite what you think, I'm old enough to know that much."

"You don't believe that this 'desire' could grow into love?" Jase asked, as he studied her intently.

Coley held her breath for a second, squelching the whispering hope that maybe he could grow to love her. Instead she replied coldly, "I'm not about to sacrifice the rest of my life for the chance. Besides, if Uncle Ben has gone so far as to concede that he'll give you title to the ranch if you marry me, then you're only a step away from getting it without any strings. You might as well take that step, because I'll never consent to marrying you."

"Suppose I told you that I already have title to the ranch? That it was made over to me this morning?" Jase said, glancing at her sideways.

"On the condition that I accept your proposal tonight," Coley finished with a superior tilt of her head.

He studied her quietly for a minute. "Would you consider a temporary engagement? Until I can persuade Ben around to your way of thinking?"

"No," she spoke quickly before the tempting idea could take hold. "No, that wouldn't work at all."

"So be it," said Jase, shrugging his shoulders. "You know he had his heart set on doing this for you." Coley glanced up quickly. His face was hidden in the shadows of the night.

"I'll explain to him," she said. "He'll understand, I'm sure he will."

"I wish I was half as sure as you are. He hasn't fully recovered from his heart attack, despite the improvements he's made." His voice drifted quietly to her, but the words seared deeply into her mind.

Jase only wanted the ranch, she thought bitterly. And he was not above using emotional blackmail to persuade her to fall in with his wishes.

"I don't care, Jase," she spoke sharply, fighting the whirlpool he was sweeping her into. "I will not be your fiancée under any circumstances."

"I once accused you of being too sensitive." His lips curled sardonically as he spoke. "That drowned kitten I rescued from the rain has turned into a regular wildcat . . ."

"Please don't remind me. I was just naive," she cried, hugging her long arms about her to ward off the shiver as she wished for the security of his arms. He jerked her around to face him, his fierce grip almost hurting in her arms.

"What happened to that girl who was more frightened of me than the storm? Where's the girl who was afraid of water, who was scared of the view from the top of a horse? Where did she go?" he demanded, shaking her as he spoke.

"She was too shy and too frightened to ever oppose you. But she grew up fast," Coley shouted. "Did you expect her to not see what goes on around here? Hey, I hate the way I'm being used by the two of you and I want to be wanted for myself, not for a piece of property I might bring into a marriage." She was trembling from the violence behind her words as she glared up at him, "You didn't really believe I could stay as innocent as I was that first night?"

"No," he replied, the word coming through tightly pressed lips. Slowly his fingers uncurled from her arm until she was standing freely in front of him. "You have everything all figured out, Coley. But you still don't know everything there is to know. Think hard on what's been said tonight. Later you'll be apologizing to me." His expression was almost smug as he gazed down at her.

"If you think for one minute that I'm going to apologize to you . . ." Coley began, enraged by his calm statement.

"Don't say any more that you might regret," he interrupted. The light of anger shone briefly in his eyes. "I'll be going back to the house now—to do some celebrating with Ben. I don't think you're in a very festive mood, so I won't ask you to join us. Good night, Coley, and sweet dreams,'' he added with a mocking lilt to his voice before nodding arrogantly towards her and striding off into the darkness.

She stamped her foot as she glowered at the retreating figure. She had wanted to spite him, to hurt him as she had been hurt. The bitterness had demanded it, and now even that was denied her. He had walked away, so sure that she would be running after him to apologize. Never, never as long as she lived—no matter how much she loved him—would she beg his forgiveness for the things she had said tonight.

"Coley, what are you doing out here?" Danny's voice called out to her. "Jase just told me you wouldn't be coming in to join the party."

"That's right," Coley replied in a tight little voice that threatened to betray her emotional state.

"But you of all people should be there." His forehead was creased by a frown as he studied her with puzzled eyes.

"That's exactly why I'm not." Her voice trembled with vehemence.

"Coley, I just don't understand you any more." Danny shook his head as he tried to fathom his bewildering sister. "Since the first day we arrived, you've been fighting Jase's fights, defending him. And tonight, when Uncle Ben has finally given in, you're out here sulking like a kid."

"You don't know the whole story, Danny," Coley began, hurt choking her throat at her brother's disapproval.

"And you have no intention of enlightening me either," Danny interrupted impatiently. "You've been acting peculiar all evening. What ridiculous notion have you got into your head this time?"

"You can stop the big brother act. I don't need one any more." Her lower lip trembled while her breath came with a quickened pace as she fought to hold back the silent sobs.

His eyes revealed the hurt and anger that surfaced at her words.

"I think you need a swift kick in an appropriate place!"

"Danny!" Coley called out sharply as he turned away towards the house. "Danny, I'm sorry. I didn't mean to hurt you."

He hesitated a moment before turning back to face her.

"No, I don't imagine you did." His eyes narrowed as he studied her. "But you're right. You're a big girl now. It's time you started working out your own problems without leaning on someone else. Whatever you've got yourself into, you're going to have to figure it out on your own. Good night."

She gulped down her tears while she watched him walk back towards the house. She knew what she was doing. Of course she did!

The steady drumming of rain on her windowpane greeted Coley as she woke from a restless night's sleep. The dark, sunless morning mirrored the depression that had hung over her head since yesterday morning. With stiff, listless movements she dragged herself from beneath the covers, grimacing at the growling thunder that vibrated the glass in the windows. She grabbed a pair of Levis from the drawer and with an unhurried motion pulled them on over her legs before reaching in another drawer for a sweatshirt. A very unglamorous combination, she thought, as she dragged a careless brush through her hair, but then she didn't feel very glamorous anyway. She glanced briefly at the jars and tubes of makeup lying on her bureau before shrugging at her reflection. Who cares? she thought, and ambled out of her room. Halfway down the hall, she passed the open door leading into Tony's room. She stopped, surprised to see Tony inside busily throwing clothes into a suitcase.

"Tony, what are you doing?" Coley asked in a dazed voice.

"You got eyes, princess. Use them." His voice was sharp as he continued packing without looking towards the door.

"You're leaving, aren't you? Where are you going? Why are you going?"

"Someone else has control of the kingdom and the castle." Tony walked over to the doorway, his expression twisted with anger. "I won't be sticking around to play the fool any more." His fingers turned her frowning face up to his. "You know, Coley, you not only have big eyes, you have a big mouth as well. Between you and Jase, you've finished me here at the ranch. I've got as much luck as my father had."

"I don't know what you're talking about," she murmured as Tony released her and walked back over to his bed to resume his packing.

"Go ahead, play your little games, but don't expect me to believe that you don't know about Uncle Ben's latest move." At Coley's puzzled expression, Tony slammed the lid shut on the suitcase angrily. "Oh, go on. Just get out of here. You've been a pain ever since you got here!"

Confused, she turned away from the door, hurt by the bitter contempt in Tony's voice as he ordered her from his room. The stairwell yawned before her and she made her way slowly down the steps. She hesitated briefly at the bottom. Breakfast waited in the dining room, but she wasn't hungry. Coley slipped out to the porch, jamming her hands in the pockets of her jeans as she wandered along the wooden railing. A distant, jagged bolt of lightning from the oncoming storm sent her retreating back to the safety of the house walls. She walked aimlessly along the L-shaped veranda, her desultory thoughts keeping her company, until she was halted by the echoing rap of a hand against a window. She glanced through the shadow-darkened glass to see Ben motioning insistently for her to come inside. Her mind raced to think of an excuse, to no avail. So, with a sigh, she accepted the inevitable and entered the house, turning down the hallway to Ben's study.

"You're certainly a ray of sunshine this morning," he scoffed at the sullen expression on Coley's face as she entered the room.

"It's not exactly sunshine weather outside," she retorted quickly, sending him a withering glance.

"Seems to me you used to be frightened of our thunderstorms. You were showing a lot of courage just now wandering out there on the porch."

Coley glanced out the window at the dark, rolling clouds. Their angry forms seemed to mirror her own tossing and tumultuous emotions, her unshed tears of frustration and hurt.

"Maybe I was hoping the rain would wash some of this Savage dirt off of me," she said sarcastically.

"Have you had breakfast yet?" Ben asked. At the negative shake of her head, he added, "I thought not. An empty stomach usually sharpens the tongue as well as the appetite."

"Surely you didn't call me in here to discuss my eating habits," Coley said huffily, turning from the window to face him.

"Hardly," he answered with an indignant snort. His bushy brows lowered as he studied her intently. "I was wondering why you didn't join the celebration last night."

"It must have really been some celebration," she replied with a bitter laugh. "I just saw Tony upstairs, packing."

"Don't change the subject on me, girl. I asked you a question."

"Did it ever occur to you that I didn't think it deserved an answer?" Coley answered smartly. Then she noticed the knuckles on his hand, white from gripping the armrests on his wheelchair. The memory of their last argument came bursting through her bitterness and she sighed her defeat. "I just didn't feel like celebrating the grand occasion."

"But it's what you've been wanting all along." A flicker of hurt and confusion gleamed briefly in his eyes.

"When have I ever said I wanted you to buy me a husband?" Coley asked dejectedly, her chin trembling as she fought to hold back the tears that threatened.

"I don't know what you're talking about," Uncle Ben replied, a frown creasing his forehead. But Coley noticed the brief start of guilt that had preceded his answer.

"I went over this last night with Jase, Uncle Ben,

so it doesn't do any good to play innocent." Her sad eyes gazed at him with pity. His misguided attempt to give her the man she loved had backfired. "I'm not going to marry him."

"You're not going to marry . . . Did he propose to you last night?" The hawklike look was back in his eyes.

"Not really," Coley answered. Her chin straightened defiantly as she met his eyes. "I didn't give him the opportunity."

The funny half-smile on his face disturbed her, as if he was laughing to himself. "You—uh—didn't give him a chance to explain things, huh?"

"There wasn't anything to explain," Coley strove for an air of nonchalance that didn't match her nervous movements. "He hinted that I should consider an engagement to . . . to humor you. But I refused."

"Naturally," Ben replied smugly.

"You don't seem very upset," she said, a confused frown creasing her forehead.

"Should I be?"

"Yes, I mean, I would have thought . . . wasn't that the purpose of . . ." She suddenly felt she was putting her foot in her mouth.

"I have the feeling that you were in my study yesterday morning. Am I right?" Coley nodded her head affirmatively at his question. "I take it you heard part of a conversation between Jase and myself." Again she nodded. His eyes crinkled at the corners as a short laugh escaped his lips. "Oh, Coley, nothing good comes from listening through keyholes."

"I'm certainly glad I did," she replied, slightly angered by his laughter as well as confused. "Oh, Uncle Ben, how could you sign over the ranch to

Jase for marrying me? Didn't you think I have any pride?"

He tried desperately to keep the smile from his face with only limited success. "I'd say you have as much pride as any Savage on this ranch. As for Jase, I was testing him." His expression was somber as he gazed abstractedly out the window before turning back to her. "You should have stayed for the entire conversation. Then you would have heard him refuse the ranch under that condition, just as I would have done had it been me in his place. No, Coley, I signed the ranch over to him with no strings attached." The last words were spoken clearly and concisely so that there was no misinterpretation.

She stood in silence as the full meaning of the words sank in, before she collapsed into an arm chair.

"What have I done?" Her eyes filled with tears as she turned to Ben. "The horrible things I said to him last night! Oh, Uncle Ben, what am I going to do? I love him so much!"

"The same thing I did yesterday, Coley," he replied with a tender smile. "Apologize and tell him what an old fool you've been. Except in your case, when you've been a young fool."

A glimmer of hope rose in her as she remembered Jason's words the night before—that she would be looking for him to apologize. "Where is he?" she demanded hoarsely, swallowing the pride that had made her say she would never beg his forgiveness.

The old man blinked quickly at the tears in his own eyes and glanced out the window.

"Knowing Jase, in this kind of rain, I'd be out

checking the washes for stray cattle in case of a flash flood.''

Coley leaped from her chair, her cheeks wet with tears, but her face glowing from an inner sunshine. As she dashed from the room, Ben wheeled as rapidly as he could after her, shouting instructions. ''He'll probably be over in the eastern section near Blue Rock Mountain. Cut across the lower pasture,'' he called as the screen door slammed behind the running girl. ''You should be wearing a raincoat!''

As he came to a stop in front of the screen, he chuckled to himself. She was in love. She wouldn't even notice it was raining. He pushed the door open and wheeled on to the porch. A few minutes later she came scurrying out of the barn leading a reluctant roan. Mounting quickly, she waved a hasty hand in Ben's direction before galloping off into the rain.

She raced across the flat pasture land, the tall grass giving her horse footing despite the torrential rain. The wind whipped her face, the raindrops stung her cheeks, but still she didn't check her pace. Then the land began to rise and dip as she reached the undulating foothills. Coley slowed Misty down, not wanting to risk laming her favorite mount as they began to climb the hills. Little rivulets of water were racing down and the sparse growth could not hold them back. In places, the ground was a sea of slippery, oozing mud just as it had been that first night she had met Jase.

She pulled Misty to a stop on the top of a ridge and searched the surrounding slopes and bottom land for a sign of him. A bolt of lightning flashed brilliantly in front of them as Misty tossed her head and neighed her misgivings while the earth trembled beneath them from the accompanying roll of thunder. Coley patted the roan's neck reassuringly. She shivered slightly, her clothes soaked to her skin. For a minute she wondered how she would find him, then her eyes lit up with an idea. The line shack! It was somewhere near here. Jase would stop there sometime during the day. He was bound to.

She touched the roan's side with her heel urging the horse down the sloping ridge. The dry washes at the bottom of the slopes were filling with the runoff water. Even now Coley could visualize the water rising at the highway crossings. Farther and farther she and her mount rode, crossing hills, riding down canyons, until the highway became a shiny gray ribbon in front of them. She cantered Misty along the flatland until she reached the plateau that she had climbed on foot so long ago. Giving the horse free rein, she clutched the saddle horn tightly while the roan bounded up the steep slope, muscles straining with each slippery step, until the reached the top. Minutes later the line shack loomed darkly against the morning's rolling thunder clouds. A thread of smoke mingled with the clouds and rain. With a shout of joy, Coley slapped her horse on the flank with her reins.

Huddled against the building under the overhanging roof stood the big red horse that Jase always rode. Coley dismounted quickly as she and Misty reached the building. Impatiently she tugged her horse under the roof with Jase's. Then she was off, racing around the building to the door, bursting inside with a shower of raindrops. Inside she stopped short, her happy eyes taking in Jase in the act of pouring himself a cup of coffee. Suddenly she was shy, frightened. What was she going to say? Where did she begin?

"What are you doing here?" Jase finally spoke, sitting the pot down and walking around the table towards her.

"I'm sorry. I was wrong. I was a fool." The words rushed out of her mouth. "You've got to forgive me. I didn't mean all those horrible things I said. Forgive me, please forgive me."

"You rode all the way up here to tell me that . . . in this weather?" He gazed at her through half-closed eyes, his tone mocking.

"Of course! Don't you understand, Jase? Uncle Ben explained everything to me. You see, I only heard part of your conversation with him. I thought you'd made a bargain with him to marry me." She struggled for the words that would make him understand. Her happiness evaporated with each passing second that he stood there so indifferently.

"And now that you know differently," he said blandly, "what am I supposed to do? Forgive you?"

"Yes," Coley answered breathlessly. Her eyes looked beseechingly into his. "I thought you wanted to marry me just to get the ranch, not because you cared for me."

"You don't think that's the reason now?"

"No, I mean . . . I don't know." She felt so awkward as she blinked at the tears that were forming in her eyes.

"I don't even remember proposing last night."

"Well, I'm not asking you to now." Her pride reasserted itself as the tears threatened to fall. "I just wanted you to know I was sorry, that's all. You can go back to your Tanya." She turned and fumbled with the door latch, anger and humiliation frustrating her attempt to open it.

"Coley, I don't want Tanya." Jase laughed, grabbing her arm and twisting her around to him.

"Let me go!" she shouted, twisting and turning as he took her in his arms. Finally she was pinned against his chest with no more strength to resist. He determinedly lifted her chin with his hand until she was gazing sullenly into his face.

"Don't you see, Coley," he said with a tender smile, "you were unbearably cruel last night and stubborn, too. You never even gave me a chance to explain. But, darling, I love you so much I'd forgive you anything. I've never wanted Tanya, only you." Then he was bending his head, his lips touching hers gently, almost reverently, until Coley threw her arms around his neck to give his kiss back to him.

"Oh, Jase," she sighed, minutes later as she pressed her head against his chest, "tell me again that you love me."

"I love you. That first night I had a feeling that you were going to change my life. I tried to stay away from you, to keep you from finding out how I felt, but you wouldn't let me," he answered, gently pushing the wet curls away from her face.

"I hated Uncle Ben so much when he offered you the ranch if you married me. I knew how much you wanted this land. I didn't see how you could resist such a temptation." Her face raised in glowing wonderment to his.

He touched her lips lightly before replying, "I realized I loved you more. I loved you so much more that accepting his offer meant putting a price on that love, which would have only cheapened it."

"Oh, Jase, what have I ever done to deserve you?

I can't cook, I can't sew, I can't grow roses. I'm not even pretty."

"Coley, you've brightened the days of an old man and filled a childless woman's heart with love. You give yourself, and I'll cherish you all the rest of my life." The warmest light was shining out of Jason's eyes that Coley had ever seen.

"I hope all our children have blue eyes like yours," she said before he covered her lips with a short but burning kiss. He hugged her closer to him as if afraid she would run away. "Why did Uncle Ben change his mind?" she asked suddenly, pushing away from him to raise questioning eyes to his face.

"Because of you and that argument you had with him. You must have said something to him that made him think. At least, between that and a private conversation with Tony," he answered, locking his hands behind her back to gaze down lovingly at her.

"I saw him packing this morning," Coley remarked. "But what has he got to do with it?"

"I didn't probe too deeply into the reasons, but I got the feeling that Ben has decided that Tony was there the night Rick died. The only thing that Ben would say was that he had judged too harshly and too suddenly once before and he wasn't going to do it again."

"Do you mean that Tony was. . ." Coley began, only to be silenced by a hand covering her mouth. With surprising clarity, Tony's exclamation that day in the canyon came rushing back to her with new meaning. "I was afraid something would happen to you, too."

"Hush. Too many ill feelings have been bred by the past. I agree with Ben, there'll be no judging,"

...se said sternly. Then he smiled. "Do you know you're drenched? And now I am."

Coley shivered in affirmation of his statement. "You'd better come over here and get some hot coffee in you. I'll get a blanket to put around you."

Coley followed him to the table and accepted a cup from him, before succumbing to a giggle.

"What's so funny?" he asked, walking over to remove a blanket from the cot and put it around her shoulders. She hugged it around her for a second before glancing up at him mischievously.

"I really don't know what good this blanket is going to do with all of these wet clothes on underneath," she said innocently. "The last time I was caught in the rain, there was a stranger who ordered me to take off all of my clothes."

"Not this time, Coley," Jase said, sweeping her, blanket and all, into his arms. His arms trembled about her as he gazed ardently down into her love-starred eyes. "That would be demanding too much control . . . even from a Savage."
